For Martha

This book had a lot of help from my big sister Martha, who was like no other woman I know. She was extremely social, the glue that held family and friends together, and yet chose to spend the last part of her life living in a beautiful but isolated log home. She hunted her own land and was as independent and stubborn as Olivia. She gave to me generously – love, friendship, encouragement, insight, too much fabulous food, and just enough alcohol. I miss her every day.

Acknowledgements

Special thanks are owed to my friend and "overseer" Jane Abramowitz, who never fails to go the extra mile for her friends. I also received invaluable support and feedback on the books in this series from Tina Foley, Rasana Atreya, Carol Kean, Linda Scharaga, Mark Thomas, Michael Greenberg, Bobbi Dekay, Erik Cross, Michal Weissman, Yvonne Schumacher Strejcek, and Henry Tobias.

The Way the World Is

Book 2 of the Olivia Series

Yael Politis

The Way the World Is

CreateSpace Edition

Cover photo by Yulia Kazansky
Cover design by Tatiana Vila

The Way the
World Is

Chapter One

Five Rocks, Pennsylvania – March, 1842

Olivia Killion sucked in her breath and grimaced, waiting for the contraction to pass. Eighteen and unmarried, she was sitting at the bottom of the stairs in the home of Jettie Place, the woman who had been her father's mistress.

A few more hours and it will be all over, she thought. I'll know. She closed her eyes and prayed, Please God, let it be Mourning's. But how will Jettie react if the baby is colored? I don't care. Let her throw us out in the snow. It has to be Mourning's. Then she bit her bottom lip and forced herself to accept the other possibility. White or black, I am responsible for this helpless little baby. No one else is going to take care of him, stick up for him.

Jettie rushed in and gathered up the blankets and pillow that lay on the steps next to Olivia. "I'm taking these out to the buggy," Jettie said. "I'll be right back. You sit there and wait for me. Don't you move. Them steps out there are fearsome slick."

Jettie's voice had grown steadier and she no longer sounded on the verge of hysteria. When she came back in she pulled a thick knit hat over Olivia's head and wound a scarf around her neck. Then she all but carried her down the steps, hustled her into the backseat of the buggy, and covered her with the blankets.

"You don't have to suffocate me." Olivia struggled out from under the blankets and set the pillowcase in which she had stuffed her belongings on the seat next to her.

Jettie got in the front seat and turned around to train a frown on her. "You sure you want to do this? It's a long drive to Weaverton, and we don't even know if that old goat of a doctor is at home. What if we lose a wheel? It's dark already. Ain't gonna be a soul on the road."

"Jettie, I told you, I didn't spend nine months hiding in your house so everyone in Five Rocks would know I had a baby. Quicker you stop talking and drive, quicker we'll get there."

Jetty hung a lantern on the post and said, "Giddap." She hunched forward, peering into the black ahead of them. "I can't see a darn thing. Not five paces in front of me."

"You don't need to see five paces ahead. All you need to see is the spot where the horse is going to put his foot down next." Olivia quoted what Mourning Free had told her, when she'd complained about driving at night.

The back seat was deep, with plenty of legroom. Olivia knew the next contraction would come soon and turned around to kneel on the floor, with her arms and head resting on the seat.

Jettie turned in her seat again. "What's the matter, you gonna be sick?"

"No. Stop worrying about me and watch where you're going. I just want to see if it's easier to take the pain like ..." Her own low cry cut her off as the contraction took her by surprise.

It was close to ten o'clock by the time they knocked on the doctor's door.

"Yes?" Only his nose was visible through the crack.

"Thank God you're home. It's her time." They huddled on his dark porch, Jettie holding onto Olivia as if she were a rag doll.

"You brought a birthing mother here? In the middle of the night?" He didn't open the door any wider.

"Yessir, that's what I did and here she is."

"No, Madam. No. No. I deliver babies in the mother's home. You should have sent for me. You don't get a woman in labor out of her bed, and I'm not running a hospital. Or a hotel."

2

"Well, we're here now and her contractions are coming right quick."

Olivia bent forward as the next one hit her.

The door didn't budge. "Certainly you have relatives or friends who can accommodate you."

"We had family hereabout, we sure wouldn't be on your front porch," Jettie said, losing patience. "Can't you see she's fixing to drop her baby right here on your doorstep?"

He pulled the door wider, but did not invite them in. "Look here, I can't be delivering babies in my home every day. I wouldn't have a towel or blanket left in the house."

Jettie put her foot over the threshold. "We ain't plannin' on coming every day. And we got our own blankets you can spread on the bed. Is it more money you want?"

"You certainly can't ignore the inconvenience, not to mention the expense of the laundry or replacing the bedding."

Jettie let go of Olivia and stepped toward him, looking like she might take a swing. He shuffled a few steps back.

"How much?"

"Let's see ... two dollars might just about cover it. Of course, that would be in addition to my regular charge of a dollar and a half."

"All right. Just show her where she can lie down."

"You said you have blankets?"

Jettie left Olivia hanging onto the doorjamb and rushed back to the buggy for the blankets, pillow, and towels.

"Come with me," the doctor said.

He gripped Olivia's arm with obvious distaste and she moved down the hall with him, taking tiny steps. He was apparently unmarried. At least no wife came rushing to assist him. That's good, Olivia thought. One less mouth flapping. Jettie followed them into a room

3

that held only a single bed, a nightstand, and a small table and chair. The doctor released Olivia's arm and removed the coverlet and sheets from the bed, heaping them on the table. Then he spread one of Jettie's blankets on the mattress and gestured for Olivia to lie down.

"There you go," Jettie said. "You lie yourself down there. Everything's going to be all right now." After Olivia was arranged on the bed, Jettie fiddled in her pocket and handed the doctor some coins. "There's four dollars," she said. "I know we can count on your discretion."

He pocketed the money and for the first time looked at Olivia's face.

"Oh, it's you. *Mrs.* Springer." He sniffed. "Yes, I thought you might be back, wanting me to clean up the mess." He turned, gathered up his precious bedding, and left the room.

While the doctor was gone Jettie helped Olivia remove her clothing, except for the shirt of her long johns, and covered her with the other blanket. He soon returned, carrying his doctor's bag and a stack of towels. While he spread a white towel on the table and arranged his instruments he muttered a string of unkind words – young girls can't keep their legs together, it's always a man's gotta suffer for the stupidity of some female.

"I left a pan of water on the stove," he said to Jettie. "Go wait for it to boil and bring it here."

His voice was harsh, but by now Olivia was in such distress that she didn't care how mean-spirited he was, as long as he got her through this alive. It went on until after three in the morning. All Olivia remembered later was the tremendous relief of that last push. She hadn't asked anything about the baby, didn't care if it was white, black, boy, girl, or frog – as long as it was out of her. But there was no need to ask what color it was.

Jettie had been next to the doctor, down there

4

between Olivia's legs, saying, "Come on, girl, push, you're almost there, just once more, you can do it, that's a good girl." But a moment before that last tremendous flood of release Jettie grew quiet. There were no shouts of joy when Olivia felt the doctor pull the baby away from her. So she knew it was colored, even before Jettie laid it across her chest. The room was silent except for the doctor coldly instructing her to push once more so he could finish up down there.

"It's a boy, Olivia," was all Jettie whispered.

The doctor soon stood and ordered Jettie out into the hall. Olivia squeezed her eyes shut at the ugliness of his words – "nigger bastard ... slut ... worst kind of trash ... respectable house." Then she heard Jettie declare that she'd had no idea.

"Here," Jettie said to him, "take another two dollars and keep your trap shut. We'll be gone before dawn."

Olivia gently put her hands on the tiny wrinkled creature – who had no idea he was the object of so much hatred – and lifted her head to look at him. "Hey Boy," she said softly and moved one hand to his head. "Don't you pay him any mind. Are you feeling all right Little Boy? You ought to be. You could have had a monster for a daddy, but the one you got is a wonderful man."

The doctor never returned to the room. Olivia pulled the blanket over the baby and lay still, terrified of hearing the sound of Jettie's heeled boots as she stomped out to the buggy and abandoned them. But when the door opened Jettie was there, carrying a bucket of hot water. She said nothing as she lifted the baby from Olivia. He fussed while Jettie cleaned him up, but made more contented sounds when she wrapped him in the clean towel that had been warming on the stove.

"Here, lean forward so I can tuck this behind you." Jettie was cradling the baby in one arm and holding out a second pillow in the other.

5

When Olivia was settled, Jettie lowered the baby into her arms. Olivia peeked at the tiny face hidden in the folds of the towel. He was the same lovely color as Mourning, black coffee with a touch of cream. Soft black fuzz covered his head. She had never smelled anything so lovely and new.

"I'm gonna see to you now, so don't you turn all shy on me," Jettie said.

She pulled the bloody blanket away, wetted a rag, and washed Olivia as best she could without getting everything sopping wet. Then she rolled up a towel and shoved it between Olivia's legs, pushed her knees together, and covered her up with the blanket.

"You're gonna bleed. That ain't nothing to worry about," she said and then poked Olivia's shoulder. "Nudge over a bit, will you."

Jettie rested her hip on the bed and neither of them spoke. Olivia felt she should say something, apologize for lying, but she was so tired. She slouched back down in the bed, with the baby lying across her chest. Before she dozed off, her eyes flew open. "The horse. We left the poor horse outside in his harness."

Jettie stroked her forehead. "He's all right. I seen to him. You get some sleep."

It seemed that barely a moment passed before Jettie was shaking her. "Olivia, wake up."

"Go away. Leave me alone." Olivia turned on her side. She could hear some horrible squalling, but it seemed to be coming from far away.

"Come on now. There's a good girl. You want all this howling to stop, you got to give that little feller something to suck on."

Olivia pushed herself up in bed, blinking. On the table was a drawer Jettie had taken from somewhere and lined with towels, to serve as a tiny bed. Jettie tucked a pillow under Olivia's arm and then picked up the baby and settled him with his mother.

"Just look at him, will you? Latched right onto you

like a tick. Most girls have a time of it, till they get the first one feeding."

"How would you know?" Olivia asked grumpily as the baby clamped down hard on her tender nipple. "Ouch! This baby was born with teeth!"

"You're all sore and sensitive now, but it'll get easier, don't you worry."

Olivia collapsed into the pillow with her eyes closed, grimacing. "What time is it?" she asked.

"Don't know. Sun ain't up yet." Jettie sat at the foot of the bed. "So, it would appear that you and Mr. Mourning Free were slightly better acquainted than you let on. At least now I understand why you were so set on having this baby anywhere but Five Rocks."

Olivia felt her face flush and was ashamed to look at Jettie. "It only happened with Mourning one time. Just the once. I got real sick with the fever and he took care of me. Then after I was feeling better ... it just happened is all. A day or two after that I went over to the Stubblefields and that's when they ... you know, like I told you. Everything I said about that was true. I swear."

Jettie patted her leg. "Sure it was. Ain't no girl gonna make up a story like that, 'bout some monster raping her over and over."

"I couldn't tell you about Mourning. I promised him I'd never tell anyone. You know what some folks would do to a colored for being with a white girl. I didn't mean to lie to you, Jettie. Honest, I didn't. I just thought it was likely to turn out to be Filmore's baby anyway, so there was no reason anyone ever had to know about Mourning. I'm sorry for keeping it secret from you."

"Best you did, child. Best you did. You go on holding that secret. You ain't done nothing wrong by not telling me. Best thing for you, nobody knows you been with a colored. I ain't judging you, but it sure is best that no one else know."

"You probably don't believe that it only happened

with Mourning the one time."

"Yes I do. I think I do. And a damn shame at that." She slapped Olivia's thigh and grinned. "That Mourning Free is a right handsome fellow. Got that strong chin and all them muscles. I don't think I'd have lasted past the first time I saw him take his shirt off. He did take it off, didn't he?" She opened her eyes wide.

"You're awful." Olivia giggled and looked at Jettie with something close to adoration. After a night without sleep and with her face unpainted, Jettie looked tired and used up. Everything on her that could sag did. But Olivia had never seen a more beautiful face.

She always says people never fail to surprise you by behaving worse than you imagined they could, Olivia thought. But she keeps surprising me the opposite, by how good she is. No one but Jettie could have gotten a laugh out of me today. Poor Jettie. She was so hunched over all the way here, her back must be killing her. And now she has to drive all the way back home.

"You're the best friend a person could have," Olivia said. "There was a time I felt sorry for you, but I don't any more. The ones who need feeling sorry for are all those mean-hearted women who don't talk to you. Not one of them will ever have a Christian heart as big as yours."

That was the only time Olivia ever saw tears in Jettie Place's eyes.

They both dozed off, Jettie seated in a chair with her head resting on the foot of the bed. The baby's fussing soon roused them. Olivia felt a pleasant tug in her stomach with every suck he took. She lowered her head to breathe in his sweet milky scent and ran her fingers over the soft fuzz of his hair, marveling at the little hand poking out of the towel. He had the tiniest pink fingernails. When he fell asleep she loosened the towel and ran her fingertips over his soft body. His skin was perfect except for one small mole on the side of his neck. That was when Olivia started crying, her resolve from the night before abandoning her. How on earth was she going to look out for a black baby?

"Oh Jettie, what am I going to do? Who's going to take care of this poor little boy?"

"Shh ... shhh." Jettie stroked her head. "Right now you are, darling. You brought this little feller into the world and you're going to give him the best start you can. You got plenty of time to think about what's to come. Right now you got nothing but time. No hurry about anything. You rest and get your strength back and let that baby get working on turning into a person. One day at a time. For the both of you. That's all you got to worry about."

The house was still silent when Jettie said they'd best be leaving. First she went into the kitchen and made two cups of tea and sliced some bread.

She set Olivia's cup and plate on a chair next to the bed and said, "I bet the good doctor ran off to stay somewhere else, waiting for the white trash slut and her nigger bastard to vacate his respectable premises." She reached for the baby so Olivia could eat.

"He left us all alone in his house?" Olivia asked as she hungrily devoured the bread. "Two strangers?"

"Probably figured the last thing these two strangers are looking for is the trouble and attention they'd stir up by stealing anything."

It was a long way home. Not wanting to arrive home before dark, Jettie turned in the opposite direction, thinking they could stop for a few meals and while the day away. She soon realized how exhausted she was and how ridiculous it would be to drive around in the cold with a newborn.

"To hell with this," she said and turned the buggy around.

The baby seemed to like the rocking motion and

slept when he wasn't nursing. Jettie stopped once for dark ale, which she told Olivia would help her produce milk, and brought bowls of beef soup out to the buggy. Then she headed for home, worried that they might find customers waiting outside her bake shop. But there was no one in sight when she pulled the buggy close to the back door and hurried Olivia and the baby through the kitchen and into the parlor.

"You sit. Let me take the baby up first," she ordered Olivia.

Jettie held him tightly to her breast with one hand and clutched the banister with the other. Afraid of tripping on her long skirt, she stopped on the third step and reached down to grab a handful of fabric and wrap it around the handrail. Olivia had never seen Jettie's legs and noted how shapely they were. Then she closed her eyes in exhaustion.

Jettie laid the baby on Olivia's bed and removed a drawer from the bureau. She emptied it, lined it with towels, and managed to settle him in his new bed without waking him. Then she went back down to help Olivia up the stairs. On her third trip up, she carried two pitchers of water. On the fourth, she had rags and towels tucked under her arms, a lantern and matches in one hand, and a plate with a piece of pie and two slices of bread in the other.

"I got to go return that buggy to the livery and then I got to lie down. I'm sorry, but you'll have to do with just that to eat."

When Olivia woke to feed the baby the next morning Jettie's door was still closed. The clock in the hallway said it was almost 10. Wincing in pain with each step, she tiptoed downstairs to light the stove. Then she peeked out the window and wondered how many customers had come today and found the Closed sign still on the door of the bakery. How many days would Jettie's house have to remain closed up and silent before any of those good women would think to knock on the door and see if she needed help? Later Jettie came down and poured a cup of the coffee Olivia had made. The baby was awake on the table in front of Olivia, surrounded by rolled up blankets and towels, he and his mother cooing at one another.

"Look at that. He's looking right at me," Olivia said.

"He can't see you yet. Can't see nothin' but shadows and light." Jettie worked the pump for a glass of water.

"Then he's looking right at my shadow. His skin isn't all that dark, is it?"

"Dark enough." Jettie set her water and coffee on the table next to Olivia and sat down. "Sure is a cute little feller."

"But people could think he's a dark-colored white person. Like an Italian or Greek or something. With real curly hair."

"Don't you even try to convince yourself of such foolishness. That child is colored and ain't no one going to mistake it for nothing else. That nanny goat doctor knew the minute his poor little head started crowning. Don't you let your mind go in that direction, Olivia Killion. Not for a minute."

"But there *are* dark-skinned white people that aren't colored. Arabs. What about Egyptians? Don't they have dark skin?"

"Maybe a dark-skinned Egyptian ain't exactly colored, but he sure ain't white and ain't gonna be asked to tea in any parlors in Five Rocks. You can't pass this baby. Not in this world. Don't even think about it. You'd only break your heart trying. And his."

Olivia bit her lip and fought tears. "At least he didn't turn out to be Filmore's," she said, her voice shaky. "I wouldn't be able to stand to look at him if he were Filmore's." She leaned over and put her elbows on the table, both palms on her baby's head.

Chapter Two

Olivia kept her son with her at Jettie Place's house for three months, but never gave him a name. Jettie referred to him as the baby; Olivia called him Little Boy. Jettie had made a point of mentioning to one of her customers that her niece and the niece's baby were staying with her for a while, in case anyone heard him crying.

One June night Jettie put down her needlework and peered at Olivia over her eyeglasses. "It's good you kept the baby this long – he needed his mother's milk. But it's time to let him go to folks what can be parents to him. He can't stay locked up in this house forever and you got to get on with your life."

Little Boy, sticky and sweet, was in Olivia's lap, laughing as she made faces at him. Olivia had no interest in what was left of her pathetic life. She had been clinging to one hope – that Mourning would come back and raise Little Boy up. Olivia would give them money. All the money she had, and Uncle Scrugg's farm, and she'd get a job. She daydreamed about Jettie hiring Mourning to help in the bakery. Olivia would go on hiding in Jettie's house and look after Little Boy during the day. Mourning would take him to his own home at night. After folks got used to the idea that Mourning Free had a son Olivia could "come back" from Michigan and take a job as Jettie's housekeeper. They could all be together and Olivia wouldn't have to hide anymore.

"I'd say the sooner was the better." Jettie interrupted her thoughts. "For the both of you."

Olivia felt numb. She blurted out her daydream about Mourning coming back.

Jettie let out a deep sigh and picked her needlepoint back up, speaking as she worked. "Sure. That ought to work out just grand. So what if the two of you disappeared from here at the same time? Who's gonna notice Mourning coming back with a motherless child and you turning up just in time to all but adopt that child? Nothing strange about that. Person would have to be a real busybody to pay any attention to that. It's not like you and Mourning was ever friends or anything. Like any of them ladies ever thought you was too good a friends. Lucky we don't got any nosy ladies like that around here."

"So I'll move to some other town, someplace no one knows anything about Mourning. With the orphan child I'm bringing up –"

"Stop it, Olivia. Ain't no point to that kind of dreaming. Strange white girl in town with no family and her bastard nigger child. Neither one of you'd have any kind of life at all. You got to let him go. He needs to be with his own kind."

"Who says colored is his kind? He's just as much white as he is colored."

"Longer you wait, harder it's gonna be."

"I can't do it. How can I let him go?"

"How can you not? Why would you want to do that to him? Look, it ain't like I don't know how hard it's gonna be on you. But you know better than most that life is hard. The choices we got to make ain't hardly ever between good and better. You did a stupid, irresponsible thing, lying down with Mourning Free. Now you got the results sitting in your lap. So do what you gotta do to make it right. Give that child a chance to live his life like a whole person, not half of anything. What *you* want to happen don't count for nothing."

Olivia stared at the floor for a long while. When Jettie spoke again the stern look on her face and the harshness of her voice had relented.

"Who knows, you might get to see him after he's grown. His new daddy might work here in Five Rocks, like Goody Carter done. Or maybe Mourning *will* come back and want to go get him. But you can't hold this child prisoner, waitin' on that happening."

"I know, Jettie." Olivia laid the baby down on the rug and hugged her arms to her chest, feeling empty. "Let's do it tomorrow," she heard herself say. "Let's just get it over with."

"Tomorrow? You can't do it tomorrow. You got to learn him how to eat something 'sides what comes outa your titty. I suppose there'll be plenty of wet nurses in whatever nigger town he ends up in, but what's the little feller going to do between the time you leave him and the time he lands with his new parents? That ain't gonna happen in five minutes."

"All right, we'll start teaching him that tomorrow," Olivia snapped and clomped up the steps, leaving the baby with Jettie.

The next day Jettie came in for her noon break and set what looked like a misshapen ceramic teapot on the kitchen table. It was white with a pattern of delicate blue flowers, though that was barely visible through the layers of crud that encrusted it, and its spout was long and open.

"What the heck is that?" Olivia asked.

"It's a pap feeder. For the baby. I got it out of a crate of my mamma's old things."

Olivia frowned at it.

"Oh, stop looking like that. Course it's dirty. It's only been up in the loft for about a thousand years. But while I'm out in the shop this afternoon, you're going to get it all cleaned up. Nice and shiny. And get some pap ready. Then this evening I'll show you how to use it."

"Pap? I don't even know what that means. How am I supposed to know how to make it?"

"Ain't no thing. Just grind a bit of cornmeal, fine as you can get it, and mix it with water." She turned to reach up to the cupboard for the pestle and mortar. "Then you grind up some walnuts to add to it. Little Boy here is gonna like it just fine, aren't you darling?"

After supper Jettie said, "You nurse him a bit now.

14

Enough to keep him from fussing, but not so much that he ain't got no appetite left."

While Olivia obeyed, Jettie squinted at the bowl of pap Olivia had prepared, stirred some more water into it, and poured the mixture into the pap feeder.

"You just put this in his mouth." She pointed to the spout. "And then you tip it up like so." She demonstrated and a few blobs of pap fell into her palm. "It also has this special spoon." She held it out for Olivia to examine. "See how the stem is all hollow? That's so you can blow into it, case the pap ain't getting into his mouth."

Olivia looked dubious and her skepticism proved to be justified – her first attempts resulted in gobs of mush dotted all over the baby and his shirt. As far as she could tell, nothing had gone into his mouth.

"You keep at it," Jettie said as she began grinding more corn meal. "Once you get the hang of it, we can try putting some milk in there."

"Cow milk?"

"That too. But mostly yours. You gotta learn how to squeeze it out, less each day, till it dries up."

Over the next two weeks Little Boy gradually got more pap and milk from the feeder and less nourishment at Olivia's breast. Then one evening Jettie announced, "I think I'd best get a buggy tomorrow."

Olivia nodded, walked silently upstairs, got into bed, pulled the covers over her head, and tried to convince herself what a good thing this was. By this time tomorrow I'll be free – as if none of it ever happened. This baby is nothing but a rock around my neck and I should be celebrating. The best for him is best for me too. Besides, colored is colored and white is white, and this child and I would never understand one another. He doesn't belong with me.

She fell into sleep, but started awake in the middle of the night and sat up. Who says he doesn't belong with me? Why doesn't my half count for anything?

"I'm not going," Olivia said the next morning.

Jettie had risen before her and there was already a buggy standing outside.

"That would be best," Jettie replied, avoiding Olivia's eyes, "but I can't see me managing both the reins and the baby."

"I didn't mean I want you to go alone. I meant I'm not going to abandon him."

They were standing in the front hall, Olivia at the foot of the steps with her arms crossed, Jettie with her back to the open front door. Jettie stared at Olivia for a moment and then loudly sucked her front teeth. She reached behind her to push the door shut, went to her chair in the parlor, and sat back, eyes closed.

"I can't, Jettie." Olivia stood in front of her. "He's mine to care for. I'm the one who's supposed to stick up for him. Like Mr. Carmichael always stuck up for Mourning."

Looking exhausted, Jettie opened her eyes. "Don't you see that you're the one person on earth what can't do that? Because he's yours. If he'd been born to someone else, you could be that kind-hearted stranger lady, always willing to lend him a hand. But being his mother, you won't be able to do that. All you'd bring him is grief. Let him go, Olivia. If you really care for him, you'll let him go."

It was a long drive to South Valley, where a community of coloreds lived in The Bottoms. Neither woman had anything to say on the way. Olivia held Little Boy limply, as if he were a bundle of napkins. Jettie had no trouble locating the colored section of town. Find the unmarked turn-off that's never been graded. The one that leads to a cluster of weather-beaten cabins.

They were soon parked facing the colored Baptist

16

church, but far enough away to give Olivia some privacy. She handed Little Boy to Jettie, climbed into the back seat, and opened the buttons of her dress to express milk into the feeder, which she carefully set in the baby's basket. When she had finished and climbed out of the buggy she took Little Boy back from Jettie.

"Hullo!" she called into the empty church. "Hullo! Anybody here?"

Jettie strode past the altar and peeked around the corner. "Don't seem to be no one. Let's have a seat for a few minutes." She nodded at the simple pews.

They sat in silence, staring up at Jesus. "Died for our sins," Jettie muttered. "Lot a good that done, way folks keep replenishing the inventory. And I ain't talking about you."

Olivia said nothing. Neither did she smile at Little Boy when he wiggled to get her attention.

Finally Jettie spoke. "Might be best if we left him up there on that table in front of the altar. I'll go get the basket out of the buggy."

"We aren't going to go off and leave him, Jettie. What's the matter with you? There's no one here."

"Someone's bound to hear him crying and come before long. The door ain't locked."

"Have you lost your mind? I'm not leaving him here all alone. Suppose there are rats in here? Or some nasty old cat gets in?"

"Can I help you ladies?" a deep voice said from behind them. It belonged to a heavy-set colored man whose stained white collar proclaimed him to be the preacher.

"Hullo, Reverend." Jettie rose and nervously stepped into the aisle. "Pardon us for barging into your church, but the door was open. We were looking for you, hoping you could help us. You see we found this baby." She turned and nodded at Olivia and Little Boy. "Poor thing was totally abandoned. Someone just left him lying in a basket, right by the side of the road. He was crying his little heart out, so we stopped and picked him up and drove right straight over here, hoping you'd know some good Christian colored family might be willing to take him in."

The preacher walked toward them. "Where did you say you found this child?" he asked and looked down at Olivia, who was still seated holding Little Boy. The Reverend's eyeglasses were so thick she couldn't see the expression in his eyes, but his voice was kind.

Olivia looked into his face as she spoke. "By the side of the road. In a basket. There was a bundle of clothes, too. We've got those and the basket out in the buggy." She held the baby up for him to see. "He's a real sweet little thing."

"Yes, I can see that." He emitted a soft grunt as he sat down on the pew next to her. "It happens there is a couple in my congregation that hasn't been blessed with children of their own."

"That's plain wonderful," Jettie said, looking ready to run out of the church like a bank robber making his get-away. "So I guess you can arrange everything."

"It's not that simple," the Reverend said. "This baby has parents somewhere. Perhaps they didn't abandon him. Could be someone stole him from them, or he was left at the roadside by accident and they're looking for him, frantic with worry. Please, come into my office, so I can make a note of the exact place you found him and any other details you can recall. I'll have to post advertisements. Someone may well show up to claim the child for their own. I'll need your names and addresses too, so we can get in touch with you, need be."

"Reverend, we'd like to accommodate," Jettie said and edged toward the door, "but we're in an awful hurry. We didn't have the time it took to bring him here. This was way out of our way."

"I hate to impose," the Reverend said, his voice revealing the anger he was trying to hide, and stood up with another soft grunt. If Olivia hadn't been so miserable, she could have smiled at the way he had Jettie shaking. Not many folks managed to intimidate Jettie Place. "But you have to understand. I can't ask anyone to adopt a baby I know nothing about. How do they know that a year from now someone won't show up wanting to claim him for their own?"

"Reverend ..." Olivia struggled to her feet, one arm around the baby and the other hand on the back of the pew in front of her. She looked directly into his eyes. "This child's mother is never going to come to claim him. She couldn't, even if she wanted to. Not in this world." She was sure he understood what she was saying and held Little Boy out to him. "I hope they'll be good to him."

The Reverend reluctantly accepted the baby. "I must insist that you give me your names. There are authorities I need to notify. It will only take a few minutes."

"I'm sorry, Reverend, but we gotta be on our way," Jettie said. "We got all the way back to Philadelphia to go. We could have just left him here by the altar. Probably best you tell them authorities that's what happened. You found him right there." She took Olivia's arm and dragged her out of the church. "Get in that buggy and let's go."

"I've got to give him the basket with the clothes and things."

"Never mind about that. Let's get out of here, 'fore someone else comes along wanting to know our names."

"I'm not leaving him here without any clean clothes. Without a thing to eat!" Olivia angrily yanked her arm out of Jettie's grip, leaned into the back of the buggy to retrieve the basket, and strode back to the church.

"He's three and a half months old and perfectly healthy. His birthday is March 24. These are his clothes." She turned to leave, then stopped to ask,

"What's your name, Reverend?"

"Jameson. Reverend Harold Jameson."

"Thank you, Reverend Jameson. I can't –" Her voice broke, but she didn't cry. "The name of this baby's father is Mourning. Mourning Free. He has no idea that he has a son. But Little Boy should know who his father is and be proud of it."

The Reverend stared at her.

"There's money in the bottom of the basket. Fifty dollars. It's for Little Boy, when he's grown. Or if this couple – his parents – come on hard times, it's to help them through. There's milk in there too. In one of those pap feeder things."

Without looking at her son again, Olivia turned and fled.

Chapter Three

Jettie drove away from the church as fast as she could. Olivia sat behind her in the back seat, her lips clamped in a tight frown and her gaze frozen on the scrubby fields they passed. At first she felt nothing. Then she turned her head slightly to glare at Jettie's back, wanting to pound her fists against the older woman.

The old bag can't wait to get out of here, Olivia thought. Just can't wait to be rid of Little Boy, have my bastard colored baby out of her house. Why did I listen to her? She doesn't care two cents about what's going to happen to him. She pretends to be so nice, but look how she shamed my mother, didn't care if the whole town knew she was "Old Man Killion's whore." The busybodies are right not to speak with her. The selfish bitch made me give my little baby away. No one would ever have known that Little Boy was in her house. Not in a million years. Someone would have to visit her for that to happen, and no one does. Everyone hates her. I hate her. How did I spend a whole year with her?

Olivia did not speak a word. Neither did Jettie. Again Jettie pulled close to the back door. Again Olivia slipped into the house while Jettie drove off to return the buggy. But this time Olivia was unencumbered. Her arms and heart were empty.

She dragged herself up the stairs and shut the door to her room with a soft click. She removed her outer garments, leaving them as they fell, and crawled into bed, where she remained for the next three days. She shed no tears. When she sank into sleep it was dreamless. Mostly she lay awake, either curled on her side, hugging her knees to her chest, or stretched on her back with her hands clasped behind her neck.

July 15, 1842. That was her first coherent thought. She mustn't forget the date. She had to write it down. The day she'd gone to the South Valley First Black Baptist Church and placed her three-month old baby boy in the arms of Reverend Harold Jameson, a man she'd never before laid eyes on. She could still hear the crunch of gravel under the wheels of the buggy as they fled the churchyard. Lord, what kind of mother abandons her baby to his fate, just because his skin is the wrong color? She felt sick, remembering how she had handed Little Boy over and walked away without looking back. She could think of nothing worse a woman could do. Why should she trust the Reverend? Just because he was colored? That didn't mean he couldn't do something terrible to a colored baby. What was to stop him from selling Little Boy to one of those slave catchers? Some people would do anything for money. She'd heard there were even free colored folks down south who owned other colored folks as slaves. She'd laughed the first time she'd heard that ridiculous notion, but Avis said it was true. A free colored man was entitled to own property same as a white man, including slaves. She broke into a sweat, imagining the Reverend's kind features contorted into evil ones. Lord, how had she left her helpless Little Boy with a complete stranger?

She remembered the rage with which she had glared at the back of Jettie's neck, at the wisps of gray that escaped the bun of blond hair. But Olivia's anger – and the need to blame someone else – had quickly passed. She burned with shame. Jettie had shown her nothing but great kindness. Olivia had no call to blame Jettie for the mess she had made of her life. No, she could find fault only with herself.

She felt ill with longing, remembering the tiny face, the way his bright eyes opened wide whenever she picked him up. So trusting. Never suspecting his mother capable of such a grand betrayal. But Jettie was right about one thing – if she tried to keep him, she'd likely be doing him more harm than good. She needed a plan.

I no longer have to hide in Jettie's house, she thought. I'll go home, but won't stay with Avis and Mabel for long. I'm free to waltz around wherever I please. I'll ask everyone in town if they know where Mourning Free has gotten to. I'll say I need him to do some work for me. Surely Little Boy will be all right with the good Reverend long enough for me to do that. He looked like such a kind-hearted man. And if I can't find Mourning and tell him he has a son? Then I'll go back and get Little Boy. I'll rent a buggy and tell Avis and Tobey that I intend to drive to all the towns around here, see if any of them are looking for a schoolteacher. And that evening I'll return home with a little colored baby. Say I found him abandoned by the roadside. I promised Reverend Jameson that I'd never come back, but he'll just have to understand. Little Boy is my blood.

Olivia had grown accustomed to blaming Iola and Filmore Stubblefield for every bit of the disaster her life had become. The overly-helpful, nosy, Bible-thumping couple she'd thought herself lucky to have as neighbors had violated her, humiliated her, and tortured her. Tried to force her to bear a child for them. Probably would have succeeded, had she not already been carrying Mourning Free's son. She had no idea what they'd done to Mourning, except that it had been awful enough to make him flee in panic, leaving her alone and vulnerable.

Yes, for all those things the Stubblefields were to blame, she thought. But the rest? What happened between Mourning and me is nothing to do with them. If we'd never met the Stubblefields, I still would have borne Little Boy, and still be unable to care for him. The blame for that is all mine. It was my big mouth that talked Mourning into leaving Five Rocks, the one place he felt safe, and going to Michigan with me. And then it was me went and put my arms around his neck. I chose to lie down with Mourning Free. No one made me do that. He would have stopped any time. All I had to do was say, "No, we can't do this." I could see him waiting for me to say that word. "Don't." But I never did.

She closed her eyes and remembered his scent and the warmth of strong arms around her. It was a memory she found impossible to regret. How could that be a sin? But she knew the answer: because it begat a child who was now alone in the world.

But it isn't our fault the world is filled with stupidity and hatred. Isn't that the real sin? And if I hadn't lain with Mourning, Little Boy wouldn't have been there to protect me, to make my womb safe from Filmore's assault. And how did I repay that sweet baby? Left him to grow up just like his father – on his own, from meal to meal.

Jettie waited patiently. Each mealtime Olivia heard her set a tray out in the hall, rap lightly, and tiptoe away. Olivia always waited for her tread on the stairs before opening the door. Then she ate some of the food, barely tasting it.

23

Toward noon of the fourth day Olivia descended the stairs, her breasts painfully swollen and large wet circles staining the front of her nightdress. Jettie was in the kitchen preparing a meal, and Olivia stood silently in the doorway, waiting for her to look up.

"There you are. Hungry?"

Olivia shrugged.

"Sure you are. Come sit. Ain't you been doing nothin' about that?" She nodded at Olivia's chest.

"I will."

Olivia dished herself a bowl of the beef stew simmering on the stove top, too hungry to politely wait for Jettie to join her at the table.

"How was business this morning?" Olivia asked between bites, as if this were any other day.

"Oh, same as usual. I miss your help, I can tell you – " Jettie stopped abruptly and turned from the counter where she was slicing bread. "Not that I mean … I want you to get all the rest you need. I was just saying … you been a big help and good company, and I miss having you out there." She took the few steps to put her arms around Olivia.

"I smell bad," Olivia said, leaning away.

"My nose has survived worse. You should a smelled old lady Sommers this morning. Her girl must be off, or she'd never drag her old bones all that way for a loaf of bread. Must be years since that woman had a good scrub." She ladled a bowl of stew for herself and sat down, slipping into a stream of idle gossip and occasionally sneaking a wary glance at Olivia.

Oblivious to Jettie's chatter, Olivia devoured the stew as if she hadn't eaten in weeks. She mopped the bowl with thick slices of Jettie's rye bread and then stood to get herself a second helping.

"I want you to wake me for work tomorrow," Olivia said when she had finished, pushing her chair back.

Jettie put a firm hand on Olivia's arm. "You stay put. You ain't leaving this table yet. I got a peach pie out there, got your name all over it, so stay stuck to that chair while I go get it."

The door banged behind Jettie as she hurried out to the bakery in the barn. Olivia stared blankly at the pictures tacked to the kitchen wall, feeling hollow. Iola and Filmore had carved a hole inside her, but this new one, the one Little Boy left in her heart, was a gaping void. Olivia thought it would tear her to pieces. She suddenly felt faint with exhaustion and rested her forehead on the table.

She was in no hurry to leave Jettie's house. There was no place she wanted to go, no one she had any desire to see. She could imagine her brother Tobey's face and the boyish grin that would spread across it when he saw her. And then she heard herself feeding him a fat pack of lies. Him and everyone else.

By the time Jettie returned with the pie, Olivia was sobbing.

"Oh honey." Jettie came to stand at Olivia's side and rub her heaving back. "There, there, now. Everything's going to be all right."

Olivia lifted her head and turned to put her arms around Jettie's waist, clinging to her. "No it's not. Nothing is ever going to be all right. I wish I could just die."

"None of that now. What a thing to say. You got a whole life ahead of you. And you got your family. Course you're feeling awful low, but you'll see, it'll get better with time. You got to put Little Boy out of your mind. I'm sure he's gettin' all kinds of good care. Most all colored folk I ever known are right kind-hearted. Must come of havin' so many troubles of their own. I bet his new mamma's got him out in the yard right now, enjoying the sunshine. All the neighbor kids are crowding around to see him, giving him a tickle, and he's laughing the way he does. He's fine. Believe me. Much happier than he was here, no one but the same two women to look at, and never a breath of fresh air. I don't mean to say that you ain't done well by him. You made him a wonderful mamma. You ought to be feeling nothin' but proud for having the love and courage it took to do right by him. And you did the right thing. You know that without me telling you."

Olivia sat up straight, dry-eyed. Her mouth was set in a hard line, and she said nothing. Courage, she thought. It takes all kinds of courage to discard a tiny baby in a basket.

"You'll go back to your life and before long you'll have your own family. You'll still think of him every day, probably till the day you die, but it won't hurt so much. And who knows, maybe when he's grown or after Mourning comes back, you might get the chance to see him. See how good he turned out. How happy he is."

She continued to rub Olivia's back for a few more minutes, then said, "I got to get back to the shop, or I'm gonna have Mrs. Brewster banging both fists on the back door, yelling for her bread pudding. Meanwhile, you see how much of that pie you can put away. And about gettin' up for work tomorrow ... you best go on taking it easy for a while."

"I don't need any more rest. You wake me. The busier my hands are, the less time I'll spend crying." Olivia paused and then asked with a quiver, "Jettie, did I say anything mean to you?"

Jettie opened her eyes wide and shook her head. "I don't know what you mean, child."

"I was ... while we were driving back, all I could think was mean things about you, for taking me there. Like it was all your fault. I was so mad. I'm sorry for even thinking like that, but I hope I didn't say anything out loud to hurt your feelings."

"No, child, you didn't. You had your teeth clamped so tight, horse couldn't a dragged an unkind word outa that mouth."

The next morning Jettie rapped on Olivia's door and they slipped back into their old routine – baking together in the barn in the early morning and Olivia cleaning the house and preparing their meals in the afternoon. Olivia stuffed rags in the front of her dress and expelled less milk each day, waiting for her breasts to realize that there was no longer any need for what they yielded. When she'd been dry for two days she stood staring at herself in the mirror. Now there was nothing. The last remnant of Little Boy was gone, as if he'd never existed. She attempted to garner some appreciation for the freedom she would soon reclaim. I am a nineteen-year-old woman with my life ahead of me. She tried to smile, but her face seemed to be set in stone.

The next evening at supper Olivia said, "I've got my things packed to go home tomorrow. I'll wait until after dark, say I came on that delivery wagon."

Jettie paled and froze for a moment, then carefully arranged her knife and fork across her plate and wiped her mouth with her napkin. "Yes, it does seem to be time." She looked up, smiled brightly, and began chattering about Mrs. Reese and Mrs. Monroe. Her voice was so strained, just listening to it made Olivia's throat hurt. After a few minutes Jettie rose, left the dishes to Olivia, and went upstairs. Later she came back down to sit with Olivia in the parlor. She peered at a piece of needlework and mumbled about how good it felt to be off her aching feet.

"It's awful, the way I've got to say good-bye to you," Olivia blurted out. "Tomorrow I'll still be living right here in the same town, but it feels like I'll never see you again. I mean, not the way it is now."

"No." Jettie looked at Olivia over her glasses and spoke stiffly. "You won't. Not like now. You gotta go back to nodding when we pass on the street. At least you never used to cross to the other side when you saw me coming, like them other ladies."

"Oh no, Jettie, I can't ignore you like that. We'll be friends. Maybe not right at first, but we'll find a way to spend time together. We have to."

"That brother of yours and his Lady Mabel ain't never gonna let that happen. You can bet your life on that."

"I don't give a whit what Avis and Mabel think."

"I know you don't want to care but, like it or not, them and Tobey are the family you got."

Olivia rose and went to kneel by Jettie's chair, so she could rest her head in the older woman's lap.

"You've been more of a family to me than they ever were. You're the only person in the world who's ever made me feel like they'll always be on my side. No matter what. No one else would have taken care of me the way you did. You're the smartest, strongest, kindest woman I've ever known. Best thing I could hope for myself is to turn out to be as good a person as you are."

"Thank you for saying that, child." Jettie softly stroked Olivia's back. "Seems you're all the family I got, too. Best thing Seborn Killion left to me was this friendship with you." Then her voice lost its wistful note and she gave Olivia a pat, saying, "You get on up now. You'll have us both blubbering. Heavens, you ain't goin' but three blocks over. You'll come to visit. You get yourself up off the floor. I'm way too old for this kind of carrying on."

Olivia lifted her face up before she rose. "Jettie, are you still so sure it was the right thing to do?"

"More than sure. Far more than sure."

The next evening they ate most of their supper in silence. Then Jettie said, "I think I feel like going up early tonight. I'll leave these dishes for you to do up, if you don't mind. Before I turn in, I'll bring the wagon around to the back door, help you load your things onto it."

That afternoon Olivia had emptied her two wicker

baskets and lugged them down to the parlor where she repacked them. Now Olivia and Jettie each grabbed one of the handles of the first basket, carried it outside, and balanced it on the hand-drawn wagon that Jettie used to bring her groceries from Killion's General. It was a lovely night, the air cool and crisp. Olivia took a deep breath, deciding to take the bracing weather as a good omen. They went back for the second basket and then Olivia sank down on the back steps and said, "I think I'll sit out here for a while. Collect my thoughts."

Jettie gave her shoulder a squeeze and said, "I'll be saying my good night then. You keep safe."

"I *will* come to see you," Olivia promised before Jettie disappeared into the kitchen.

Olivia waited for the house to grow silent before going in to do the washing up. Then she paced in the dark, impatient for the time to pass. By 10 o'clock she could stand it no longer and donned her cloak, pulling its hood so far forward that she almost tripped down the back stairs. Wouldn't that be perfect – after hiding in Jettie's house for a whole year – to fall and break her leg now, on the very last day? After she caught her balance, she set both feet firmly on the path, bent for the handle of the wagon, and dragged it toward the road. Before emerging from the shelter of Jettie's backyard she stopped and threw her head back – one hand holding the hood in place – and gazed up at the night sky. Masses of dark clouds had begun to gather and the stars that were still visible shone like bright saucers against the blackness. She wondered what kind of sky Mourning was under.

Once out on the road, she moved quickly. When she reached Main Street she paused and squinted into the black shadows, but saw no one. All the downstairs windows were dark and no curtains seemed to be moving. Then a door creaked open, causing her heart to thump frantically. The willowy figure of Mr. Carmichael emerged from his office. He descended the steps and halted when he caught sight of the hooded creature lurking farther down the street.

Olivia remained motionless, not daring to draw a breath. The lanky lawyer paused a moment before he nodded, put a finger to his hatless forehead, and said a clear "Good evening." Then he turned and walked in the other direction. Olivia exhaled slowly as she watched the familiar gait of his long, thin limbs, knees jutting out to the sides, looking like a spindly-legged water bird. Like a crane, she almost giggled, remembering how the school children always shouted "Ichabod Crane" when he passed.

She assured herself that he couldn't possibly have recognized her. Not at that distance, in the dark, with her face half-covered. Anyway, she calmed herself, better to have been seen by Ichabod Crane than by anyone else in this town. At least he knew how to mind his own business.

Someone had torn out the bushes that used to grow around the sign in front of the Episcopal Church, so she dumped her baskets by the shrubbery along the side of the building. Then she dragged the empty wagon up Main Street and lifted it onto the wooden sidewalk outside Killion's General. Jettie would find it there early the next morning, allegedly abandoned by the mischievous children who had taken it from her yard. Then Olivia stood in the dark, back pressed against the side of the church, waiting for the arrival of the delivery wagon. For once she was not impatient. She felt painfully alone and disconnected, not yet prepared to make an appearance on the street as Olivia Killion.

When she heard the clop-clop of the horses she opened one of the baskets and removed the straw bonnet that she had packed at the top of it. She plopped it on her head and then wadded her cloak into the basket and closed it back up. The delivery wagon drew near and the driver reined in the horses and climbed down to let them drink from the trough. Luck was with her; he had no passengers. Olivia watched from the shadows, waiting for him to finish spitting tobacco and scratching himself. After he drove away she stepped out into the moonlight. Now all she had to do was walk up the street.

A light rain began to fall, but she didn't mind. She clamped one hand to the crown of her bonnet and turned her face to the sky, opening her mouth wide and savoring the warm drops. For a moment she felt like a little girl again. In the morning the street would be swarming with juicy pink worms. Ugh. She could smell them already. She walked out to the middle of Main Street and studied the town. Everything seemed to be the same, so why did it look so foreign?

There was the store, where she had sat at her father's feet playing jack-stones. She turned and looked behind her. From where she stood she couldn't see even the roof of Jettie's barn. Was Jettie asleep already? Olivia imagined her waking in the morning, once again alone in the empty house. She let out a sigh and walked slowly past Killion's General, up to the next corner. There was Avis's house, just a few steps away. All she had to do was knock on that door.

Chapter Four

Olivia stared at her old home with a puzzled expression and counted the number of houses from the corner. Yes, she was standing in front of the right one. Why didn't it look right? Then she realized what it was. The door was supposed to be black, but had been painted a rich olive green. It also boasted a shiny brass knocker that looked like it could crush rock. The unfamiliarity seemed to be mocking her – See, you don't belong here any more.

The steps and porch boards squawked under her feet, but the inside of the house remained silent. Olivia lifted the knocker and tapped three times. More silence. She took a few steps aside to peek in the front window, but no lantern glowed behind the drawn curtains. They must be asleep already. She lifted the knocker again and pounded, producing a series of loud metallic clanks. She glanced around, half-expecting the neighbors to rush out brandishing shotguns.

A minute or two passed before she heard a door open and close. Heavy steps thumped down the stairs and someone peered through the peephole. It was Mabel who pulled the door open, looking half-circus clown, half-ghost in her billowing white dressing gown, with her hair tied in clumps around white rags. She was holding a lantern high, but quickly bent to set it on the boot box, freeing both hands for her assault on Olivia.

"Olivia Killion, as I live and breathe, is that really you! Why bless my soul. Get yourself in here and let me give you a big hug!" She pulled Olivia into the front hall and closed the door behind her. "Lord, we've been so worried about you. How could you go off like that? Avis! Avis! Guess who's here! Your baby sister Olivia. She's here. She's standing right here in front of me. She's finally come to her senses, remembered where her home is."

She clamped her arms around Olivia and then pulled back to put her hands on Olivia's shoulders and hold her at arms' length. "You look just fine, thank the good Lord. We couldn't imagine what kinds of things you might be getting up to. I'll never understand how you could go off like that. Not let us hear a word from you. Not a single word. What were you thinking?"

Mabel vigorously shook her head, jiggling the ends of the strips of cloth she had knotted around her curls. She looked like a talking mop and Olivia had to suppress a giggle. She had yet to utter a word.

"Hullo, Olivia." Avis had come to a halt halfway down the stairs.

He was wrapped in their father's red and gray

flannel robe and even wore Seborn's slippers on his feet. He stood still as a statue, feet on different steps, looking hesitant to venture all the way down. Olivia stared up at her older brother, braced to see anger and censure on his face. Instead she saw – what? Insult? Shyness? His own fear of rejection? She had never perceived this big brother as vulnerable, but at that moment he looked almost afraid of her.

Olivia took a step and smiled up at him. "Hullo, Avis. You're looking fine."

He descended to the bottom of the stairs, awkwardly squeezed her shoulders, and pulled her briefly to his chest. He seemed to have put on some weight. Olivia stepped back to look at him and imagined him sitting with Mabel in the parlor after supper, him with his newspaper and her with her knitting. In the picture in her mind he looked at home. Comfortable. Like a man who has found the place he belongs.

Of course he feels comfortable, Olivia thought, feeling old resentments begin to simmer. He waited all his life to be the one in charge, and now he is. He has Killion's General, the house, Mabel to see to his needs, and Tobey to do all the dirty work at the store.

"You're looking fine yourself, Olivia."

Olivia stared into his face for a moment. He did appear to be glad to see her.

"Well, what are we all standing around here for?" Mabel herded them into the parlor. "I don't know where you've just come from, but wherever it is, I bet you're exhausted. You sit yourself down and I'll get you a nice cup of tea. Are you hungry?"

None of the furnishings in the room were familiar. Olivia perched on a short sofa upholstered in pink roses. Her brother settled himself into a black leather easy chair, lit the lantern that stood on the round end table next to him, and put his feet up on the footstool.

"No, thank you," Olivia replied to Mabel's question.

33

"I've eaten. But a cup of tea sounds good."

When Mabel left the room Olivia actually missed her presence. She couldn't remember the last time she'd had a conversation with Avis. Had they ever done more than exchange bits of information?

She looked around the room. For as long as Olivia could remember, it had held one simple divan, her father's ratty easy chair, and an unfinished rocking chair that creaked so loudly it startled people who sat in it the for the first time. Two straight-back chairs had stood in the corners and could be called into service on the rare occasions that company called. Now the room was crowded. Besides the enormous easy chair that Avis occupied – which was obviously his – there were two small sofas and three smaller easy chairs, all covered with the same fabric of pink roses and big green leaves. A similar pattern was repeated in the rug that now covered the once-bare floor. Olivia almost laughed out loud when her eyes came to rest on it; it was identical to the rug that lay in Jettie Place's parlor. Olivia nodded approvingly at the lacy white curtains that had replaced the heavy green velvet drapes.

"You've been gone a long time." Avis reached for something from the end table.

"Yes." Olivia untied her bonnet, set it next to her, and smoothed her hands over her hair.

She waited for the interrogation to begin. The glare of disapproval. But he squirmed in his chair and turned his attention to the pipe he had taken from the table, busying himself with cleaning and filling it. When he finally did begin asking questions, they were hesitant. Awkward.

"So, what have you been doing all this time? Where you been at?" He picked a long stick of something off the table, leaned over to touch it to the flame of the lantern, and used it to light his pipe.

"I went out to Michigan, to work Uncle Scruggs' place. I put in a crop, so I could make a claim on it, like it says in Father's will."

She was worse than a liar, trying to cheat her brothers, but felt little guilt about that. Neither Avis nor Tobey had wanted the land, and it wasn't her fault that she and Mourning hadn't been able to finish planting. Anyway, Avis already had everything he'd ever wanted and she would find a way to make it up to Tobey.

Avis puffed on his pipe, filling the room with sweet, pungent smoke, and voiced no objection. He nodded and didn't even look surprised. It occurred to her that he might be relieved by the prospect of Olivia going to live in far off Michigan, out of his hair and home.

"Uncle Lorenzo's cabin is still standing then?"

"Yes."

"What kind of crop did you put in?"

"Sweet corn. And winter wheat," she lied. "Not much of either, but all the will says is 'a crop.' It doesn't say how much of one."

"I didn't ask because … Tobey and I have discussed this matter." Avis sat up straight, looking more at ease, now that the conversation had taken this turn. "He thought that might have been where you'd gone. You know …" He paused and shook his head. "You didn't have to go all the way out there, Olivia. All you had to do was ask; both of us would have agreed to sign that land over to you, if we'd known you wanted it so bad."

Olivia stared at him for a moment, realizing she owed him a tremendous apology. Why did she always expect the worst of him? "That's generous of you," she said softly.

"Neither of us has any use for it." He sniffed his nose.

"But you could have sold it."

"None of that matters now, does it?" He settled back in his chair. "You went out there and earned it fair and square. But how did you manage on your own?"

She was stunned to see something that resembled admiration on his face.

"I hired one of the neighbor men to do the heavy work. And I bought a team of oxen in Detroit."

"What do you know about picking out a team of oxen?"

"Nothing. Lucky for me there was only one for sale and they turned out to be good animals."

"You're back for good though, aren't you?" He turned back into the serious, responsible older brother. "I mean, you don't plan to go back out there and live in the middle of nowhere, all by yourself, do you?" He sounded truly dismayed at the thought.

Olivia was spared from having to respond as Mabel stormed the room with her tea tray. She set it on the table at Olivia's elbow and half spun around, hands out. "So how do you like what I've done with the house?" she asked. "There's so much light in here now, without those dark old drapes. Course, you can't notice that now, but wait till you get up in the morning. Sun shines right in onto my new rug. Don't you just love those big roses? How do you take your tea? Here." She offered a plate of cookies to Olivia. "You've got to try these. Everyone says I ought to open a bakery of my own, put that horrible Place woman right straight out of business."

Mabel poured cups of tea and handed them to Avis and Olivia, offered them each a bowl of sugar cubes with a pair of tiny tongs, and then seated herself with her own cup of tea. She perched primly on the edge of the chair, her head still covered with the knotted rags.

"It looks real fine, Mabel. I can see you've put a whole lot of work into it."

"So," Avis said, looking uncomfortable. "How are you, Little Sister? You've got to tell me everything about being out there in the west."

"I'm fine. There's not much to tell. I've been doing a lot of hard work. Nothing more exciting than that."

"Well, my, it must have been just awful," Mabel said. "I've heard how things are out in those places."

36

She leaned over to place a hand on Olivia's arm. "Judith Webster and her husband went out to Ohio last year to visit a cousin of his. She said those folks had plenty of money, but couldn't get any help at all. Seems no one out there wants to hire themselves out. Everyone is king of the castle. This cousin had beautiful carpets on all her floors, but had to do all the cleaning all by herself. Just imagine that. You must be glad to get back to civilization. That's no kind of life for a delicate thing like you. We'll have to start thinking about some suitable gentlemen to have to Sunday dinner, now that you're finally home."

"How is Tobey?"

"Oh, he's fine," Mabel said. "Took himself a room over at Mrs. Monroe's. He knows he's perfectly welcome to stay here. More than welcome. We'd both love to have him, instead of him throwing away nine dollars a month, but that was his choice, and we got to respect it. He's still keeping company with his lady friend. You remember Emma O'Keefe, don't you? Sweet little thing with long blond curls? I'm sure he'll be settling down soon enough."

"Yes, I remember Emma. So how's business?" Olivia turned to Avis.

"Store's doing well. We've put in some new lines of merchandise. Ladies' hats, for one."

"And a complete line of footwear," Mabel added proudly. "Twice as much as we used to carry. That was my idea. I've also been thinking of stocking a few wedding gowns. They have them ready-made now, you know. I got the idea when I was over to Alanton shopping for my own." Mabel went on to tell Olivia much more than she wanted to know about their wedding, though to Mabel's credit she did manage to refrain from criticizing Olivia for not having been in attendance.

"You two ladies will have plenty of time to talk tomorrow." Avis tapped his pipe in an ashtray and rose.

37

"Aren't you about ready for bed, Olivia?"

"Yes, I am pretty tired." Olivia set her teacup on the tray and also stood. "May I assume it's all right for me to spend the night here?"

"What a question!" Mabel looked as if she intended to hug Olivia again, but was finding it difficult to maneuver past the table. "Of course it's all right. Of all things. You'd have to fight your way past me to get out the door. You're staying right here with us, and I don't mean just for tonight. I wouldn't hear of anything else. How can you even ask such a question? What are you thinking? We're your family, Olivia."

"Thank you, Mabel, for making me feel so welcome." Olivia turned to her brother. "I left my things over by the church. Two big wicker baskets. They're around the side, by the bushes. They're too heavy for you to carry by yourself, but do you think tomorrow morning you could send someone for them with that push cart you have at the store?"

"Bosh, you can't leave them there all night. I'll go get them now."

"I was hoping you'd say that." Olivia smiled. "I'll come help."

"No, no, no need for that." Mabel started hustling Olivia toward the stairs. "Avis can manage a couple of baskets. You must be good and tuckered. Let me show you right to the guest room, so you can get yourself comfortable. Anything you need, you just tell me."

When she reached the top of the stairs Olivia automatically turned toward her old room, but Mabel took her by the elbow. "That's my sewing room now, Olivia. You'll be staying in here, in Avis's old room. We use the master bedroom of course. We had to get rid of everything in there after your poor father, rest his soul … Would you like to see what I've done with it? No, you're tired, poor dear, there's time for that in the morning. We breakfast at seven." She led Olivia into the guest room.

"I'd as soon not get up for breakfast." Olivia sat on the bed, watching Mabel run her finger over the nightstand and lower the blind.

"Oh, you don't want to miss breakfast. Avis says it's the best meal in this house. Well, a person can't go off and work all day on an empty stomach, now can they? Of course, I suppose I can understand, just this once, you wanting to sleep in a little late, after a long journey."

"Thank you, Mabel. Good night."

Olivia lay back on the bed, her legs over the side and her shoes still on, and closed her eyes. She was soon roused to a sitting position by Avis's knock on the door. He set one of the baskets in the room and turned to go back down for the other.

"Is this everything?" he asked with a huff as he set the second one down, obviously unaccustomed to physical exertion.

"Yes, that's everything. Thank you, Avis."

"Good night, Olivia. You get some rest."

"I will. Good night ... and Avis."

She reached out to touch him, but he was already out of reach. When he turned to face her, her arm hung limply in the air between them.

"I do want to thank you ... for everything."

He took a step forward and awkwardly put his hands on her shoulders. "I'm just glad to have you home."

Then he turned abruptly and shut the door behind him.

Chapter Five

An insistent rap woke Olivia at noon the next day. She peeked out, saw Tobey standing there, and flung the door open to throw herself into his arms.

"You're all wet." She stepped back to muss his hair.

39

"You brung the rain with you. We been praying for it and now look at it coming down out there." He stepped into the room, she handed him her towel, and they sat side-by-side on the bed. "So ..." He looked at her open baskets, clothes trailing out of them. "You back for good?"

"I haven't decided what to do with myself. I don't want to go back and be a farmer. That cabin is pretty bad, like you said. But I don't want to live here and work in the store either." She wrinkled her mouth and nose like a rabbit. "So here I am, back where I was a year ago. But at least now I'll have a piece of land in my name. That's something."

"Sure it is."

"I mean, Avis said you had agreed, that both of you will sign it over –"

"Sure we will. Woulda done that anyhoo, you'da bothered to ask. Neither of us got no use for a farm."

"Thank you, Big Brother. Seems like there ought to be something better than that to say, but thank you is all I can think of. So what about you? How have you been getting along?"

"'Bout like you'd expect. Mabel ain't such a bad sort. Means well anyhoo. You just gotta train your ears not to hear her. And I ain't never had no trouble getting along with Avis. He ain't like you make him out."

"I know. When I turned up on their doorstep last night he was so ... so nice."

He stuck his lips out to make a smacking sound and then said, "I figured that's where you'd got to. Out there to Michigan. I thought about getting on a steamship myself, going out there to make sure you were all right."

Olivia rose and went to the window to raise the blind. While her back was to him she said, "No need for you to have done that. Just because your sister runs off like some fool, that's no reason you should have to go chasing after her." She turned back around. "Anyway, truth is, you can't ever be sure a body's all right. You can go checking on them all you want, but five minutes after you leave, you've got no guarantee they're still all right. Look at Uncle Scruggs. He was perfectly fine, right up until the second that horse kicked him in the head, and then he was dead."

"Can't argue with that. Well ..." He put his hands on the bed and pushed himself up. "You passed up a good breakfast, so you better get some clothes on 'fore you miss out on Mabel's fried chicken for dinner."

The door closed behind him and that was that. Olivia was home.

For the next few days she didn't venture outside. The first time she found herself home alone she went to the little room off the kitchen and stared up at the rafter. Olivia had never noticed it before. In all the years she'd lived in this house, all the times she'd opened that door, she'd never looked up and paid any mind to that beam, open, exposed, just waiting for someone to throw a rope over it. She did not imagine her mother hanging there; she barely remembered what her mother had looked like in life. She turned quickly and never entered the storeroom again.

She spent some of her time helping Mrs. Hardaway, who still came to the Killion's three times a week to clean and do laundry. In the afternoons, even when it was raining, Olivia sat on the front porch reading. Mrs. Sorenson from across the street tried calling a tentative hullo, but Olivia responded with only a quick wave and returned to her book. Let them wonder, she thought.

One afternoon Tobey's girl, Emma O'Keefe, joined Olivia on the porch. She had soft blonde curls and skin so white and thin her veins showed like a road map. Olivia made tea and found it not unpleasant to sit with Emma, chatting about nothing and wondering how Emma and Tobey spent their time together. No one would ever have to tell Emma to simmer down, that was for sure. Olivia had to lean forward and strain to

41

make out what she was saying.

"Emma was here for a visit today," Olivia told Tobey that evening while they were sitting in the parlor waiting for supper. "Do you love her a lot?"

He sucked on his front teeth. "Sure … of course I love her. She's my girl, ain't she?"

"Do you think about her all the time?"

"I think about her enough," he replied stiffly.

"Do you think life would be dreary and unlivable without her?"

"What're you asking all these questions for?"

"I don't know. I just want you to be happy. Do you think you'll ever have any secrets from each other?"

"Secrets? What should we have secrets about?"

She shrugged. "You shouldn't. But people do. Sometimes they have things they're afraid to tell the other one. Afraid they wouldn't understand."

"You can rest your busy mind. I don't think either of us got any of those. If anything, we got the opposite problem." He grinned. "Probably know way too much about each other. I get women coming into the store to tell me they heard her cough."

Olivia leaned back in her chair and closed her eyes for a moment. When she opened them she said, "I'm just saying – I hope you're going to be best friends. That's what a man and his wife should be to each other – special angels. Put on God's earth to show kindness to one another," Olivia quoted Jettie.

"Dint know you'd gone and got to be a big expert on married life. So tell me what you didn't like about farming." Tobey changed the subject.

"It's awful hard work and in the winter that cabin was so cold the snot froze in my nose. But I guess the main thing was how lonely it gets."

"Warn't there no neighbors to keep you company?"

She almost bleated then, but feigned a cough and talked about the Indians she hadn't seen, the grizzly bears that hadn't attacked her, the snakes that hadn't bitten her, and the wolves she'd only heard at night. Finally Mabel called them to the table.

The next day, after a dinner of chicken and dumplings, the Killions were having apple cobbler while Mabel worked her way around the table with the coffeepot.

"Olivia," she said, "it's grand to see you have such a healthy appetite. There's nothing I love better than for a body to enjoy my cooking the way you do, but you better take care. Looks to me like you've gotten a little thick around the middle."

Mabel set the pot on the stove, smoothed her apron, and sat down. Olivia ignored the subtle insult and the irony of it being Mabel, who had twice the girth of Olivia, who delivered it.

Olivia folded her napkin in her lap and said, "I'm going to see Mr. Carmichael this afternoon. I intend to tell him you both agree that I've satisfied the conditions of father's will and have no objection to him putting the deed to Uncle Scruggs' property in my name."

Both her brothers nodded, staring at their plates and chewing with great concentration. Olivia watched her sister-in-law out of the corner of her eye. Mabel threw a sharp glance at her husband, but bit her lip and held her peace.

An hour later Olivia made her way up Main Street, nodding at the women who gave her curious stares, but stopping to talk to no one. When she knocked on Mr. Carmichael's door, he opened it himself.

"Ah, Miss Killion, I've been hearing whispers that Five Rocks is once again graced with your presence. How may I be of service?" He turned to pull the chair out for her.

"You remember that farm we talked about, out in Michigan?" she asked after they were both seated.

"You aren't going to tell me that's where you've

43

been."

"I surely am. And now both my brothers agree to you getting that land signed over, put in my name."

"Astounding." The lawyer shook his head. "Quite astounding." It seemed to take him a moment to recover from his astonishment. "Well, as far as you're concerned, it should be a simple matter. Your brothers will both have to come here and sign some papers. I'll let Avis know when they are ready. But all you have to do now is wait patiently. The process is sure to be a lengthy one. It will take weeks for the documents to reach Michigan, and I couldn't guess how long it takes a county clerk in Michigan to record a transfer of title. It likely requires the signature of a judge, and out on the frontier that may mean waiting for the arrival of a judge riding the circuit. Then their paper work will be in the post for another few weeks. Once it arrives, all you'll have to do is come here to affix your signature, with me as a witness."

"Can't I just go there and sign the paper?"

"Certainly that's possible, if you choose to make that long trip again." He looked appalled at that idea. "But I can't advise you to put yourself at such risk. Why take that on yourself, when you could simply wait here for another few weeks? Your farm isn't going anywhere. And your presence in Michigan won't make the judge arrive any faster."

"But the post is so slow. I'd rather get it over with," she said, which was true enough, though the bigger reason was of course her eagerness to go back to Michigan and look for Mourning.

"In any case, don't go rushing off for a while. Not until I've made inquiries as to the procedure in Michigan. Do you know the name of the county your farm is in?"

"No. It's not far from Detroit. Isn't the name of the county on the deed?"

"That deed was written up years ago, before

Michigan even joined the Union. And these new states redraw county lines every Thursday. There's no point in you going anywhere until you know for certain which office, in which county, has to record the transaction."

She thanked him and leaned forward, as if she meant to rise. Then she sank back in her chair.

"I was wondering ... has Mourning Free been around to see you?" she asked.

"No, not lately. He was in town quite a while ago. Sometime in February I believe it was. In fact, he asked me if I had seen you."

"Oh. Did he happen to tell you where he was going?"

"No."

She studied the wall behind him and he waited patiently through a long silence.

"Is that confidentiality thing still going on between you and me?" she asked.

"Certainly. As long as you are my client, anything you confide in me is privileged."

"Then I would like to hire you regarding another matter."

He lifted a hand, palm up, as if to say "welcome."

"Are you sure you can't tell anyone?"

"Did I not say so?"

"Yes, I'm sorry, you did, but ... it's just ... I have to be sure." Her body felt stiff and heavy, and her voice quivered when she began speaking again. "What I would like to hire you to do is write a paper, telling about certain things that happened. And for you to keep it, together with the last will and testament I want you to write for me."

His face remained blank and he waited for her to continue.

"Only ... I don't exactly ..." She blinked, afraid she might cry.

"You don't have to tell me," he said gently. "Actually, it would be better for it to be written in your own hand. You can do that alone, in your own time and with all the privacy you need. I don't even need to know what the paper says; I will simply bear witness to your signature. Just write everything down and I'll sign that I saw you put your name to each page. Then we'll put your document in an envelope, seal it, and lock it up in my safe. A note on the outside of the envelope will state to whom it is to be given or under what circumstances it is to be opened."

"Does Billy Adams get to look at the stuff in your safe?" She referred to a former classmate that she knew clerked for Mr. Carmichael.

"No. Absolutely not. No one has a key but me and an attorney in South Valley. That attorney has clear instructions regarding what is to be done with the contents of my safe upon my disability or death."

She sighed with relief and stared at the floor for a moment. "All right. I'll go home and write it down, like you said, but, fact is, I want you to read it. There are things ... things that someone has to know about, so they can tell Mourning without me having to be dead first. I mean, what if I leave for Michigan and the next day Mourning turns up here? No, someone has to know and it best be you. There's no one else in this town that a person can trust not to blab everything all over. And if Mourning does come back, he'll be sure to pay his respects to you, seeing as you were always so good to him and all."

Neither spoke for a moment.

"If you've got the time, I'd just as soon start with part of it right now," she said.

"I have all the time you need." He opened a drawer for paper and pen, drew the inkwell closer, dipped the quill into it, and looked up at her expectantly.

She took a deep breath, looked away from him, and blurted it out in a rush. "So the first thing you need to know is that I birthed a baby. A little boy. And the father of that baby is Mourning Free."

She paused and turned back to face him, chin

46

raised, poised to withstand a scornful glare. Mr. Carmichael's eyes had frozen on the paper in front of him and his hand was still. When he finally met her gaze, she saw only sadness on his face.

"Only Mourning doesn't know a thing about the baby," she added. "Neither does my family. And they can't know."

"That is quite a problem you are carrying on your young shoulders." He spoke softly and set the pen down. "I'm sorry." He looked helpless, trying to think of something to say.

"I guess it isn't easy being you. What's the fun of knowing everybody's secrets, if you can't tell a soul?" She tried to keep her voice light while the nail of her index finger nervously picked at the cuticle of her thumb, drawing blood.

"I am truly sorry to hear these troubles of yours and would derive no pleasure from divulging them to anyone." He placed his palms in the praying position she remembered from the first time she visited him, after her father died. Then he pushed his chair back and folded his hands in his lap. "Do you mind if I ask where this baby is? Where you were when you gave birth to him?"

"No, I don't mind. You have to know. When Mourning comes back, you've got to be able to help him find the baby. And you've got to put all the details about him in the will I want you to write for me. To make sure any money I have goes to that baby. I guess I'd better tell you from the beginning."

He nodded and wrote slowly during her monologue, occasionally lifting a finger to indicate he needed more time to keep up with her.

"Well, you know I wanted to go out to Michigan to get that farm and I needed someone who could do all the things I couldn't. So I talked Mourning into going with me. You see, once we'd gotten Uncles Scruggs' farm for me, I was going to help him buy his own land.

47

We were partners. I had six hundred dollars that Uncle Scruggs gave me and his land with the cabin he built, and Mourning had ... just being him, knowing how to do everything and fix everything. And things went well for us at first." She again fixed her gaze on the wall above his shoulder. "But then one day we ... you know ... just that one time. We both swore it would never happen again. We didn't need that kind of trouble, neither of us. But then there I was, carrying his child. Course, I didn't know that until later." She paused and put the tip of her thumb in her mouth, running her tongue around the nail to stop the bleeding. "Then something else happened. Nothing to do with Mourning. It's something I can't sit here and tell you. That would be too hard. I'll have to go home and write it down, like you said." Her throat was tight, as if someone's hands were squeezing the breath out of her. "But after I bring it back, I want you to read it. Not with me sitting here in front of you, but before you close it up in that envelope. I want there to be another person on God's earth who knows the truth about what happened to me."

She hadn't come to the lawyer with the intention of telling him about the Stubblefields; she'd only wanted him to know about Little Boy. But while she sat there, feeling somehow comfortable and protected in the presence of this strange-looking man, she couldn't stop talking.

After a short pause she looked directly into the lawyer's eyes. "Mourning always said you treated him the fairest of anyone in town. It meant a lot to him, you trusting him enough to let him sleep here in your office, giving him a key and everything. You were the reason I had such a hard time talking him into leaving Five Rocks. He felt safe here, knowing you would always stick up for him."

Mr. Carmichael shifted his weight, looking embarrassed.

48

"Anyway," Olivia said and broke eye contact with him, "after Mourning and I, you know, something happened that made him run away. I don't know what, but something must have scared him real bad. And then ... then the thing that I'll go home and write about happened to me. And after that I came back here. But I was afraid I might be with child and didn't want to see my family until I knew. So I came on the delivery wagon, after dark, and instead of going home I walked down to The Circle, by Mrs. Place's house. She came out looking for her kitten and saw me standing there and asked me to come in for a cup of tea. Just like that, like we were best friends or something. She said I should stay with her until I knew whether I was going to have a baby. And then, after I knew I was, I just stayed on at her house. All those months. She was real good to me." Olivia spoke in a monotone, revealing no emotion. "Took me to a doctor in Weaverton for the birthing. We brought Little Boy back to her house and took care of him till he was about three months old. Then a few days ago we drove over to South Valley and left him there, with Reverend Jameson in the colored Baptist church." As she spoke the last sentence, tears escaped the corners of her eyes. She quickly wiped them away and continued her story.

"I'll write down the date of birth and the name of the doctor, though he'd be likely to lie about it. He was a horrible man. Called Little Boy a black nigger bastard and good as threw us out of his house. Jettie had to give him a lot of money just to let us stay till morning." She busied herself with her bonnet and stole a glance at Mr. Carmichael. His expression hadn't changed. "I'll write down the name of the Reverend too and a description of the basket Little Boy was in and all the clothes we left with him and the pap feeder. And I put my family Bible in there too, so he'd have proof of where he'd come from. Avis and Tobey might not like to admit they recognize that Bible as mine, but they've both got one

49

exactly like it, with our mother's handwriting on the front page, just like mine."

Mr. Carmichael was busy making notes on his pad. "And in your will you want to leave all your property to this Little Boy?"

"Yes." She paused for a moment. "Or maybe I'd best leave it to Mourning. He'll need money to raise Little Boy up."

"When making a will you must also consider the possibility of you outliving your Little Boy."

"Lord, I surely would hope not. But if I do, then I want to leave the land in Michigan and six hundred dollars to Mourning Free and anything else I own to my brother Tobey."

"All right. I believe I understand your wishes. I will prepare a draft of the will and start the process of putting the land in your name. Why don't you come back ..." He paused to consult a black notebook. "A week from today? Would that give you time enough to write about ... the other matter?"

She nodded, tied her bonnet, and rose to leave with a feeling a great relief. The lawyer hurried around his desk to pull the door open for her. She paused with one foot on the sidewalk, put her hand on his arm, and said, "You are a very kind man. Lord, what a different place the world would be if all the people in it were like you."

She was out the door when she remembered and turned back. "I almost forgot. I need one more thing. Could you make me two copies of that Free Man of Color paper for Mourning? I know he got one from you, but I'd still like to have another one with me when I go back to Michigan, just in case I find him there and he needs it."

"Of course."

Chapter Six

From Mr. Carmichael's office Olivia walked to the grassy bank of the Saugata River. The stones she tossed into the water made a series of loud plunks, punctuating the way she imagined Jettie scolding her for sharing her terrible secrets with Mr. Carmichael. Maybe Jettie was right and Olivia would live to regret it, but for now all she felt was some measure of relief. Those secrets created a high wall around her. Each tiny crack in the wall admitted a bit of light into the dark space in which she lived. Anyway, she thought as she batted mosquitoes away, I had to tell him. If Mourning comes back for a day or two he's not going to come calling at the Killion residence and could be gone before I'd ever know he was here.

On her way home Olivia stopped at Killion's General and both her brothers said there would be no problem; they would go to Mr. Carmichael's office whenever he told them to. Then she went home and set the table. During their noon meal none of the Killions seemed to have much to say. Not even Mabel. The brothers kept their heads bent to their plates, complimenting Mabel's food as they hurriedly scooped it into their mouths. No one seemed inclined to linger in the kitchen over coffee. Once the dishes were draining in the tray and the house was empty again, Olivia curled up on one of Mabel's sofas with *Don Quixote*.

Late that afternoon Mabel returned from her Girls' Club and carried a tray of tea and oatmeal cookies into the parlor. Olivia sat up and watched her warily, wondering what she wanted. Mabel made a great fuss of pouring, sweetening, and stirring the tea before she settled into the easy chair opposite Olivia and contemplated her sister-in-law through a short uneasy silence.

"I know you been through a lot," Mabel spoke at last. "It was hard on the boys, losing their father, but harder on you. Left you in what you see as a difficult situation."

Olivia, unprepared for this conversation, stiffened and broke into a light sweat.

"I know I'm not your cup of tea, and don't think you got to argue with me about that." Mabel shook her head and raised a hand, palm facing Olivia. "We're family now. Beyond telling lies for the sake of manners. I always thought you could try a bit harder, about a lot of things, and though I'm of my own mind about your brothers letting you take them eighty acres, I held my tongue. I do care about you, Olivia. I always wanted a sister, and I understand you better than you think. A small town like this is hard on anyone who is the least little bit different. I know what it's like to be made fun of. You remember what they started calling me in school?"

Olivia shook her head. She had no schoolyard recollections of Mabel.

"Moo-bell." Mabel provided a loud demonstration – "Mooooo-bell" – and Olivia couldn't help smiling.

"It was that rotten, stuck-up, little Calvin Sorenson what started it. The next day he brought a rusty old cow bell to school and clanked it every time I got out of my seat. Just because I was a teeny bit on the plump side. Then during recess that moron Billy Adams and him started shouting, 'Anyone seen Moo-bell? She can't be far, they's a fresh trail of cow pies going right down Broad Street.'"

"I don't remember that." Olivia shook her head.

"Well, that's just like you. You were probably too busy sulking in the corner to notice. And it didn't go on for but a few days. I put a stop to it."

"How? I hope you smacked them good."

"No. Not that I couldn't have. That Billy Adams warn't even my age. More like yours I think. I could have easy sent both them little runts to Doc Gaylin. But I didn't. Why give the other boys something to jabber about? How poor Calvin looked like he'd been trampled by a whole herd of cows or some such. Best thing for me was to just ignore them."

Olivia shook her head again. "I ignored the kids who said my mother was crazy or called my father a miser, but that never stopped them."

"Because you ain't never had no friends was gonna stick up for you. My friends started leaving unpleasant things on Calvin's chair and accidentally bumping into him. You got to have enough people on your side, make the little villains think twice. Never let them think you're ascared of them or care one whit what they say. But that warn't you – you was always easy pickings. Ignored them because you were ascared to do anything else. Me and my friends ignored the little brats like they warn't nothing but cockroaches, just like my mamma taught me."

Olivia bit her top lip, remembering Mabel's mother coming into Killions General, a large, formidable woman with swishy skirts, who looked at everyone she encountered as if they were bugs, even when she was saying polite words. All she'd have to do was pass by the school yard and give those boys one of her looks, Olivia thought.

"And my mamma always invited my classmates' families over and made sure the conversation turned to the shameful behavior of some of them children at school. She even scared Reverend Dixby into mentioning it in one of his sermons. Then she gave me extra desserts to take to school for lunch, so I always had some to share. But you ..." Mabel shook her head. "You were a sweet child. Never an unkind word for anyone. And when them yobs were mean to you, you looked so surprised. But you never gave nothing back. Just curled up inside yourself and never learned – being nice only goes so far. Even your friends got to be

53

a little bit afraid of you."

Olivia drank her tea and said nothing.

"I can imagine your opinion of me and my Girls' Club. You think I don't know that Rose Tanner is a silly cow and Molly Van Dyke is about as smart as a caterpillar? But who do you think tells them what committees to serve on? When the church rummage sale is going to be? What kind of Christmas wreath to hang on their door?" Mabel stopped to drain her teacup and then set it down. "Nowadays Calvin's cow of a wife can't be sweet enough to me. Those Sorensons." Mabel tilted her head in the direction of the house across the street, looking as if she had a vile taste in her mouth. "They might rake a pile off that brewery, but what are they? Saloon-keepers in expensive suits." She leaned forward in her chair. "I can tell you one thing – my children ain't never going to be bullied in this town. No one opens their yap about me or Avis, not unless they want their credit cut off. Your father could've helped you. Everyone in town was beholden to him, always begging to buy on tick. Smallest hint would've done it. But he was like you, paid no mind. He was the same with everyone – tight-fisted and ornery. Made no difference how any of 'em behaved toward him and his. And your brothers ... Avis was never around to be made fun of, always running back to the store, even during recess. And Tobey ..." She waved a hand in dismissal. "He warn't no better than you at getting his in." She reached for Olivia's empty cup. "But that ain't why I come in here to talk to you. I want you to know that you are truly welcome here. More than welcome. I'm going to be real upset if you don't stay. Avis too. I guess you don't believe me, but that's the truth." Mabel didn't wait for a reply. She patted Olivia's shoulder, rose to pick up the tray, and left the room.

Olivia remained seated, letting her mind pick its way through the idea of staying in Five Rocks. The indomitable Mabel would bully a path into society for her ill-behaved sister-in-law and could probably even scare up a husband. Olivia could join the Girls' Club and see how bossing is done by an expert. It took but a moment for her to close her eyes and shudder. But she did go to the kitchen to put her hand on Mabel's shoulder and thank her for the kind words.

Then Olivia tied her bonnet on and went out. She walked toward the river, taking a detour through the cemetery. When she was a little girl the gravestones used to fascinate her. She'd close her eyes and pick one, see how old the person had been when they died, and spend the rest of her walk making up the story of that life.

It was the best hour of day, the last rays of sunlight slanting over the earth, and her favorite kind of weather – sunny and brisk – but she didn't take her usual pleasure in being outdoors. The conversation with Mabel had left her feeling exposed, and she couldn't help seeing herself as others did. Even Mabel thought she was pathetic. There she goes, that Killion girl, all alone again. Poor thing. What can you expect?

Perhaps the edgy, empty feeling in the pit of her stomach had nothing to do with the Stubblefields or her longing for Little Boy. It was just the way she was. Always had been. Always would be. Sulking in the corner. Alone. No one to walk with. No one to do anything with. The only company she kept was with her books.

Mabel is dang right about one thing, she thought. If the Stubblefields had been even one tiny bit afraid of me, they never would have dared. No. No, no, no, she silently protested. I'm not going to let my mind go back to that place. It wasn't my fault. They were evil. It wasn't my fault. It wasn't my fault.

She walked until dark. When she arrived home she said she wasn't hungry and went up to bed. Mabel came to put a hand to her forehead, but Olivia pretended to be asleep.

The next day after breakfast Olivia waited for her brothers and Mabel to leave for the store and then sat at the kitchen table with pen, ink, and paper, attempting to find words to describe for Mr. Carmichael what had happened at the Stubblefield farm. The page remained blank. Then she remembered her journal. Not the one she had bought in Detroit and filled with her silly sketches and the optimistic, naive stories of a child. The other one. The one Jettie had given her for Christmas. The one with the little lock, in which Olivia had already written it all down. One cold January afternoon she'd sat at Jettie's kitchen table and found herself scribbling furiously. After she finished she'd put it away and never looked at it again. Now both journals were upstairs, under her mattress.

Why write it all over again? she thought. I'll just give him the journal. Better to get it out of the house anyway. You never know when Mabel's going to go on a cleaning rampage and decide to turn the mattresses. I'll give him both journals. The first one will also be safer with him. Little Boy might read it one day, learn something of his parents.

She went upstairs and retrieved them both, then opened the second and ruffled through its pages. It was easy to see where that part began. The cramped scratches looked nothing like her usual neatly slanted handwriting. But they were legible. Mr. Carmichael should be able to understand what was written there. She inserted a slip of paper to mark the page and closed the book. Do I need to read this, she wondered. Did I write down anything about finding the Stubblefields' bodies? Or thinking Mourning might have killed them? She frowned and thought carefully. No, she distinctly remembered being careful not to mention any of that.

She opened the book again and turned to the empty pages at the back. There she recorded the details of Little Boy's birth and painstakingly described the white flannel leggings she had sewn for him, the matching

56

hats and booties Jettie had knitted, and Jettie's masterpiece – the blanket of royal blue and white diamonds. She recorded every detail of Little Boy's basket, clothing, and even the pap feeder.

She took special care describing the Bible she had tucked in the bottom of the basket. Its cover was bumpy black leather, embossed with gold letters. In the top left corner it said "HOLY BIBLE" all in capital letters, the H and B larger than the others. "Olivia Killion" was in smaller letters in the bottom right corner. She copied a list to keep for herself of the marriages, births, and deaths that her mother had recorded on its front pages, including the additions Olivia had made – the deaths of her mother, Uncle Scruggs, and her father, Avis's marriage, and the birth of Little Boy. This Bible would be the only real proof Little Boy would have of who his mother was. When she finished she returned the journals to their hiding place and put on her bonnet. On the front porch she met Mabel, who was just coming back from the store to start preparing the noonday meal.

"Hullo Mabel. I don't seem to have much appetite, so I think I will not be joining you at table. You've been feeding me too well," Olivia said, placing her hands on her stomach. "And you're right. I do seem to have put on some weight."

She quickly slipped past her sister-in-law, giving her no chance to object. Olivia turned right on Main Street and walked toward The Circle, keeping her chin high and a smile on her face, feeling lighter than she had in a long time. She greeted everyone she passed. "Good day, Mrs. Monroe, isn't it lovely weather? Hullo, Mrs. Brewster, how nice to see you. Mr. Sorenson, hullo, you're looking well. So nice to see you." She glided past them all, allowing none of them the opportunity to respond.

Through the front window of Jettie's shop she could see customers – two women and a little girl. She opened the door and entered with a cheerful "Good morning," directed to the room in general. The little girl insinuated herself into the skirts of one of the women, a homespun-clad farmer's wife whose name Olivia did not know. The other woman was Rose Tanner, one of the members of Mabel's Girls Club, with whom Olivia had never exchanged more than a few words.

"Hullo, Mrs. Place," Olivia said, perhaps a little too loudly. "It's good to see you looking so well. I certainly have missed your baking. No one makes a peach pie like you do."

Chapter Seven

Olivia knew it was time for Jettie to close for her noon break and waited for the customers to leave. She and Jettie were soon seated at Jettie's kitchen table with steaming bowls of chicken stew in front of them.

"I've decided to go back to that church tomorrow, find out exactly who took Little Boy from Reverend Jameson," Olivia said and held out her left palm in anticipation of vigorous objections. "Don't worry. I don't intend to try and take him back. I just have to know where he is. Who's taking care of him. And when he's old enough, I want him to know there's someone he can come to, if he ever needs help. Someone who will always be on his side. I'm going to save up my money, keep it for him."

Jettie stared at the table, uncharacteristically silent.

"Don't you have anything to say?" Olivia put her hand on Jettie's. She didn't remember the older woman's skin being so slack and yellowish.

"Ain't going to argue with you, if that's what you think," Jettie replied. "I told you before, I been fretting about him myself. It's a terrible thing, leaving a child in the hands of a stranger. I'm regretful if I pushed you into it. I didn't see you had no choice."

"No, you were right. I'm just sorry I didn't have the courage to tell the Reverend straight out that I'm Little Boy's mother. But there's nothing for you to feel regretful about. It was you saved us both. What would I have done without you?" Olivia squeezed Jettie's hand.

"You want me to come with you?"

"No. It's good of you to offer, but it's something I have to do on my own. No one else to blame." She rose to leave. "And there's another thing I want to tell you. I've made my peace with never being invited to join the Girls' Club. Folks can talk all they want, but they're just going to have to get used to me coming to visit with you. I don't give two cents what any of them think."

Early the next morning Olivia hired a buggy and set out for South Valley. She cursed under her breath as she turned onto Broad Street. She would have preferred sitting astride a horse to having to handle one in harness, but thought the more respectable her appearance, the better she'd fare with the Reverend. The only vehicle she had ever driven was the heavy farm wagon she and Mourning had bought out in Michigan, but it had been hitched to a team of broad-backed, slow-going oxen. Now she feared the flimsy buggy might go into the ditch at the first curve in the road. Luckily, the horse did not share her anxiety. He calmly clop-clopped up Broad Street, over the covered bridge, and out of town.

"There's a good boy." She relaxed. "I don't know what I'm so scared of. You've got no reason to go jumping into the river or dragging this danged contraption through a corn field, now do you?" She spoke softly to him and gently tugged on the reins when they came to the turn to South Valley.

It was a hot, dry day. As she coughed and waved the dust away, she suddenly found her mind filled with pictures of Mourning's parents. She had never given them much thought, but that day they became real to her – two young black figures, running north to freedom, on a road just like this one. How old had they been? She pictured his mother, probably not any older than Olivia, heavy with child, stumbling along the dirt road in the heat, her husband constantly looking back, listening for the dogs.

Olivia couldn't imagine being that kind of alone, not even knowing where they were. Any person they encountered was as likely to throw a net over them as offer a dipper of water and crust of bread. Had they carried any food and water with them? Did they have shoes? Where did they sleep, curled up in the long, itchy grass? Olivia felt a deep sense of shame. The two of them had kept on going – destitute, nothing but the rags on their backs, risking a terrible whipping or worse – because they'd wanted their baby to be born to freedom, safe from being sold away from them. That was how a mother behaved. She didn't toss her child to the winds of fate because the Girls' Club wouldn't approve of the color of his skin.

Approaching South Valley, Olivia turned down the hill toward The Bottoms and there, on its hill slightly above the cluster of huts, stood the rickety wooden church. She led the horse to the trough and stood watching the children playing in the clearing. Those homes were so mean-looking. The porches and roofs sagged and the yards were of dirt and scraggly weeds. Come winter, they must be awash in mud. Even from a distance the clothes that flapped on the lines looked pitiably faded and worn. She hadn't noticed any of this before. She hadn't cared. All she'd wanted was to rid herself of her burden and run away.

What is the matter with me? How could I have done that?

She felt as if her bones were losing their rigidity and she might melt into a puddle, but she forced herself out of the buggy and walked to the church. There was no lock on the door, but she knew before pushing it open and calling out that there was no one inside. She sat in one of the pews, prepared to wait as long as necessary. Why hadn't she thought to bring a book? But she didn't think it would take long for someone to notice the strange buggy standing outside the church and call for the Reverend. She was right.

"Can I be of help to you, Ma'am?" Reverend Jameson asked, as he strode through the door in work clothes and boots.

Olivia stood and turned to offer her hand. A curtain of disapproval and suspicion closed over his face as he politely greeted her.

"You do remember me?" Olivia asked.

"Of course I remember you."

"I know I promised you that no one would come back to ask about that baby, but I ... all I need is to know where he is. Who's taking care of him."

The Reverend frowned. "Why don't we go into my office?" He led her to the small room at the back of the church and held his arm out, inviting her to take one of the chairs in front of his desk. Then he seated himself behind it. "Can I offer you some water?"

"No thank you." Olivia said nothing else, hands clasped in her lap, every muscle taut, her head throbbing, and her dress suddenly hot and itchy.

"You don't need to worry none about the child. Same day you left him here a lovely couple stopped for the night, on their way to join a wagon train. They been praying for a child and, praise the Lord, you answered those prayers."

"You mean he isn't here?" Olivia's voice trembled.

"No." He blinked and stared at his hands, which were flat on the desk.

"Some people came driving through, and you just gave him to them? To people you don't even know?" She felt panic rising, though she was sure he was lying. But why?

"They be good people, on their way to make a new

life out west. A better life than he'd a had here in The Bottoms." Reverend Jameson stood up, still avoiding looking at Olivia.

Olivia remained seated. "What was their name? Where were they going?"

He ran his tongue over his bottom lip and hesitated too long before answering. "Washington. I believe that was their name. On their way to Kansas. Or maybe Nebraska."

He stepped around the desk, obviously anxious for the conversation to be over.

"You're lying." She rose from the chair. "He's here, and you're lying."

He stood stiffly, shoulders back, and his face grew hard. "I have to ask you to leave."

"You can't just lie to me like that. The day we brought Little Boy to you, you said there was a nice couple living right here that would be blessed to have him. You said! You can't just make up some story now. I can bring the law. They'll make you tell me where he is."

"You do what you need to, Miss. You can make a pack of trouble for us, that what you want. But there's no abandoned baby here. And you be making a bigger pack for yourself." Now he looked angry rather than guilty. "You got no cause to complain and threaten me with the law. How many times I aks you for your name? Now you come back, all worked up 'bout a negro baby? What you want with him? You best be getting back to your own people. You got no business here."

She sat down so hard she thought the chair might collapse beneath her. Elbows on her knees, she covered her face with her hands and took several deep breaths. Then she straightened and looked up at him, imploring.

"I'm sorry for saying that about the law. I would never do that. Never. I promise." Her voice grew pleading. "The last thing I want is to make trouble for you. But I have to know where my son is. I'm his mother. He's my Little Boy."

She stopped speaking and watched him. Distress flickered in his eyes, but his face remained closed up. A cliff of black granite.

"Please, I don't mean to take him away from anyone. We both know I can't take him home with me. I just want to see that he's being cared for. I want him to know who I am, in case he ever needs anything."

"They were real nice couple. Said they got 'nuff money to get a business going. He be all right. You don't gotta worry."

"Don't you think he deserves to know who his parents are?"

"He gonna have real parents. Kind what feed and clothe him."

"Look, you have to believe me. I won't make any trouble. All I want is to help him. To help them, the family. With money."

He shook his head and took a step toward the door. Olivia reached out for his arm. "No, you can't just leave. You have to tell me!"

"I already told you. That baby's gone to Kansas with his family. Now I got work waiting on me. I'm sorry, but I can't help you. You best not be coming back here."

"At least let me write down my name. You can give it to the parents and when he's older —"

He shook his head. "When I aks for your name, you been too busy. Too late for that now. I told you. That family ain't here. I got nobody to tell your name to."

"It's Killion. Olivia Killion. From Five Rocks," she said. "Let me give you some money." She slipped her hand into her pocket. "For him. For his parents."

He raised both hands and averted his gaze. "Sorry. That be like stealing, since I got no one to give it to." He turned and strode from the room.

Olivia stood motionless, stunned. She had been fretting over how she would approach the family for the first time, what she should say, imagining his adopted

63

parents, the wary glances they would exchange, the way she would slowly gain their trust, make them see how good it would be for Little Boy to have a kind-hearted white lady looking out for him.

But Little Boy gone? No way to find him? Who could imagine such a thing? She sat, waiting for the Reverend to return. He couldn't just leave her like that. He had to come back and tell her the truth. He had to.

"I'm his mother," she shouted at the ceiling. "I'm his *mother.*"

No footsteps came running; she was alone in the office. She pressed her palms to her cheeks, trying to find the energy to rise from the chair.

He can't do this. There are laws. I'll go to Hillsong, get the sheriff. I have Jettie as a witness that Little Boy belongs to me.

But she didn't want to make trouble for these people. Anyway, the sheriff was unlikely to have much sympathy for a white slut searching for her nigger bastard. And even if he wanted to help her, how could he disprove the Reverend's claim? Wagons passed through all the time. The whole world seemed to be going west. If the sheriff was of a mean and nasty character, he could decide to teach Olivia a lesson and arrest her for confessing to child abandonment. And she still wouldn't know where Little Boy was.

Finally she gave up waiting. She knew that not a soul would come near the church as long as her buggy stood outside. She rose, drew a gold quarter eagle from her pocket, and placed it in the empty center of the Reverend's desk. Outside, she stared down at The Bottoms. It looked deserted; the playing children had vanished. Even the chickens seemed to have fled from sight. Before climbing back into the buggy, she stood for a moment with her arms around the horse's neck. Then she drew back to speak to him. "Don't you be thinking this is the end of it. I'm going to find my baby. You just wait and see."

64

Avis was coming out of Bellinir's Feed & Grain and stared open-mouthed as Olivia drove past him, down Broad Street toward the livery. Olivia forced a smile and waved, but kept her eyes straight ahead. After returning the buggy she came back out onto Main Street, relieved to find Avis gone. She walked east – toward Jettie's – and found the shop open and empty of customers.

"He won't tell me where Little Boy is," Olivia said before the door had closed behind her. "He just stole him."

Jettie waved her around the counter, into the bake room at the back of the old barn, and they sat at the work table while Olivia described every detail of her encounter with the Reverend. She was interrupted only once, when the bell announced Rose Tanner's entrance. Jettie went out to sell her an apple pie and returned.

"I know he's lying." Olivia picked up where she had left off.

"Probably so." Jettie returned to her chair next to Olivia. "You keep your spirits up, though. Look on the bright side. The good Reverend is only trying to look out for him."

"Look out for him? By lying to his mother about where he is?"

"Try and see it the way he does. Two white women turn up in his church with a colored baby and promise no one will ever come looking for it. Then not a week goes by and one of them not only comes back, but starts threatening him with the law –"

"I said I was sorry for that. And I told him I'm Little Boy's mother and that I wasn't trying to take him back, that all I wanted was to know where he is. Give him whatever help I can. I told him all that."

"What reason he got to believe anything comes out of your mouth? Most every word you said to him the first time was a big lie."

"But why would I lie about being his mother? Why

would I want to know about him, if I wasn't his mother?"

"A colored child fetches good money on a block in Kentucky."

Olivia paled. "You think he thought I was trying to get him back so I could sell him into slavery?"

Jettie lifted one shoulder. "Why not? You think that ain't never happened? Ain't no limit on the evil people can do. You think there's some kind of line a human being wouldn't cross, but there's always some villain eager to jump over it. Say two white women found this abandoned baby and took it to the nearest black church. Then they're telling their friends about the good deed they done and those friends say, 'You fools, that's valuable merchandise you handed over.' So one a them women concocts a story to get him back."

"Lord. You think that's what he thought of me?"

"Couldn't say, but the possibility may have crossed his mind. Or maybe you started thinking about what a good little servant you coulda raised that child to be. His keep for the first few years gonna be the best investment you ever made. Your own little home-grown slave, getting around the law and without paying a cent for him." She paused and Olivia sat still, fighting back tears. "Look, it ain't nothing about you in particular. Nigra folk don't trust any of us. What cause they got to? They live their lives on the edge of a cliff, always expecting one of us to come along and push 'em over. And even if he did believe you, why take the risk? Just to be able to tell this little boy he's got a white mother? Colored man might not think that's such joyous news."

"So what am I supposed to do?"

"Trust in God that the Reverend is a good man and that some lovely couple over in South Valley is right this minute thanking that same God for bringing Little Boy into their lives. Go on living your own life. One of these days Mr. Mourning Free will turn up, and maybe Reverend Jameson will trust him with the truth. Or

66

Mourning will be able to find it out just by making friends over there, talking to folks."

Olivia sat with her chin resting on her fist, thinking this over, before she rose and hugged Jettie. "I guess you're right." She sighed. "You always seem to know the right thing to say. If Mourning does come back to town and you see him, you be sure to tell him that Mr. Carmichael has some papers for him."

"What kind of papers?"

The bell jingled, and Jettie patted Olivia's hand before rising to tend to her customer. Olivia was grateful for the interruption; she was too exhausted to stay and defend her decision to tell Mr. Carmichael about Little Boy.

Chapter Eight

Olivia returned home exhausted and famished, glad she was just in time for the noon meal. She found genteel table manners difficult to maintain and ate like a starving person. She could feel Avis glancing at her, his eyes full of questions where she had gone in the buggy, but he refrained from asking. The older brother she had always considered annoyingly predictable kept surprising her. Olivia focused her attention on her plate, wondering where Avis was imagining she might have gone, trying to enjoy her new role as mysterious traveler, comings and goings unexplained. No more the timid little sister who rarely left the house.

After the meal she went up to her room and searched her bureau for the pair of Mourning's trousers she had brought back from Michigan. She ran a thin piece of rope through the belt loops, pulled the trousers on under her dress, slipped out the front door, and walked back to the livery. This time she asked Mr. Ferguson for a horse, stipulating that she would be riding western, not side-saddle. The toothpick in his mouth bobbed up and down, but he took her money and saddled up Rachel Jackson, a gentle mare Olivia had often ridden as a child. Mr. Ferguson turned to hand her the reins and stood watching her with undisguised curiosity. Olivia ignored him, reached down to lift her skirts, mounted, and quickly rode up Broad Street and out of town. She spent the afternoon and early evening visiting all the farms within a twenty-mile radius of town. At each she inquired if Mourning Free had come around looking for work, and at each she received a negative response.

"Well, if he does come around, please tell him that Mr. Carmichael has some papers for him. It's important."

After a restless night she woke well before dawn and lay reconsidering the plan she had devised while tossing and turning. Despite Jettie's advice, it seemed to Olivia the only thing she could do. She rose and donned a simple work dress with no petticoats, pulled Mourning's trousers on under it, and slipped into her work shoes. Downstairs, she yanked one of Tobey's flannel shirts out of the heap of laundry and grabbed his rust-colored floppy felt hat from one of the pegs. Then she reconsidered the hat and exchanged it for the less conspicuous beige corduroy flat cap that Avis never wore. She hurried out of the house, driven by frustration, anxiety, and determination. Today she was going to find her son. She would hide in the woods near that shanty town and wait, all day if she had to. Eventually the woman who had Little Boy would emerge from one of those cabins, bringing him out into the sunlight and air.

No one was at the livery yet, so Olivia climbed over the back rail and saddled up Rachel Jackson for herself. She scribbled a note to leave on Mr. Ferguson's desk and rode up Broad Street and out of town. In the shelter of the covered bridge she stopped, dismounted, and hurriedly pulled her dress over her head. She put on Tobey's wrinkled shirt, rolled the dress up, and stuffed it into the saddlebag. Her hair was tied back in a pigtail that she tucked under the flat cap. Who would pay any mind to a lone male rider? From a distance she would be taken for a young man.

Before she reached the fork in the road that led to The Bottoms, she turned into the woods. When she thought she was fairly close, she tethered Rachel Jackson to an oak and crept toward the cabins, remaining well behind the tree line. She found no hiding place from which she could see the doors of all the homes, but she did have a clear view of the large central yard and the well. She began her vigil squatting on her heels, but soon sat cross-legged on the ground, batting away mosquitoes and horseflies.

As she waited for the sun to rise higher in the sky she practiced what she would say to Little Boy's new mother. She scolded herself for not having brought any money, but then thought, no, that might appear crude. Insulting. Anyway, once she won the woman's confidence, she would come back often, bring them all kinds of things. She imagined herself striding out of the woods to introduce herself. She must walk confidently, but not too fast. She didn't want to alarm anyone. She'd take off her hat, so they'd see she was a woman, and keep both hands in sight, clearly no threat. But she'd go right up to her. Hullo, my name is Olivia. Please don't be frightened. I only want to help you. I'm the mother of that baby in your arms. Would the woman run away? Or would Olivia finally get to look into Little Boy's face again, feel his fist close tight around her finger?

A new fear made Olivia's throat close up. What if she didn't recognize him? She remembered how quickly he had changed, one morning to the next, eyes opened wider, face first grown thinner then cheeks filled out, fuzz on his head grown thicker and darker. It had been over three weeks since she'd left him. If someone put three colored babies in front of her, was she sure she'd be able to pick him out? It was a distressing question, but she calmed herself. She was being ridiculous, and anyway there was always that little mole on the side of his neck. She'd know him by that, even at a distance.

Soon a heavy-set woman in a white bandana emerged from one of the cabins and carried a bucket to the well, where she set it down. She placed her palms on the small of her back and stretched, before bending to draw water. She poured the first bucket into the trough near the well, and Olivia bit her lip, wondering if poor Rachel Jackson was thirsty. No matter. This wouldn't take much longer, now that people were beginning to stir. More women came out to draw water, take in firewood, and toss handfuls of grain to the chickens pecking in the dirt.

Soon afterward men began to appear in the yard, yawning, stretching, and studying the sky. Most of them went back into the houses, presumably for breakfast, and then came back out carrying tools. They walked in small groups toward the fields to the west of the shanties. A few headed up the road toward South Valley. The heavy-set woman made Olivia's heart leap when she reappeared carrying a basket, but it was filled with laundry that she began shaking out and hanging over the lines stretched between two trees.

Olivia got to her feet and was shaking her legs to get the kinks out when she heard a baby crying. Sharp stomach contractions surprised her, and she looked down at her shirt to see tiny damp circles beginning to emanate from her nipples. I should have listened to Jettie and bound my breasts, she thought as she pulled the flannel shirt away from her body. She inched closer to the edge of the woods, and a young woman in a brown work dress and bright blue apron came into sight. She was pushing something and Olivia moved aside for a better view. It was a small homemade cart with large front wheels and legs in place of the back wheels, so it stood level when the woman let go of the long handles.

"Laisha, bring me one a them swaddles," she called behind her.

Another young woman appeared, handed over a piece of white cloth, and then seated herself on the slanted surface of the chopping block, her face turned up to the soft rays of sunlight. Laisha's head was wound in a white cloth, like a turban, and her striking profile reminded Olivia of the ancient Egyptian queen in her history book. She wore a raggedy white shift with a red and gold cloth belt twisted around her waist. The woman in the blue apron spread the cloth Laisha had given her over the bottom of the cart and then returned to the cabin. When she came back out she was carrying a baby.

A cry nearly escaped Olivia's throat, but she choked it back. The woman was bending down, the child in her outstretched arms, and Olivia didn't want to startle her. The moment the baby was safely in the cart, Olivia plodded through the undergrowth, hat still on her head, oblivious to how she must look. The woman looked up and stepped in front of the cart, shielding the child from the strange apparition descending upon them. Olivia stopped a short distance from them, swept the cap from her head, and forced herself to speak in a normal tone of voice, instead of shouting what was in her mind, *Little Boy, Little Boy. My baby. That's my baby. You've got my baby.*

"Please. Don't be afraid," Olivia said.

"What you want here?" The woman straightened up, raised her right hand, and began waving it vigorously, high over her head.

"My name is Olivia. Olivia Killion. From Killion's General over in Five Rocks. On July 15th I left a baby here. In the church with Reverend Jameson."

"What you talkin' 'bout?" Her hand waved frantically.

71

"That baby." Olivia nodded at the cart. "I'm his mother. I couldn't keep him, so I left him here with Reverend Jameson. All I want … I just want to know –"

"This here ain't no white baby. This *my* baby."

"Please." Tears came to Olivia's eyes. "I only want to see him," she whispered. "I won't try to take him away. Even if I wanted to, I'd have nowhere to go with him. Just let me hold him. I'm going to get a job, save all my money for him."

"Lady." The woman's voice softened and she no longer looked frightened. She did continue waving her hand. "I don't know what you talkin' 'bout, but this ain't your baby. This ain't no him."

Some of the men out in the fields had gathered together, and one of them was pointing at Olivia. The young woman called Laisha stood up. There was pity in her large dark eyes as she studied the white lady in men's clothing who had walked out of the woods. Olivia saw Laisha's eyes go to the milk stains on her shirt. Embarrassed, she crossed her arms to hide them. Three of the men had begun hurrying toward them.

"I know you're only trying to protect him –" Olivia said.

"I told you, lady, this ain't no him. This my baby girl, Jayleen, and I sure dint git her from the Reverend. I been in thirty-three hours of pain bringing this sweet child into the world, and she be *mine*."

"A girl?" Olivia repeated. "It's a girl?" She could be lying, Olivia thought desperately. "Can I see her?"

The woman looked over her shoulder and saw that the men would soon be at her side. "Okay, you can have a peek at her, but I gotta aks you to stay right there. Nice and calm. Nothin' to git excited 'bout. Don't be comin' no closer." She held her palm out in front of her, watching Olivia, before she bent to pick up the baby.

She came within a few paces of Olivia and held the baby up. Olivia squinted at the child in the woman's arms. How could she know if the woman was telling the truth about it being a girl, short of asking her to remove the swaddling and diaper? But then the child stirred, and the women raised it to her shoulder, completely baring its neck to Olivia. Olivia took two steps closer. The woman pulled back, but not fast enough to prevent Olivia from seeing that there was no mole on the baby's neck.

"Oh," was all Olivia could say.

The rigidity left her body. She slowly dropped to her knees and fell forward, oblivious to the thorny weeds, her forehead and fists on the ground. Desolate, she couldn't think. Couldn't move. Finally she sat back on her heels and looked up at the woman. "You're right, that's not my baby. I'm sorry. That's not my baby."

"Everthin' all right, Anna?" asked the first of the men to reach them.

"Everthin' be fine. This poor lady just be needin' a nice drink of water. Laisha, you go fetch her one. She real upset, thinkin' someone here got her baby. I told her ain't no white woman left no baby with our Reverend."

The men exchanged glances and then avoided looking at Olivia while she clumsily got to her feet.

Anna laid the baby back in the cart, approached Olivia, and placed a hand on her shoulder. "Maybe you just in a confusion. Maybe they ain't no baby. Maybe you had a bad dream."

"I'm not crazy." Olivia looked her in the eye. "I think you know that. You were clever enough to let them know who I am and what you told me." Olivia nodded at the men. "But you can't change the truth. I had a baby. He's my baby, but he's not white. He's as black as you are. He's more than four months old now, and he has a mole right here." She placed her fingertip on her neck. "I gave him to Reverend Jameson, and then when I came back to ask who was caring for him, the Reverend told me he gave my Little Boy to some couple on their way to join a wagon train. Are you claiming not

73

to know anything about that?" Olivia slowly turned her head, studying each of their faces. Laisha and the men all avoided her gaze.

"That right. Ain't none of us know nothin' 'bout that," Anna said. "Maybe you thinkin' 'bout a different church."

"No, that's the church up there. How do you think I know your Reverend's name? And even if the Reverend told me the truth, even if my baby was only here one night, you all have to know about him. In a community this small, you all heard. You're a mother," she looked directly at Anna. "How can you lie to me like this?"

"Who you callin' a liar?" one of the men demanded. "You best git from here."

"Hush," Anna said, waving a hand at the man who spoke.

Olivia continued speaking to Anna, as if they were alone. "I swear, I don't mean to cause harm or trouble. I did a terrible thing, abandoning my baby. I was afraid, didn't want anyone to know. I didn't know what else to do. I was scared for the father too, what might happen to him if white folks found out he had a child by a white woman. But I know you aren't going to tell any white folks about this. You wouldn't do that. For his sake. I'm still scared, and I still don't know what to do, but I want to make it right for my baby. As right as I can. I only want to look out for him. See that he never wants for anything."

Again, Olivia looked at all of them, one after the other. They were a silent wall, ranks tightly closed. Laisha's eyes were soft, but she wasn't going to tell Olivia anything. She looked away and then went to fetch a dipper of water. Defeated, Olivia accepted it and drank.

"Could I ask you for the use of a bucket to water my horse?" She looked into Laisha's face. Even in her distress Olivia couldn't help noticing how beautiful the young woman was.

74

Laisha nodded and went to draw water from the well. Olivia thanked her, trudged back to Rachel Jackson, and then returned with the bucket. Two of the men were still standing protectively on either side of Anna as she jiggled the baby's cart.

Olivia set the bucket down by the well and once again ignored the men, speaking to Anna. "If you should ever decide that a mother and her child ought to know one another, remember my name. Olivia Killion. From Five Rocks. I own a farm in Michigan that will go to the boy, along with all my money, if only I can find him and know what name he's been given. His daddy's name is Mourning. Mourning Free."

She thanked them for the water and walked away.

Chapter Nine

After breakfast the next morning Olivia took one of the cloth hold-alls Mrs. Hardaway kept on a peg in the kitchen, slipped both of her wine-colored journals into it, and walked to Mr. Carmichael's office. Billy Adams opened the door and Olivia couldn't help staring, trying to picture him ten years old, in torn and dirty overalls, with a runny nose and shouting, "Moo-bell. Moo-bell."

Mr. Carmichael rose from behind his desk and invited her in.

"Is this a good time?" she asked.

"Yes. Mr. Adams was just leaving to run some papers over to the brewery for me."

When the door had closed behind Billy, Olivia declined the offer of a chair and drew the journals out of the cloth bag. She set one down on the desk.

"That one's from when we first got to Michigan," she said. "I brought it to you for safekeeping. I'd like to think that Little Boy might have it one day. You can read it or not, as you like. It just tells about me and Mourning working the farm."

She clasped the second journal for a long moment before she resolutely placed it on the other and took a step back, as if it were a dangerous viper coiled between them.

"I wrote what's in there after I came back from Michigan, while I was staying at Mrs. Place's house." She bobbed her nose at it. "Everything I wanted to tell you is already in there, so I didn't bother writing it down all over again. That paper sticking out marks the place where I start telling about the thing that happened. And I added all the details about Little Boy in the back. It's got a lock." She reached into her pocket and set the tiny key on top of it, next to the latch.

"And you haven't changed your mind about wanting me to read this?"

"No, but Billy –"

"You needn't worry. Mr. Adams has no access to the documents in my safe."

"All right, then. You read it and lock it up. Next time you see Mourning, you can give it to him to read. I think he ought to know, since what's in there must have had something to do with him disappearing the way he did."

She turned to leave and then stopped. When she spoke again it was in a rush, anxious to have the telling over with. "I twice went back to The Bottoms looking for Little Boy, but no one there will tell me where he is. Mrs. Place says Mourning could probably find out. So you see, I have to find him. And if you see him, you have to tell him everything."

"Yes, I do see." The lawyer sat still in his chair, his face expressionless except for the intensity of his eyes upon her.

She turned and took another step, then stopped again, to say over her shoulder. "And by the way, there's something else that occurred to me about my father's will. He left that other piece of land, the one in Kentucky, to his first-born grandson. That's Little Boy."

76

From Mr. Carmichael's office Olivia went to Killion's General. She fingered calico fabric for what seemed forever, while waiting for the store to empty of customers and Avis to be alone behind the counter.

"I have to go back to Michigan," she told him. "To register the deed to Uncle Scrugg's farm with the county clerk out there. And there are a few other things I have to take care of."

"Traveling out there all by yourself again ..." His voice trailed off. "But once you're done with all that, you're going to come back here, aren't you?"

He is slightly in awe of me, Olivia thought, finding it difficult to get used to his attitude toward her, wishing she could see herself the way he suddenly seemed to. Can I simply decide to be brave and adventurous rather than desperate and lonely, she wondered.

She might have done the easy thing – lied and told her brother that yes, certainly she would come back – but found herself reluctant to tell him more untruths than necessary.

"I don't know. I still don't know what I want to do with my life. But I have to get that paper work taken care of anyway. While I'm waiting for that to be done, I'll have time to think about what comes next."

"I wish you wanted to make your home here with us. So does Mabel."

"I know. She told me the same thing. You've both been good to me. More than I deserve. I know I've acted like a spoiled child lots of times."

"No one ever thought that, Liv. How could we, the way you took such good care of our father?"

Olivia's mouth stretched into a thin smile. "Our father." She drew in a long, deep breath. "Did you ever call him Pappa or anything like that?"

His upper lip covered the lower, and he shook his head.

"Not even when you were little?"

"No. I'd guess the first word out of my mouth was

probably, 'yessir.'"

"Do you think he used to be different? That he changed, after our mother –"

He cut her off abruptly. "No, I can't say I remember him being different."

She leaned over to put her fingers to his cheek, half-expecting him to pull away. But he didn't, and she let her hand linger there for a moment. "I don't want to talk about that either," she said, not wanting to be asked how long she'd known about their mother hanging herself and who had told her.

"Would you like me to come with you? Out to Michigan?" he asked, looking so apprehensive that Olivia thought him likely to faint if she accepted his offer.

"Oh, no, there's no need for that. There's nothing dangerous about it. Just a ride on the stage and then a longer one on a boat. And you can't close the store for that long. But thanks for offering. And I promise not to disappear again. I'll either come back or write and tell you where I am." She paused for a moment. "What I'd mostly like to thank you for is not asking a lot of questions when I came back. Not trying to pry into my life and tell me what I ought to do."

"By what right would I do that?"

He looked pleased but embarrassed, and she guessed he would be glad for a customer to come in and force an end to the conversation. So she turned away from him and commented on how much better the store looked with the changes they had made.

"Do I still get free sucking candy?" she asked, her hand already in the tilted glass jar. "How about if I help out a bit? I could straighten up these shelves."

"You don't have to do that. Mabel will get to it."

"You mean she'll rearrange it all anyway," Olivia smiled, and her brother flushed. "Doesn't matter. I just feel like I need to do something useful."

"Suit yourself."

She busied herself for a while and then the bell did jangle, but it announced the one customer Avis was never glad to see.

"Hullo, Mrs. Place," Olivia greeted Jettie warmly. "It's good to see you again."

"Why hullo, Miss Killion. Nice to see you too." Jettie glanced nervously at Avis. "And good day, Mr. Killion. I've brought your pies. They're out on the wagon."

Avis went out to fetch them and then handed some coins to Jettie.

"I feel like taking a walk by the river," Olivia said when Jettie had pocketed her money and was ready to leave. "Mind if I walk along with you?"

Avis's face was blank as his eyes darted back and forth between the two women.

Jettie flushed, but smiled and said. "Certainly, I would be glad of your company."

When they were out on the sidewalk, Jettie's wagon clanking along behind them, Jettie said, "You're only hurting yourself, you know, not helping me. You being friendly with me ain't gonna shine up my tarnished reputation none. Rub a muddy hand up against a clean one, all you get yourself is two muddy hands."

"That's not what I ..." Olivia paused, considering her words. "I remember my father always telling Avis to choose his battles. I've decided to choose my lies. I don't want to pretend or lie about anything that I don't absolutely have to. I don't want to go on sneaking into your shop, waiting for you to be alone before I dare speak to you. Besides, if I'm not going to live here, what difference does it make? And if I am going to live here, I'll probably come begging you for a job and people will just have to get used to us being friends."

When they came to The Circle where Jettie lived, Olivia stopped by the trail that veered down toward the bank of the Saugata.

"I do feel like sitting by the river for a while. I just wanted to tell you that I'll be going back to Michigan soon," Olivia said and then looked into Jettie's face. "Are you feeling well? You look awfully peeked."

"Just been a busy day."

"How's that cough of yours?"

"Same as always. My body insists on reminding me that I'm getting older is all. What are you going to Michigan for?"

"Settle the deed to that land, but mostly to look for Mourning."

"Then what?"

"I don't know. Depends on if I find him, I guess."

"Well, you get yourself back here. I know you think this town is about the last place on earth you want to be, but a person needs their family. And folks ain't no better anywhere else. There's small-minded, hard-hearted villains wherever you go. Might as well stay with the devils you know."

Olivia smiled and gave her a quick hug before turning to start down the path to the river.

"Why the heck did they have to build Michigan so far away?" Jettie called after her.

Olivia was startled to find "her" spot on the bank of the river occupied. There sat Mr. Carmichael, right on the ground, gangly knees pointing to the sky. Olivia would have turned and fled, but it was too late. He had already looked up and seen her.

"Oh, hullo Mr. Carmichael."

He nodded, but did not return her greeting. He seemed reluctant to speak to her, and she paled, realizing he must have already read her journal. She had blanked out those thoughts – when would he read it, what would he think, how would he look at her the next time he saw her? She had handed the terrible story over and then pushed it out of her mind. He must have started reading the minute she left his office. Only an hour or two had passed since then.

The lawyer slowly got to his feet and brushed

himself off. "Good afternoon, Miss Killion ..." He floundered for appropriate words. "I ... You needn't worry ... Your journal is locked away in my safe." His voice was low, even, and both he and Olivia averted their eyes.

He is so disgusted he can't even look at me, Olivia thought. It's like Jettie said.

She tried to escape, saying, "I guess I'd better be getting back home. Good day to you."

"Miss Killion." He raised his voice, and she turned to face him again. "I read what you wrote. Those people ... they must be brought to justice. You wrote nothing about that. Is there not a sheriff in Fae's Landing? Or in some other town nearby? I can only assume that you told no one in Michigan what they did, but –"

"No!" Olivia said too loudly. "No, you can't tell anyone. Not ever. No sheriff. You've got to promise."

"Please, don't be upset." He took a hesitant step toward her. "I would never do such a thing against your wishes. But they must be punished. People can't just get away with –"

"Yes, they can," Olivia said, her voice low and back in control. "They can. They did. Who do you think would believe me?"

"Why would the sheriff think you are lying? What reason could you possibly have for making up such a thing?"

She smiled wryly and looked away, partly mortified to find herself discussing "the thing that happened" face-to-face with her father's attorney, partly relieved to be talking about it with anyone. Sometimes she thought that all the censure and pointing fingers in the world could not be as bad as the pain of keeping it all locked inside.

"Do you feel like sitting back down?" Olivia asked, somewhat astonished by her own familiarity, but tired out by the two of them awkwardly facing one another, shifting their weight from foot to foot.

"Certainly." He offered her a hand and then sat at a respectable distance from her.

"If a doctor examined me he could tell I've had a baby," she said. "Then people would say I got myself in trouble and went looking to blame it on some poor innocent man."

"No one who knows you would believe that you would do such a thing. I could go with you, as a character witness. Help you find a good local attorney."

"That's awfully kind of you, but it wouldn't do any good. Even if there ever got to be a trial, I'd have to account for myself, say where I'd been all that time – staying at Mrs. Place's house, getting ready to have a baby. And they'd want to know where that baby is, so everyone would find out it was colored and I gave it away. Then who would believe me about the Stubblefields? I'm amazed you do."

"Why, I've watched you grow up. I have no doubts regarding the goodness of your character."

He looked so helpless, Olivia almost felt sorry for him.

"Anyway," she said, "if folks found out about Little Boy, you know what they might say about Mourning. Thing like that could get him hurt. Killed."

He pursed his lips. "Of course. I hadn't thought of that. Still –"

"I appreciate you wanting to help. But there's nothing for me to do but try and forget it all."

He looked away from her, toward the river. "You know," he said softly, "I have found that prayer can lift the spirit of even a non-believer. Or an I-don't-know-what-I-believer." He glanced at her, shook his head, and looked away again. "No, I have never been a religious man of the church-going variety." He paused. "But I do believe that our whispered, secret prayers, those we voice only to our own ears ..." He stopped, cleared his throat, and began again. "To find peace of mind, to live a life of purpose, a person must bind their life to a world larger than that we are capable of seeing."

Olivia stared at the light shimmering on the water and wished she had paper and pen so she could write down the words he'd said and try to decipher them later. She had longed for a conversation like this, but was in too much inner turmoil, was having too strong a bodily reaction to the memories, to be able to make sense of his words. And Mr. Carmichael now looked uncomfortable, probably regretted having spoken them. He cleared his throat and brought them back to more pragmatic matters.

"But you said you plan to go back to Michigan. What if those criminals see you?"

Olivia's eyes rose to the sky, as she remembered the flies buzzing around Filmore, the little sparrow pecking at Iola's eye, the sickening smell in the barn.

"Oh I won't have to go into Fae's Landing. I'll just go to the county clerk in Detroit or wherever you say. There's no danger of running into them there."

"Actually, your land no longer seems to be in Wayne County." Mr. Carmichael's voice gained confidence, back on safe ground. "I sent Billy Adams over to our county seat. I don't know how reliable their national records are, but the best Billy could make out was that your uncle's farm is now part of the newly drawn Washtenaw County. So you'll have to pay a visit to the county seat there. It's in a little town called Ann Arbor."

"Thank you for finding that out so quickly." It had only been a week since she'd gone to him with her request. "How come you didn't tell me that when I was in your office before?"

He seemed taken aback. "I assure you, I didn't mean to keep the information from you. But the documentation you require is not yet fully prepared. And I have written to Detroit, to make sure this information is correct. I certainly wouldn't advise you to go off before I receive their confirmation."

"Oh. I didn't mean I thought you were trying to hide anything. I was just asking." Olivia felt terrible for having insulted him. "Sorry. Lady Mabel is always telling me how tactless I am. Guess she's right. And I guess I'd better get home for dinner. She'll have one of her conniption fits if I'm late."

Twenty-seven days later Mr. Carmichael informed her that he had received a response from Detroit. "You do have to go to Ann Arbor," he said. "To the Washtenaw County Courthouse, at the corner of Huron and Main Street." He handed her the documents she required, and she thanked him.

She was disheartened, having spent those twenty-seven days riding out to farms, farther and farther from Five Rocks. She'd also visited the colored section of every town she passed and left a note in every church and store: Mourning Free, please contact Mr. Carmichael. Important!!!. But she'd met no one who knew anything of him.

While walking home from Mr. Carmichael's office she looked at her not yet official deed to the land. Her name appeared on one of the top lines, in big black letters. Here was her dream come true, and she felt nothing. She showed the papers to Avis that evening.

"So you're set on going back there?" he asked.

"Yes."

"Then you'd better have this." He rose and took a leather pouch from a drawer. "There's $200 in there. In coin. I wish I could give you more, but lately folks have been buying everything on tick."

Her first impulse was to refuse it, but then she thought, why not? Why shouldn't he help me? He got everything else. She graciously accepted the money, again feeling ashamed for always having such low expectations of her brother.

The next day she boarded the stage to Erie. Never in her life had she felt so alone.

Chapter Ten

Before Olivia stepped onto the pier she paused to stare at the steamboat, searching for its name on the bow. Yes, it was *The Windsong*, the same boat she and Mourning had taken to Detroit. She thought it looked even more crowded this time, but otherwise the scene was identical – sweaty stevedores shouting, black stallions and red and white heifers balking at the plank, and a small man in a black jacket and cap, waving aboard strangely attired people who spoke in harsh-sounding foreign languages.

Her cabin – the cheapest they had to offer – was on the main deck. She was carrying only one case, and there was no ladder to maneuver, so Olivia assured the man in the black cap that she needed no help finding her accommodations. The door to her cabin opened only halfway before banging into a lonely-looking bed covered with a worn patchwork quilt tucked tightly under the mattress. On the wall next to it a shelf held a lantern and a single brass candlestick. Most of the white candle in it had already melted into long drips of wax that spilled over the edge of the shelf.

Olivia set her case on the bed and removed a blue and green gingham pouch from her pocket. It held a pistol, which she had resolved to keep on her person at all times. The hard wood and metal banged against her thigh as she walked, but a few bruises were worth the comfort of knowing the weapon was there, easy to put her hand on. She decided she was unlikely to be assaulted on the deck of the boat and tucked the pistol under the mattress.

Then she opened the case and changed from her tight, high-laced shoes into her beaded moccasins. Comfortable at last, she left the cabin and wandered to the rear area of the bottom deck, where she and Mourning had spent their journey listening to the thump-thump of the engine. She watched ten or twelve colored families arranging their rag-tag belongings and pictured herself and Mourning among them. How young and hopeful she must have looked back then – not even a year and a half ago – and how glaringly out of place, with her pale face, new shoes, and store-bought clothes. She almost laughed out loud, remembering how she'd thought no one would notice her.

Nearest to her was a five- or six-year-old girl with rows of tight braids sprouting from her head and bound in different colored ribbons. Olivia took a step forward, and the little girl looked up at her with frightened eyes and edged into the generous homespun folds of her mother's dress. The woman glanced down and then up at Olivia and placed protective hands on her child. The mother was young and plain-looking, with a colorful flowered kerchief covering every strand of her hair, tight over her forehead and knotted at her nape.

"Hullo," Olivia said and ventured closer. "My name is Olivia Killion." She offered a hand, and the black woman hesitated a moment before taking it. "Josie Mumford," she said, eyeing Olivia warily.

"I was wondering if any of you might be heading for Backwoods."

The woman did not respond, but continued staring at Olivia.

All she sees is a white face, Olivia thought. That's all it takes for her to think I might wish her harm. For a simple question to arouse her suspicions. But Olivia forced herself to smile. "I'll be going there myself in a day or two. I'm trying to get in touch with a friend of mine. A colored man by the name of Mourning Free. I think he may have gone to Backwoods looking for work, a little more than a year ago."

The woman shook her head. "Ain't never met no one go by that name."

"Oh, I didn't expect that you might know him. But perhaps you could ask the other colored passengers, if any of you are going to Backwoods, or wherever you do go, to ask folks about him. If anyone runs into him, tell him that he needs to get in touch with Mr. Carmichael, from his home town – Five Rocks. It's about his son. It's important. Please."

"What you say his name be?"

"Mourning. Mourning Free. From Five Rocks Pennsylvania. Tell him Olivia Killion told him to go see Mr. Carmichael as soon as he can. There are some important papers there for him."

"All right. I aks my husband to tell everybody that."

Olivia thanked her, smiled down at the little girl, and turned back toward her cabin. She felt exhausted and depressed. Used up. This trip was a bad idea, she thought as she removed her moccasins and sat on the hard bed, hugging her knees and sapped of energy. The only way I am ever going to find Mourning and Little Boy is if Mourning comes back to Five Rocks. Why didn't I listen to Mr. Carmichael? Why did I get on this stupid boat? I don't want to be here all alone.

The cabin grew chilly, and she yanked the quilt away from the mattress and wrapped it around her shoulders. Soon she began to feel better. I've got three days on this boat with nothing to do but rest. Then I'll spend another night at that nice hotel in Detroit, and it's probably only an hour or two to Fae's Landing when you're on horseback, no wagon to pull. I'll go to my cabin first, to check to see if Mourning found my note and his tools, and then I'll pay a visit to Jeremy, find out what kind of stories folks are telling about what happened to the Stubblefields. Then on my way to Ann Arbor I'll go to that Backwoods place to ask about Mourning. What's so hard about that? I might not find Mourning, but at least I'll know where he isn't.

This time the trip to Detroit was longer – four days – and seemed like weeks. The engine began grinding and wheezing, so they stopped for repairs in Cleveland. Olivia disembarked only to buy food. On board she wandered the deck for hours, but seldom exchanged words with anyone. During the greasy meals that were served almost cold she made polite conversation, but formed no friendships. When she encountered the colored woman she had asked about Backwoods they smiled and nodded to one another, but didn't speak. Olivia thought the other passengers must be staring at her, elbowing one another, tsk-tsk, just look at that poor thing, all by her lonesome. She found herself desperately wishing for company – Mourning, Jettie, Tobey, Avis. Even Mabel. Anyone who knew her name and would notice if she fell overboard.

It was early morning when they docked in Detroit, and Olivia was one of the first passengers off the boat. She strode down the pier and up the muddy dirt road, heading straight for the American flag over the entrance to the United States Hotel. There she asked for a room overlooking the street. After quickly freshening up, she went out to wander the streets, enjoying being on solid ground and anonymous in a crowd.

I might like to live in a busy city like this, she thought, if it weren't for the stink. The piles of horse manure were overpowering, the open drainage system gave off unspeakable odors, and she never seemed to escape the stench of so many outhouses, so close together. And then there was the constant racket of wagons and the shouts of their drivers. But it was exhilarating to walk the noisy streets, lined with so many different types of shops and businesses, trying to guess what language the foreigners were speaking.

She passed groups of men who dressed, behaved, and cussed in a manner that would have been cause for a town meeting back home. Detroit seemed much more male – and free – than Five Rocks. Olivia doubted that many eyes here would blink twice at a woman in trousers with a rifle slung over her shoulder. There were, however, enough good women in poke bonnets to maintain a sense of order and decency.

She turned onto Jefferson Avenue and paused to watch three raggedy men trying to install an enormous pane of glass in the front window of one of the stores. They unsuccessfully tried to fit it into the frame and then set it back down. The one closest to Olivia looked far too old to be lifting anything. He took off his cap, wiped his brow, and winked at her.

"Biggest piece of glass west of New York," he said, bobbing his pockmarked nose at it. "Five foot high and seven foot wide."

"Old man Doty shelled out three hundert dollars for it," one of the other men added.

"Three hundred dollars? For a piece of glass?" Olivia said.

"Paid in gold." The man nodded.

Olivia stood and watched as they tried once again and this time succeeded. She gave them an encouraging smile, but walked away in dismay. Three hundred dollars for a window. She used to feel so rich with the six hundred dollars her Uncle Scruggs had left to her, but was beginning to realize how much in life depended on having great sums of money.

She continued her walk and stopped to stare at a prim, side-gabled, five-bay colonial with a spacious, wrap-around front porch. She had never seen such a well-maintained home. Everything looked as if it had been freshly painted that morning – light grey walls, darker gray trim, and black shutters. Next to it stood an even larger home of red brick. It had no porch and so was less inviting, but was equally imposing and well-kept. She continued up the street, wondering how so many people got enough money to build such fancy homes. They all had two chimneys and many boasted bay windows, front doors surrounded by colored glass, decorative cornices, and columned porticos. A broad wooden sidewalk separated these wealthy homes from the well-leveled dirt road. She smiled wryly, remembering the way folks in Five Rocks called Maple Street "where all the fancy, rich folks live." Compared to these mansions, the Killion residence was humble indeed.

She found herself gravitating toward Fort Street, to *Chez Mademoiselle Lafleur*. She hadn't forgotten how kind Michelle, the owner of that dress shop, had been to her when she'd passed through Detroit on her way back to Pennsylvania. A peek in the window revealed the shop to be empty, but Olivia heard voices and continued up the sidewalk to the alley that ran along the side of the shop. A woman with bottle blonde curls like Michelle's had her back to Olivia, one elbow resting on a large wooden crate.

Two men stood facing Michelle, leaning against a large Conestoga wagon. The wagon was fitted with three bows, but had no canvas cover and was piled high with wooden barrels and boxes. One of the men was ragged looking: tall, thin, pock-marked, and sporting a fringed deerskin shirt and a long scraggly mustache. The other couldn't have been more different. Short and stout, with a neatly trimmed rust-colored mustache and beard, he seemed to be attired for church or a funeral. His shirt was white and his knee-length frock coat, cravat, trousers, and broad-brimmed hat were all black. He laughed at something Michelle was saying and then took a box from the wagon and handed it to her. Michelle set it on the crate beside her, and he handed her a second one.

Olivia ventured a few steps closer and could hear what Michelle, with not a hint of her French accent, was saying: "... and the fool went home with five boxes of –" Michelle paused mid-sentence when scraggly mustache noticed Olivia and nodded in her direction.

"Can I help you?" Michelle turned around, giving no sign that she recognized Olivia.

"Good day. I didn't mean to interrupt. I just stopped

by to say hullo." Olivia was reluctant to speak in front of the men, but thought that if she didn't say it now, it would never get said. "I was in your shop once. You probably don't remember. It was over a year ago. Last July. You were very kind to me."

Michelle squinted. "Oh sure, I remember you. Indeed I do." Her voice grew soft. "The sad girl with the cuts and blisters all over her hands. Good to see you back up to nick."

Olivia flushed. "I'm going to be in Detroit for a day or two," she said. "It would be my pleasure to invite you to share a meal with me."

"Sure, why not?" Michelle surprised Olivia by how readily she agreed. "How about we meet at The Shades? Around seven?"

"That would be grand." Olivia smiled. "What street is that on?"

"It's over by King's Corner." She turned to the man in the black frock coat. "Hershey, which corner is The Shades Tavern at? Jefferson and Griswold?"

He nodded. "That's right."

Olivia's eyes had widened. "It's a saloon?"

"Uh-huh. Why? That a problem? You one a them temperance terrors?"

"No. No. I never knew women were allowed in saloons, is all," Olivia said, doubting that Mrs. Brewster, Mrs. Monroe, or even Mrs. Sorenson (now that she thought of it, especially Mrs. Sorenson) had ever frequented Sorenson's Saloon in Five Rocks.

Michelle smiled. "Tavern keeper ain't gonna refuse money from no one. Wouldn't bat an eye if a nun walked in and told him to pour her a brandy. But don't worry, The Shades is a restaurant too. Plenty of respectable folks eat there. Pretty thing like you might not feel too comfortable on her own, but you'll be fine with me. I know all the mugs in there."

"This one, she is knowing all the mugs everywhere," the man in the frock coat said as he removed his big black hat to wipe a handkerchief across his balding head. His face was round, and when he smiled his almond eyes almost disappeared.

Olivia smiled at the man and turned back to Michelle. "Perhaps I could bother you with a question," she said. "I'm looking for a friend of mine who may have passed through here, on his way to a town called Backwoods. I don't suppose you know many colored people?"

"Enough." Michelle shrugged. "And they's easy enough to find in this town. Don't many of 'em live west of Randolph. Why, he a nigger, this friend of yours?"

"Yes, he's a very good friend who happens to be colored," Olivia said stiffly.

Back in Five Rocks more people than not had referred to Mourning as "the nigger boy," even those who were kindest to him. Olivia had grown up used to it, but now it was unbearable for her to think of anyone calling Little Boy a coon, nigger, or sambo.

"His name is Mourning Free," she continued, "and I have an important message for him. That he needs to go see Mr. Carmichael. Get some papers he's holding for him."

Before replying Michelle took a crumpled cigarette from the two that lay on the crate beside her, bent her head as the scraggly mustache man struck a match to light it, and exhaled a long stream of smoke. "You best start asking in the shops on Congress or Larned." She put her finger to her lip and flicked away some loose tobacco. "Come to think of it, I can tell you the best place to leave a message." She grinned. "Nigger name of James Slaughter keeps a bawdy house. Runs it together with his fancy woman. White lady, she is." Michelle raised her eyebrows. "You can bet they get plenty of colored trade in there. White or black, any man traveling through Detroit's gonna be knocking on that door way before mine."

"Isn't that ..." Olivia began timidly, "against the law?

92

A place like that?"

"So you do know what a bawdy house is." Michelle's grin grew wider. "No, it ain't against the law. Not that some of the aldermen wouldn't like it to be. One of them tried to put a sign up in front of it." She raised a hand, palm out, and moved it as if running it over said sign. "'House of Ill Fame for the Commission of Fornication and Adultery by Permission of Court.' But the city wouldn't do it."

The man in the frock coat said, "Those aldermen, they have a serious job to do. I bet a few of them are over at Mr. Slaughter's house right this minute, looking for evidence."

He winked at Olivia, who mumbled her good-byes.

Chapter Eleven

Olivia was flushed with embarrassment as she walked away from Michelle and her friends. She felt awkward and had no idea how to talk to this unfamiliar breed of people, but couldn't help smiling. Imagine, a man dressed like a minister making jokes about a bawdy house – and in the company of women. Had he actually winked at her? One thing for sure about Detroit, it wasn't boring. Tired of being alone, she was pleased to have the evening with Michelle to look forward to.

She decided to put off her search for Mourning until the next day, preferring to idly ramble until it was time to go back to the hotel to get cleaned up and have a rest before supper. She spent the next hour wandering through quieter, more modest streets and then past the railroad yard and noisy mills. The last hovels she saw were perched on piles, looking as if the slam of a door might send them splashing into the water. She quickly turned away from that depressing sight.

Her feet had been complaining for a while when she

passed a lopsided wooden sign marking the city limits. She continued a bit farther, and the familiar sounds of the woods confirmed that she had indeed left civilization. When she had dressed to go out it had seemed silly to carry the heavy pistol all about the crowded city, but now, feeling vulnerable, she regretted leaving it in her room.

She turned around to retrace her steps and soon saw an uncovered Conestoga wagon coming toward her. Though she knew the driver had probably already seen her, she instinctively stepped off the road, into the trees. But as he drew closer his black coat and hat made it easy to recognize him as Michelle's friend. He was turning to the right, onto a private road. Only then did she notice the large house standing back from the road, at the top of a gentle slope. It was partly concealed by three towering oaks, and she had passed it before without noticing.

The house was painted a light blue-gray and dripped an astonishing amount of lacy white trim – along the railing of the wrap-around porch, as well as around the door and all the windows. Elaborate wooden carvings hung from the roof of the porch, as well as from the projecting edges of the front-gabled roofs that covered the second and third stories. Olivia couldn't stop staring and wished she had bought a new journal and pencils and could make a sketch of this enchanting home.

She stepped back into the open and reached the private road in time to see Michelle's friend knock on the front door and disappear inside. Halfway up the drive she turned to look behind her. The fairy tale dwelling stood on the first poor excuse for a hill she had seen in the relentlessly flat state of Michigan, and its view of the river was only partly hidden by the trees. She stood and watched a large steamer and three schooners in full sail gracefully plow the waters.

Near the front porch the faded red letters of a

weather-beaten sign declared: **Rums Fer Let, Daley Or Wekely**. Olivia tsk-tsked the spelling mistakes and sloppy lettering. If she had a beautiful boarding house like this, the sign would be bright and cheery, repainted every spring. Then the newer sign planted next to it caught her eye: **Fer Sale**. And there it was – a respectable way that Olivia could make her living had presented itself. Why hadn't she thought of it before? She was certainly capable of running a boarding house, and then she wouldn't have to choose between living all alone or under someone else's roof. Her boarders would be like a family.

Olivia's thoughts rushed ahead. There was no reason she couldn't hire a colored handy man. Hadn't Mourning worked at Mrs. Monroe's? So he could work for Olivia. And of course the poor widowed handy man would keep his little boy with him, right there in the house. Olivia already knew how to sweep floors and change beds; all she had to do was learn how to cook. She would write to Mabel, ask for all her recipes. She had no idea where the money would come from, but her mind was made up – she was going to buy a boarding house.

The idea of acquiring one in Detroit was tantalizing. Imagine living in this exciting city on a river, with its broad avenues, stately homes, bustling markets, and endless rows of shops. There were all kinds of restaurants and people chattering in every language you could think of. Even Indians walking around in feather head dresses. With all those steamboats coming and going, how could there ever be a shortage of folks looking for a place to lay their head? I'd be only a boat ride from Five Rocks, she thought. Someday Avis might come to visit and see all those boats, all that cargo passing in and out every day, and decide to open a store in Detroit. Mabel would never dream of moving away from her precious Girls' Club, but Avis could leave Tobey here to run it for him.

95

Of course, I'll never be able to afford anything as grand as this house here, she thought. But once Uncle Scruggs' land is registered in my name I can sell it. Maybe that, together with what's left of Uncle Scruggs money and what Avis gave me, will be enough to buy something small. She sighed and stared at the dream home in front of her. It was perfect – a place she could picture herself living, sitting on that shady porch shucking corn, peeling potatoes, or slicing apples, while she watched the boats float by on the river. What harm could there be in enquiring about the price? She continued toward the wagon and stopped to bid a good day to the horses, one black with white markings, the other a sorrel with a thick yellow mane. She was stroking the neck of the sorrel when the front door opened.

Michelle's friend had spent barely a minute inside and came out looking angry. The door didn't slam, but was shut resolutely behind him. He clomped down the steps toward the wagon, muttering. "Miserable *alte yachneh. Kish mir en toochis.*"

Olivia raised a hand and said, "Hullo."

"Oh, hullo. I didn't see you." He squinted at her. "You're the girl who came to see Michelle."

"Yes. My name is Olivia." She offered a hand. "Olivia Killion."

"Hershel Abraham." He smiled, but only stared at her hand, looking embarrassed. "Pardon me for no handshaking, but my hands, they have axel grease."

She pulled hers back. "Do you mind if I ask – was that German you were speaking?"

"Sort of." He moved toward the wagon, not looking nearly as friendly as he had back at Michelle's shop.

"You've got a beautiful team of horses."

He stopped, forced a smile, and put his hand on the nose of the black horse. "Yes, that's the truth. These two are pulling me around, all over Michigan. Ohio and Indiana too."

96

"This isn't your house?" she asked.

"No." He shook his head with a wry smile. "I was asking about a room."

"Oh. So they're full up?"

"No, not full. Empty rooms the gracious lady has. Just not for a man of my religion."

Olivia's chin jerked up, her eyes open wide. "She turned away an Amish man? I've never heard of such a thing."

He again smiled and wagged a finger. "Not Amish."

Olivia stared blankly at him for a moment. "Oh. So what are you?"

He seemed amused rather than offended by her bluntness. "Dear young lady." He removed his hat and bowed. "I am a Jew."

Her face went from blank to a frown. "I've never heard of that," she said, though she did have a vague memory of that word and tried to dredge it up.

"Maybe you are calling them the Children of Israel."

"You mean like in the Bible?"

He nodded.

"You're fooling me."

"No. No fooling."

"There are still Children of Israel? I thought those people – the Pharaohs and all like that – are just, you know, in the Bible."

"No more Pharaohs. *Kaput*. But Jews there are. We outlasted them. But plenty of Christians are wishing we didn't. Like that lady in there." He jabbed his thumb over his shoulder. "She is describing her respectable establishment as 'No place for coons, crooks, or Christ-killers.'"

Olivia kept the frown on her face and asked, "So Jews aren't a kind of Christians?"

"No. Definitely not Christians." He fiddled with the horses' harnesses.

"It sure is interesting to make your acquaintance." Olivia took a step closer to him. "I've never known anyone who wasn't a Christian. I mean, I know plenty of folks who never stick their nose inside a church. My father was like that. And I don't go much. But I guess we still think we are Christians of some shape. Then there are folks who do all manner of evil, but can't stop bragging about how they never miss a Sunday service. Big liars is all they are, to call themselves Christians. Like that lady in there. I wonder if she thinks Jesus would have turned you away." She was surprised by the flow of words that kept tumbling out of her mouth.

"Well, it is my honor to make your acquaintance, Miss Killion." He lifted his hat again and bent at the waist. "I better ... what is it people say ... make my breast clean? I don't want that you are thinking I am a big liar, but I did say a lie about why I didn't shake your hand. The truth is that my religion forbids me."

"Now why on earth is that?"

"It forbids touching any woman who is not my wife. Even her hand."

Olivia digested that for a moment. "Well, I guess that sounds like a pretty good rule. All the women in the world ought to get busy converting their husbands into being Jews. Can I ask what you were saying before? In sort of German?"

"Nothing very nice. I called her an *alte yachneh*. That means ... mmm ... an old hag I guess you are saying. Then I invited her to ... never mind."

"All-ti-yak-nay?" Olivia tried to mimic him.

"Close enough." Mr. Abraham smiled broadly and climbed up onto his wagon. "You have a good day, Miss Killion."

"Oh, you too," Olivia said, wishing he would stay to talk more. "Listen, I'm looking to buy a boarding house and was just going to ask about this one. Would you have any advice to offer me about how much a house like this sells for?"

He leaned back in the seat. "A number I can't to say, but the last years the price of land fell to hell. I can to give you one good advice – don't let that witch know you're interested before you asked around town."

"All right." Olivia nodded. "One thing for sure – if I do buy a house I promise you'll always be welcome to stay there. So long as you don't mind staying in the same place with coloreds, because I wouldn't turn them away either. I'd put up a new sign – everybody welcome."

"I'll keep peeling my eyes for it." He took up the reins and said, "Back," to the horses. "You take good care."

Olivia stood and watched as Mr. Abraham eased the wagon back down onto the road, but then he stopped and sat still for a moment, as if trying to make his mind up about something. Finally he put the brake on, sprang down, and walked back toward Olivia.

"Listen, if you are wanting to buy this place, you should to speak with a fellow I know. He is working in a bank and I think he can to tell you what is a good price."

"Oh, I'd love to talk with him," Olivia said eagerly, though she felt like the biggest liar of all – a pauper pretending to be of means.

"You're having your supper with Michelle at The Shades?"

She nodded.

"I'll talk to him. Maybe we can to come there also, but later, just for having coffee with you lovely ladies."

"That would be wonderful. Thank you so much."

"Least I can to do for my future landlady. You want I should take you back to the city?"

"Oh yes, thank you."

During the short ride he questioned Olivia. Where was she from? Why was she in Detroit? Why did she want a boarding house? Who was her colored friend? She didn't mind answering and lied only when necessary.

He stopped to let her off at the corner of

Woodbridge Street. As she watched him drive away Olivia's memory suddenly perked up. She took quick steps and said to his back, "I just remembered. I have heard of a Jew before. In *Ivanhoe*. That Isaac of York fellow was a Jew, wasn't he? And his daughter, the Jewess Rebecca."

"See, I told you," Mr. Abraham replied over his shoulder and gave a last wave of his hand. "We are everywhere."

All-ti-yak-nay, Olivia repeated to herself. Every time I see Mr. Abraham I'm going to ask him to teach me a word in Jewish.

Chapter Twelve

The Shades tavern was easy to find, and Olivia timidly pushed the door open. She was a few minutes early and relieved to see Michelle already seated at one of the heavy wooden tables, a glass of golden-brown liquid in front of her. Like many of the dresses Michelle sold in her shop the red and white one she was wearing showed ample and impressive titty, but to Olivia's surprise the four men seated on stools at the bar did not seem to be paying her any mind. Though Michelle was not a conventional beauty, Olivia thought she was stunning. Her blonde curls and light olive skin glowed, her lips were always shiny, and Olivia had never seen lashes as thick and dark as those that fringed Michelle's large brown eyes. The warmth of her wide smile made Olivia feel welcome.

As Olivia seated herself, Michelle pointed at her glass. "One for you?"

"Oh no ... I mean, I have drunk whiskey before. I just don't care for any at the moment."

"It's brandy," Michelle said. "*Eau-de-vie* to folks around here. But suit yourself. The best thing they got to eat here is fried chicken and potatoes."

"That sounds fine," Olivia said.

"Hullo, Slim Johnny my love, can you bring us two plates?" Michelle called to the man in a grease-stained apron behind the bar. Olivia recognized him as the scraggly man who had been in the alley with Michelle and Mr. Abraham. Then Michelle turned back to Olivia. "So what brought you back to Detroit?"

"I need to register a deed, for some farmland I inherited from my father."

"That where you got all them cuts and blisters you had?"

"Yes. In order to inherit I had to put in a crop." Olivia nudged her chair closer to the table and arranged her skirt. "But that's not the only reason I came back here. As I told you this afternoon, I'm looking for a friend of mine."

"Oh right, you were asking about Backwoods. You know, after you left I remembered a friend I've got over there. He keeps a dry goods store on Main Street and knows everyone in town. If you go over there looking for your friend, you should talk to him. Name's Zach Faraday."

"Is he colored?"

Michelle nodded, took a sip of her brandy, and glanced up at Slim Johnny, who had appeared with two plates of food. The chicken looked burnt and dry and the potatoes were limp with grease. I should open a restaurant, Olivia thought, if this is their idea of good food.

"Better dig in while it's hot," Michelle said and hunched over her plate.

They chatted while they ate. Olivia asked a few questions about Michelle's shop. Michelle asked a few questions about Olivia's farm. Then Olivia asked, "Are colored people in Detroit allowed to own businesses?"

"Sure." Michelle drained her glass and raised it, signaling Johnny to bring another.

"Is it true that white people shop in their stores?"

"Course. Whites buy from coloreds, coloreds buy from whites. Why wouldn't they? I know a colored doctor who's got white patients. I guess we don't keep so separate out here, not like back east." Michelle cocked her head and thought for a moment. "Except in church. Coloreds got one of their own. They can go into a white church if they want, but they got to sit up in a special gallery."

"What about schools?" Olivia asked. "Do colored children go to school?"

Michelle stuck out her bottom lip, shook her head, and shrugged. "Couldn't tell you about that. People are always talking about the old days, when the French were still in charge, how there was just the one school for everybody. Half-breeds, full-blooded Indians – those Jesuits didn't turn anyone away. But I don't know how it is today, with the Yanks running things. That's a question for someone what's got kids."

Olivia's brow creased slightly; she couldn't get used to the way people had started using the word for baby goats to refer to children. "But you wouldn't say there are a lot of white people who hate coloreds?" she asked.

Michelle gave Olivia a curious glance. "I guess I'd say anywhere you go you're gonna find plenty of folks what hate plenty of other kinds of folks."

Michelle took a packet of matches and a roll of fabric from her pocket, unrolled the cloth to remove one of the cigarettes inside, and lit it. Then she leaned back and stared at Olivia, studying her as if she suspected her of something or was trying to work out the answer to some question. After a long pause she spoke. "I'll tell you one thing, all the ones what do hate 'em must write for the Free Press. That paper – white bankers in this town can rob us all blind and the editor ain't got a word to say about that, but let a colored man steal an apple from a cart, it's all over the front page, like he took an axe to someone. They're always running editorials, wanting to pack 'em all off to Liberia."

Olivia changed the subject. "You're not really French, are you?"

"New York City." Michelle raised and drained her glass, as if toasting her hometown. "Real name's Joan. Joanie Johnson of Marble Hill. Tourists fall real easy for the whole French thing. The stupes. Come out here and dress up in buckskin, get a guide to do their hunting for them. I tell 'em that the dresses and hats in my shop are the latest fashion, straight off a ship from Paris, France. Every one of the fools buys a couple to take home to his wife."

Olivia studied her half-full plate, finding it difficult to hide her shock. She'd never heard anyone admit to lying like that. But, she asked herself, where is the harm? Michelle's customers go away pleased, and their wives are probably thrilled with their new Parisian creations. She raised her head and smiled at Michelle, seeing her as a younger version of Jettie. For a moment Olivia felt a tinge of aversion – Why did she seem to be drawn only to women of questionable character? – but she pushed that unworthy thought aside. She knew both of them to be kind and generous. So some women broke the rules, so what? A lot of those rules needed breaking. Neither Jettie nor Michelle was hurting anyone. They were surviving.

"I've thought of changing from Michelle to Monique. Whad'ya think?"

"I like Michelle better. It's softer sounding."

Michelle nodded and then called to Slim Johnny, "Bring us two more of these." She held up her glass. "You got to celebrate our new friendship," she said to Olivia.

Olivia smiled her agreement. Why shouldn't an adventurous traveling woman take a drink with a friend? She wasn't a child any more.

"So where do you get the dresses?" Olivia asked and set her plate aside.

"I draw 'em and got two ladies what stitch 'em up

103

for me. Sometimes they even come out looking like the drawings."

"You draw them yourself? Really? They're so beautiful."

"I copy some of 'em out of journals. My ladies cut 'em with wide seams, so they're easy to let out for the big girls," Michelle said proudly. She put out her cigarette and immediately lit another one.

"What about the hats?"

"I buy plain straw bonnets by the dozen. From Hershey." She raised her eyebrows and pointed a finger at Olivia. "You met him today. In the black hat."

"Oh yes, Mr. Abraham. Actually, we met again. At a boarding house outside of town. Some horrible lady refused to rent him a room."

"Poor Hershey. Bless his soul. Good thing he don't take none a that to heart. Anyway, he sells me all my fabrics and straw bonnets. Gets them in all different sizes and shapes. I just stick some ribbon, feathers, or silk flowers on 'em, add a lace curtain or ruffle in the back and one of my *Chez Mademoiselle Lafleur* labels, and *Voila*." She made a circle with her right hand.

"I forgot to tell you, Mr. Abraham may join us here with a friend of his. That boarding house is for sale and his friend works at a bank, so he might know what the price of a house like that should be."

"You looking to buy a house?" Michelle asked.

"Thinking about it."

Slim Johnny silently set a glass of brandy in front of each of them and drifted away. Michelle raised hers and waited for Olivia to do the same.

"To women in saloons," Michelle said.

Olivia touched her glass to Michelle's and added, "To women who are true friends to one another."

While Olivia slowly sipped her drink, Michelle gave her an education in women's fashions. Olivia noticed that Michelle never mentioned any family or home and was again reminded of Jettie. Olivia wondered how many women were out in the world, struggling all alone.

"Isn't it hard to pretend to be French all the time?" Olivia asked.

"Don't do it all the time. Just when a strange face pops into the shop."

"But what if a local person comes in at the same time?"

"Don't matter none, they all know I do it. Stand there and enjoy the show. Ain't no one going to snitch on me."

"Still, don't you think the men would buy the latest fashion straight from New York? Or London?"

"London. Peh." She made a dismissive gesture. "Who wants to be like the English? No romance in that. You ever seen any a them French voyageurs?"

Olivia shook her head. "I don't know who you mean."

"Frenchmen in striped shirts, all different colors, rowing and paddling their big voyageur canoes up and down the river. The steamers are driving them off, but there's still a few around. You must have seen some on the way."

"Oh them – you mean the men who wear those funny pointed caps with tassels at the end." Olivia remembered the man in the canoe who had clutched his cap to his heart and sung to her, while she stood at the rail of the steamboat that brought her to Detroit for the first time. She had since seen a few more of the large canoes and always wondered why they made them in such a funny shape, with the front and rear curling up toward the men, like the toes of shoes worn by dwarfs in a book of fairy tales.

Michelle nodded. "Well, not all of them wear those hats, but yes, that's who I mean. They got all those pretty cushions in their boats, and awnings and flags. That's the French. Bright and colorful. Singing and enjoying themselves. Never too late for another drink.

Never too tired for another dance. Even the Yanks who look down their snooty noses at them for being too friendly with the Indians still sit around sighing, talking about the good old days when you could hear those light-hearted Frenchmen singing their love songs as they went by at sunset." Michelle extinguished her cigarette and let out a sigh of her own. "Then look at the Yanks with their drab clothes and God-awful noisy steamers. All they do all day is work. Grub, grub, grub after money. The French know how to live. But –" she said and leaned forward, stabbing the tabletop with her finger, "those Voyageurs are no lazybones. They work harder than any Yank. Spend weeks out in the wilderness, with not much to eat."

"What do you mean about the French being too friendly with the Indians?" Olivia asked.

"They were the first white men out here and since there warn't any white women, they took up with the Indians. Lot of 'em married squaws – sometimes more than one – and had a passel of half-breeds. And like I told you, even the ones what lived in town and had white children didn't see nothing wrong with sending them to school together with Indians."

"And colored children."

"Sure. Them too, I guess, if there were any of them in Detroit back then."

"So out here it isn't against the law to teach a colored person to read and write?"

Michelle puckered up her face. "Is that against the law back east? I never knew that. Why would anyone make a law like that?" Then she smiled broadly and began waving at someone behind Olivia.

"Hershey," Michelle called out, rising from her seat.

Olivia turned and saw Mr. Abraham, accompanied by a paper-thin, meek-looking man wearing a silk top hat.

"Mademoiselle Lafleur." Mr. Abraham smiled, strode quickly to the table, and gave a curt bow.

"Together with Mademoiselle Killion. A miracle. The two most beautiful women in Detroit at one table."

Michelle turned to Olivia. "So I guess you and Hershey are old friends. I can't believe you asked the bandit what's been robbing me blind all these years for financial advice."

Unsure what good etiquette required of her, Olivia rose from her seat. "Good evening, Mr. Abraham. It's good to see you again."

"Wonderful to see you. Please, let me to present Mr. Richard Guffey Wentworth. He's a Protestant Minister, but don't mind about that. He's still a wonderful fellow. Men like him are giving Christianity a good name. And about making money and hanging onto it, no one is knowing more."

Mr. Wentworth shook hands with Olivia and greeted Michelle – with whom he seemed to already be acquainted. Then they all seated themselves and ordered coffee. Everyone except Mr. Abraham also asked for apple pie.

"How did you and Mr. Abraham become acquainted?" Olivia asked Michelle, though she was more curious to know how on earth Mr. Abraham and Mr. Wentworth had become friends.

Mr. Abraham made himself sloppily comfortable, obviously enjoying the opportunity to relax and exchange small jibes with Michelle. Mr. Wentworth's back did not touch his chair as he waited for the chit-chat to be over with.

"This thief started overcharging me for the rags he sells a long time ago," Michelle replied to Olivia.

"If she wasn't too stubborn to do what I am telling her and hire a dozen more sewing ladies," Mr. Abraham said, "I can to be the thief who is making a wealthy woman of her, who is selling her hats and dresses all over Michigan, Ohio, and Indiana."

"This fool thinks women are going to buy dresses out of the back of his wagon." Michelle rolled her eyes.

"Their husbands probably would," Olivia said. "If you gave them a fancy wrapper. Same as the men who come into your shop."

Mr. Abraham nodded and pointed at Olivia. "Exactly what I am telling her." Then he turned to Michelle. "And you never saw how I am selling. I convince everyone."

"I can certainly attest to his powers of persuasion." Mr. Wentworth joined the conversation, still expressionless. Then he turned to Olivia. "I understand you have some interest in a business venture of your own."

Olivia felt slightly uncomfortable under his scrutiny, as if he were trying to assess her. He probably can tell I don't have much money, she thought.

"I don't know if I can afford it," she replied, as the coffee and pie was delivered to the table, "but I did notice a boarding house for sale – on the southwest side of town, up on a hill."

"Yes, I am familiar with that property. I considered investing in it myself. The owner, Mrs. Rafferty, has to sell. She's eager to go back east to live with her daughter, but has proven to be entirely unrealistic regarding the price. Her father bought the lot back in '35, when land prices were still in the sky. Then he sunk another fortune into the building. All those pretty-pretty bargeboards and other nonsense. He had teams of carpenters working for months carving all that gingerbread." He sniffed.

"I think it's beautiful," Olivia said.

"I suppose." He sniffed again. "If you like that sort of thing. Myself, I prefer a good solid colonial, with nice straight lines. Mr. Rafferty insisted it was all the rage in London. Queen Anne style he called it. He wasn't a young man and had only the one daughter, so no one could imagine why he needed an enormous house like that in the first place. Now his daughter seems incapable of understanding how far prices have fallen since then. She'll be lucky to get a fraction of what he put into it."

Olivia vaguely knew that something called "the panic" had caused markets to collapse all over the country, though it never seemed to have affected her father's business. As Avis said, folks still had to buy flour and oil.

Mr. Wentworth studied Olivia's blank expression for a moment and then continued in the voice of a patient schoolteacher. "You see, years ago the price of land in Michigan started rising and just kept going up, higher and higher. Some rise would have been only natural, following the opening of the Canal and the influx of so many new settlers. But the unfortunate fact is that rising prices always attract speculators, and once they get involved there are even steeper increases. Out here the railroads also contributed to the disaster – managed to take over vast tracts of land intended for homesteaders. Insurance companies too." His nasal voice grew indignant. "They'd get people with absolutely no intention of farming to stake a claim on a piece of land and mortgage it to them. Then as soon as it was proved up and they got the final certificate, the owner would pocket the mortgage money and turn the property over to the insurance company."

Olivia's eyes had glazed over and she took a bite of her apple pie. The crust was hard and dry, the apples hadn't been peeled, and she could barely taste the fruit for too much flour and sugar. Forget the restaurant, I should open a bakery, she thought. She drifted from Mr. Wentworth's drone into her own thoughts, seeing herself in the large, sunny kitchen of her boarding house, baking extra pies and frying fritters to sell to the hotels and restaurants.

"I think what Miss Killion is wanting is a number – what a fair price for that property would be." Mr. Abraham broke in, interrupting Olivia's daydream,

Olivia nodded, looking relieved. "Yes, that's true. I

109

don't understand much about business ... I don't even know what a speculator is."

Mr. Wentworth seemed unable to resist explaining. "A speculator is a person who buys something not because he needs or even wants it, but because he thinks he'll soon be able to sell it for more than he paid. Then it's a cycle – the more land the speculators buy, the higher the price keeps rising, so more speculators buy more land. They drive the price up so high that no farmer can afford to pay it, so now there's no real market at all. Nothing but a flock of greedy parasites trying to outguess each other about when to start selling. And that's what happened all around Detroit," Mr. Wentworth said. He ran his napkin over his mouth and folded it. "Paper cities, we call them. Enormous amounts of land were purchased, but to no purpose. When the speculators realized that the market was deplete of buyers, all of them wanted to be the first to sell. Now none of them can get their money out of that land. So it's what we call a buyer's market."

"But what does it all mean? How much is it worth now?" Olivia asked.

Mr. Wentworth's expression seemed sad as he said, "I can remember, in the fall of '36, an insurance man out of New York paid $12,000 for a few acres of farm land – part of one of those ribbon farms stretching back from the river. Today you can take ownership of a fair-sized lot for $200. Even less, if the seller is really pressed."

Olivia's heart stopped for a moment when he said $200, but she fought against getting her hopes up. "But it's not just a lot," she said. "There's a house on it. That big house with all those fancy trimmings. And a barn and things."

"In today's market, with so many men looking for work, you could put up a regular house that size, and all the out buildings, for somewhere under $2000. And that house is seven years old and needs some work. As far as those fancy trimmings – well, a thing is worth whatever some fool is willing to pay for it. I wouldn't give a red cent for all that lace. If I bought that house, I'd pay someone to take it all off, save me having to paint it every year. So I wouldn't pay more than $1600. And since the owner is pressed to sell, I'd try to get it for a few hundred less than that. Start out offering a thousand. But who can say? Someone who thinks they just have to have a Queen Anne house might pay a lot more."

Olivia wiped her mouth and pushed her chair back. "I guess I've been wasting your time. All I have is an eighty acre farm and $420."

"Is the money in state scrip or gold coins?"

"Gold," Olivia replied.

To her surprise, Mr. Wentworth nodded his approval. "That's more than a decent down payment. You shouldn't have any trouble arranging financing, though you must have noticed how many of the banks have closed their doors."

"I've had no need of a bank, so no, I hadn't noticed."

"Nearly all of them have gone under. The Michigan State Bank and then Farm and Mechanics were the first to go, back in '39. The few left are about to get their charters annulled. I'd wager that the Michigan Insurance Bank is the only one that's going to survive."

"Just by chance, he is sitting on their board," Mr. Abraham said from behind the back of his hand, as if divulging a secret.

"It was not by chance that we refused to behave as irresponsibly as the other banks, foolishly approving mountains of mortgage applications with ridiculous terms."

"What did you mean by arranging financing?" Olivia asked, embarrassed to reveal the extent of her ignorance about these matters.

"A mortgage," Mr. Wentworth said, and seeming perplexed that Olivia's face remained blank he gently added further explanation. "A loan from a bank. You pay it back with interest over a number of years, making a payment each month."

She remembered Jeremy's plans to give people mortgages and end up owning their property and asked, "What happens if you can't always make the payment?"

"You can try to refinance new terms. That means you ask the bank to let you take more years to pay it back, with smaller payments. But if you can't comply with the terms of your contract, ultimately the bank will take possession of the property."

"Oh." Olivia no longer saw herself humming about her bright kitchen, but lying awake at night, terrified of losing everything.

"I am in a position to assure you that the bank would give you favorable terms. For instance, you might want them to defer payment for the first six months or year, however long you think it will take you to start turning a profit. And we would prepare a business plan – estimate how much income the boarding house can be expected to generate as opposed to expenses – and keep the payments safely within your ability to pay."

"How long does it take to pay off one of those mortgages?"

"That depends, of course, on the size of the loan and the size of the payment. You must also understand that for at least the first two or three years you would be paying only on the interest, not gaining any equity in the house."

"You mean I'd be giving good money to the bank every month, but it wouldn't be going toward making the house mine?"

"Yes, that is correct. Not for the first few years anyway."

"Why on earth would I want to do that? I might as well rent myself a room and let someone else do all the work and worrying."

Michelle laughed and Mr. Abraham smiled and shook his head.

"The difference," Mr. Wentworth said and sniffed his nose, not amused, "is that you would go on renting forever, with no chance of ever owning anything."

"Do you know where Fae's Landing is?" Olivia changed the subject. "About forty miles west of here? I'm asking because I've got those eighty acres there to sell and wonder if you'd know what it might go for."

"Not enough," Mr. Wentworth replied, shaking his head. "And in any case I would strongly advise you to hold on to it. It's not close enough to either the Territorial Road or the Chicago Road or to any planned railroad route to fetch much now. But if you can hold off selling for five or ten years, that will change."

"But the price of land could keep going down, couldn't it?" Olivia asked.

"No. Not in the long run. It's at rock bottom now and you know what they say – the reason you can count on land going up is that God isn't making any more of it. And Michigan is developing. Fast. Right now the state is on the verge of bankruptcy, so they aren't laying track or leveling roads, but that will change soon. Boatloads of people keep coming, and they're all going to need transport for their produce, timber, copper, whatever. Fae's Landing is close enough to Detroit that it is certain to eventually get a properly graded road and a railroad stop. When that happens your farm will be worth ten or twenty times what you'd get if you sold it now."

"Oh."

"If you don't want to take out such a large loan, there are many smaller properties for sale, whose owners are more realistic. I could give you a few addresses to look into."

"That's very kind of you, Mr. Wentworth. I have to go to Ann Arbor to register the deed to my farm in Fae's

Landing, but when I get back I would surely like to look at those other houses."

"Then I'll look forward to seeing you again," Mr. Wentworth said and passed her a card with his address on it.

Chapter Thirteen

Out on the sidewalk Olivia shook Mr. Wentworth's hand again, thanking him for taking the time to talk with her. "You certainly have given me a lot to think about," she said.

She said her goodbyes to Michelle and Mr. Abraham, hoping Michelle might walk along with her. But Michelle remained behind, discussing fabrics with Hershey.

"Send me a note when you get back from Ann Arbor," Michelle called to Olivia's back. "I'll come see you at your hotel."

"All right, I will." Olivia gave her a smile over her shoulder and turned left at the first corner, for some reason anxious to be out of their sight.

Owe money to a bank. The thought was distasteful. Seborn had always railed against the banks, calling them a gang of blood suckers and crooks. She'd also heard Avis brag that he would never go hat in hand, begging for the pleasure of paying them interest. But what if there was no other way to buy a property? And Mr. Wentworth had seemed eager to help her, said he would make all the arrangements for a mortgage. But that was bothering her. Why would he offer to do that? She was a complete stranger to him, as she was to Michelle and Mr. Abraham. Avis always said nobody does something for nothing, so what did he want of her? Could Mr. Wentworth somehow take her down payment and then have the bank foreclose on her property, so she lost everything?

114

But surely she could trust Michelle. Michelle hadn't had any hidden motive for being so kind when they first met. It was ridiculous to suspect the three of them of being in cahoots, trying to cheat her. Olivia had taken an immediate liking to Mr. Abraham, and Mr. Wentworth, stiff and humorless as he was, struck her as a good man. Besides it was impossible for Michelle and Mr. Abraham to have planned any of this. Olivia had met him purely by chance.

Then she shuddered, remembering – I thought Iola Stubblefield was a good woman. Olivia stopped to lean against the wall. So am I to go through the rest of my life suspicious of everyone? No. I trusted Jettie and that was no mistake. If I'm going to run any kind of business, I've got to trust my own judgment, stop thinking of myself as a helpless idiot.

She turned left twice more, heading around the block, back toward the corner on which The Shades stood. She cautiously peeked around the edge of the last building on the block, curious to know if her new friends were still huddled under the streetlamp. Yes, there they were, their three heads together in the halo of light. What on earth could Michelle be whispering to Mr. Wentworth? Olivia felt certain they were discussing her, but suddenly felt too exhausted to think any more. I'm going to spend two days alone on a horse, she reminded herself. I'll think about it then. I don't have to give him an answer until I come back. Or even then. I can take as long as I want.

Before collapsing in bed she wrote a short letter to Avis and Mabel, telling them not to worry if she was gone for a month or two, as she planned to remain in Detroit and look into some business opportunities. She also asked Mabel if she wouldn't mind writing out a few of her best recipes, especially the one for her fried chicken. The letter ended with an enthralled description of Woodward Avenue. "It is wider than any street you ever could dream of and will soon be entirely paved," she wrote. "On both sides it is lined with beautiful homes and stores of every kind. Some of the buildings are three or even four stories high. The most beautiful sight you can imagine is standing in the middle of that broad avenue and watching the busy port. There is always a steamer either arriving or departing. Graceful schooners and canoes float up and down the river, their sails billowing. You would do well to pay a visit to this city. It is entirely civilized and has excellent hotels."

The next morning she asked the desk clerk where she would find the post office building.

"It isn't a building," he replied. "The mail resides with whoever happens to be Postmaster. At the moment that means Mr. McKnight, who lives on the southwest corner of Jefferson and Brush. Big brick house. I think he may have put up some kind of sign. A flag or something, though I don't rightly recall. I can have a boy run your letter down there for you."

"No, thank you, I'll take it. I have to go out anyway."

Never having had anyone to exchange letters with, Olivia had no idea how the postal service functioned, but thought it time she learned. Finding the Postmaster was easy. The streets of Detroit were never empty of people, and no one was ever too busy to offer directions

She handed her letter to Mr. McKnight and asked how much it would cost to post it.

"The person you're sending it to pays the postage," he informed her.

"Oh. And how much would that be?"

He squinted at the address. "Five Rocks, Pennsylvania? Well, Miss, I don't know where that is at, but if it's more than four hundred miles from here, the charge will be 25 cents."

"And how long will it take to get there?"

"At least two weeks."

"And the same for the reply?"

116

"Yes."

"And how will I know when a reply has arrived?"

"If it's addressed to you at your hotel, I'll send a boy to leave a note up there, so you'll know to come pick it up."

"I see."

"Course, the boy don't always make the rounds of the hotels right away. If you're in a special hurry, you best come check for yourself, when the postal rider comes in."

"And how will I know when that happens?"

"He carries a horn with him. Gives it a few good loud toots when he gets here. Even if you don't hear it, you'll know. Everyone on the street will be telling each other that the mail come in."

She spent the rest of the day alone, roaming the wards where the colored folks lived, asking shop owners about Mourning and leaving notes on every available board. No one had any recollection of a man named Mourning Free. She trudged back to her hotel, exhausted and discouraged.

She rose early the next morning, had breakfast in the hotel, planned her journey over a second cup of coffee, and then went out to do her shopping. The Archdiocese ran a thrift shop, and in the boys' section she found two pairs of trousers that looked her size. She also bought a boys' woolen jacket that would be just as warm as her coat, but more comfortable to ride in. It was mid-September, and the evenings could get chilly. In a dried goods store she purchased a stub-handled shovel, a bedroll, and water skins. Then she walked to the market for bread, cheese, pickled meat, and apples. On her way back to the hotel she passed a bookstore and, after a slight hesitation, stepped in to purchase a copy of *Ivanhoe*.

Back in her hotel room she changed into a work dress over trousers and packed into her case everything she wouldn't be taking with her. She set *Ivanhoe* aside,

117

with the necessities she would have to fit into the saddle packs. She left her case with the desk clerk and told him she would be back in two or three days. She was wearing her flat cap and knew she made a strange sight, but the clerk seemed to be well-practiced at not pretending not to notice such things.

The boy at the livery had a harder time of it. He kept sneaking peeks at her while he packed up a bag of feed and put a bridle and western saddle on a bay mare named Silly Sally. Olivia fastened her pistol to the saddle horn and crammed the rest of her belongings into the saddle bags. Then she hitched up her skirt, slipped her work boot into the stirrup, and threw her leg over the horse's back. She took the long way out of the city, detouring to take another long look at what she already thought of as *her* boarding house.

She stopped in the road and looked up the slope, knowing her mind was as good as made up. No matter how much she hated the idea of being in debt to anyone, let alone a bank, she had to have that house. She was hopelessly in love with it and would have to work hard at concealing that fact when she went to talk with Mrs. Rafferty. She remembered what Mr. Abraham had said during their conversation last night. "I'm not knowing so much about finance like Mr. Wentworth here, but one thing I can to tell you. The more you're wanting something, the more it's costing you. The only way to make a good deal is to be willing to walk away with no deal."

She did want it badly; she could already see herself sitting on that shady porch with the breeze off the river caressing her face. It felt wonderful to want something, even if it was only a structure of lumber and nails. This could be the way to heal, she thought, to make a life you can live. Start out loving a place, then discover you are capable of caring for a cat, a horse – and someday another human being.

I'll ask Mr. Wentworth to do the negotiating for me,

she thought. That man may look sort of puny, but I bet those piercing blue eyes of his could stare down a stampeding buffalo. I'm going to make a decision to trust him. And Michelle and Mr. Abraham. Even if that makes me a fool.

For the first few miles Silly Sally's hooves clattered on the plank road, and Olivia was relieved when the wood and gravel gave way to dirt. She had always loved the clop-clop of hoof against soft earth and the familiar rhythm was calming. The time passed quickly and she was surprised to find herself at ease – no fear of bandits, bears, or wolves. The few wagons she passed were loaded with farm produce or cord wood. The drivers nodded amiably and Olivia did not so much as put her hand on the pistol.

She had braced herself for the trip, expecting a sense of dread to descend upon her when she took the turn toward Fae's Landing. But in this of all places she found herself admiring the beauty of the world, the rays of light straining through the treetops, the busy rustle of small furry animals. Soon these woods would be ablaze with color and she was grateful she would be alive to see it.

Chapter Fourteen

The day had turned chilly and Olivia didn't want to get wet crossing the river, so she took the long way, around the north side of Fae's Landing.

"Easy girl, this thing only looks like it's going to collapse." She stroked Silly Sally's neck as they crossed the rickety bridge. "We'll be just fine." Olivia smiled when the horse stepped back onto solid ground, next to the staked ropes that had given Pier Street its name. Some pier, a rope to tie your raft to, thought Olivia, feeling very much a Detroiter.

"Good day to you, sirs," she said, as she passed two

men. They touched their hats and their gaze followed her as she went by.

There were few other people on the streets, and none of them gave her more than a curious glance. Fae's Landing was as sorry-looking as she remembered, but now she considered it through Mr. Wentworth's eyes. It was right on a river that was wide and deep enough to accommodate rafts and canoes. And even when the river was frozen, the little town was not too far from Detroit. A loaded wagon could probably make the trip in five or six hours, even allowing for a long rest for the animals. Once the roads were improved, travel would be faster. At the rate boatloads of immigrants kept pouring into Michigan, it wouldn't be many years before Fae's Landing turned into a real town. Olivia knew she had a good piece of property. Uncle Scrugg's land was nice and flat, and Mourning had declared its soil to be rich. The branch of the river that ran through it stayed at least waist-deep all summer. Mr. Wentworth was right; she would be a fool to sell it now.

She rode straight to the farm. Weeds had grown high around the cabin and someone had stolen their lovely door, but otherwise everything appeared to be as she had left it. The empty water barrel still stood by the door. The remains of the wood pile peeked out from around back. Even her clothesline still swayed in the breeze. She dismounted and led Silly Sally into the barn. A half bale of hay was still there, mostly strewn about the floor, and two water buckets lay on their sides by the trough.

"Looks like you're going to have better eating than I thought," she said to Silly Sally and bent to set one of the buckets upright. "And you won't even have to walk down to the river for a drink of water." She removed the mare's saddle and bridle, rubbed her down, and left her free to munch on the hay. Then she went to the river to fill the buckets, emptied one into the trough, and left the other for herself. "I'll be right back," she said to the horse as she pulled the barn door, rattling it closed on its rail.

She checked again that the pistol was loaded and looked at the sky, guessing she had about two hours of light left. She tramped into the woods and headed for the tree in which Mourning had hidden the rifle, praying for it to be there. If the gun was still tied to the branch up there, but the note to Mourning she had hidden in its barrel was gone, she would know for sure that Mourning had gotten her message. Her heart ached when she looked up. No rifle. She circled back, searching the area several times, hoping she had gone to the wrong tree. But she hadn't been mistaken. This was the one; she remembered the shape of its branches. Now she knew nothing. Mourning might have taken the rifle, but so might anyone else.

She strode back to the barn to see if Mourning's precious tool box was still where she had buried it. She cleared the hay from where the bales had been stacked and began digging with the shovel she had bought. She dug deeper and wider than she knew should be necessary. Her hands quickly blistered and she was dripping with sweat by the time she finished creating a large square hole, but she leaned back on her heels, smiling. Mourning's tool box was gone. So it was him who had taken the rifle. He'd found the note telling him where Olivia had hidden his "most precious belongings" and dug them up. Then he had acted wisely and taken the time to fill in the hole, careful not to leave anything that would seem strange, set folks to wondering. She did the same.

Then she went out to the bucket and splashed water over her face. The sun was almost down, and the woods would soon grow cold. She hurriedly pulled some of the weeds from around the fire pit, noting the familiar scratches that soon covered her hands. Two of their stump chairs were half burned, but the other two stood where they had been. She quickly laid a fire with kindling from the woods and logs from the woodpile and went to her saddle pack for her punk wood, flint, and knife. Then she sat enjoying the warmth of the fire and the sound of the crackling logs, not afraid to be alone. She did, however, keep the loaded pistol on her lap, just in case. She gazed up at the pale moon that hung low in the gray sky and then looked over at the other stump, imagining Mourning sitting there, whittling or playing his harmonica. It should be such a happy memory, she thought, and felt hatred seep up from the soil and fill her soul. Being dead wasn't punishment enough for them.

What would Mourning and she have done, she wondered, if there had been no Stubblefields? A scared young white girl and equally terrified black man who found themselves about to become parents. There would not have been much need to conceal her pregnancy; they'd had no friends, other than Jeremy. They could have stayed here almost until the end, and then she could have gone to one of those places. She stared at the fields in the dusk, imagining a dark-skinned man and his son ending their day of work, gathering up their tools.

She shook herself. No point crying over that now. She toasted some bread on a stick and when the fire burned out went to the barn for her bedroll and the saddle blankets. Then she entered the cabin for the first time. It was pitch dark, but she could see the deeper shadows of the bed and table. Trappers must have begun using the cabin again and chose to preserve the furniture rather than burn it. She spread her bedroll on the dusty bed and laid the pistol next to it. Getting ready for bed consisted of removing her shoes.

She tightly wrapped the two blankets around her, like an Egyptian mummy. It felt strange to be lying there looking up at the roof. She had slept on this bed under the open sky for only a few nights, until Mourning got the roof on, but that was one of the best things she remembered – hugging her luxurious quilt to her as she counted the stars.

She quickly fell asleep and when she woke with a start the sun was already up. Outside she kicked around in her overgrown garden, but found only the remains of a few rotten tomatoes. Then she remembered the cellar and climbed down into it. There she discovered the last jar of sugary peaches and went outside to greedily slurp them down. She decided not to bother with the dress and put on a shirt and trousers and tucked her hair under her flat cap. Mounted on Silly Sally, Olivia surveyed her little kingdom and nodded to herself. Someday it would make someone a good home. Maybe that someone would be Little Boy.

There was no reason for her to visit the Stubblefield place. It wasn't part of her plan and she told herself it was a bad idea, but an irresistible force seemed to pull her up that trail. She became unaware of time – it seemed only a moment ago that she had tapped her heel against Silly Sally's flank to turn onto the trail, and they were already emerging into the clearing.

Someone had boarded up the door and windows of the cabin, but they'd made a poor job of it. One of the boards dangled by a single nail. Olivia sat limp in the saddle for a long while, before dismounting and hitching Silly Sally to the post. She scowled at the cabin door and then tugged at one of the boards. It easily gave way, as did the next. She pushed the door open and found the cabin empty. All that remained of the furniture was one of Filmore's handmade cabinets. The ladder to the loft lay broken on the floor.

She went back out and pulled the door closed behind her. She didn't know what she had expected to feel, but not what she did. Nothing. One day another family will probably live in this house, she thought. Would it matter to them what happened here? No, why should it, she shook her head. People being what they are, the commission of some horrible crime probably stains every inch of the face of the earth. Anyway, evil lives in its doers; it doesn't stake its claim in the soil. The rain makes everything new. A breeze sweeps the past away. She didn't know if she found that thought heartening or unsettling.

The barn door was closed, but not locked, and she slid it along its rail. She hadn't prepared herself for its metallic rattle and clenched her teeth. The barn too was empty; not so much as a bloodstain where their bodies had lain. Had someone bothered to scatter clean earth? The air still carried a faint scent of hay. Sparrows flitted from one rafter to another. Olivia walked to the far wall and found the nail on which she had cut her arm. She touched one fingertip to it. It was just a nail.

She went outside and squatted in the sun, hands on her knees. She still felt no definable emotion, only the need to suck in deep breaths of air. It was an empty barn. Pieces of wood nailed together. Next to her foot she noticed some rusty pieces of iron rod, probably remnants of the farm implements Filmore had piled outside, to deprive Olivia of anything sharp to use as a weapon. Here was tangible proof that she hadn't imagined the whole thing. Sometimes she almost believed it couldn't have happened; it was all a horrible nightmare.

She straightened, went into the woods, and kicked through the brush. The two by four that had killed Filmore was where she had tossed it, hidden in a tangle of ferns. The dark stain on one end had survived the rain. She picked it up and threw it deeper into the woods.

Back at the hitching post, ready to mount Silly Sally, she noticed two mounds of earth behind the cow shed. Two simple wooden crosses marked the graves. She strode over and looked down at them. What words had the minister said over their remains? And what fool had decided to bury them here? Who would want to live on this farm, now that it was a cemetery? Anyway, they didn't deserve a Christian burial. She yanked up the crosses, took quick steps, and flung them into the woods. In time the land would flatten out. No one would remember the rotting flesh that lay beneath it. Iola and Filmore Stubblefield had been blotted out.

Chapter Fifteen

Olivia mounted Silly Sally and rode to the home of her only other neighbor, the elusive Mr. Jeremy Kincaid. His cabin stood silent and she resigned herself to a long wait. She led her horse into the barn, and there stood Jeremy's big red horse, Ernest.

"Hullo, fella," she said and introduced him to Silly Sally.

So Jeremy was on foot. But that didn't mean he couldn't be gone for hours. He was probably out watching bears or some other wild animal. She considered firing a shot to get his attention, but decided against it.

She took *Ivanhoe* from her saddle pack and settled into the rocker on Jeremy's porch. She had begun reading it in school, but made it less than halfway through, preferring the more modern works of Charles Dickens. Now she flipped through its pages, re-familiarizing herself with Isaac of York and his beautiful daughter, the Jewess Rebecca.

It wasn't long before she saw Jeremy loping up the trail. He was unshaven, in a long linsey-woolsey shirt, and empty-handed, not even a rifle over his shoulder. She stood to greet him, and when he came close his face broke into a smile of recognition.

"Olivia?" He eagerly mounted the steps.

"Yes, it's me."

"I hardly know you, you've been gone so long." His eyes ran from her cap to work shoes, but he did not comment on the way she was dressed. "Sit, sit back down," he said and pulled a chair out to face her. "This is a wonderful surprise."

She returned his smile. "It's good to see you. I thought I might have to wait all day, if you'd gone out chasing after rabbits."

"No, no, I was just baiting one of my blinds. Thought I might try to take a deer this afternoon. You should have let yourself in and made coffee. You hungry?"

"No, thank you, I've already eaten," she lied. "I did take the liberty of letting my horse into your barn, and Ernest graciously agreed to share his hay and water."

"So what brings you back here? Have you decided farming isn't so bad after all?"

"No. But I'm going to put Uncle Scruggs' farm in my name, and I have to go to the courthouse in Ann Arbor for that. I couldn't come all the way to Michigan without stopping at my cabin and saying hullo to my old neighbors. I've just come from the Stubblefield place, but it was all boarded up. Did they move away?"

"Oh now, that's a story. First let me get the kettle on."

A fire smoldered in the stove on his porch, and he opened the door to poke at it, added a few logs, and then went inside to grind coffee. Suddenly chilly in the shade of the porch, Olivia nudged her chair closer to the warmth of the stove. Yes, Jeremy Kincaid was a clever man, doing his cooking outside and rigging pulleys to draw water from the river.

Jeremy came out to put the kettle on the stove and went back inside, returning with a bowl of apples. He set it on the table, picked one up, and offered it to Olivia. When she shook her head he rubbed it on the sleeve of his shirt and took a bite. After crunching and swallowing he said, "The Stubblefields – now there's a sad story. They're dead, both of them."

"Dead!"

He nodded. "Closest folks could make out, a pack of

wolves – or even a bear – got Filmore in the barn. Then Iola must have come running, but whatever it was got her too." He shook his head, took another bite of his apple, and nudged the bowl closer to her. "You should have one. I got them from McVays, over by Dearbornville. Best apples in Michigan."

Ignoring his last remark, Olivia shuddered and exclaimed, "I can't believe they're dead. Both of them. How awful. When did it happen?"

"No way of knowing. Last anyone remembers seeing either of them was middle of July, year ago. Filmore had borrowed Emery Meyer's horse and brought it back. It was Emery came around to see why they hadn't been to town and found what was left of them. Which wasn't much."

She shuddered again. "When did he find them? I mean, how long after –"

"Wasn't till the middle of August. So they could have been lying there for close on a month. Or they could have been killed just a few days before he found them. No way of knowing. Course, since she hadn't brought any eggs to Norma Gay at the store, the Sheriff assumed it must have happened sooner, not later." He rose to pour the coffee.

"Sheriff? Fae's Landing has a Sheriff?"

"Noooooo. One rode over from somewhere. Maybe Detroit. I couldn't say."

"Didn't anyone think it might have been Indians? Or robbers?"

"No reason to. They didn't have much of anything worth stealing, and none of what they did have was missing, far as anyone could tell. Even Iola's egg money was still in the jar she kept it in. And it's been a good couple of years since there've been any Indians around here, except for that peaceful lot over in the village. What would make them want to kill the Stubblefields?"

"Didn't they have folks somewhere around here? Pontiac or Mount Clemens?"

127

A sickening thought occurred to Olivia. Filmore's rifle and watch. She'd taken both of them. Hadn't anyone noticed they were missing?

He shook his head. "Sheriff was going to look for kin, but I couldn't tell you if he found any."

"But no one else came around, wanting to find out what happened?"

No one with a personal interest, she thought, who might notice something like a missing watch? She felt close to vomiting, but then the muscles of her stomach relaxed. Emery Meyers, who had found the bodies, was the only one who could have known for sure what was in their cabin that day. And after discovering the half-eaten bodies of his friends, he surely wouldn't have been of a mind to take inventory. He'd have run straight back to town. After that, a lot of folks must have come to gawk. Any of them could have appropriated a watch and a perfectly good rifle.

"No one that I heard about," Jeremy said.

Olivia had to fight the urge to heave a huge sigh of relief. "What will happen to their land?" she asked, for lack of anything better to say.

"Apparently they owed some on it. If no family turns up, I suppose the state will take it back."

"What about all their things?"

"They grew legs. Meyers was always complaining about Filmore owing him money, and I'd guess it was him took it all. If no relatives turn up, who's going to complain? Anyway, the cow was the only thing they had that was worth anything. You know, it was the strangest thing – Filmore had taken everything out of the barn, had it all piled outside, all his tools, plow, everything."

"Why on earth would he do that?"

Jeremy tipped his chair back on its hind legs and took a sip of coffee. "No one could figure it out. He was pretty far behind on his taxes, so some folks thought maybe he was planning to give up farming, auction it all off. But if that's the case, he never told anyone.

Emery said he could have been planning to get horses or more cows, and cleared that stuff out so he could put in stalls and troughs. But he didn't have the lumber ready for a job like that, just a few pieces lying around. Anyway, where's a man who can't pay his taxes going to get money for livestock?" He lowered the legs of his chair and set his tin cup on the table.

"I didn't know they were so hard up. He seemed to know so much about farming."

Jeremy shrugged. "I know I shouldn't speak ill of the dead," he said, "but I can't say I ever had much use for them. He was all right, I suppose. Bit of a dullard. But that Iola, something about her wasn't right."

"What do you mean?"

"Ask me, religious fanatics are usually the biggest sinners."

Olivia cocked her head, wondering if he suspected anything, and thought it best to change the subject.

"So how is your work coming along? Have you written any new articles?"

"One every two months, and every one of them's been published." He rose, went into the cabin, and returned with a sheaf of papers. "Listen," he said as he handed them to Olivia. "I've got three fish, already cleaned, in a crate in the river. I'll fry them up and see if that doesn't bring your appetite back."

He poured oil into a frying pan, set it on the stove, and went down to the river for the fish. She half-heartedly glanced through the sheets of paper, another article about the black bears of Michigan. Jeremy was soon back on the porch, and the smell of the frying fish made her ravenous. She joined him at the table and ate hungrily.

"Delicious." She made no attempt at good table manners, picking the bones out and licking her fingers.

"So what did you think?" he asked.

"About what?" Olivia blinked.

He nodded at his papers, which were still on the

table.

"It was real interesting. It's amazing how you find out all the things you do about animals. You sure have a special talent for that."

"Which part did you like best?"

Her mind went blank; she had scarcely paid any attention to the words on the page. Then she remembered one fact that had stuck in her mind.

"I guess the part about how a bear's pulse gets way low when it's hibernating."

"Yes." He nodded approvingly. "It drops considerably, down to between eight and ten."

"How can you possibly know that?"

"Like I said in my article. By counting."

"I guess I didn't get that far. You walked up to a bear and asked to take its pulse?"

"It was hibernating, and I had a gun in the other hand. They don't truly hibernate, you know, not like some other animals. They do sleep all winter – deep enough for their temperature to go down and their pulse rate to drop – but it's not all that difficult to wake them up. Sometimes they even get up and go out looking for food."

"Do the fathers bring some home for their babies?"

"Not hardly. A male bear is the biggest danger to a cub, even its own. The females refuse to mate so long as they have their young with them, so I guess it's easier to kill the cubs than go scare up another female."

Olivia smiled. It was interesting, what he learned about animals. Too bad his style of writing was so tedious. She studied his hands; they were as lovely as she remembered them. And there was that enticing vein on his forearm. She again remembered sitting on the riverbank with him, watching a mamma bear and her cubs play in the water. The only thing that had mattered to her that day was the possibility of his arm brushing against hers. The way emotions can change is frightening, she thought. A woman could go to the altar thinking she's marrying her perfect soul-mate and then find herself having breakfast every day across from a tiresome, chicken-chested man with straggly hair.

"That article is going to get me a job at the university in Ann Arbor," he said, obviously expecting her to be impressed.

"You want to go live in a city?"

"Oh, I won't have to live there. It's not a full-time job. They have a faculty of Natural Science, but so far there are only four professors in the whole university and they teach everything. But they'll bring me in as a guest lecturer from time to time, and my articles might be collected into a text book."

"That's wonderful. Congratulations."

"And that may lead to a job. The university is growing fast. The professors used to hold their classes in their homes, but they've built a four-story building for offices and classrooms. They're going to need a lot more professors."

"I'm glad for you," she said sincerely before turning to the topic that had brought her here. "I wish I knew where Mourning had gotten himself to." She tried to keep her voice casual. "I wonder if he went to that Backwoods place to look for work."

"Say, I'd just about forgotten, lucky you brought it up. Not long after you left I was in Northville playing cards, and a fellow at the table turned out to be from Backwoods. I asked him if he'd heard of a colored, name of Mourning Free, and wouldn't you know, he said, 'Yes, I believe that may be the name of one of the niggers I got working for me.'"

"What was the man's name?"

Jeremy frowned for a moment. "Abbey? No, Abbot. That's right it was Abbot. Mr. Linus Abbot. Took five dollars off me."

"And he lives in Backwoods?"

"Not in the town. Has a farm somewhere around there. You know, I might have to move to Ann Arbor some day, if things work out with the university. I'd still keep this place, for the summer, but I'd have to get a bit more civilized. Think about settling down."

"I can just see you, standing in front of a class in a frock coat." Olivia rose. "Thank you for the lunch, Jeremy. It was good seeing you again."

"You can't leave now," he objected. "You're not likely to make it to Ann Arbor before dark. You stay here in the cabin. I'll sleep out in the barn."

"Thanks for the offer, but I have to be on my way." She walked toward the barn to saddle Silly Sally, with Jeremy following her.

"You can't seriously be thinking of sleeping on the trail."

"Sure I can. It won't be the first time. You forget how we first met."

"That was different. You had your boy with you."

Olivia bristled at him calling Mourning "your boy," but managed a smile. "Don't worry. I've got a gun and fire. I'll be fine. Oh, I almost forgot to fill my water skins."

Jeremy helped her with that and gave her a sack of feed for the horse.

"What about you?" he asked. "Do you have anything to eat?"

"I'll be fine. Someone just fed me a wonderful meal, and it's only one night." She put on her woolen jacket.

"Wait, at least let me get you some of McVay's apples." He returned with a bag of four apples and half a loaf of bread. "If you change your mind, I'm hoping for a dinner of roast venison tonight."

She mounted Silly Sally, anxious to be on her way. "Another time, perhaps. By the way, if you should hear anything else about Mourning, I'd appreciate you letting me know. Care of the United States Hotel in Detroit." She raised the reins, but paused. "It was great having you for a neighbor," she said. "And I'm thinking of buying a boarding house in Detroit, so who knows,

132

we may see each other again."

She could see that he was about to say something else, but flicked the reins and rode off.

Chapter Sixteen

Olivia's heart thumped as she rode away from Jeremy's. She had to get to Backwoods. She had decided to go to Ann Arbor first and stop in Backwoods on the way back to Detroit. But what if Mourning was at that farm right now and then left while she was piddling about at the county clerk's office? That would be a grand joke on her. So she turned onto the trail that led northeast. It was a longer ride to Backwoods than to Ann Arbor, and she would certainly be spending the night in the woods.

She tried to prepare herself for disappointment the next day. It had been over a year since Jeremy played poker with that farmer, and the chances of finding Mourning at the Abbot farm were slim. Olivia had never known him to work more than two or three months at the same place. Still, someone he had worked with might still be there, might be able to tell her where he had gone.

The sun sank low in the sky; she would risk missing the turn if she didn't stop soon. She found a clearing of buffalo grass to sleep on and looked for the best place to light a fire. Then she noticed how dry the grass was, remembered that it hadn't rained for the past two weeks, and sighed. She hadn't thought to bring enough extra water to put out a fire and so didn't dare light one.

"It's going to be a cold night, Killion," she muttered.

She saw to Silly Sally, munched Jeremy's apples and bread, and then wrapped herself in her blankets and lay down, certain she would not sleep that night. But it had been a long day and she quickly drifted into dreamless sleep. A cold drizzle woke her just before sunup, and she got slowly to her feet, frozen and miserable.

"Guess I didn't have to worry about setting the woods on fire," she grumbled to Silly Sally.

She was soon on the road to Backwoods, one of the damp blankets draped over her head and shoulders. Wet wool was one of her least favorite smells, so she was glad when the drizzle damped down to a light fog around Silly Sally's ankles and she could stop to roll up the blanket and try to make herself presentable. Being dressed in men's clothing was bad enough; she could at least comb her hair. She was glad she had when she entered the tidy little town of Backwoods. Sturdy wooden sidewalks lined both sides of its Main Street, shielding brightly painted houses and stores from the mud in the road. The more she saw of the world, the more Olivia realized what a shabby little town she had grown up in.

She rode slowly up the street, waiting for people to begin stirring so she could ask for directions to the Abbot farm. Judging by the color the faces that began appearing on the sidewalks, she decided that the south end of Main Street must be the colored section. She stretched her upper lip over the lower and nodded in approval; it was adjacent to and did not look less prosperous than the white area. And there did not seem to be a discernible line dividing the two. No shanty "Nigger Town" here. She allowed herself to become more optimistic. Why wouldn't Mourning have stayed in a nice place like this, with all these well-kept, colored-owned stores? She might even go into one of them and find him clerking behind the counter.

The town slowly came to life. A heavy-set colored woman in a corduroy dressing gown stepped outside and swept the sidewalk in front of her house. Another set wicker chairs on either side of her door, creating a porch of sorts. A white man yawned, stretched, and turned to rub his sleeve over smudges on the front window of his shop. Then Olivia noticed a sign –

Faraday's Dry Goods. She had forgotten about Michelle's friend. That's who she should ask. She tethered Silly Sally to the post and waited for the "Closed" sign on Faraday's to flip over to "Open." When it did she ran her hands over her hair and tried to smooth the wrinkles out of her shirt before going in. The man behind the counter was indeed colored, but light-skinned, like caramel candy.

"A very good morning. What can I help you with, Ma'am?" He managed to sound cordial, though he barely glanced up from his newspaper.

Olivia took a few awkward steps toward him, and he put the paper down. Though his wiry arms and neck were taut and muscular, he was so thin that the strings of his white bib apron circled his body twice and still left enough to make a large loopy bow over his flat stomach. His black-brown eyes contemplated Olivia from behind wire-rimmed spectacles that rested on a narrow, pointy nose. Soft fuzz covered his head, as if it had recently been shaved, accenting his striking features.

Olivia wondered if he might be a mulatto, like Little Boy. She would ask Michelle. Perhaps some day she could talk to him about what it had been like, growing up black with a white mother. But the moment that thought entered her mind, Olivia realized how stupid it was. If this man had a white ancestor, there was slight chance that it was his mother. More likely the plantation owner who had raped his mother or grandmother. She cringed with shame and wondered if she would ever feel comfortable around colored people.

"Hullo," she said. "Good morning. Are you Mr. Faraday?"

"Yes. I'm Zachary Faraday." He tensed and his face closed, turning suspicious. He stared at Olivia the way the colored women on the boat had.

"I'm glad to meet you," she offered a hand and he took it. "My name is Olivia Killion. A friend of mine

135

from Detroit, Michelle Lafleur –"

"Ah, Miss Killion." His face broke into a warm smile, and his hand tightened around hers. "Yes, yes, Michelle told me you might be stopping in. Welcome."

"Told you? How? I mean, it was only three days ago that she met me."

"And the day after you dined with her, I had the pleasure of her company in Detroit. The women of Backwoods also wish to be attired in the latest fashions, straight from Paris, France." He swept an arm in the direction of a rack of dresses. Olivia recognized some of Michelle's hats perched on the shelf above the rack. "Michelle told me you are trying to locate a friend of yours."

"Yes, that's right. A young man named Mourning Free."

He shook his head. "I'm sorry. As I told her, I don't recall meeting anyone by that name. But if you can stay in town for a while, I'd be glad to help you make enquiries."

"That's kind of you, but I know where to ask first," she said brightly. "Someone told me that last year Mourning was working a farm around here, so that's where I'll start. The Abbot farm. Mr. Linus Abbot. Do you know him?"

"I know of him, but would not call him a friend of mine."

"Could you tell me how to get to his place?"

"Nothing is easier than that," Mr. Faraday said. "Take Main Street north out of town and stay on it about, oh say half an hour, until you see a big white silo with a flag painted on it. That's the Abbot farm. You couldn't miss it if you tried."

Suddenly they heard shouts outside, the voices of angry men, and both Olivia and Mr. Faraday glanced toward the window.

Olivia was anxious to be on her way to the Abbot farm and said, "Well, thank you for your help."

136

"Certainly. So this young man, this Mourning Free, he is a good friend of yours?" Mr. Faraday seemed to be studying her.

"Yes. We grew up in the same Podunk town. Back in Pennsylvania."

"And your parents? They had no objections to your friendship with a colored boy?" Mr. Faraday raised an eyebrow.

"Truth be told, I don't know what they thought about it. Except once, my father stuck up for me when one of the women complained about me teaching Mourning to read."

"Perhaps your parents are Abolitionists?"

More voices joined in the shouting outside, as an angry mob gathered. Olivia ignored Mr. Faraday's question and went to the window. "My stars, what's all the commotion out there?"

A jostling crowd of men, both white and black, had gathered outside one of the stores a few doors up. Groups of women huddled on the sidewalk opposite, yelling as fiercely as the men. Everyone seemed to be shaking their fists or pitchforks at the two white men who stood in the middle of the street, wearing wide-brimmed white hats.

"Excuse me, Miss Killion," Mr. Faraday said. "You best stay in here." He went out and strode up the sidewalk to where the turmoil was.

Olivia followed him outside, but hung back by Silly Sally. Someone had begun clanging the fire bell, and by now there were thirty or forty men, many of them wielding farm implements, and more kept coming. Three white men broke away from the crowd and hastened toward Mr. Faraday. The four of them stood apart, heads together, and Mr. Faraday seemed to be doing most of the talking. Then one of the white men, a pasty-faced redhead in a grimy buckskin shirt, slapped Mr. Faraday on the back and disappeared up the alley between the stores. Olivia was curious to know what the fuss was about, but more concerned about how she was going to get past all those ill-tempered men. She took hold of Silly Sally's reins and led her to the other side of the street, toward one of the knots of women.

"What's all the hubbub?" she asked one of them, though she doubted anyone could hear her above the shouting. Olivia caught only fragments of what the men were yelling – "I been giving my hospitality to these lying bastards – Take your stinking carcasses back down south – You ain't going nowhere but to jail for kidnapping – Oughta tar and feather 'em."

"Private agents." A white woman in a blue poke bonnet answered Olivia, nodding toward the two men in white hats, who by now were surrounded by the increasingly unruly mob. "Come up here looking for runaway slaves."

A second white woman clasped her friend's arm. "I heard they're chasing after poor Caleb and Maribelle Greenstreet."

"The Greenstreets? Why they been living here for I don't know how long. It must be five years now, going on six."

"I know. Imagine coming after them now, after all this time. Their little Josiah just had his fourth birthday. Maribelle was in my shop, wanting red ribbon for his present."

"Josiah been born here, so that boy be free even by their account," a young black woman said. "What they think, they gonna drag his parents back to their plantation, leave him here all by hisself?"

"You bet they gonna try and take him too," a second black woman said. "Another two-three years, they got him in those fields, twelve hours a day."

Olivia caught bits of what the men in white hats, who appeared surprisingly unafraid, were shouting back. "Private property ... the law clearly obliges you ... have the lot of you arrested ... I want all of your names." One of them removed a small notebook from his coat pocket.

A coarse-looking white man in workman's clothes shoved his face in that of the agent. "Put mine right at the top of your cursed list, in capital letters. G-O-R..."

"So there really is such a thing as slave-catchers," Olivia said, more to herself than to the women.

"Sure as they's vipers and jackals," the black woman said.

Olivia took Silly Sally and tried to edge around the crowd, but someone pushed someone and the mass of bodies surged toward her. "Back," she said softly to the horse and retreated a few dozen paces down the street. She looked back and guessed that by now there were over a hundred people in the street.

The red-haired man in the buckskin shirt who had slipped up the alley returned and whispered something to Zachary Faraday, who nodded. Then Mr. Faraday looked down the street behind him. His eyes fixed on Olivia for a moment before he turned back to the circle of men.

Olivia considered trying to find another road that went around the town, but decided she'd best look for a quiet place to wait it out. She hitched Silly Sally to a post far from the mob and returned to Mr. Faraday's store, hoping he wouldn't mind her sitting in the straight-backed chair he kept just inside the door. Then she heard gunshots and leapt to her feet to look out the window. A tall man was waving a pistol in the air. He had a badge pinned to his coat and seemed to be trying to calm things down. Mr. Faraday was on the sidewalk, hurrying back to his store.

"I saw you come in here," he said.

"I just wanted a place to sit. I hope you don't mind."

"No, of course not. But I need to talk to you." He paced. "Sit back down. Please."

She obeyed, and he stopped in front of her, hesitating before he spoke. "I assume someone out there told you about the Greenstreet family?"

"One of the women said those men in the big hats are slave-catchers, looking to take them back down south."

"That's right. Those two villains have been in town for weeks, claiming to be land agents of the Michigan Central. Said they were mapping out a route to lay down track and looking for people willing to sell their land for a good price. They went around knocking on every door, and everyone in town talked their heads off to them. There's another one of their like, been pretending to be a census taker. So he came knocking too, wanting to know who all is living in every house and for how long. All they were doing was making sure the Greenstreets are who they thought they are, before they arrest them."

Olivia shook her head in dismay at the evil of men, but had no idea why he was telling her these things.

"Terrible what people can find the heart to do to one another." She got to her feet to look out the window, where she saw the crowd beginning to disperse. "Looks to be over. I guess I can be on my way to the Abbot place. Thank you for the directions. I hope this ..." she waved her hand, "... works out all right. That poor family."

"Can I ask you to sit down again, Miss Killion? For just a minute."

She reluctantly obliged.

"The Greenstreets are safe for the next few hours. Our lawyer convinced the Sheriff to arrest those slave-catchers for assault, battery, housebreaking, and attempted kidnapping, but he won't be able to hold them for long. The law is on their side. Our lawyer will take his good time arguing to the judge that public sentiment is above the law. It won't hold water, but it will give us time. An hour or two. Longer if the Sheriff can be convinced to jail those devils for their own protection, considering the way they got folks so riled up. That gives us time to get the Greenstreets out of town. All we need is someone to drive them to Detroit."

"Oh, I'm glad to hear that. I'd hate to think of those awful men trying to tear parents away from their child."

"Well, folks down in Carroll County, Kentucky are of a different mind about colored families. The reason the Greenstreets ran away in the first place was because their owner was planning to sell Maribelle off to another plantation, three counties over."

Olivia shook her head, still with no glimmer as to why he was telling her all this.

"Someone has gone to bring a wagon to the road outside town. It won't be but a few minutes before it's there, ready to take them." He paused and stared at her. "Problem is, none of us can drive it. The minute those slave-catchers are out of jail, they'll be searching every road and trail out of here. Them being on horseback, they'll catch that wagon up in no time. And after two weeks of them pretending to take their census and trying to buy land, they know every face in this town. The minute they spot anyone from Backwoods, they'll take that wagon apart splinter by splinter."

So now she knew. She stared at her feet, knowing she couldn't do this. She had to get to that Abbot farm and couldn't risk ending up in jail.

"Why don't the Greenstreets go to Detroit by horseback?" she asked. "They'll have a good enough head start."

"We can't know that there aren't more agents, already out there watching the roads toward Canada. The Greenstreets will be well-hidden in the wagon, but I can't drive it. Neither can anyone else from town. But a nice white lady like you," Mr. Faraday continued, "a nice white lady they've never seen before, who doesn't live anywhere around here, a nice white lady carrying a wagonload of goods with a bill of sale showing purchase in Everson this morning? All they'll do is ask her if she's seen anything."

"I'm sorry, I wish I could help, but I can't go to

Detroit now. I have to go ask about my friend and then be on my way to Ann Arbor. Anyway, I couldn't make a trip like that in a wagon." She got to her feet as she searched for excuses. "What if I lost a wheel? I don't know how to repair anything on a wagon. I don't even know how to manage a team –"

"That's why your younger brother will be with you."

"I don't have a younger brother."

"We've got one for you. Nice young fella from Everson. We're lucky he happened to be in town this morning. He's only thirteen, but that boy is strong as a horse and handles a team better than any of us. And he knows the way. You won't go direct. He'll take you to the southeast first, get on a different road, so by the time they catch you up, it will look like you started out from Everson. It's a better road, too. You'll only have to worry about the mud for the first ten miles or so. There's a plank road after that."

"If you've got this nice young fellow who knows how to do all that, you certainly don't need me." She reached for the handle of the door.

"A boy that young, on the road alone. It doesn't look right." He stared at her for a long moment and then turned his gaze out the window. "All right." He turned away. "I've wasted too much time here. I can see you don't want to help us out. You're too busy, looking for that colored friend of yours."

She froze, and they were both silent for a moment before he spoke again, this time in a softer voice. "There's some danger in it. I won't try to tell you there isn't. You could be arrested, but no judge around here is going to put a young white woman in jail for that. He'll give you a fine, maybe a large one, but there are men here in town, wealthy men, who have already said they will pay that fine for you."

"I'm sorry. I would like to help you, but I just can't."

"All right." He raised both palms and took a step back from her.

142

She hurried out of the store and back toward Silly Sally, rationalizing her refusal. *I've already made one horrible mistake, leaving Little Boy at that church. I'm not going to make another one and take the chance of missing Mourning. I know how awful those plank roads are. You could lose a wheel every five minutes. And with the weather so unpredictable? Anything could happen. And why me? They've got a whole town full of people. He can't tell me those slave-catchers remember every single one. And they've got that boy from Everson. It isn't fair to ask me. Why is any of this my problem?*

She had walked only a short distance when she suddenly felt as if a physical presence were holding her back. She could almost see Mourning standing in front of her, Little Boy in his arms. At first he simply glared. Then his voice was in her head, scolding. "You gonna go and make another horrible mistake, just so you can boohoo 'bout it later? Ain't you learned you don't get no second chances? You gotta do the right thing when it be there in front of you, begging to get done. How you gonna feel, you don't help these folks? You wanna be the reason someone else's child got dragged off to slavery? Or left alone like me? Like Little Boy?"

She stopped short and shook her head. *What am I thinking? How would I ever face them?* She turned on her heel and strode back to Mr. Faraday's store, almost bumping into him on his way out.

"All right," she said, "I'll drive the wagon. But my horse comes along, and you're going to have to get me some ladylike clothes."

Chapter Seventeen

Mr. Faraday let out a breath, placed his hands on her shoulders, and said, "Thank you. Thank you." Then he seemed infused with new energy and said, "A dress is not a problem. Come on." He turned and took her elbow between his thumb and forefinger. "We'll have you fixed up in a snap, and that wagon is going to look a whole lot better with you on it. Those agents will definitely stop you. They won't miss a chance to make goo-goo eyes at a pretty young lady. But don't let them put a fright in you. Once they see a bill of sale for what you're carrying, they aren't likely to roust you. Don't give it to them too quick, like you were waiting to be asked for it. Pretend you don't remember where you put it. That's your horse?" He nodded at Silly Sally.

"Yes."

"I'll see that someone rides her back to Detroit for you. No sense giving them something to wonder about, why you're trailing a horse all the way to Detroit. Where do you stable her?"

Olivia opened her mouth to object, but heard herself say, "She doesn't belong to me. I took her from the livery on Beaubien."

"Don't worry. I'll see that she's returned and paid for."

A small cluster of men remained in the street, the pudgy red-haired man among them. Mr. Faraday motioned for him to come over and whispered in his ear while nodding at Silly Sally. The red-haired man took the reins and started walking away, but Olivia hollered, "Wait," and hurriedly retrieved her pistol, possibles bag, and the saddle packs. Then Mr. Faraday led her down an alley and up a flight of stairs to one of the apartments over the stores. A heavy-set, middle-aged black woman let them in.

Olivia stuck out her hand. "Hullo, my name's –"

"No need for you to know each other's names," Mr. Faraday interrupted her.

"We need you to make her respectable," Mr. Faraday said to the woman. "Nothing new and nothing too fancy. Please be quick about it."

The woman rolled her eyes. "I know, I know. Ever thing with you folks always be one big rush and hurry." She turned and waddled toward another room, muttering, "Greased lightning, that be me." She stopped and looked back at Olivia. "Girl, you gonna stand there all day?"

Olivia followed her into the other room. The woman looked her up and down and pulled a blue and green flowered work dress from a wardrobe so filled with clothing that the doors didn't shut. Olivia slipped into it and rejoined Mr. Faraday, who had the saddle bags draped around his neck and the rifle over his shoulder. He handed the possibles bag to her and steered her back down the stairs.

"How'd you know she'd have something that would fit me?" Olivia asked as he led her up the street.

He stopped for a moment and looked into her face. "I understand that you want to ask a lot of questions. Please don't. Now we need to hurry."

Almost at a run, he led her out of town, through a strip of woods, across a stubbly cornfield, and through large stand of pine. Finally they emerged into a clearing bisected by a muddy road on which a farm wagon stood, its box filled with rows of barrels. Two white people stood next to the wagon – the dough-faced man in the buckskin shirt and an adolescent in a long black frock coat that was more patches than original fabric. The boy was pale, with short, straw-like blonde hair. He looked calm but intense, his forehead creased.

"I'm not going to tell you his name," Mr. Faraday gestured toward the red-haired man. "And he doesn't need to know yours."

145

The man stepped forward, shyly handed her a document, and said, "Man what sold you them pickles is Frances Carpenter, and you're called Rebecca Erlich."

Olivia looked the document over and then tucked it into the pocket of her dress.

"You have a safe trip," the red-haired man said to Olivia and turned to leave. "See you next week, Zach."

Mr. Faraday gave a quick wave of his hand.

The blonde-haired boy was left standing alone by the wagon.

Mr. Faraday nodded at him. "This is your brother, Phillip. Phillip Erlich."

Olivia nodded and smiled at the boy. The corners of his mouth jerked up for a moment, but he did not look directly at her.

"So what's your name?" Mr. Faraday asked Olivia.

"Rebecca," Olivia answered. That would be easy for her to remember. Ivanhoe's beautiful Rebecca. Lovely, black-eyed Rebecca. "Rebecca Ehrlich of Everson."

"Okay, Phillip, meet your new big sister. I know you don't need anyone telling you what to do." He turned back to Olivia. "Phillip will explain some things to you once you're on your way."

Phillip put thumb and forefinger to the corners of his mouth and gave a sharp whistle. A tall, thin-as-a-beanpole black man and his willowy, terrified young wife appeared from behind a heap of partly-burned stumps that stood a dozen paces off the road. A small child emerged from the woman's skirt, clutching her hand. So these were the Greenstreets. Caleb and Maribelle and their son Josiah. They all looked exhausted and disoriented.

Olivia smiled sadly and bent to look into the child's enormous dark brown eyes. "What a sweet boy you are."

"Plenty of time to tell him how sweet he is once you're in Detroit," Mr. Faraday said and clapped his hands. "Let's get them in."

146

Only then did Olivia notice the open lids of three of the barrels – two in the last row in the back and the first one in the first row, right behind the driver.

"You mean they have to ride in those?" she asked. The barrels were wide, but Caleb and Maribelle would have to fold themselves up, knees to their chests, and even so it would be tight.

"There are holes for air. Whenever Phillip thinks it's safe, he'll stop to let them out. Lids look like they're nailed shut, but Phillip knows how to open and close them back up."

"A little boy inside a dark barrel all by himself – he'll be so scared. What if he starts crying?"

Mr. Faraday stared into her eyes. "Miss Ehrlich, you have got to stop asking questions. We don't have time for it, and you have no say about what is happening here. These people need to get away from here and are willing to suffer a few hours of discomfort in exchange for the rest of their lives in freedom."

Caleb Greenstreet nodded. "That be true."

"Now you have to get moving. Those agents will be out of jail soon, saddling up to start searching."

Olivia was still eyeing the open barrels. "But why hide them in the outside rows? Isn't that the first place they'll look?"

Mr. Faraday took a deep breath, obviously struggling to keep his temper in check. When he spoke, his voice was patient. "No, those agents are so smart. They always look in the middle, as long as it isn't too much trouble for them to get to the middle. That's why we left so much space down the center. They never open but one or two. That seems to be sufficient exertion for a Kentucky gentleman when he has no slave to do his work for him. They'll be watching your faces while they do it, so make sure you look angry or impatient, not scared. The only thing on your mind is all those pickles you just paid good money for." He clapped his hands again. "Now no more questions. You

147

folks have got to get on the road."

"I ain't gonna cry," the little boy suddenly spoke.

Olivia looked down at him and lightly ran her hand over his head.

"I ain't," he repeated.

"I know you ain't," she said. She smiled and gave his shoulder a squeeze. "All right then." Olivia felt a surge of energy that drove away the fear. "Let's get going. The sooner we're out of here, the better." The moment the words left her mouth she knew Mr. Faraday must be longing to roll his eyes, but he gallantly refrained.

Mr. Greenstreet pulled down the ladder and climbed up first, before helping his wife and son. Then he lifted the boy into a barrel, handed him a skin of water and a small bag of food, and set the lid in place. Phillip climbed up, inserted two wooden pegs, and thumped on the lid.

"You all right in there, pal?" he asked.

There was no answer, and Mr. Greenstreet nodded proudly. "We told him that once he be in that barrel he can't make no noise, no matter what."

Mrs. Greenstreet was next. Her husband held her while she slipped her feet into the open barrel. Olivia didn't think she would ever forget the woman's terrified eyes as she folded herself up into that wooden container. Mr. Greenstreet then fit himself into his, and they were ready to leave.

"First thing, Phillip will tell you about your family," Mr. Faraday said. His eyes were constantly moving, checking all directions. "Where your store is, where you get the cucumbers, who you're selling the pickles to."

Olivia stepped closer to him and asked in a whisper, "Is there a way for them to open the lid from the inside?"

He shook his head and replied softly. "You and Phillip have to make sure they don't need to. If those agents do catch you up, the most important thing for you to remember is not to turn around to look at those

148

barrels. Not a glance."

Olivia bit her bottom lip and shook her head, imagining a barrel falling off the wagon and rolling down a steep hill. Thank God Michigan was so flat. But she went on thinking of other horrible things that could happen – the wagon catching on fire or falling off a bridge into a river.

Before climbing onto the seat she held out her hand to Mr. Faraday. "Thank you for asking me to do this," she said.

"God speed." Mr. Faraday patted the flank of one of the oxen and gave Phillip a quick salute.

Phillip was talkative as long as he was imparting information and instructions – telling Olivia the name of the Ehrlich's store, where it was, what they sold, who worked there. He also made her recite the names of some of the prominent citizens of Everson, as well as the Erlichs' neighbors. Then he carefully explained what they must do when they stopped.

"When it looks safe, we'll pull to the side and let them out. It's got to be in a place that's around a bend and where there's lots of trees. We got to be able to hear their horses before they can see us. But that still don't leave enough time for all of 'em to get back in the barrels and me to put the pegs in. So they only get out one at a time. If I hear a patrol coming and don't think there's enough time for whoever's out to get back in, I say 'Go.' That means they run far into the woods and hide, and I peg up the empty barrel. Every time we stop, you got to get down, so it looks like we made the stop for you."

Olivia marveled at the youth, who had seemed so awkward but now spoke like an adult, confident and matter-of-fact.

Phillip continued, "But if I say 'In,' that means the patrol is far enough away, they have time to get back in the barrel. And you get back up on the wagon. It's best if we're moving by the time the patrol comes on us."

They rode in silence while Olivia pondered these instructions. What a world we live in, she thought. Her pistol was on the seat beside her. She looked at it, unable to think of one good reason for not shooting any agents who rode up. She knew she wouldn't, but they had it coming, same as the Stubblefields.

"Do you still think they're likely to come on us, now that we're on this road?" she asked.

"Pretty much."

"Why is that?"

"They's three of them. They gonna split up, and there ain't that many roads."

Neither Olivia nor Phillip spoke much for a long while, until they came to a place between two bends in the road.

"We'll stop here," Phillip said.

Olivia climbed down, and Phillip let Mr. Greenstreet out first. He groaned when he tried to pull himself up to stand and needed a few minutes to stretch and shake out his legs before he could lift them to get out of the barrel and climb down. Sweat was pouring off his face, and his shirt was soaked. Olivia hadn't thought of how hot and airless it must be in there.

"You remember 'Go' and 'In?'" Phillip asked.

Mr. Greenstreet nodded, and Olivia handed him a water skin. He took a long drink and poured some of it over his head.

"Okay, you know you got to stay right close by the wagon 'less I say Go," Phillip said. "And don't forget what I told you – sometimes these agents want to ride along with us for a while. If you're hiding in the woods and that happens, you stay put and don't worry. We're gonna come back and whistle for you, soon as they's gone, even if that's a good long time. So when you run into the woods make sure you got your food and water with you. And no matter what, don't go trying to catch us up. Stay exactly where we left you. I promise we'll come back for you, but we might have to go all the way to Detroit to get rid of those bastards before we can."

Olivia was busy unlacing her shoe to remove a pebble and did not respond when Phillip addressed her as Rebecca.

"Rebecca," Phillip repeated loudly, and she finally looked up. "You got to remember your name," Phillip said impatiently. "Go into the woods, Rebecca."

"What for?"

"You gotta give him some privacy." He raised his eyebrows toward Mr. Greenstreet, who was doing squats. "You know what we stopped for, but he gotta stay close to the wagon."

"Oh. Yes. Of course." She flushed and obeyed, careful to keep her back to the road until Phillip called, "You can come back now, Rebecca."

Mr. Greenstreet re-inserted himself into the barrel, and they repeated the process with his wife. Phillip had to lift her out and hand her down to Olivia.

"Move your legs. Shake them," Olivia said, holding Mrs. Greenstreet under her arms. When Mrs. Greenstreet could stand, Olivia moved around to face her and said, "I'm so sorry for all you have to go through."

This time Phillip went into the woods. Olivia went to the other side of the wagon and kept her back to Maribelle.

"Those agents just barged into your house this morning?" Olivia asked.

"They tried, but we got a big, thick crossbar, put it on every night. Neighbor heard 'em banging. They's two of them pounding on the door. Third one watchin' out back, so we can't go out the window. Neighbors run that one off with pitchforks, so we climbed out. Made it to the neighbors' house without any of 'em seein'."

"You're lucky to have neighbors like that."

"Backwoods a good town. Folks always help each other." Maribelle came around to where Olivia stood and reached for the water skin. "I flew out that window in my nightdress. Neighbor give me these clothes and shoes."

"So you climbed out the window with nothing, and that's how you're going to Canada? With nothing?"

"Zachary gonna write a letter to a friend he got in Windsor. Let us know what the judge say. Maybe we gonna be able to come back. If we can't, Zachary gonna pack up for us, send our things over the river." Mrs. Greenstreet looked nervously up and down the road and reminded Olivia that she needed to call Phillip back. "Got to put me away, let my boy out."

Josiah had fallen asleep, but Phillip woke him, gently lifted him out of the barrel, and told him to drink and make pee. Olivia climbed up and peeked into the barrel. Someone had thought to put two large pillows in it, so perhaps Josiah would sleep all the way to the Detroit. Olivia smiled; in the end it was the child who was having the easiest time of it. Josiah was safely back in the barrel before they heard the horse's hooves. Philip and Olivia scrambled onto the wagon seat and rounded the bend before they saw the lone rider approaching, a large white hat on his head.

Chapter Eighteen

"Good day," the rider greeted them, removing his hat and bowing toward Olivia.

"Good day to you, sir." Olivia's smile was accompanied by a little giggle. Wasn't that the way the girls in Five Rocks had flirted with boys? Tittering like fools, about nothing?

In fact, she didn't have to pretend feeling flirtatious with this incredibly good-looking man. She couldn't stop staring at him. He reminded her of the statue of some Greek person's head they had in the library back in Hillsong. Symmetrical features, high cheekbones, perfect nose, strong chin. His dark eyebrows were not bushy, but thick enough to dramatically set off his eyes, which were a vivid violet-blue. Long, wavy dark brown hair formed a lustrous mane around his face. His mustache was both rakish and well-trimmed. Under it, his lips curved into an easy smile. He was dressed for the parlor of a plantation, not chasing around on dusty trails – ruffled white shirt, red waistcoat, and black frock coat. His speech was as polite and proper as his attire. Not at all the monster Olivia had expected.

"My apologies for interrupting your journey," he drawled. "Jared Dansbury."

"I'm Rebecca Erlich. And this is my brother Phillip."

"Pleased to make your acquaintance. I have been commissioned by the State of Kentucky to return fugitive slaves to their rightful owners. As such, I carry papers granting me the power to search travelers suspected of harboring such fugitives. So I need to ask you folks – what you are carrying back there?"

"Pickles," Olivia said, smiling and eager-to-please.

"Pickles that y'all made?"

"No, we bought them."

"From whom?"

"Mr. Frances Carpenter. In Everson."

"And you're taking them ..?"

"To Detroit."

"Are you in possession of a receipt?"

Olivia looked flustered and turned toward her brother. "Phillip, where'd you put that Bill of Sale?"

He scowled. "I didn't put it anywhere. He gave it to you."

"He did? I don't remember that. When did he give it to me?"

"When we was loading up. He handed you a piece of paper. I seen it."

"Well, goodness, I can't think what I did with it. Do you have to see it?" She looked up at the agent.

"It would be a great help, Miss."

"Oh well then, let's see." She stood up and turned to

rummage through the cloth hold-all that was behind her, in the box of the wagon. Next to it was a large tapestry bag that she hadn't noticed before and she searched it too, noting that it contained the type of things two people would pack for an overnight journey. That Mr. Faraday certainly was clever, she thought. He thought of everything and got it organized in a jiff.

"Hmmm, it's not in there." She stood up, hands on her hips, and frowned at the rows of barrels. "Where could it be? Oh, I know. I must have stuck it in one of those bags back there." She went to the back of the wagon to look through two more hold-alls. "Philip, are you sure he gave it to me?"

"Yes I'm sure." He was slumped down in the seat and replied in the voice of a sullen teenager who resents having to answer to his older sister.

We're good at this. I bet this fellow can't wait to get away from us, Olivia thought, almost having a good time and surprised that she wasn't frightened.

"Oh, look, here's that hairbrush I was looking for."

"Miss?" the agent said. "The Bill of Sale?"

"Oh, I'm sorry. I didn't mean to hold you up. It's got to be in here somewhere." She removed the contents of both bags, studied every piece of paper in them, and looked up at the agent with a look of absolute bewilderment on her face. "I can't imagine where it's gotten to. But I give you my solemn word we've got one." She went back to the front of the wagon and climbed up to reach for the first bag she had searched. "Let me take another little peek in here. There's just so much ... Phillip, why do you always have to cram everything in here? It's such a mess, a person can't see a thing." While the agent studied the horizon, she retrieved the folded paper from her pocket and waved it triumphantly. "Oh, here it is." She handed it over to him. See, I told you I had it."

He glanced at it and handed it back. "I'm going to need a crow bar to open those barrels."

"Open them? You're allowed to do that?" Olivia asked.

"Yes, Miss, I surely am." The agent swung down off his horse. He was even more impressive standing, tall and trim in his tight pants and shiny black boots.

"But what if it was raining? You could ruin the lot of it."

"But it isn't raining, now is it?" The agent's voice began to show impatience.

"But if it were. I mean, it doesn't seem right. States shouldn't go around authorizing people to damage other folks' property. We're just as entitled to our pickles as you are to your slaves."

"Miss, why don't you get down and step away from the wagon." He turned to Phillip. "You want to help me with that crowbar, son."

Phillip climbed down and made a great show of looking. "I don't believe we got one a them with us, sir. You're welcome to look for yourself."

"Y'all go out on the road without any tools?" the agent asked.

"I guess I forgot to put 'em back," Phillip said. "I was using 'em this morning before we left ... and don't you start on me." He scowled at Olivia. "You was the one asked me to fix –"

"Well, I didn't ask you to leave all the tools out in the barn, now did I? Honestly, Phillip Erlich –" Olivia sighed. Then she turned to the agent and suggested brightly, "Why don't you ride along to Detroit with us? The buyer there is bound to open some of them, save you the trouble. I forgot, what is it you said you're looking for?" she asked as she climbed off the wagon and went around to stand near the agent.

"Fugitives."

"Oh, yes, that's right. Slaves."

"Yes, Miss. Runaway slaves that y'all here in Michigan seem to feel entitled to steal away from their rightful owners."

155

"People in Michigan keeping slaves?" She turned to her brother. "Goodness me Phillip, did you hear that? They must have changed the law. I thought Pappa was kidding about buying me one for my birthday."

"He *was* kidding, Rebecca." Phillip rolled his eyes at the agent. "Mister, if you really gotta open them barrels, we could try using a branch. I got a good sharp knife and could whittle a point."

"That wouldn't be much help," the agent said. "Not the way you've got those lids nailed down." He studied the ground for a moment and then raised his gaze to Olivia. "You wouldn't mind selling me one of those barrels, now would you? For the price you got there on your Bill of Sale, and I'll add a ten per cent profit for you." His eyes challenged her to meet his dare.

"You mean when we get to Detroit?" Olivia asked.

"No, I mean right here." He pulled the pistol from the holster on his belt. "I'm of a mind to have a little target practice."

He walked around the wagon, reaching up to tap the butt of his pistol on a few lids. "Some of them sound sort of hollow, don't you think?"

"You want to shoot one of my pickle barrels?" Olivia said. "Are you gone loony?"

"I will reimburse you for it," he said. Then, watching both Olivia and Phillip, he raised the pistol and pretended to take aim, first at one of the middle barrels in the last row and then at the one next to it, the one Caleb Greenstreet was in. "First," he said and lowered the weapon, "I need you to sign a declaration for me, giving your solemn oath that these containers are not being used to transport fugitives. So if there does happen to be a darky in there, you will be responsible for whatever injury he may sustain, both legally and financially."

"Listen Mr. Whatever-your-name-is –" Olivia said.

"Dansbury. Jared Dansbury." He smiled.

"Well Mr. Dansbury, you want to waste your money

shooting at a pickle barrel, that ain't no thing to me. Take your pick," she said. "But you ain't doing it while it's sitting on my wagon. You'll scare my team to kingdom come, not to mention your bullet could go right through and damage the barrels behind it."

"Oh, there's no need to worry about that. I won't shoot through like this." He placed the pistol against the side of Caleb's barrel, right about where his head would be. "I'll shoot straight down." He put a foot on the ladder and stepped up so he could aim the mouth of the pistol's barrel straight down against the lid.

"The devil you will," Olivia said. "Not unless you plan on buying the whole dang wagon. I got to haul a load of wheat next week, taking it loose. You think I'm gonna leave a trail of grain from Everson to the mill, you *are* loony. Shoot whatever you want, but first give me my money and take your target off my wagon. And then wait till I get my team up the road."

She had slipped her pistol into her pocket and could feel it through the fabric of her dress. Her mind was made up. If that agent unloaded one of the barrels in which the Greenstreets were hiding and aimed his pistol at it, she was going to shoot him dead.

"All right, son." He nodded to Phillip. "Lower the end gate down and help me take this one off." He patted the barrel next to Caleb.

Olivia's stomach relaxed, though she'd been fairly certain he wouldn't choose Caleb's barrel. The way the wagon was packed, he couldn't have taken Caleb's barrel without first removing the one next to it. She couldn't help wondering if it had cost the life of some poor fugitive for Mr. Faraday and his friends to learn that trick. But no matter which barrel the slave-catcher was pointing at now, Olivia decided she must strenuously object. Once one was down, who said he wouldn't decide to go on and shoot another?

"You'll do no such thing, Phillip Erlich," Olivia said. "We are law-abiding citizens, but just because this lunatic has a piece of paper what says he's allowed to search our wagon, that don't mean he can boss us or we got to do his job for him." She turned to the agent. "My brother ain't one of your slaves. You want the dang barrel off, take it off yourself. After you pay me for it." She held out her hand.

Mr. Dansbury pushed his hat back on his head and studied her. "I'm sorry y'all are feeling so uncooperative. But that being the case, I guess I best be on my way," he said. "You folks have a safe journey." He tipped his hat again.

"We wish you the same," Olivia said, her voice dripping sweet sarcasm.

After he rode off Olivia reached for the water skin at her feet and poured a long stream down her throat. Now that he was gone she suddenly felt weak with fear.

"I'll tell the Greenstreets he's gone and everything's all right." She turned, intending to climb into the back of the wagon.

"Don't." Phillip grabbed her arm. His voice was sharp but low.

"Don't even look at them barrels," he said. "Just get back on the seat and keep your eyes straight ahead."

She obeyed. Phillip picked up the reins and said, "Giddap." Then he ordered Olivia between gritted teeth, "I mean it. Don't look behind you, Rebecca."

"Why?" she whispered.

"I'll tell you later. Just go on talking like you was before, like you're my idiot sister. Loudly."

She complied. "That fellow sure wasn't blessed with much patience. And the audacity, making me search and search for a silly piece of paper he warn't hardly even going to look at. And then getting all out of sorts cause we ain't got no crowbar. Ain't no law says you got to have one. If he can't do his job properly without a crowbar, I say he's the one ought to be carrying one around. What on earth would we want one for, so we can stop on our way to have a pickle? And imagine him thinking you could hide a person in there. Who'd want to eat them pickles after a darky's been floating around in 'em?"

She kept up a stream of mindless chatter, thinking Phillip was taking caution to a ridiculous extreme, but amazed at how easy it was for her to play this part. I should go back to Five Rocks and pretend to be Rebecca Erlich, she thought. I'd probably have all kinds of beaus. When they next rounded a bend Phillip whispered through taut lips, "There, up ahead, see the tracks? Horse went into the woods. He's been waiting on us. Could have tracked back and been listening. Now he's going to follow behind. All he needs is to see you having a conversation with the lid of one of them barrels."

"Oh." Olivia's stomach turned over. Idiot, she scolded herself. Stop thinking you're so smart and do exactly as Phillip says.

She continued chattering, having a one-sided discussion of how good-looking that agent was, those blue eyes, and when he got off his horse, oh my. Too bad he chose to be such an unpleasant man. And southerners are supposed to be such gentlemen.

Phillip didn't speak again until they came to a patch of road that was far from the tree line on both sides, so that no one hidden in the woods could have heard him.

"They're gonna have to stay in there the rest of the way to Detroit," he said quietly. "Ain't no way of knowing if he's still behind us. At least the sun's out now. The road should dry up fast and we'll make better time. Gonna be hot in them barrels, though." He shook his head.

It was a long while before either of them spoke again. Then Phillip said, "I'm gonna look for a shady place to stop. Team needs food and water."

Olivia kept quiet. She had receded into her own thoughts, imagining the agent prying the lid off a barrel and pulling poor Maribelle out by her hair. Josiah sobbing. And she was troubled by Jared Dansbury's good looks. She'd always thought of evil people as ugly.

"You did good," Phillip said in a whisper, while they stood waiting for the oxen to drink. "Real good. Ain't never seen no one handle 'em better."

She smiled, feeling proud. "I thought so too. Surprised myself. Wasn't sure I'd be able to think straight."

"Never know till you're in it. But you did real good."

"It doesn't make any sense, him wanting to shoot at a barrel. Why would he want to kill one of the slaves he came across three states to catch? Destroy the property he wants back so much."

"Guess that don't matter naught to his kind. He figured that if the Greenstreets were hiding in them barrels and he didn't do nothing, all three were gonna make it over to Windsor. Might as well kill one and capture the other two. And most of them agents would rather kill a slave than see him go free. They hate us too. Come up here acting all polite, but they'd like as put a bullet in your head if they think you're helping a slave get away from 'em."

Olivia sighed. "Do you think the team is ready to get going?"

She no longer dared offer an opinion about what they should do; Phillip knew best. But she couldn't stop thinking about the Greenstreets, how hot and close it must be in those barrels, roasting in the sun, while she and Phillip stood cool and comfortable under the trees.

"Spose so."

When they were back in the wagon he continued to keep his voice low. "You know, that Mr. Faraday, he got them agents outsmarted ever which way. Same time we left, he sent everyone in Backwoods what got a wagon driving in a different direction. Anyone stop them, they put on a show like they's all nervous." Then he abruptly stopped speaking.

Olivia glanced over at the young boy. He's worried

he blabbed too much, she thought. He's obviously done this before. Many times. That's how everything got arranged so quickly. They all belong to some sort of organization. Mr. Faraday and the red-haired man. And that fat colored lady, Mrs. greased lightning, with the wardrobe stuffed full of clothes. It's all secret and they have no reason to trust me. She remembered her initial refusal to help and felt ashamed.

She remembered Avis reading from the newspaper about the Underground Railroad. Her girlish mind had imagined a long chain of black people being carted through a scary, deep, dark tunnel, from down south all the way up to Canada. But of course there couldn't be any such thing. Underground Railroad must be nothing but a funny name for people like Mr. Faraday and Phillip. Plain old people doing the right thing.

She thought of Mrs. Brewster back in Five Rocks. With her pinched face and schoolteacher manner, Olivia had always dismissed her as another annoying old busybody. But when Mourning's parents escaped slavery and came stumbling into Five Rocks, it was Mrs. Brewster who made a bed up for them and brought them hot meals. Her Quaker friends lent a hand, but there had been no organization, no wealthy men offering to pay the fine if she got caught. And no one had needed to ask Mrs. Brewster to help them. To convince her. Doing what was right and decent came naturally to her.

Something that never seems to happen to me, Olivia thought. How could I have said no to Mr. Faraday? What's wrong with me? She imagined how she'd be feeling now, had she ridden off to Ann Arbor. Hating herself.

They never saw another sign of the agent; nothing but wagons and riders headed in the opposite direction. Phillip nodded in greeting, sometimes stopping to exchange a few friendly words. When they came upon a wagon stopped by the roadside, Phillip pulled over to help its driver reset a wheel. It seemed to take forever and Olivia found it difficult to hide her impatience. How long could the Greenstreets stand to be cramped in there, half-suffocated?

It was dark when they finally drove onto Fort Street. Phillip turned up Griswold to State, where a long, low barn of multi-colored brick stood. Someone must have been watching for them; the barn door slid open at their approach, and Phillip drove straight in. A man emerged from the shadows and offered Olivia a hand to help her down. He wore a wide-brimmed hat that was pulled forward on his head, so she couldn't see his face.

"I'm sure it's been a long ride for you, Miss," the man said. "You'll be glad to get back to your hotel. You go right on. Don't worry none about your horse. She's back at the livery."

She stared at him blankly for a moment; then all she said was, "My pistol."

Phillip retrieved it and her water skin, possibles bag, and saddle bags. He shyly draped her belongings over her – the saddle bags around her neck, the possibles bag over one shoulder, and the water skin over the other. He held out her pistol and said nothing before he stepped back into the shadows.

She wanted to ask so many questions, but this was obviously not a time and place for that; the man was herding her toward the door. She turned back to look at the wagon. What were they waiting for? Why weren't they letting the poor Greenstreets out? But Phillip was standing still, watching. He raised one hand in a kind of good-bye, and it seemed that what he was waiting for was for her to be gone. The man took her elbow and gently led her outside.

"Good night to you, Miss." He tugged on the brim of his hat, stepped back inside, and rolled the door shut.

She was stunned to find herself out on the street, alone. She wanted to see the Greenstreets freed from their horrible confinement and help welcome them to this safe haven. To see little Josiah in his mother's arms. She'd thought she might be enlisted to help on their next step of the journey. She should at least have had the chance to wish them good luck. There was also a part of her that expected to be thanked.

For a moment she stood in the dark, blinking. Then she turned and pounded her fist on the door. When no one responded she banged more loudly.

It rolled open a few inches, and she knew he could see it was her. "Yes?" the man asked.

"What about the dress? It doesn't belong to me. I have to return it to a woman in Backwoods."

"Don't worry none about that." The door slammed shut.

Chapter Nineteen

Olivia stood in the street, unable to understand why she felt so miserable. Shouldn't she be relieved that it was over with? Glad to get back to solving her own problems? But her empty hotel room was a dreary prospect. A bath and a meal would be welcome, but she dreaded being alone. She'd grown accustomed to having Phillip at her side. She wanted to talk with him about what they'd been through together. Now that they were safe, they could have had a good laugh, remembering the look on Mr. Dansbury's face. She sighed. Now she had one more thing that she couldn't tell anyone about. So what was the point of seeking companionship? The last of her energy drained away.

She trudged up the dark street that led to the hotel with the feeling that someone was following her. Had the slave-catchers been behind them all the way? Had they seized the Greenstreets in the barn and now come to arrest her? When she stopped and spun around the street behind her was empty, but she remained ill at ease until she entered the lobby of the hotel. She asked

163

the clerk to send up a bath, followed by something to eat.

"I'm not sure what we can arrange at this hour," he said.

"Anything hot would be lovely," she said. "Soup or even some fried potatoes. But cheese and bread will do, if you've nothing else."

In her room she took off her shoes and plopped down on the bed. She hadn't been lying there long when someone knocked at the door. That was fast, she thought, wondering how on earth they had heated the water for her bath so quickly. When she opened the door, however, she found Michelle standing there, emanating a strong flowery scent of perfume. She was wearing a plain blue dress, but had some kind of silvery threads woven through the elaborate arrangement of her hair.

"Michelle, hullo, come in." Olivia moved away from the door, glad to see her, though puzzled. "How did you know I was back?"

"I happened to be walking past the hotel and saw you come in. So did you finish up your business?'

"Yes ... Well, no, not all of it. I have to go back to Ann Arbor again."

"What for?" Michelle made herself comfortable on the bed.

"The man who takes care of the deeds wasn't there, so I'll have to go again."

"So what've you been doing all this time?"

"I went to my farm. Visited my old neighbors." Olivia pulled the chair next to the bed and sat.

"Oh. I thought you must have gone to Backwoods."

"No. I went to Ann Arbor first. Wanted to get the paperwork over with. Then after I found out I was going to have to go back there again, I decided I might as well stop in Backwoods on the next trip. So how have you been?"

"You do that very well," Michelle said.

"Do what?"

"Lie."

Olivia blanched and froze. Could Michelle be one of those horrible agents? Or their informant?

"That's good." Michelle smiled. "So do I."

Olivia stared at her, unable to think of anything to say.

"You asked how I knew you were here. Finney told me."

"Finney?"

"The guy what owns the barn you just rode into on a big old wagon."

"What barn?" Olivia tried to keep her voice evenly moderated and sound bewildered. "I don't know what on earth you're talking about. What would I want with a wagon? I rode to Fae's Landing and Ann Arbor on a horse I took from the livery."

Michelle's face lit up with amusement. "Oh Lordie, ain't that rich. You're worried I might be the law."

"Michelle, I don't know why anyone would make up a story like that, but they have me mixed up with someone else."

It wasn't difficult for Olivia to look baffled. She was. She rose, turned her back to Michelle, and went to look out the window while she tried to think. What if Michelle – and maybe Mr. Abraham and Mr. Wentworth too – were in cahoots with those slave-catchers? That could have been what they were talking about, huddled under that street lamp. The way Olivia had shown up, blabbing about her colored friend and how she would let coloreds stay at her boarding house, they'd thought she was an Abolitionist agitator. And Michelle might have always suspected her customer Mr. Faraday of being in the Underground Railroad. That's why she'd told Olivia to go see him, to see what would happen. And then today, after all the commotion, one of those slave-catchers had ridden straight to Detroit, told Michelle someone would be

165

bringing a family of fugitives to Finney's barn. So she'd been watching all day, waiting to see who would drive into that barn.

"Look." Michelle rose and walked over to put a hand on Olivia's arm. "It's all right. You don't gotta pretend. It was Zach Faraday what rode your horse back here, told us to get ready for the Greenstreets."

Olivia turned to study her face. No, she couldn't risk trusting Michelle. Hadn't she just admitted being a good liar? Didn't she put on a show for her customers? And Olivia was too exhausted to play this game tonight.

"I'm tired," Olivia said at last. "They're going to bring me a bath soon, and something to eat. And then I want to sleep. I don't know where you got all these wild ideas. You must have had too much whiskey. Why don't you get a good night's sleep, and I'll come see you tomorrow morning?"

Michelle pressed her arm again. "All right. You get your rest. But don't bother coming to look for me in the morning. I'll join you here for breakfast. Please don't go anywhere before we talk."

The next morning Olivia finished her breakfast and asked for a second cup of coffee, hoping Michelle was going to show up soon. Anxious to be on her way to Backwoods, Olivia was about to get up and leave when a halo of golden curls sailed through the door. It wasn't until Michelle was almost at her table that Olivia noticed someone following behind her: Mr. Faraday.

"Feeling better?" Michelle bent to give her a hug.

"Good morning, Miss Killion." Mr. Faraday lifted his cap and gave a stiff bow before seating himself opposite Olivia. "And more than good to see you well. The Greenstreets asked me to express their gratitude to you."

"So you've seen them?" Olivia asked. "They're all right?"

He leaned forward and glanced at the empty tables

on either side of them before speaking. "Safe and sound in Windsor. We had a barge waiting to take them over. We don't like to do that at night, but in this case the river seemed less a peril than that crew from Kentucky. And frankly, until Michelle followed you back here, we couldn't be sure you wouldn't go straight from Finney's barn to the authorities."

Olivia opened her mouth to speak, but he held up a hand, palm out, and continued. "I'm sure you can understand my concern that perhaps your initial refusal to help reflected your true feelings, and you only changed your mind after recognizing an opportunity to help catch a gang of abolitionists."

"If I were on the side of those agents, I would have turned the Greenstreets over to the one that stopped us," Olivia said.

"Not if you wanted to see where we were taking them and find out who helps us in Detroit."

Olivia smiled wryly. "Oh. Yes. I see. The same way I thought Michelle might have been watching that barn to see who would turn up, so she could turn them in."

Mr. Faraday nodded. A waiter approached the table and they asked for coffee.

"The world we live in ..." Olivia said after the waiter moved away. "Everyone suspicious of everyone else."

Mr. Faraday raised his eyebrows and shoulders. "Better than the cost of trusting everyone and being wrong just once."

"So now you think you can trust me? I passed the test?"

"You passed the test." He smiled and nodded. "Phillip is a hard boy to convince, and he trusts you. By the way, he says you're the best actress he's ever seen."

Olivia smiled at the compliment, and then her baffled look returned. "But I don't understand." She looked back and forth between the two of them. "You planned this whole thing with the slave-catchers? That's why you told me to go see your friend in

Backwoods?" She stared at Michelle.

They all maintained an awkward silence while the waiter served the coffee.

"Are you gone loony?" Michelle said. "How could anyone know that was going to happen? And I didn't know if you were going to Backwoods at all, let alone when. All I wanted was for Zach to meet you some time, so I could hear what kind of impression you made on him."

"We're sorry for putting you in it that way," Mr. Faraday said. "That situation simply arose, and there you were. We need the help of folks like you." He leaned forward again and looked into Olivia's eyes. "It's not enough for someone's heart to be in the right place. We need people who can keep their senses about them and their mouths shut."

"So ... you need more drivers?" Olivia asked.

"No. Not drivers." Mr. Faraday looked at Michelle and she nodded. "I understand you spoke to some people about buying a boarding house."

"Yes, that's right."

"Mr. Wentworth, from the bank, he's been looking at that place for a while."

"Yes, that's what he said." Olivia nodded. "Only the lady was asking for too much money."

"That's not the only reason he hasn't bought it. He doesn't want his name on the deed, seeing as he's a prominent member of the Anti-Slavery Society."

Olivia looked at him blankly.

"Besides, Wentworth don't want to run no boarding house," Michelle said. "And then you turned up. You warn't wanting to buy it for an investment. You actually wanted to live there and take in boarders. You were perfect. And the way you met up with Hershey at the house –"

"Yes, that was quite a coincidence."

"Some folks might call it a coincidence; I call it a sign."

"Sign?"

"Fate," Michelle said and tapped her index finger on the table. "Then, on top of that, you started yapping about how you'd let Jews and niggers stay there –"

Olivia broke in. "Why do you have to use that word?"

"That got you worried? A word ain't nothing but a word. Anyway, person who's helping spirit slaves over the water to freedom don't want to get a reputation for being a nigger lover."

Olivia shuddered. "I hate that word." She blinked and stole a glance at Mr. Faraday, but he kept his expression carefully blank.

"All right." Michelle leaned back, took out a cigarette, and lit it. "You started saying you'd let *coloreds* stay in your boarding house. Suit you better?"

"Words hurt," Olivia insisted. "Hatred starts with words, doesn't it?"

"We could argue about that." Michelle stuck her bottom lip out and exhaled smoke at the ceiling. "Maybe you're right. People brung shiploads of slaves over from Africa cause words taught 'em to hate people with black skin. Me, I think it's the other way around. They didn't want to have to bend down and pick their own cotton and those black Africans were defenseless, so they took them. The hating came later, when they needed an excuse for why it warn't a sin to throw a net over someone, steal them away from their home, force them to work in your fields, and whip them near to death if they try to get away from you. Ask me, the words came last. But that's not what we were talking about."

"The boarding house." Mr. Faraday nodded.

"Yes. The boarding house," Michelle said and looked at Olivia. "I s'pose you've heard of the Underground Railroad?"

Olivia nodded.

"Then you must have figured out that Finney's barn

169

is one of the Detroit stations. But the agents are starting to get too curious about it, which is a shame cause Finney's got a good situation. Same time he's got packages hiding in his barn, he's often as not got the agents what have been chasing after those packages right next door in his hotel. Pours them whiskey and listens to them moan about how awful it is, the way those damned abolitionists think they can steal another man's lawful property." Michelle put out her cigarette. "That's why Wentworth wants someone like you to buy the Rafferty place. He needs a new station and thinks that house is perfect. Not in the middle of town, like Finney's. No nosy neighbors and a barn out back."

"I see." Olivia remained silent for a long while.

"That's why Hershey brought Mr. Wentworth to meet you."

"What's Mr. Abraham's part in it?"

Mr. Faraday broke in. "We never discuss one another's activities unless it's necessary. You'll figure things out, but you'll also learn it's best to talk as little as possible. To know as little as possible."

Olivia's attention was no longer focused on what he was saying. She took a deep breath and let herself feel it – some of the terrible heaviness leaving her body. They were offering her a thing worth doing. Something right and good. And something that by chance would also provide a home for Mourning and Little Boy when she found them. They would be so proud of her.

It had never occurred to Olivia to seek an active part in such an organization, but now that the idea had been placed in front of her, she knew it was the one thing that might take her mind off herself. What was it Mr. Carmichael had said? To find peace of mind, to live a life of purpose, a person must bind their life to a world larger than that we are capable of seeing. Olivia didn't know if the Underground Railroad led straight to God, but it certainly led somewhere away from her own troubles.

170

Michelle had gone on talking. "Mr. Wentworth has all the money in the world, but like Zach said, he's a fire-breathing abolitionist dragon, so the deed would go in your name straight away. He'll put up the money and have a private contract written up, where you'll make payments to him. But the house will be all yours. He won't want any say in running the place. And since he's got all the money in the world, you won't have to worry about him foreclosing on you. Long as there's slaves running north, he'll want that boarding house open."

"Stop," Olivia said.

"Just hear me out."

"You can stop trying to convince me," Olivia said, "because I don't need convincing. I want to do it. I'll go talk to Mr. Wentworth as soon as I get back from Backwoods and Ann Arbor."

"Oh, that's grand. I knew you would. You can count on me to make sure you always have clothes for new arrivals. See, that's another thing about having a station in a boarding house – you can have mountains of laundry lying around – men's, women's, children's, all different sizes – no one's going to think a thing of it. Won't wonder why you buy so much food, either." Michelle paused to take a deep breath. "So, it's all settled. I'll tell Mr. Wentworth to come by this afternoon. You'll just have to put your trip off for a day or two. You know they got a stage coach goes all the way to Ann Arbor? Leaves every day, from right in front of the Steamboat Hotel. There's a train too, though I can't say how often it runs."

"I prefer to ride."

"Well, that's up to you. You know, with Wentworth's backing you'll be able to offer cash money. Gold. No months of waiting for a loan from the bank and no scrip. That should clinch the sale. I heard old lady Rafferty has gotten even more anxious to sell. Can't wait to go back east and live with her daughter."

"That's all fine, and I'll be grateful to meet with Mr.

Wentworth, but not today. I'm already packed to leave for Backwoods."

"That's gonna have to wait a few days," Michelle said. "Wentworth heard someone from Dearbornville in the bank, asking about a mortgage, planning to make Mrs. Rafferty an offer. You got to make sure the old bag knows there's another offer on the table – in cash – before she goes and signs a contract with him."

Despite her desire for the gingerbread house to be hers, Olivia shook her head. "No, I've got to get to that farm where Mourning was working. I was willing to put it off to help bring the Greenstreets here, but not for a pile of lumber. Not that I don't want that house. I've never set foot in it, and I love it already. But I've got to go today."

"I'm returning to Backwoods today," Mr. Faraday said. "What if I go to that farm to ask about your friend?"

Olivia shook her head. "No. Thank you, but I want to be there. Why can't Mr. Wentworth go ahead and make an offer in my name? He's a minister and an officer of the bank. Mrs. Rafferty certainly isn't going to doubt his word."

"Don't you want to look at the offer he's drawn up?" Mr. Faraday asked.

"I'll look at it when I get back. I'm prepared to trust you people to come to a fair arrangement for me. What do I understand about banks and loans anyway? And if the old bag doesn't want to believe Mr. Wentworth, and I lose the deal, so I lose the deal."

"I don't see you thinking straight on this," Michelle said.

Olivia stared into Michelle's eyes. "Believe me, this is the straightest thinking I've ever done. I've made mistakes in my life. Big mistakes. Because I was scared, or plain didn't think, or told myself I'd always be able to fix whatever stupid thing I was about to do. But there are things you can spend the rest of your life trying to put right. So I might miss buying that beautiful house, and that would be a shame. But there will always be other houses. Plenty of other houses. But Mourning – there's only one of him."

Chapter Twenty

Olivia asked the boy at the livery to saddle Silly Sally for her. The weather was good and the ride to Backwoods uneventful. She watched her reflection in the window as she passed Faraday's Dry Goods, wondering how he felt about Michelle saying "nigger." It was such an awful word. Coon and Sambo were terrible things to call someone, but if you didn't know their meaning, they sounded all right. Cute even. Let's dance the Sambo. He won two dollars playing Sambo. But nigger didn't need any context to sound ugly. Without knowing what it meant, you knew it was something nasty.

She continued north out of town, following Mr. Faraday's directions to the Abbot farm. He was right. You couldn't miss the weather-beaten silo, embellished with the peeling remnants of a painting of the American flag. Newly harvested fields fanned out around the house and barn, and a few black men were busy sinking fence posts in one of the far sections. As soon as she turned into the drive, a rotund, tobacco-chewing white man emerged from the barn. He put a hand on Silly Sally's bridle and introduced himself as Linus Abbot. Olivia returned his greeting and introduction and then inquired about Mourning Free.

He scratched his head. "You expect me to remember the names of all the Nigras what come around looking for work?"

"I thought you might remember a name as unusual as that."

"More of 'em got unusual names than what got

usual ones. If they bother to tell me what they're called. Fer what do I gotta know their names?"

"Have any of those men out there been working for you since last year?" Olivia nodded at the fields.

"Might a been. What you want with this fellow?"

"I have a message for him. Regarding his family. Would it be all right if I left my horse to have a drink and went to talk to them?" She tipped her head toward the trough and then toward the men in the field.

"Suit yourself." He spat a large brown wad onto the ground and turned to waddle back into the barn.

Her heart beat fiercely as she trod slowly over the damp earth in one of the furrows. The men continued working, but she could feel their eyes glancing off her, sense their tension as they wondered what this strange white woman wanted of them.

"Good day. I'm sorry to bother you, but I'm looking for a man named Mourning Free who worked here for a while last year."

No one answered, but one thin young man was keeping his eyes trained too steadily on the ground. Olivia lowered her head to the side and addressed him directly. "I assure you I mean him no harm. I only wish to bring him news of his family."

He glanced at the others before replying. "Yes Miss, a fellow go by that name been workin' here. I 'member him playin' his harmonica come evening."

"That's him," Olivia said eagerly. "He always ended with 'Amazing Grace,' didn't he?"

"That right." He nodded. "He warn't here but a week. Day he come aksin' for work, Abbot warn't lookin' to take on no more hands, but that fella said he'd work for his keep. Like I said, only stayed a week. Maybe two. One morning he be gone."

"Did he give you any idea where he might go?"

"No, Miss. Ain't gave me no idea of nothin'. Kept to hisself, far as I remember. Just worked, ate, slept, and played that harmonica."

"And you never saw him again?"

"No, Miss."

"Well, if you ever do see him, please tell him Olivia Killion is looking for him and that she's staying at the United States Hotel in Detroit. And that he should get in touch with Mr. Carmichael."

Olivia turned her gaze on each of the other workers, but none of them had been working there long enough to remember Mourning. She was aware of Mr. Abbot's beady little eyes on her as she trudged back to her horse. She had to bite her lip to keep from crying.

Disheartened, she had no desire to continue her journey to Ann Arbor. What did it matter, anyway? Without Mourning she'd never find Little Boy, and without him what did she want with a farm? But after she mounted Silly Sally and returned to the plank turnpike, she turned west. She'd come this far, turned her life upside down trying to get her hands on that piece of land, she might as well make it hers. She stayed on the soft dirt shoulder, which was kinder to Silly Sally's hooves, and after a while stopped by a small clearing at the side of the road to give the horse some oats. Then she opened her saddle pack to check once again that she had all the documents Mr. Carmichael had prepared for her: the deed to the farm, copies of Uncle Scruggs' and her father's wills, signed declarations by both her brothers, and a long document signed by Mr. Carmichael and bearing the seal of the County Court in Hillsong.

Less than two hours later she passed the last neatly laid-out farm, turned off the turnpike onto a dirt road, and found herself on a quiet, shady street. She stopped at the next corner to contemplate the tidy rows of freshly-painted wood and brick homes. Ann Arbor was a frontier town? For as far as she could see, the yards were trimmed and well-cared for, bordered by sturdy sidewalks. The streets were unpaved, but looked as if someone had recently dragged a two by four over them.

Even the few log cabins looked civilized. Why was a town that hadn't even existed twenty years ago so much nicer than Five Rocks?

She rode a few blocks, looking for someone to ask for directions. Finally a man in paint-splattered work clothes emerged from one of the houses.

"Excuse me. A good day to you. I wonder if you could tell me how to get to the corner of Huron and Main?"

He squinted into the sun as he looked up at her, appearing puzzled. "These streets got names?" he asked, revealing that he was missing four front teeth. "Never knowed that."

"Thank you anyway."

"Hold on. What is it yer lookin' for?"

"The County Courthouse."

"Well, sure I can tell you where it's at. Right smack in the middle of town. Courthouse Square they call it. When this street stops, turn right, then left. Take you straight there. It's right across from Bloody Corners."

"Bloody Corners?"

He displayed a toothless grin. "The tavern ..." He waved a hand. "It's a store too. Tavern and a store. They got ever kind of thing in there. Even got rooms to put you up in, you be needing. Folks call it Bloody Corners count of first someone painted his house red, and then they painted the tavern the brightest red you ever seen. Redder than my blood, I can tell you."

Olivia easily found the way. The store-hotel-tavern was indeed a landmark one could not miss, a four-storied block of startling red. Shade trees, flower beds, and wooden benches filled the central square in front of it. Most of the town's business seemed to be conducted on this square. Apart from the store-hotel-tavern, there was a post office, barber shop, law office, bank, restaurant, and a number of other stores and offices. A sign identified the three-storied building across from Bloody Corners as the County Court. A number of

176

horses were already tethered to the split-rail fence that surrounded the square and Olivia led Silly Sally to join them.

She removed her documents from the saddle bag and timidly entered the courthouse building for her first encounter with bureaucracy. The entry and corridor were empty, as were the first two offices she poked her head into. A clear-faced young woman, more pleasant-looking than pretty, sat behind a desk in the next office. Her pale blonde hair was tied back so tightly it hurt Olivia to look at it.

"Can I assist you?" the young woman asked, articulating every word with great care, in what Olivia by now recognized as a German accent.

"Yes, I need to register a deed in my name. Do you know where I can do that?"

"Has the land been surveyed and marked?" the young woman asked, pronouncing "marked" as if it had two syllables.

The question made Olivia feel exhausted and almost queasy. *Lord, this is going to be worse than I thought. Am I supposed to take someone to Uncle Scruggs' farm and try to measure it? How could anyone walk a straight line through those woods? And then what, I have to run some kind of a marker around it?* She imagined the farm tied up in a big red ribbon.

"If no, then you need to start at the Title Office," the young woman said. "I can show you where it is, right here on the square." Confronted with the look of distress that came over Olivia's face, the woman's voice softened from efficient to sympathetic. "But what are all these documents you are holding? May I please look?"

Olivia gladly relinquished the papers and watched the woman flip through them.

"Oh, I see, I must to apologize. I made you worry for no reason. I did not understand. Of course, this land has been surveyed and granted. You already have a

177

deed!" She held it up, as if it were a proud accomplishment. "You are inheriting this land, so I think the judge only must to look at these papers, and then he can write the change of ownership in the Book of Deeds."

"Oh my, that's a relief." Olivia returned the woman's smile. "I thought I was going to spend the rest of my life taking care of this."

"No, no, don't worry. I take care of you. Come with me to Otto. He is the clerk for the judge. He will help you and you will see that everything will be easy. Otto is a very good friend of mine."

She led Olivia into the office of a young man with white-blonde hair and orange freckles, who, if not for his frock coat, would have looked more in place in a schoolyard. The woman whispered something to Otto and he nodded, obviously eager to be more than her friend. He perused Olivia's papers, declared everything to be in order, and disappeared through a door with them. When he reappeared he picked up a heavy ledger titled "Book of Deeds, Land Entry Case File" and led Olivia into a wood paneled room.

A bearded man sat behind a table, smelling of whiskey and looking as if he hadn't slept or bathed in months. Otto proffered a Bible and Olivia placed her hand on it and swore before God and the court of His Honor Ramus Jackson that all the statements and signatures on the documents were genuine and true. Then Otto opened the ledger and filled in the columns – county, township, section number, township number, range number, previous owner, and new owner. He entered the information in two rows, one passing ownership from Lorenzo Scruggs to Seborn Killion and one from Seborn Killion to Olivia Killion. Then he set the book in front of the disheveled man and pointed to the two spaces where his signature was required.

"Now," Otto said as he turned the book toward Olivia. "You sign here ... and here." He pointed. "And now I will sign as witness." He did so with a flourish, shut the book, and nodded his head toward the door.

Olivia looked at the man at the table, who had not spoken a word during the entire proceeding. "Thank you, Judge. I mean Your Honor."

He did not reply, but raised his forefinger and pointed it at her, in some sort of acknowledgement.

"Doesn't he talk?" Olivia asked in a whisper when Otto closed the door behind them.

Otto opened his mouth, but apparently thought better of what he had been about to say and snapped it shut.

"Why don't you go have your dinner?" he suggested, taking a watch from his pocket and clicking it open. "Come back in an hour and I will have a new deed for you, with your name on it. Usually this takes a week, even two weeks, but for special cases I can give higher priority." While saying this he smiled proudly not at Olivia, but at the young blonde woman, who was still waiting in Otto's office.

"You also keep a copy, don't you?" Olivia asked. "In case I lose mine?"

"Yes, that is correct."

Olivia fed and watered Silly Sally and then followed Otto's suggestion. After her meal she went into a candy store and bakery, where she purchased two bags of brightly-colored sweets. When she returned to the courthouse she found Otto true to his word. The deed was ready; **Olivia Killion** leapt out in thick black letters.

"Thank you for preparing it so quickly." She placed one of the bags of sweets on his desk. "And it's a comfort to know there will always be a copy here."

"Long as the courthouse doesn't burn down," he said, raising his eyebrows almost to his hairline and then smiling.

Olivia set the second bag of sweets on the young woman's desk and thanked her profusely. Then she mounted Silly Sally and decided she had time for a tour of Ann Arbor. Her first impression did not change; it was an extremely pleasant little town. Not exciting like Detroit, but pretty, quiet. Open, she thought, though she couldn't have said what she meant by that.

Two crossed wooden signs told her she was at the corner of State and South University Streets. The name "University" drew her attention to two identical houses that stood side by side. She rode a short way up South University to get a better look at one of them. It was large: two-stories, five bays, and chimneys at both ends. The roof of the wide covered porch was supported by six white wooden columns. On the outside, a partially roofed staircase led up one side, apparently providing a separate entrance to the rooms on the second floor. These had to be the professors' houses that Jeremy had told her about. Their students must go up those steps to the classrooms. A ride around the block confirmed this to be true. Two more identical houses stood on North University Street, backed up against those on South University.

Next she found the University Building Jeremy had told her about. He'd said it would be the first of many, but she couldn't imagine any school needing more classrooms than that. The building was four stories high, and she counted fourteen windows across the front and two on the side. That makes 112 classrooms, she thought, 28 for each of the four professors. Jeremy's right, they're going to have to give jobs to people like him. Someone has to fill up all those rooms. And they aren't scrimping; that University Building cost a heap of money. It's just like the Town Hall in Hillsong, double brick covered with that stucco stuff. Father always griped about what a waste of money that was, scoring the stucco to make it look like stone.

Olivia rode back to North University Street and sat outside one of the professors' houses. If I put my mind to it, she thought, I could end up living in a house like that with Jeremy – serving him his dinner, nodding and smiling while he tells me about his day, drinking afternoon tea with the other professors' wives, just like Mabel's Girls' Club. He's no longer afraid of matrimony. Talking about settling down. Probably thinks he'll need a wife to fit in here. All I'd have to do is buy one of those corsets that push your titties up to your chin. That and getting Michelle to teach me how to fix my hair should about do it. Save Jeremy the trouble of having to look around for a presentable woman. I'd have to practice giggling whenever he says something he thinks is funny, prepare his meals, and leave him alone when he doesn't want to be bothered. That doesn't sound so difficult.

For some reason that scenario repelled her. She scolded herself, almost speaking out loud. Are you telling me you'd rather spend your life changing sheets and preparing meals for a bunch of grumpy strangers, who will surely complain about every little thing? The surprising answer was, "Yes, I think I would."

She squared her shoulders and looked up at the sun. She should head back to the store-hotel-tavern to ask about a room. But no, it wasn't going to rain and she didn't need one. As long as she got on the plank road before sundown, she could probably ride all night and find her way back to Detroit in the dark. But she didn't want to do that either. She felt like sleeping under the sky one more time. It may be the last night she'd ever spend rough on the trail, now that she was going to become a respectable homeowner.

With no reason to hurry, she decided to complete her tour. She stopped to contemplate "The Misses Clark School for Young Ladies," wondering if there would someday be schools for girls everywhere. Not far from it a sign outside a church announced the next meeting of the Anti-Slavery Society. When she passed the office of a local newspaper, *The Signal of Liberty*, she stopped and went in. As she had assumed from its name, it was an abolitionist paper. She asked if she could pay in advance to run an ad once a month for the next two years: *Mourning Free, Mr. Carmichael has important papers and information for you. Olivia.* Then she rode back to Bloody Corners and put up a similar notice in every business that would allow her to.

When she climbed back on the horse she could think of no other reason to linger in Ann Arbor and was suddenly exhausted. Why did her insides feel as if they had been pummeled on a washboard? Trying to fight the despondency that had begun to coil itself around her, she forced herself to count her many blessings. I am young and healthy. I have all my teeth and have not been marked by the pox. I have a family. I know Mourning is alive, and sooner or later I will find him. The farm is in my name and will some day belong to Little Boy. I may soon have a business that will not only be my home, but will also help rescue people from slavery. I have Michelle and Jettie. I am going to live in an exciting city, in a beautiful young state full of lakes and rivers.

But she felt empty. She had done everything she could think of to find Mourning and Little Boy. With no more tasks to cross off a list, tomorrow would be an entire day, twenty-four long hours, with nothing to do but live her own small life. And the day after that. And the day after that. She wondered if she would manage to take any interest in it.

That night she rested her head against the saddle, stared up at the stars, and fell quickly asleep. She dreamt of Mourning, of lying in his arms. She awoke in tears, tormented by frightening thoughts of who might have her Little Boy.

Back in Detroit the next day, she slung her saddle pack over her shoulder and walked straight from the livery to *Chez Mademoiselle Lafleur*. Through the front window she saw Michelle at the counter, working on one of her creations. Olivia pushed the door open, saying, "So how are things?" Michelle put down the piece of lace she'd been fiddling with and rushed from behind the counter to give Olivia a hug.

"We got the house," Michelle said. "We did like you said – Mr. Wentworth went to see the old bat and made an offer, conditional on you viewing the property and approving. Would you believe, she was ready to accept it right on the spot? For the whole place, as is, furniture and all. I guess she got some letter from her daughter and can't wait to get out of here."

Olivia nodded.

Michelle pulled back to arms' length and looked into Olivia's face. "What's wrong? You don't look happy. Is it all happening too fast? You still want to do this, don't you?"

"Yes. Yes, of course I do. That's wonderful news. I'm just tired, is all."

"Didn't find that friend of yours, did you?"

"No."

"Well, that's too bad." Michelle said. "But don't worry, he'll turn up. You've told half the population of five counties that you're looking for him and where he can find you. It ain't but a matter of time till they get around to repeating that message to the other half. You'll see. Not everyone gallivants across the state and back like you. It'll take time, but he'll get your message. He'll come find you."

Michelle went behind the counter and pulled a bottle of brandy from beneath it. Olivia remained long enough to toast her new enterprise and made an effort to look more excited than she felt.

"You go get some rest," Michelle said. "I'll ask Hershey to come get you tomorrow morning, take you to close the deal."

Olivia dragged herself back to the hotel. She ate alone in the dining room and then again asked the clerk for pen and paper and sat in the lobby writing to Avis and Mabel. She told them her good news and asked

183

Mabel if she could please, please send some of her recipes, since everybody knows she is the absolute best cook in Pennsylvania.

See, Olivia told herself as she folded the letter, how hard is it to go heavy on the flattery? I could easily do that for Jeremy. My dear, that article you wrote is the most interesting thing I've ever read, I simply could not put it down. Except Mabel really is a superb cook – and that stuff Jeremy writes – truth be told, I'd rather eat those pages than read them. And faking a smile is a lot harder than I thought. Look at how bad my face hurts after the last half hour with Michelle, trying to look happy.

Chapter Twenty-One

The next morning Mr. Abraham's round face appeared in the doorway of the hotel dining room. He surveyed the tables, his eyes almost disappearing in two almond slits. Olivia wiped her mouth with her napkin and pushed her chair back, raising her hand to wave him over.

"*Mazal tov*," he said, removing his hat and bowing at the waist. "That means congratulations. My wagon awaits. But sit, sit." He motioned her back to her chair, nodding at her plate. "Finish your breakfast. I don't mind to have a coffee with you." He waved to the waiter.

"It's kind of you to come take me, but I could have walked. It's not far to the lawyer's office."

"Who said something about taking you to the lawyer? Not yet. First to the boarding house," he said, his tone implying that should be obvious.

"Oh, we don't have to go all the way out there. If you know what time we need to be at the lawyer's, I'll ask the clerk to send a boy to tell Mrs. Rafferty to meet us there."

184

He stared at her, perplexed. "I thought you said you never put your foot inside her house."

Olivia smiled. "I haven't."

He turned his palms to the ceiling and jutted his face toward her, features all wrinkled together. "A house you didn't see, you're going to buy?"

"I've seen the outside. Don't worry," she said. She reached out as if to place her hand on his arm, but then she remembered the rule about not touching and pulled it away. "I love the outside, and I'm sure anything wrong with the inside can be fixed."

"No, no, no, *mammelah*, you can't do that. A house you're buying. A house. Not a cupcake. The first and maybe only one you'll ever own. One of the biggest decisions a person is making."

"Mr. Wentworth has looked it over, hasn't he? He knows way more about houses than I ever will. What does 'mammela' mean?"

"*Mammelah* means sweet young thing. Like you."

"Will you teach me some words in Jewish? I remember 'all-ti-yak-nay.'"

"On our way to the boarding house."

"I told you, I trust Mr. Wentworth's opinion."

"Is Mr. Wentworth going to live in it? Suppose there are snakes in the cellar? Bats in the attic?" He moved his hands in ways that he presumably considered snake- and bat-like.

"I think he would have noticed." Olivia smiled.

"Ah, but he is seeing with the eyes of a man. You ladies have your own delicate ways. According to my wife, anyway. Your home must to suit you, have the special little touches you need."

"You mean like walls, roof, doors, and windows?"

He raised his palms again and rolled his eyes to the ceiling. "Where were you hiding all my life? Finally, a woman who is thinking like a man, and she must to be a *shikseh*."

Olivia flushed. "Maybe thinking like a man is what's

turning me into an old maid."

He shook his head. "Don't worry, the right man will come. You must to wait for the kind of *mensch* that you are deserving." He pointed his finger at her. "Now there's a Jewish word for you. In English you don't have a word like this. A *mensch* is a man, but a man who is behaving the way God is saying he should. But you changed the subject. You must to look at the boarding house. If for no else thing, we'll make the *alte yachneh* sweat a bit, get her worried that you might change your mind. If you act like you hate a lot of things, maybe Wentworth will make the price less."

"All right." She pushed her chair back and put her napkin on the table. "What did you call me before? A chicksie? Like a little chicken?"

He laughed. "No, no. A *shikseh*. A not Jewish girl. Usually a young and beautiful not Jewish girl. God put them on earth to torture Jewish men."

Olivia raised her fist to gently punch his shoulder, the way she used to with Tobey, but once again pulled back and said, "You know, this rule about not touching a person is a lot harder than you'd think."

"Dear girl, that is the best thing a *shikseh* ever said to me."

When Mrs. Rafferty saw Mr. Abraham standing on her front porch her bottom lip jutted out, and she moved as if to slam the door in his face. Then she noticed Olivia at his side and froze.

"You wouldn't be Miss Killion, would you?"

Olivia nodded and Mrs. Rafferty stepped outside to put a hand on Olivia's arm. "Come in, come in." She began a long monologue about her wonderful home, how happy she had been there, how sorry she was to be leaving it.

Olivia moved away from her grasp and imperiously swept through the rooms. She looked down her nose, ran her fingertips over the furniture, and murmured disparaging comments to Mr. Abraham, just loudly enough for the landlady to hear – "That will have to go. Where do you suppose she got that monstrosity? How could anyone think this was a good place for a wall? These windows hardly open and close. They'll have to be replaced, unless the cost of doing so is taken off the ridiculous price she's asking. How unfortunate that the rooms are so very, very small."

In fact, she loved every inch of the house. The front door opened to a small entry. Beyond it were the stairs and a corridor that divided the ground floor in two. To the left was a spacious parlor and behind it a large bedroom with an attached private dressing room. This room would obviously be Olivia's. It had a wide fireplace, which backed up to the one in the parlor and a beautiful bed with an intricately carved headboard. It was large enough to also accommodate a sofa, two easy chairs, and a low table.

Across the hall from Olivia's room, the kitchen was spacious and sunny, with still another fireplace and a large iron stove. The sink pump was old and rusty, but three strokes of its handle produced a stream of cold water that reeked of minerals and reminded Olivia of home. The heavy table was homey and inviting, with six chairs around it. Olivia ran her hand over the smooth wood, remembering the table in Jettie's kitchen.

"Now here at the front used to be a formal dining room," Mrs. Rafferty explained as she opened the door to a bedroom. "But my guests always preferred taking their meals at the table in the kitchen. Nice and cozy warm by the stove and fireplace. Sight easier for you serving too. So I cut the dining room into two bedrooms. Gives you nine rooms to let – these two here, five on the second floor, and two up on top. The house'll give you a right good living. You got room out in that barn to board six horses and keep a few buggies. I always kept a milk cow out there."

"The table in the kitchen," Olivia said. "There are

only six chairs. How do you seat all your boarders at it?"

"That ain't no worry. It opens up to seat twelve or twenty, and there's two stacks of chairs in the storeroom."

Wide wooden stairs led to the second floor. Olivia ran her hand over the smooth mahogany rail and admired the elaborate balustrades. The man who built this house had certainly spared no expense. The rooms upstairs were of a good size and comfortably furnished. Only two of them had windows that looked out on the barn. The two rooms on the third floor were smaller, due to their slanting ceilings, but Mrs. Rafferty had arranged them nicely. Their windows faced the front, toward the river. So, Olivia noted, Mr. Wentworth was right. Only two tenants would have a view of any "parcels" being delivered to the barn.

On their way out Olivia stopped for a moment to sit on the shaded wrap-around porch and watch a steamer chug up the river. She couldn't wait to sign the papers, but when she rose to leave she sniffed her nose and leaned close to Mr. Abraham, pretending to think Mrs. Rafferty couldn't hear. "I believe Mr. Wentworth has come to some kind of agreement about that other property he was talking about. But even if not, the price of this one will have to come down, unless she's willing to make improvements."

Mr. Abraham waited until Olivia was settled next to him on the wagon seat before offering Mrs. Rafferty a ride to the lawyer's office. She grunted her acceptance, and he politely looked away from the sight of her struggling up the ladder into the box of the wagon. Olivia was half-turned, about to say, "Wait, let me go back there, you take the place on the seat," when she glanced up at Mr. Abraham. He gave his head a tiny but almost violent shake, and the glare on his face was as clear as if he had spoken – "Don't you dare give your seat to that cow." The wicker basket Mrs. Rafferty chose to settle on disappeared under her bulk and wide skirts. She stared ahead, clutching the side of the wagon with one hand and her hat with the other. Once they arrived at the offices, the three of them sat silently in an outer room, waiting for both the lawyer and Mr. Wentworth to become available.

Finally both men emerged from one of the offices to greet them. Mr. Abraham drew Mr. Wentworth aside for a whispered consultation before Olivia was introduced to the lawyer and whisked into the inner office with him, Mrs. Rafferty, and Mr. Wentworth.

"Good to make your acquaintance," were the first and last words Olivia spoke, until it was time for her to sign a pile of papers. She sat in bored silence as Mr. Wentworth insisted on the addition of numerous clauses to the contract, presented a long list of repairs required, and amended Olivia's offer. Two hours later Olivia emerged from the office clutching a signed contract for $300 less than Mr. Wentworth's initial offer. The sale included all the furnishings, as well as the contents of the outbuildings, and gave Mrs. Rafferty two weeks to vacate the premises. Olivia effusively thanked Mr. Wentworth and the lawyer, wished Mrs. Rafferty a good trip back east, and stepped outside where Mr. Abraham was waiting for her.

"My best congratulations." He bowed again. "A woman of property. First a country estate, and now a house in the city. A real aristocrat." He straightened up. "Come, I will deliver you back to your hotel, but first allow me to take you for a ride."

He drove to the river and stopped by one of the piers. "It's only a mile wide here," he said, staring at the water. "I don't know if you are understanding how absurd is the world. Here we are sitting on what they call free soil," he said, pointing to the ground and sounding angry. "A democratic republic. Feh. Where is the freedom? Over there." He bobbed his head toward Canada. "The king is protecting them, not our president." He turned toward Olivia and stared earnestly into her face. She had never seen him look so serious.

"What you are doing, it is a worthy thing," he said. "You must to know that. In this time and place it is the most worthy thing a person can do."

Olivia stared at the ground, not knowing what to say.

"This isn't my first wagon," he said quietly. "The first one also was with a double bottom. Three black men I was hiding in it. Even down in Kentucky, I wasn't afraid of the patrols. I delivered many parcels before and thought I was very clever – the way I was chatting with the agents, making them laugh, always keeping some dresses for their wives and bottles of whiskey for them. But one day there were many of them, and they were coming with dogs. They weren't asking anything. Weren't saying a word to me. Just pulling me down off the seat and tying me to a tree. They let the horses to go free and then in the box of the wagon they made a pile of the dresses. When they were striking matches I thought it was a bluff – they were waiting for me to confess about hiding the slaves. It was taking them so long to kindle a fire. By the time there was a flame I was crazy, shouting, telling them the men were there, how to let them out. How to get their property back. They didn't mind. They took all the whiskey off the wagon and were sitting on the ground, passing a bottle. When the horrible screams began, they laughed. It lasted so long, that shrieking. You can't to imagine how long a person can to suffer. The smell of a human being, slowly roasting. Those black men died the worst death I can to imagine. And their fellow men thought this is entertaining. 'Oh-ho' one of them was raising the bottle, like he is making a toast, when a specially loud scream went to the sky. After, when it was quiet, they started to pile branches at my feet. Said they will burn me too. Then they pulled my beard and were laughing while they rode off."

Olivia found no words.

"I didn't tell you this to make you sad. Yes, I know it is a terrible story. But the reason I told it to you ... you must to know how evil these men are. How dangerous. And you must to know how worthy it is, the thing you are doing. Trying what you can to change a world that isn't changing." His voice sounded tired.

"Don't you believe the slaves will be freed some day?"

"Yes. Yes, I believe. Some day." He let out a long sigh. "But human beings will still be monsters. They will find new ways to torment one another." He sat straighter and forced a smile to his face as he took up the reins. "But don't let an old man to spoil your happy day. You must to remember always that you are not personally responsible to repair everything that is wrong with the world. There is a saying of the Jews – a person who is saving a single soul, it is as if he is saving an entire world."

"That's a beautiful concept." She stared at her hands and then asked, "Would you mind if we sat here for a while longer?"

He put down the reins, and Olivia turned his saying over in her mind. It was the perfect response to people like her brother Tobey. People who thought that since you can't change everything, you might as well not bother trying to make anything better. And to Christians who used that verse about the poor always being with us as an excuse for never giving charity to anyone.

"It also means ..." She finally looked over at Mr. Abraham. "That if you don't help a person, and that person dies, then it's like you destroyed a whole world."

He nodded. "That's right."

"Thank you." She smiled. "I've been looking for a saying like that."

Mr. Abraham nodded. "So now we are finished to

191

discuss the evil in the world. Now it's time to celebrate the new life you are beginning. May you find much joy and comfort in it." He raised an imaginary glass.

Olivia was glad to shake off the sadness. She returned his make-believe toast and smiled. "I'm going to buy a horse," she said. "I thought of it before, while we were at the house. It has that big barn and everything."

"An excellent idea." He told her to go to Thompson's Livery and say she was a friend of his. "And now, since you are still horseless, maybe I am taking you for a drive."

When they passed the park called Campus Martius, Olivia asked where its strange name had come from.

"It's Latin for something like Military Square," he said. "I think it's because the Brady Guards are marching around on it, all dressed up in their blue uniforms. It was the center of the plan for the way they wanted to build the city again, after the big fire."

"What big fire?"

"Detroit was burning to the ground in 1805. Three hours was all and the whole town was gone. Poof. *Kaput.* Only a couple chimneys left. So since they must to start over from nothing, they made a map, all the streets going out from a big park, like the spokes of a wheel."

"Who's 'they,'" Olivia asked.

"What?"

"You said 'they made a map.' Who gets to make a plan for a city?" Olivia asked, thinking that sounded like a wonderful job.

"Don't know. Some are saying it was old Judge Woodward, but no one likes to give him credit for doing anything good."

"Why not?"

"I think he wasn't so popular. A reputation he had – for taking a lot more drinks than baths."

Olivia shook her head and wondered if all the judges

in Michigan were drunkards. When they passed the Berthelet Market she asked him to wait for her to buy some fruit.

When she returned he asked, "What should I show you now? How about the Female Seminary? You can probably be a teacher there."

"I know that building. The big yellow one. I noticed it the first day I came to Detroit."

"So maybe the old Catholepistemiad?" he said, making three false starts on the pronunciation of the name. "Don't laugh. I'm not the only one who isn't saying it right. Everyone is saying the 'Cathole-what's-its-name'. They say Governor Cass was calling it that, back when they first built it."

"Places here certainly have strange names."

"That's what you are getting when you let Jesuits do the naming. But that name, at least I know what it means: universal science. It was before the University of Michigania, but that moved to Ann Arbor. Now I think they got a library in there. Or I can to show you the Fireman's Hall on Larned Street. They have dances up on the top floor," he said, "for young people like you."

Olivia smiled. "The truth is, I'm starting to feel tired. Would you mind taking me to Michelle's now?"

"No, that's good with me. I also must to get myself ready to leave tomorrow. Off to Ohio and Indiana."

"Oh, I'm sorry you won't be here. Well, at least you'll get to see your family in Cleveland. Do you ever bring them to Detroit?"

"Not so far."

"Well when you do, you'll bring them to stay at *my* boarding house."

Outside of Michelle's shop Mr. Abraham said, "So I wish you again much, much success and I see you in two months, a crabby old landlady by then. By the way, that sign you are wanting to put up, that in this house everyone is welcome –"

"I know. I won't do anything to call attention to my house. But I'm not going to start calling colored people niggers either."

He smiled. "I don't think it's a requirement."

Michelle came out of her shop, asking, "Sooo?"

"We signed," Olivia said as she climbed down. "It's mine. Mr. Wentworth wants to do some renovations." She put her lips near Michelle's ear. "Put in some storage spaces for parcels." She leaned away. "But he said that wouldn't take more than two months and that someone from the Society will pay for that part. I only have to pay back the cost of the house and for painting it after everything else is finished."

Mr. Abraham interrupted. "You ladies must to forgive me." He tipped his hat.

"I want a promise that when you come back you're going to stay at my house," Olivia said to him. "By then I'll have my sister-in-law's recipes, and I'll be the best cook in Detroit."

"Don't bother for him," Michelle said. "He ain't gonna eat nothing you cook."

"Why not?" Olivia stared up at him.

He looked amused. "Once I explained to Michelle the very simple Jewish dietary laws. She can to tell you," he said and chuckled.

Olivia turned curious eyes to Michelle.

"Believe me, you don't want to know," Michelle said, shaking her head.

"Good-bye, ladies." Mr. Abraham tipped his hat again and drove off, repeating to himself, "Michigan, *mishuggeneh*, Michigan, *mishuggeneh*."

"Crazy," Michelle said. "That other word he's saying means crazy in Jewish. So what, you're going to be in that hotel for another two months?"

Olivia nodded.

"That's silly. You can stay in one of the rooms in the back of my shop. Just shove the junk out of your way. You can sleep on the massage bed and come upstairs to use my kitchen."

Though surprised by the offer, Olivia readily accepted it. She remembered the day she and Mourning had crossed the river, the way he had been there to catch her before she fell. That day she had thought, so this is what it feels like to have a friend. Now she slipped her arm through Michelle's and relished that feeling again.

Then she went back to the hotel to get her things. She once again asked the clerk for paper and this time wrote a letter to Mr. Carmichael, informing him that she was leaving the hotel and letters should be sent to her care of *Chez Mademoiselle Lafleur*, on Fort Street.

Chapter Twenty-Two

Olivia had been glad to accept Michelle's hospitality, but later that night, alone in the room, she found the lingering scent of lavender disturbing. It evoked too vivid memories of the first time she had chanced into *Chez Mademoiselle LaFleur* – only a day after she'd discovered Iola and Filmore Stubblefield dead in their barn. Three days after Filmore raped her for the last time. Olivia had been in a daze and covered with cuts, scrapes, and bruises. Michelle gently persuaded her to lie on this bed and succumb to "her girl" Sara May, who slathered Olivia with lavender oil and massaged some comfort into her damaged and exhausted body. In recent months Olivia had gained some distance from that broken version of herself. Now the scent of that oil brought it back.

How long ago did it all happen? That day, she thought – the day Iola tricked me into going to their place – must have been right before the Fourth of July. I remember her cackling like a witch, "Yoo-hoo, Happy Independence Day." What a laugh on me. The day I lost my freedom forever. Now there's a strange turn of

195

phrase – lost my freedom. As if I misplaced it. No one's freedom is lost. It is stolen, ravaged, obliterated. Today is the twentieth of September. So it was more than a year ago – the middle of last July – that I fled to Detroit, on my way back to Pennsylvania. Olivia's heart pounded and she found it difficult to lie still. She needed to go back in time, to confront them.

Why did someone else have to go and kill them, she thought. It should have been me. Or I should at least have taken a crowd of people to their place, accuse them, witness their shame. Even if no one believed me, I still should have shouted it. I should have. I should have.

She sat up and hugged her knees, rocking back and forth, her anger swelling and then subsiding into despair.

Everything is gone, she thought. There is no Mourning. No Little Boy. No dream of a big yellow dog running alongside my wagon full of laughing children. I'll never marry and have a family. What am I doing in this room? This city? I don't belong here. I don't even know this Michelle person who pretends to be French and drinks whiskey. Why am I sleeping in her bed? Only because she feels sorry for me. Takes pity on the girl who is no one. I pretend to be Olivia Killion, but there's no such person. There's nothing but a big lie.

The bed stood in the center of the room, cold and exposed. She rose and shoved it up against the wall, wincing at the loud rasp of its legs scraping over the floor and hoping she hadn't woken Michelle. When Olivia climbed back onto the bed it felt a bit more comforting. She calmed herself and banished the Stubblefield barn from her mind, but too quickly focused on a new source of distress. Why on earth did I sign that paper? How could I put myself so deep into debt? What if I can't make the payments? What do I know about running a boarding house?

The first rays of sunlight were showing before she

was able to focus on her immediate future. What was she going to do for the next two or three months, while she waited for the *alte yachneh* to vacate the boarding house and then for Mr. Wentworth to finish having it renovated? She was unfamiliar with the concept of leisure. School, chores at home, and helping out in the store had filled her days, the minutiae of daily life consuming whatever hours remained. During the two years her father had been bedridden she was often idle, awaiting his next demand, but that time had felt anything but "free." She filled it with sketching and reading, leaving the house only to run errands for Mrs. Hardaway or take a walk during Seborn's afternoon nap. She didn't know how to face the prospect of waking on sixty or more mornings with no clear picture of what she was supposed to do that day.

When the sun was up she washed, dressed, and peeked into the shop. The window in the door was still darkened by the green blind, but Michelle was already on her stool behind the counter, bent over a newspaper, her blonde curls a halo in the light of the lantern beside her.

"Good morning," Olivia said brightly as she stepped into the room and surveyed Michelle's little empire. "How can I be of help?"

Michelle raised her head and squinted at her guest. "Help?" She looked around the shop. "I don't know. Ain't much needs doing."

Olivia's cheerful face fell, and Michelle straightened up and frowned. After a short silence she said, "On second thought, there is one thing. You feel like it, you could undress them two dummies in the windows and get something else on 'em. Been a while since they changed their clothes. I ran out of ideas. Your new eyes would be a big help."

Olivia stepped toward the windows. "I guess I could do that. I mean I could try. I don't know about clothes the way you do."

"You wear 'em, don't you? I'm sure you'll do better than that." Michelle waved her hand in the direction of the window. "But first go upstairs and get something to eat. You're welcome to whatever you can find." She waved her hand again, this time to shoo Olivia in the other direction, and turned back to the *Detroit Free Press*.

Olivia climbed the stairs, expecting Michelle's kitchen to be a shambles and planning to clean it, but found all its surfaces surprisingly spic and span. She had a hasty breakfast of corn bread, jam, and coffee and returned to the shop. Michelle had left the door ajar and was outside, humming *Blue Eye'd Mary* and sweeping the sidewalk. Then she tugged on the blind to roll it up and flipped the "Closed" sign to "Open."

"*Bon, mon chèri,*" Michelle trilled and batted her eyelashes before switching back to her regular voice. "We're officially open for business."

Olivia smiled and stepped outside to study the front display. In each of the two tall, narrow bay windows stood a wire dressmaker's frame, clothed in one of Michelle's designs. The dummies were simple hourglass shapes, with no heads, arms, or legs. Michelle had set brooms inside them, upside down, and plopped hats over their bristles.

"How would you like them dressed?" Olivia asked.

"Colorful. Give one of 'em a neckline that shows a bit of titty. That gets the men's attention. Don't seem to matter none that the titty's made outa chicken wire."

Olivia flushed and Michelle continued. "Make the other one more respectable. Something they'd dare take home to their crabapple Yankee wives."

Olivia took her time deciding on a frock for the "what they wish they had" display. She went through all three racks, holding each dress up to herself in front of the mirror, before selecting an off-the-shoulder evening gown of royal blue silk with flounces of white lace to the elbow. She carefully laid the dress over a chair and then lowered one of the dummies to the floor and removed the broom from it. The shoulders of the mauve and yellow day dress it wore were gray with dust. Olivia pulled the frock off and gave it a good shake. When she held the blue gown up to the frame she realized that since the frame had no arms and the dress had no shoulders or sleeves, there would be nothing to hold it up.

"I don't suppose I could sew this onto the frame?" Olivia asked Michelle.

"Watered silk? I don't think so."

Olivia pulled up a chair and sat down to study the problem. Then she fingered the lining of the gown's bodice and asked, "Do you have any long johns? If there were some cloth on the frame, I could pin the lining of the dress to it. That should hold it up. Would that be all right?"

"Sure, long as you don't go stickin' no pins through the silk. There's some long johns back in that corner, where the men's things are at." Michelle looked at Olivia with a mixture of curiosity and amusement. "But I don't think they've come into fashion yet."

Olivia found a set of white long underwear, shirt and leggings in one piece, the kind with a large opening across the back half of its waist, rather than a trap door. She pulled the shirt over the dummy backwards, leaving the buttons in the back and the dummy's torso covered in white up to the neck. The legs of the underwear dangled on the hind side, and she rolled them up and pinned them where a bustle would be. Then she wadded up sheets of old newsprint to stuff into the sleeves, creating arms. With the help of a few strategically placed pins to secure the lining of the bodice to the long johns, the gown did indeed stay up. Olivia fastened the arms in a coquettish arrangement, both bent at the elbow, one wrist to the back of the "head" of broom bristles, the other resting on the hip. Then she went to her room and removed the white case from the pillow. She took it into the shop and slipped it over the broom, using more crumpled newsprint to shape it into a round head, and tied a string around the bottom.

"As long as you're being so generous with the newsprint," Michelle said, 'You might as well ..." She put her hands under her breasts and made an uplifting motion.

Olivia flushed, but stuffed wads of paper down the neck of the long johns, using her other hand to mold it into a pair of generous breasts that almost matched in size and shape. When she took a step back to study the effect, she noticed a well-dressed man watching her through the window. Cheeks red again, she turned the dummy to face into the store and willed the man to go away. From the corner of her eye she saw him put a finger to the brim of his top hat and walk off smiling.

Finally satisfied with her endeavors, she went to the storeroom and picked some red silk roses from Michelle's hat-making materials. These she tucked into the bodice, peeking over one of the newly enhanced breasts. A delicate shawl of sheer red completed the ensemble and almost hid the buttons up the back of the long johns.

"What kind of hat does a lady wear with an evening gown?" she asked Michelle.

"None. A real person − I mean a head with hair − would stick a couple of ostrich plumes or some ribbons in it."

"We could put one of your wigs on her."

Michelle shook her head. "You know what them things cost? Ain't no one going to buy one's been sitting on a dusty old broom."

Two men stopped to peer through the window and entered the shop. Michelle greeted them in her French accent and spent the next hour selling them dresses, hats, scent, shawls, and ostrich plumes. Long before the transactions were completed she had shed her French accent, but the men didn't seem to pay it any mind. They're too busy staring down her cleavage, Olivia thought. She couldn't get over the irony of tourists from back East coming out to the frontier to buy the "latest fashions from Paris, France."

Olivia clothed the second dressmaker's frame in a conservative day dress of two shades of green. She gave it arms that she pinned together in front, a green and white shawl draped over them. She placed both dummies in the windows and went outside to study the result. They need hair, she thought. If they had hair, I could cut circles of paper and sketch pretty round faces for them. But faces would look plain stupid without any hair.

She found no yellow yarn in the back room and told Michelle she was going out to buy some. She spent the rest of that day and much of the next arranging the "hair" in buns at the crown of the dummies heads and gluing it into corkscrew curls to ring the faces she drew on circles of white card paper. To the lady in the royal blue evening dress she gave thick lashes and red lips. She wove both ostrich plumes and red ribbon through her curls of yarn. Her more modest companion in the day dress wore a Mona Lisa smile and a green velvet bonnet with curls peeking out of it and a ruffle of lace at the neck.

Michelle made no comment on Olivia's efforts until she was called outside to inspect them through the window. "Well looky there, for all your wanting to gallivant around in men's clothes, you turn out to be a girly girl after all." Michelle smiled. "You must a loved playing with dolls. Ain't that lucky for me."

"They look silly, don't they?" Olivia said.

But Michelle gushed with enthusiasm. "Silly? No, they do not look silly. I can't believe how beautiful they are. Never seen windows like these. They're going to become a regular tourist attraction. Look at those faces. Just a few simple lines, but it's like they're looking right at you. How'd you do that?"

Olivia beamed. When they went back inside she asked what she should do next.

"You don't have to *do* anything." Michelle returned to her perch behind the counter, picked up a small hand mirror, and leaned her head toward the sunlight, stretching her lips back to study her teeth.

Olivia stood in the middle of the shop, watching her.

"Well, go on." Michelle lowered the mirror and made the shooing motion again. "Don't just stand there gawking at me. It's a beautiful day out there. Go enjoy what's left of it."

"I don't mind helping out." Olivia walked to a shelf, picked up a fringed scarf, and refolded it more evenly. A body's got to earn their keep, she thought, but didn't say it out loud.

"Helping out with what? Ain't nothing for me to do till a customer comes in."

"Oh." Olivia forced a smile and returned the scarf to the shelf.

Michelle walked over to stand facing her. "Look, 'fore long you're gonna be stuck with a bunch of pain in the arse boarders, and you ain't never gonna have a day off. And it's gonna get cold soon. You oughta be enjoying this weather and your freedom while you got 'em."

Olivia squeezed her lips into a fishy kiss while she thought. "I suppose I could go to that 'Cathole-what's-its-name' place. Mr. Abraham said they have a library in there."

"You don't have the slightest idea how to have a good time, do you?" Michelle shook her head and muttered, "Yankees."

"I'm no Yankee. Three-fourths Irish."

"So go find something that will make you smile. If that's a pile of moldy old books, go stick your nose in 'em. But there's a whole city out there. The non-Yankee part of you must like to do something 'sides work."

"Like what?"

"I don't know. How about a boat race? You could go ask the Boat Club if they're gonna be having any more a them. They didn't used to have but the one boat, but last year they bought another one and started racing 'em to Hog Island and back."

"How come it's called Hog Island?"

"Cause that's where all the farmers used to keep their chickens and pigs. Lot of 'em still do."

"Why?"

"Cause coyotes can't swim. Anyway, you go over to Hastings Street, ask at the office of the Boat Club. That would be a fun thing to do, specially if you make it interesting. Slim Johnny was taking bets on the last one. Or you could take a ride on a ferry. Go down to the river, you'll see signs. They go to Mount Clemens, maybe all the way to Port Huron. Ask 'em about Sundays. I'd go along with you on a Sunday."

Olivia's eyes lit up. "Yes, that is something I would like. I always hear people say how beautiful Lake Huron is. And I always meant to go over to Windsor. See what it's like to be in a foreign country."

"See? There's plenty for you to do. And how about bowling? You ever played that?"

Olivia shook her head and said she'd never heard of it.

"Phoo. That town you come from ... I guess life was one long party."

Olivia shrugged.

"Didn't they even have lawn bowling in the summer? You know where you roll a ball, try to get it closest to the little ball?"

Olivia's face remained blank.

"Well, out here they got inside bowling saloons what are open all winter. There's two of 'em on Woodbridge and another up on Monroe. I don't remember which, but one of them saloons has nights they let women play. You go ask when Ladies Night is and I'll go with

203

you."

Olivia remained rooted to the floor of the shop, feeling like a little girl about to be sent away from home. Michelle paused and studied her for a moment. After a quick shake of her head she plunged on.

"Or you could go over to City Hall, see if they got any notices about singers or piano players. Sometimes they even put on one a them shows. This one time they brought out actors, all the way from New York."

Olivia suppressed a sigh. Trying to fill up so many days with fun sounded exhausting, not to mention expensive. All she wanted was a reason to get out of bed in the morning. A way to make herself useful. Why couldn't she just work in the shop? After a long silence, Olivia came up with an idea of her own. "I guess if I bought a horse, I could take some long rides. Get to know the different kinds of trees and flowers."

Michelle couldn't help smiling and shaking her head again. "I swear, you make even that sound like a job," she said. "But never mind. Once we're all snowed in, you'll have me and Hershey in your kitchen, playing cards and getting happy."

"I know how to play Whist," Olivia said.

"Good for you." Michelle turned away and drew her accounts ledger from under the counter.

Olivia felt she was being dismissed and moved toward the door, but paused when Michelle spoke again. "I'll tell you something else you could do. Go buy yourself some good paper. If you can draw faces like what you put on them dummies, no reason you can't make pictures of Detroit. The boats on the river. People in the markets. If I could do like that, I'd get a steamboat captain to pose for me."

Olivia smiled. "Why a steamboat captain?"

"Closest thing we got to a king around here. At least they think so. Don't you remember yours?"

"I don't know that I ever saw him. I wasn't looking out for him, anyway."

"I promise you, when your boat docked in Detroit he decked himself out in a ruffled shirt and blue swallow-tail coat, brass buttons all polished. Went strutting up Jefferson Avenue in his nankeen pants and white stockings, giving us poor locals the pleasure of the sight of him. You ask one of 'em to pose, he'll think that's a most natural request. He'll keep his big tall hat on and glare at you like he's at least the Admiral of the British fleet."

"Those French men in their canoes would make a good picture," Olivia said.

"Sure would. And they'd love to have you make a likeness of them. Won't be long 'fore there ain't none of 'em left. You could make a history of the city in pictures. I bet they'd let you hang 'em up in City Hall, once you had enough."

That was an idea that appealed to Olivia, though a voice in her head nagged. Who would want to look at your silly pictures? City Hall, indeed. You aren't any good. People would only make fun. Imagine, if the busybodies could see you, how they would talk. Just look at that Killion girl dallying about, nothing to do but sit there scrawling and scribbling. Didn't I tell you she was just like that lunatic mother of hers?

Chapter Twenty-Three

Olivia left the shop feeling alone and useless, but soon convinced herself that walking up and down the broad avenues was not a waste of time. She was learning the city, making a mental catalogue of where to obtain the things she would need for the boarding house. She was beginning to tire when a steamship blew its whistle, drawing her to the fishy, oily Detroit River. She stood on one of the empty piers and watched the current sweep leaves and twigs back toward Lake Erie, connecting her to home, to the whole world. All that moving water never failed to fascinate her. It never stopped flowing, as inevitable as sunrise, part of something grand and mysterious. Watching it long enough made the problems of a tiny human being seem trivial.

She wished Mr. Abraham were at her side. He would know how to talk about such things. Perhaps to him she could say the words – it isn't just me, is it? Everyone under this sky is alone. No one is safe. Terrible things happen. If you survive, what do you do? You go on. That's all. You'll never know the reason. Why one ship sank and another weathered the storm. There is nothing to understand. It happened because it happened. You make what you can of what remains to you, like the river goes on flowing. I have a reason for getting out of bed in the morning – because I still can. Maybe that's the only reason that counts.

Tired of standing, she wandered toward the makeshift station of the new Michigan Central Railroad. The train from Ypsilanti was due to arrive, and the station had another attraction – chairs with cushions. She sat and remembered the first time she'd heard the thundering of a locomotive, a thousand pairs of horses' hooves pounding in perfect unison. It had been during one of their father's Sunday drives, and Olivia had shrieked with delight when they blew the steam whistle. She remembered the coldness she'd seen on Seborn's face when he turned and gruffly admonished her to simmer down back there.

"Why do they make that noise?" she'd whispered to Tobey.

"So folks will know the train is coming."

Sure he must be fooling, she'd waited for him to grin and punch her arm. The earth was shaking and the locomotive was so deafening she could barely hear him, but someone thought that without the whistle folks wouldn't notice?

She sat thinking about Tobey. The good brother.

Wouldn't it be hard to live this far from him? Her indifference surprised her. But what did they share? A few blurry childhood memories. She couldn't talk to him about the wrongs in the world, could imagine what he'd have to say about her planning to hide fugitives in her house. And her personal life? She'd wouldn't dare confide in him. If she needed help or advice about her business, it would more likely be Avis she would turn to. Or Mr. Wentworth. No, she didn't miss Tobey much at all, she admitted sadly.

What does it matter anyway, she thought as she got to her feet. The river will always be my lifeline. Three days on a boat and I can be home.

Hungry, she walked to the Rail-Road Hotel, which advertised daily board for 75¢ a day. She went in and asked for their special, pleased to see the poor quality of the stringy beef and lumpy mashed potatoes, thinking that even without Mabel's recipes she could do better than that slop.

While she ate she made a mental list of things she must speak to Mr. Wentworth about before he completed his plan for the renovations. First on her list was a shower. On her way to the railroad station she'd passed a tall, circular brick structure that emitted what she recognized as the hum and thud of a steam engine. She paused to stare up at it, and the next man who happened along the street stopped next to her.

"Day to you, Miss. Those are the new waterworks," he said proudly. "Started pumping a year ago last May. Tore up half the city putting in the pipes for it – four miles of iron and another ten of tamarack logs, but it's sure worth it. Put in fifty a them fire plugs too. This town ain't never going to burn down again."

She asked the man a few questions and then continued on, smiling. I've already got my own well, she thought. All I have to do is buy some pipes and set a washtub up on legs taller than me. Someone must have figured a way to heat the water and get it up into the tub. Jeremy might know how. I wonder how much a small steam pump costs. I'll ask Mr. Wentworth.

It was beginning to grow dark when she returned to Michelle's shop.

"Looks like you found something to do with yourself." Michelle glanced up from the book she was reading at her counter.

"Walked my feet off." Olivia went to her room to remove her shoes and slip her feet into the comfort of her moccasins.

"So where you been at?" Michelle asked when she returned.

"Just about everywhere. I can't believe how many shops there are. Do you know there's a whole store that sells nothing but sheet music and musical instruments? And one that sells only chairs? Imagine that. And I never saw so many dry goods and grocers and butchers. I went into City Hall, like you said, but I don't know why you'd think anyone would want to hang pictures in there, unless they're of a dead cow. The whole ground floor is crammed with butchers' stalls. It's nothing but a big smelly meat market."

Michelle shrugged. "I meant up on the second floor, where the offices are."

"If I ever do draw any pictures, I might as well hang them in my boarding house." Olivia pulled a chair closer to Michelle and sat. "The one thing I didn't see was an ice cream parlor. Don't they have one?"

"Don't recall ever seeing one, but I warn't looking."

"So come spring we can sell ice cream. Freeze it up back in your kitchen and set a little stand out on the sidewalk."

"Could try, but now that I think of it, all them hotels probably have ice cream on their menu. Seems they got everything. Do you know that Detroit is famous for having the best hotels in the country?"

"Really?"

Michelle nodded.

"And for having good food? Cause the places I've eaten at weren't much of anything."

"Those fancy hotels are a world of their own. They got menus an arm long. Green turtle soup and frog legs —"

Olivia made a face. "Who'd want to eat a frog? Or a turtle?"

"Detroit's swarming with gigantic bull frogs. Got one on display over at the market, weighs nine pounds."

"Ugh."

"Folks fry them frog legs up and think they're pretty good eating. They'll probably expect you to serve 'em at your boarding house."

"Then they're going to have a reason to complain." Olivia untied her hair and ran her fingers through it. "I went into that old French church."

"Ste. Anne's?"

"Yes. There's a portrait inside, by the door."

"That's Father Gabriel Richard. He's buried under the altar."

"Except for that big scar on his face, he looks sort of like the lawyer back in Five Rocks. The school kids call him Ichabod Crane and run away when they see him coming. That Father Gabriel is even stranger looking."

"Don't let no Detroiter hear you say a bad word about Father Gabriel."

"I didn't mean it as a bad word. It's just the truth. He is strange-looking. So is Mr. Carmichael, but he's a really good man. It got me thinking how so many exceptional people have unfortunate faces. Made me wonder if it's the burden of looking that way that compels them to good deeds, or if God makes them like that – virtuous, but not beautiful – to force us to recognize what is not important in the measure of a man."

"You talk like a book," Michelle said with a shake of her head.

"I'm just saying ..." Olivia sought the right words. "Remember I told you about that agent who followed me and Phillip from Backwoods? How he was so beautiful, with his blue eyes and wavy hair?"

Michelle nodded.

"Well, before Mr. Abraham left he told me the story about those agents in Kentucky setting his wagon on fire and burning those men alive." She waited for Michelle to nod again, indicating that she knew the story. "I keep trying to imagine that handsome-looking man as one of those agents. Passing a whiskey bottle and laughing. I guess beauty and goodness don't have anything to do with one another."

"We are what we are, no matter what we look like," Michelle said. "Oh, I forgot to tell you." She perked up, obviously glad for an excuse to change the subject. "While you were gone, a boy came over from the hotel, brought a letter for you. I put it on your bed, sort of tucked under the pillow."

Olivia recognized Mr. Carmichael's hand on the white envelope. What a coincidence that she had just been thinking about him. She sat cross-legged on the bed, turning the letter over a few times before tearing it open. It contained two sheets of paper, and she skimmed the cramped writing on the first, willing the words "Mourning Free" to leap from it. They did:

September, 1842

Dear Miss Killion,

I pray this letter finds you in good health and spirits.

Only a few days after your departure Mr. Mourning Free paid a brief visit to Five Rocks. I can imagine your distress upon hearing that you missed him by so short a time, but at least I can attest to his apparent good health. Unfortunately, I have no knowledge of his recent activities or plans for the future. As you requested, I informed him of your present situation and delivered your journals and other documents into his hand. However, he did not read them in my presence, but took them with him and a few hours later came to return them, asking me to continue to keep them in my safe. So I am unable to tell you anything of his reaction or intentions.

The second matter of which I must inform you is a sad one. Three days ago your excellent friend Mrs. Jettie Place passed away, taken by the consumption. Doc Gaylin assured me that though she had been afflicted by the symptoms in a relatively mild manner for some time, the end came upon her quickly and her suffering was not of great duration.

I have long served as Mrs. Place's attorney and drew up her Last Will and Testament. A few months ago she came to me desiring to change its instructions. Other than a few objects of sentimental value that she wished to leave to a cousin, she bequeathed all her earthly goods to you. This includes her house and bakery shop and all their contents, as well as the monies in her bank account (nine hundred and fifty-seven dollars). This matter is not known to any other person, and there is no reason it need ever be known. I am most willing to act on your behalf, if you would like me to arrange for the sale of these properties, while you, the seller, remain anonymous. If this is the case, I must ask you to sign the attached document and return it to me. It grants me your permission to act as your agent only in this specific matter.

My condolences on your loss, which I know to be great.

I remain always at your service,
L. A. Carmichael

Chapter Twenty-Four

Olivia read the page twice before letting it drop to her lap. A tangle of competing emotions paralyzed her, and it took a few moments and deep breaths to clear her mind. She forced herself to set aside the gloriously comforting certainty that Mourning knew about Little Boy. Neither did she allow herself to dwell on the implications of inheriting Jettie's estate. First she must confront the fact of Jettie's lonely death.

I should have guessed, she thought. Jettie looked so pale the last time I saw her and her cough was worse. How long had she been sick? No wonder she was so glad of my companionship. And then the moment I could, I went off and left her to die alone. After all she did for me. But I didn't know. How could I have known?

I could have paid more attention. All I ever did was worry about myself, as if no one else in the world ever had a problem. Poor Jettie. I wonder how many people were at the funeral. Doc Gaylin would have gone. And Mr. Carmichael. One of the ministers and a few do-gooders. Who had found her dead? Doc Gaylin? I hope she had a hired girl taking care of her. Poor Jettie. How many weeks did she lie there alone, waiting for the end?

Next came an unpleasant realization. What if I had known? Would I have stayed? Olivia hoped so, but closed her eyes, imagining being once again trapped in a house, waiting for someone to die. Only this time it would have been worse. I couldn't have born the inactivity, knowing Little Boy was out there. Of all the things Jettie did for me, that was the kindest – concealing her illness so well. How did she keep that smile on her face? Go to see Doc Gaylin without me knowing? Olivia searched her memory for dropped hints or unexplained absences, but could recall none.

Dear Jettie. She spared me that test and spared both of us the sorrow of me failing it. I've got no business saying, "If only I'd known." That's a lie. I most likely would have gone anyway. I would have said, "I'll be back just as soon as I can." I would have gone back to visit, but would I have stayed to take care of her? I don't know. I hope so, but I don't know. Olivia admitted that doubt with shame. Well, that's who I am. No use lying about it. And I guess there are worse things a person can be than selfish.

She summoned good memories of Mrs. Place, sitting in her chair, head bent to the lantern, squinting at her needlework. That first night, when Olivia had stood outside like a lost child, how lovely the sound of Jettie's voice had been. "Olivia Killion? Is that you?" You were a grand lady, Jettie Place.

Olivia could not for long keep her thoughts from Mourning Free and again felt ashamed. Do we grieve for the dead only according to how dependent we are upon them? Now that I don't need Jettie any more, is a few minutes of grief all she gets from me? No, that's not true. I will always remember her with love and gratitude. I will never allow anyone to speak ill of her in my presence. But there are living people to think of.

Mourning knows everything! Olivia almost clapped her hands as she put her hopes into words. He'll go ask about Little Boy and someone will tell him where he is. I'm sure to hear from him soon. She rose and paced, repeating that thought over and over. He'll probably come here and bring Little Boy with him. The boarding house will be ready just in time for them to move in. I'll use the money Jettie left me to pay back the loan, so no one will ever be able to take our home from us. There will be enough leftover to pay Mourning a salary and buy Little Boy everything he needs.

Then she allowed the unthinkable to slither into her consciousness – that big double bed in what would be her bedroom. She blushed, her face hot, as she relived those few hours she had lain with Mourning – his smooth skin, the scent of the crook of his neck, the way his fingers had played over her body. It was the first time she'd allowed those thoughts to linger in her mind. She'd been certain she would never again welcome the touch of a man, even in her imagination, but her body responded to the memory of Mourning's hands on her with shocking enthusiasm. She felt overwhelmed and laid back against the pillow. How can I think such things? What is wrong with me?

A hesitant rap on the door pulled Olivia out of her fantasy as Michelle's head appeared.

"Is everything all right? Oh, sorry, I didn't know you were sleeping."

"I'm not." Olivia sat up. "Come in. Come in." She knew she must look pale, disoriented.

"No bad news in that letter I hope."

"There was," Olivia said as she stood and shook her skirts to straighten them out. "But good news too." She touched Michelle's arm and they went out to the shop.

"How 'bout we walk down to King's for supper while you tell me about it?" Michelle suggested.

Olivia nodded, regaining her composure while they put on their hats and Michelle searched behind the counter for the key to the shop. Out on the sidewalk Olivia slipped her arm through Michelle's.

"The sad news is that an aunt of mine passed away. She was a lovely lady. I cared a great deal for her and will miss her. But there was also good news. Someone back home has been in contact with my friend."

"The colored fellow?"

"Yes. And they told him where I am, so I think I can expect a letter or more probably a visit from him soon."

"See I told you. What's so special about him anyway? And how'd a little white girly girl get to be such good friends with a colored boy?"

"We used to play together when we were little, even

though he's a few years older. He was pretty much my only friend."

"And why was that?"

"I don't know. I was always shy and quiet. And my family ... I don't think my classmates felt comfortable around me because of my father. He owned the only general store in town, and everyone's parents always owed him money. And I guess they were jealous, thinking we were rich and I could just go in the store and take all the candy I wanted. And my mother ... everyone always talked about her. She was different."

Olivia stared into the window of the shop they were passing and hoped Michelle would not pry deeper about her mother. She didn't. After a short pause Michelle asked, "Does your friend have a name?"

Olivia repeated the story about how Mourning had gotten his name – his mother dying in childbirth and the midwife wailing, "This poor mourning child. This poor mourning child."

"His stepfather used to do work for my father, fixing things in the store. Mourning did too, when he got old enough. That's how we became friends. A few years ago he married a colored girl and they had the cutest little boy, but then his wife passed away." Olivia was surprised by how easy the lies came to her. "When I decided to come to Michigan to claim my uncle's farm ... Oh here's a bench. I need to sit a moment. There's something in my shoe." Olivia was making the story up as she went along and needed a moment to collect her thoughts, to remember everything she had told Michelle in the past.

She waited for a couple strolling up the street to pass them by before she removed her shoe, shook it, and put it back on. When she rose again, she continued. "I asked Mourning if he'd like a job working the farm for me. He was supposed to meet me here in Michigan, but he never turned up. No one back home could say where he'd gotten to. So I've been awful worried about

215

him and his little boy. I just want to know they're all right. And now with the boarding house ... I could offer him a job. It would be easier for him to raise up his son on his own if he had that kind of situation."

"That's getting ahead of yourself, don't you think? You don't know that you'll be able to afford a hired man."

"Well, actually I do. That's the other good news. My aunt – the one who passed away – left me her house. And some money."

Michelle turned to face Olivia, told her how wonderful that was – about the money, not about her poor aunt dying – and gave her a hug. Olivia felt bad, counting the lies she had told her friend, but quickly soothed her conscience. Do I know where she got the money for her shop? How many men have visited her bed? If she's ever been pregnant? Same as that's none of my business, my private affairs are none of hers.

During supper Olivia steered the conversation toward the problems involved in running a business – how she would advertise the rooms for rent, whether she should offer meals only to her boarders or expand the dining room into a small restaurant, how much she would have to pay someone to help with the cleaning and laundry. Afterwards they linked arms again and strolled east on Jefferson Avenue.

As they approached the Michigan Exchange Hotel they heard sounds of a great commotion – music, laughing, clapping, and what sounded like crockery breaking. Olivia tugged on Michelle's arm, pulling her up Randolph Street and around to the back, where the dining room windows opened onto a porch that ran the width of the hotel. Inside they could see long, elaborately set tables, from which the dirty dishes had not been cleared. Around one of them stood a crowd of young women in shiny evening gowns, officers in dress uniform, and men in ruffled shirts. All eyes were on a handsome young man with a shock of white-blonde hair who had climbed onto the table to dance. Obviously inebriated, he was slowly progressing down the length of the table, doing his best to obliterate every piece of delicate china he passed. Olivia watched in horror as his boot sent a cut-glass vase of flowers to shatter on the floor. He took a stiff bow and then raised his foot to take aim at a delicate white pitcher.

"What's the matter with him? Why aren't they stopping him?"

"That's their idea of a good time. Come on, let's go."

"We have to go in the hotel, find the manager."

"I'm sure he knows. And he knows that Daddy will pay for the damage."

Olivia found no words to express her outrage. How could anyone find entertainment in the destruction of beautiful things? She imagined how the artisans who had labored long hours to create those objects would feel, watching them smashed to bits. For fun. Who was that stupid clod to kick them aside, without a thought? How he could bear to sully the white tablecloth with his boots, let alone destroy everything in sight?

"Just because he has money, he thinks he can deliberately ruin other people's things?"

"He doesn't think he can. He knows he can." Michelle turned away and pulled on Olivia's elbow.

Olivia didn't budge. She couldn't stop staring at the scene inside. One dirty dinner plate after another sailed through the air and shattered, dripping gravy and scattering bits of food on the hardwood floor. Each was followed by a lovely water goblet. The young women with their carefully coifed hair and fancy dresses gathered their skirts and stepped back, but they were all laughing. None of them seemed to find anything disturbing about this behavior.

"Don't they know there are people over at the poor house with hardly a plate to eat from?"

"Aren't you a lamb – expecting that crew to give a whit about poor folks. Come on, let's get out of here."

217

"Who are those people?"

"I was referring to rich folks in general. That particular bunch of rich folks in there calls itself the 400 Club. It's private. Very exclooo-sive. You gotta be invited to join, and that don't happen if you ain't in the swim with them nabobs. Believe me, all of that lot has enough money, they can break all the dishes they want. And that ain't the worst they do. After the river freezes they race horses on it. Don't bother them none if the ice breaks. Rider's a big hero, climbing out of the cold water. So what if the poor horse drowns? Money buys another one. They throw themselves a lot of fancy cotillions like this. Lucky for me and you, we don't gotta worry about what to wear." She looked over at Olivia, who wore a sad frown. "But if you like dancing, there's another club. They call it the Boys Club. It's for regular people. Each boy invites a girl, and they take turns having it in their homes."

Olivia seemed to have stopped listening to Michelle and shook her head. "I can imagine having lots of money and wanting to spend it on nice things for your family and friends. That would be wonderful. But to throw it away? When there are people who go hungry? And risking the life of your horse for fun?"

"Lordie, lordie." Michelle clucked her tongue. Then she stopped again and gave Olivia another hug. "You try and keep thinking like that. This can be a hard world to stay good-hearted in, but you do your best. Try to restore my faith in human nature. You come on home now. I got to get some sleep."

Before she went to bed that night Olivia signed Mr. Carmichael's document and wrote a reply to him, feeling all grown-up.

Dear Mr. Carmichael,
I was indeed sorry to learn of the death of Mrs. Place, who was the best possible friend to me.
I would be most glad to retain your services, as

218

you so kindly offered. Please sell the house and bakery and take whatever fee is due to you, both for this and for your previous assistance to me. I would also much appreciate it if you could use some of whatever money is left in Mrs. Place's account to arrange for a proper headstone for her grave. It should be of the same size and general design as my father's. The inscription, after the dates of birth and death, should read, "Beloved friend, woman of truly Christian heart." Obviously, you must also reimburse yourself for the efforts this requires of you. I don't wish to put you to trouble, but if there is a way for you to arrange, during the warm months, to have flowers placed on her grave each Sunday and pay for this out of the account, I would also be grateful for that. And yes, I would like to remain anonymous in all these transactions.

Also, there are a few items in Mrs. Place's home that I would like to have. The first is a hairbrush, wooden with carving on its back. It belonged to my mother, but I made a Christmas gift of it to Mrs. Place, as I was unable to purchase anything for her. Also a decorative comb, encrusted with stones, that was also my mother's and also a gift to Mrs. Place for the same reason. Other items I would like to keep:

Volume of Wordsworth's poetry, with an inscription from me (probably on the stand by her bed)

Shiny red dress and white feather boa (in her wardrobe)

Mantel clock (on a shelf in the upstairs hallway)

Bottle of scent (on her dressing table)

Pictures from a journal (on the walls of the kitchen)

China figurines of women from different foreign countries (china cabinet in the parlor)

Basket of needlework (next to a chair in the parlor)

There is no need to arrange shipment of these things. They can be packed in a crate and stored until the next time I travel to Five Rocks.

I would like you to feel free to keep any of the furnishings for which you can find use. There is a lovely rocking chair in the parlor that I think would be nice for you to have next to the stove in your office, or in your home if you don't already have one there. Please do me the favor of removing that and any other things that could serve you well. I hate to think of a person's belongings being discarded after their passing, rather than used by a good friend.

I intend to remain in Detroit and have completed the purchase of a boarding house. It is on the west side of Detroit (or I suppose it is actually the southwest), just outside the city limits, in view of the Detroit River. The nearest road north of it is Michigan Avenue, which is also referred to as the Chicago Road. For now, letters can be addressed to me care of Chez Mademoiselle Lafleur on Fort Street. The road on which my house stands has not yet been honored with a name and so will not have an address until either the road gets a name or I give one to my establishment. I am thinking of calling it something that includes my initials – OK Accommodations. Friends here have objected, saying that OK – the abbreviation of the ridiculous spelling "oll korrect," which as you probably know has come to be used to mean "all right" – is too humble a description. Personally, I appreciate its connotation of sufficient but not extravagant. I would value hearing your always appreciated opinion.

The banker who arranged financing for the purchase of the boarding house is Mr. Richard Wentworth of the Michigan Insurance Bank. I have no understanding of such matters, but believe there to be a way that you can transfer to me the money from the sale of Mrs. Place's property (of course, after deducting what is due to you) care of Mr. Wentworth. Any way that you can arrange that with Mr. Wentworth is "OK" with me.

I thank you in advance for your most appreciated assistance. Your friendship continues to afford me a peace of mind I would not otherwise enjoy.

Sincerely,
Olivia Killion

The next day, after she'd had her breakfast and delivered the letter to the Post Master, Olivia walked to Thompson's Livery. She told the owner that Mr. Abraham had sent her and she wished to buy an even-natured mare.

"You want to ride it or work it?" he asked.

"Ride."

"Sandy in there is the calmest horse I ever had in my care." He led Olivia into the barn and stopped by the stall of a sorrel mare with big brown eyes. "You wouldn't want to be robbing no bank and trying to make your get away on her, but it takes a lot to get her riled. Walks right past snakes in the road and hardly turns her head for a gun shot. She ain't no filly and I wouldn't harness her to a buggy, but she'll do you fine for a riding horse. I could let you have her for $80 and throw in the saddle and bridle what came with her, though I s'pose you'll be wantin' a side saddle. I ain't got none a them, but I can tell you who does."

"No, your saddle will do just fine. What would you

say to $70?" Olivia made her first attempt at negotiating.

"That could do."

Olivia stood for a moment, looking Sandy straight in the face, and then let herself into the stall and stroked the horse's neck. Sandy nodded her head agreeably. "I'll take her," Olivia said. "That is, assuming you can continue to board her for me for at least another two months."

"That ain't no problem."

"I'll have to come back in a few days with the money."

"That ain't no problem. You want me to saddle her up for you now so you can take a ride, make sure you two get on all right?"

"Yes, I would, but in just a few minutes. I saw a beautiful blue blanket in a window across the street." She turned to speak to the horse. "You want a brand new blanket, don't you girl? All nice and soft."

"Well, you go get your blanket. I ain't going nowhere."

"You don't mind if I change her name, do you?"

"Your horse. What you got a mind to call her?"

"I don't know yet. I have to get to know her better."

Olivia returned with the blanket and a bag of apples and fed one of them to Sandy. Then she saddled the horse and mounted, managing to arrange her skirts to cover her legs almost to the tops of her high boots, hiding the trousers she wore underneath. She rode north, close to the river and past Hog Island. She found a quiet place to dismount, fed Sandy another apple, and then sat near her, listening to the river as she told the horse all about Mrs. Jettie Place and what a kind, generous, and courageous woman she had been. Olivia didn't shed any tears. The words Mr. Carmichael had spoken after her father's death had stayed in her mind: that's the way the world is. It's what we're meant to do, she thought. Live the best way we can. And then we're meant to die.

After she returned Sandy to the livery Olivia went shopping. She bought another beige flat cap, three men's shirts, three pairs of boy's work trousers, and a shotgun.

Olivia's morning walks were replaced by morning rides. The trees were changing color and the autumn weather was brisk. At first she always wore a work dress over her trousers, but soon stopped bothering with it. Before long she even ventured into the hotel dining room wearing trousers and a man's shirt with billowing sleeves. The other guests stared, but she ignored them.

One evening when she brought Sandy back to the livery she asked Mr. Thompson where there was a bridge to cross the River Rouge on horseback. She wanted to explore farther south of her property, but the Rouge always blocked her path and she'd found no spot shallow enough to wade across.

"Ain't none. Always been talk of building one, but now they ain't got no money for what they call internal improvements. Not the state and not the city."

"So how do people get to the other side?"

"Swim the horses. You got a wagon, you tie two a them canoes together, get enough men together to lift it onto them."

She rode to the Rouge again the next morning, but decided to forego putting Sandy's swimming abilities to that kind of test and so arrived home early. That was the day she declared a change. No more tavern food for them. She was going out to do some shopping and from now on she would prepare their meals. She needed the practice. Michelle responded by pouring two glasses from a bottle she referred to as the best French wine, though Olivia suspected it was made in someone's backyard from the grapes that grew wild on the islands in the river.

Chapter Twenty-Five

Mr. Wentworth hired a barrel-shaped colored carpenter named Bayliss Fletcher to perform the renovations on OK Accommodations. Mr. Fletcher had a dense carpet of graying hair, bulging cheeks, and round wire spectacles. He always wore the same threadbare green frock coat and had a gray-green floppy felt hat to go with it. The muslin shirt under his coat was invariably fastened tight, all the way up to the top button.

The day after Mrs. Rafferty moved out Mr. Fletcher and three other colored men began repairing and painting the barn and the outside of the house, in a hurry to finish the outdoors jobs before the snow came. Olivia left it to Mr. Fletcher to decide what needed doing, but did have an opinion regarding colors.

"That blue-grey on the siding is fine. You can just paint over with more of the same color. And the porch columns and railing can stay white. So can the door jambs, window casings, sills, and aprons. And all that lacy stuff under the roof. But I want a bit of color. I'm going to go pick out a nice dark blue and a deep reddish-maroon. The maroon will be for around the windows. You know, the frames and those things that separate the panes." She drew a cross-hatch in the air with her index finger.

Mr. Fletcher nodded.

"And the dark blue will be for the shutters. So you'll see the maroon of the window frames, then the white of the casings, and then the blue of the shutters. Don't you think that would look nice and cheery, Mr. Fletcher?"

"Yes Miss, that sound right pretty."

"It won't be bright red. I don't mean for the house to look like a flag. It'll be maroon."

"Yes Miss."

"Leave the front door for last. I won't know if I want it to be maroon or dark blue until I see the rest of the house. And I don't know about the steps and the floor of the porch. Do you think they would look nice painted dark blue or maroon?"

Mr. Fletcher shook his head. "I don't know much 'bout look, Miss, but you paint a floor a dark color, you gonna see ever speck a dirt on it."

"Oh. So what color would you make them?"

"Same blue-gray as the house."

"I guess you've painted a lot of houses."

"Yes Miss."

"Do you really think the way I said to paint the windows will look all right?"

"Yes Miss. Real pretty. Just that much color gonna perk it up real nice."

At Olivia's expense the men were also going to add four tiny rooms at the back – two off Olivia's dressing room, intended for her precious shower and water closet, and two off the side of the kitchen to provide similar facilities for her boarders. No one had yet worked out the mechanics of how these wonders would function, but the ground outside them sloped away from the house enough that drainage shouldn't be a problem. Once the outside was finished, Mr. Fletcher would do the inside work alone. No one but he and Olivia would know which walls he had torn down and where the secret compartments were. Then he would bring the other workmen back to paint the inside.

Olivia often stopped by on her morning ride. She rarely did more than glance around, not wanting Mr. Fletcher to think she had come to oversee or interfere. She called out to wish the men a good day and then sat on the front porch, chair tipped back and feet up on the wooden railing. Mr. Fletcher eventually joined her, though he never sat without being invited. They smiled and exchanged pleasantries, but mostly remained silent, enjoying the breeze and the apple cider Olivia brought. He was proper and polite and pretended not to notice Olivia's unladylike trousers and deportment. He gave her a report on how the work was progressing without being asked. Finally, one day in November, she asked him to show her the hiding places and followed him into the barn, where he had built a storeroom. He opened the lock on its door and they both stepped inside. The right-hand wall was covered with shelves on which stood sacks of salt, bottles of oil, bars of soap and other household goods.

"This be the one you gonna use most," he said, as he moved the sack at the end of one of the shelves aside. "See this old knothole? Stick your finger in here, get it around the latch, and pull up."

She did so and the shelves swung out like a door, revealing a space that looked large enough for four people to sleep in. Mr. Fletcher went in and Olivia followed him

"Now do the same thing here." He pointed at another knot hole, on the right wall of the hiding place.

She did and a second door on that wall opened toward them, on another, slightly smaller space.

"That's clever of you." Olivia nodded in approval.

"Wait." He stepped inside. "That ain't it yet." He kicked the hay and rags on the floor aside, bent down to open a trap door, and stood aside. Olivia got down on her knees and saw a ladder descending into a dark space. She stuck her head in and looked around in awe. The floor was packed dirt, but the walls were shored up with thick beams. More beams had been laid across the floor to keep three mattresses off the dirt. They won't be able to stand up straight, she thought, but seven or eight people can probably sit down there. A small family could get a good night's sleep.

"How on earth did you do this without anyone noticing?" she asked. "That hole in the ground is enormous."

He beamed proudly. "That the first thing I done. Before you or anyone else been around. Mr. Faraday came with two men and we dug all night. Afternoon of the next day, it all covered by the storeroom."

"What did you do with all that dirt?" She looked around, still astonished.

"Dumped it down on the riverbank. Not too close to the house, up the road a bit."

"Well, I wouldn't want to have to spend much time down there, but it's amazing. No one will ever find it." She backed out of the room smiling and then frowned. "But you know they can't have a lantern down there. The whole barn could go up in smoke."

"Can't have one anyway. Light gonna show through the cracks. Couldn't make the floor too tight or ain't gonna be 'nuff air down there."

She took a few steps away and turned to study the storeroom. "But if anyone is paying attention, they'll see right away that the outside wall is way longer than what you see inside."

He seemed eager to respond to that remark. "Day after tomorrow you ain't gonna see that side of the wall no more." He walked to the right end of the storeroom and indicated the wide space left between it and the wall of the barn. "This be where you gonna store your hay. Mr. Wentworth sending a lot a wagons full a bales. We gonna stack 'em here, fill up this space, and cover this part of the wall here, where there ain't s'pose to be no storeroom. Few more rows of bales sticking out here in front and making steps right up. Bales of hay gonna cover every bit of the roof. No one gonna think they's anything here but a big pile food for your horse, stacked up right next to your little storeroom."

She nodded her head, imagining this, but asked, "Aren't those bales of hay awfully heavy? Likely to collapse the whole roof."

"Ain't no worry," he replied and Olivia could see how pleased he was to have answers to all her questions. "You can't see it from here, but I put up a nice strong frame of two by fours between the back wall of your storeroom and the wall of the barn. Ends right level with the roof. We pile the hay up to here." He stood by the front wall and pointed to the flat roof. Then we lay more two by fours over the roof, one end resting on that frame, other end on these bales of hay here. Then we pile some more rows of bales over them beams. Hay be heavy, but it gonna hold itself up."

She nodded. "Yes, that's very clever. I see you've thought of everything."

He started walking toward the back door of the house. "They's small spaces under the stairs and behind a wall in the pantry, but they won't hold but two people each and I don't guess you ever gonna use 'em. No way to put no one in there without all your boarders seein'. But there was room, so I sealed 'em off, just in case." He quickly showed them to her.

"The one in your room is the only one you gonna use, you ever got to bring people inside." He led Olivia to her dressing room. "It s'pose to hold three people. Standing," Mr. Fletcher said. "Your frocks gonna be hanging on a pole, right here in front of it, so ain't no one gonna see the door."

"I can't see it now, without anything in front of it." Olivia nodded in approval.

The knothole for the latch on this door was only a few inches from the floor. She stooped down to open the door, stepped inside, and pulled the door shut after her.

"My goodness, it's close in here," she said through the wall.

"Bigger the space be, easier it be to find. 'Sides ain't no one gonna be in there very long." He pulled the door open. "Law says you gotta let them catchers come inside and search your house. Don't say nothin' 'bout havin' to let 'em stay around all day. Specially not in a lady's dressing room."

Olivia stepped out and looked at the door again, amazed at the way it disappeared when she closed it. Then she went to her room, to the back window, opened it and stuck her head out.

"It wouldn't be so easy to climb in," she said. "I mean this window is pretty high off the ground, and if anyone ever needs to hide in the dressing room, this would be the way they'd have to get into the house."

"You wantin', I can make a little bench, set it out there."

"That would be great, if you have the time."

He nodded. "Ain't much left to do 'cept the painting and cleaning up. And you said you don't care so much 'bout moving in 'fore Christmas."

"No, I don't. In fact, even if the house is ready, I don't believe I want to move until after the holiday." Olivia watched him out of the corner of her eye, garnering the courage to ask him a question of a personal nature. "I hope you won't mind me asking you this, Mr. Fletcher, but were you ever a slave?"

"Yes Miss, I been a slave."

"And you ran away?"

"No Miss. My Master Stuart, he be a different sort of soul. He let his slaves buy their freedom."

Olivia turned to face him, puzzled. "How can a person buy anything, when they have to work without getting paid?"

"He dint pay us nothin' for the slave hours. You gotta work for him ten hours a day. Eleven when they's planting and harvest. Them be your slave hours. You willin' to work more than that, he pay you. Even let you hire out to his neighbor, you be wantin'. Me, I be good at makin' furniture. Can do that all I want in the evening, after I give him my slave hours. Master Stuart let me sell what I make, keep the money. Take me a lot of years to save up enough to buy my freedom papers, but here I be."

Olivia was relieved that the question hadn't

offended him. He appeared pleased for them to finally be having a conversation about something other than the house.

"How long have you been in Detroit?"

"'Bout a year. Mr. Herschel Abraham done bringed me. You know him?"

"Yes," Olivia said, smiling. "I met him right here at this house, the day I decided to buy it."

"I been down in Ohio when I met him, walking up a road, wondering where I gonna take myself now that I be free. Then I see this short man in a big coat standing next to his wagon, cursing like to bust a gut. He been speaking some strange language, but ain't no question – that man be cursing. Wheel come off his wagon so I help him fix it, and he tell me that Michigan be a good place for a colored man. Say I can ride along with him."

"Do you have any family?"

"Got a wife, but she still be down in slavery. Soon's I save 'nother two hundert dollars, I'm a go down there and buy her."

"Is she also working extra and saving her money?"

"No. She can't. She be slaving for the neighbor man, Master Drew."

"And Master Drew isn't unusual, like Master Stuart?"

"No Miss. He 'bout as usual a man as you ever gonna see. But Master Stuart be his friend, sort of. Got him to promise he gonna sell my wife to me, soon's I got the money." He stood up. "I best get back to work."

Olivia remained on the porch, thinking as she listened to the sounds of Mr. Fletcher's hammer. Then she rode into the city, to the Michigan Insurance Bank, and asked Mr. Wentworth if Mr. Fletcher was paid the same wage a white man would receive for the same work.

"No colored gets paid the same as a white man."

"Surely you must think they should."

"It doesn't matter what I think. That's the way

things are."

That evening while Olivia and Michelle were having their supper, Olivia asked Michelle if she believed it was common for white masters to force themselves on their female slaves.

"There probably are some what don't, but going by the stories I hear from the women passing through Finney's barn, most a them southern gentlemen surely do like to visit their slave quarters at night. But I'll tell you, those slave women aren't nearly as afraid of their masters as they are of their masters' wives. Women got a lot more cruelty in them than men. Especially if they find out a slave woman is carrying the Master's child. I've heard of one ordering the overseer to nail that pregnant woman's ear to a whipping post and cut it clean off."

"Oh Lord." The color left Olivia's face.

"How come you're so interested in this all of a sudden?"

"You know Mr. Fletcher – the colored man doing the work on the house? His wife is still down south. In slavery. He's saving up his money to go get her."

Michelle sucked her front teeth and then held Olivia's gaze and said, "I already know what you're thinking. But you can't buy all the slaves in the south."

"I know I can't. But there's not a single reason I can't help buy this one."

The next day she rode to the boarding house and called out for Mr. Fletcher. He quickly came out and removed his hat.

"Good morning, Mr. Fletcher. Yesterday you said the carpentry work was as good as finished. Do you know someone who could take over for you here? Finish up painting the inside?"

"Miss, I been doing a right good job. Come and see. You ain't hardly never been inside, ain't seen the

231

kitchen. You gonna like it."

Olivia frowned at him for a moment until she understood his concern. "Oh no, goodness, I didn't mean anything like that. I'm not dismissing you. I have looked at your work and am more than pleased with it. But there's something else I need you to do for me. That's why I was thinking that perhaps we could find someone else to finish up the painting. Do you know anyone?"

"Yes Miss. I know a lot of men be lookin' for work."

"All right then, I have a business proposition for you. I'm not going to be able to run this place by myself. I've been looking for someone to help with the laundry and cleaning, but so far haven't found anyone I'm inclined to hire. Then it occurred to me that your wife would probably be perfect, a lot more dependable than some young girl. And she'll need to work after she gets her freedom, won't she?"

"Yes Miss," he said carefully.

"Well, I can't sit around waiting for you to save up enough money. I need someone now. So I'll lend you the money and I would like you to go get her."

He stared at her, his face blank.

"You can pay me back by her working here. Don't worry. I'm not trying to trick her into some northern kind of slavery. I'll pay her a fair wage and she doesn't have to keep working here if she doesn't like it. But I'd like her to give it a fair try. And the two of you could let one of the rooms here, if you like. I won't have a job to offer you, but it would be good to have a man on the premises who knows how to fix things. That could be part of the bargain – you doing odd jobs as they come up. When you're not busy with your regular job and for pay of course. Does that sound fair to you?"

"Yes Miss. That sound right fair." He spoke softly, almost a whisper, and his eyes grew shiny.

Embarrassed, Olivia looked away and raised the volume of her own voice. "Well then, let's sit down and have our cider. Drink to our new business arrangement."

After they were seated and each had a glass of cider, she took a small pouch of gold coins from her pocket and handed it to him. "There's three hundred dollars in there. Two hundred for Mrs. Fletcher and the rest to get yourself down there and back. I'm planning to buy a buggy anyway, so I'd like you to use part of the other hundred dollars to buy one for me. Get a used one if you can, as long as it's in good repair. But it's got to have a front and back seat, so I'll be able to give my boarders a ride into town with me."

He stared at her blankly, as if unable to take in what she was saying. She plunged on.

"I don't want to buy a team to pull it just yet, so you'll have to rent one from Thompson's. Once you've got a buggy it shouldn't take you more than a week to get to where your wife is and back, should it?"

"No Miss. Not 'less they's problems."

"You mean like Master Drew refusing to sell her?"

He nodded.

"Or with the patrols?"

He nodded again.

"You've got your Free Man of Color paper, don't you?"

"Yes Miss."

"Good. But I won't have you going down there alone. We'll hire a white man to ride along with you. I'll ask Mr. Wentworth to find someone trustworthy who could use a few days pay. Someone young and strong who knows how to use a gun." Someone like young Phillip, she thought.

She paused and lifted the skin to pour them both another glass of cider. "Is there anything else you can think of that you'll need?"

"No, Miss Killion." He bounced the bag of coins in his palm, as if weighing it.

"Well," Olivia handed him his glass of cider and

lifted hers. "Let's drink to Mrs. Fletcher soon being a free woman."

"Maryam," he said. "Her name be Maryam. And I called Bayliss."

"I know." Olivia nodded and clinked her glass against his. "Here's to Maryam. I look forward to meeting her." She drained her glass quickly. "Now let's get back to our old business. Is the shower room finished?"

"Yes, Miss, but like I told Mr. Wentworth, I don't know nothin' 'bout layin' down no pipes and puttin' in no steam pump."

"No matter. We'll get someone to do that later. An expert. Might be best to wait till the spring anyway, after the ground thaws out. All that matters is that the rooms are sealed up tight before winter."

In any case, she now had barely enough money left to buy food to start feeding her boarders, let alone pay someone to put a shower in. That would have to wait until Mr. Carmichael sold Jettie's property and sent her the money.

Olivia smiled at Mr. Fletcher and said. "You know, now that I think about it again, if you're only going to be gone a week or so, there's no point in getting someone else to work here. Why risk someone nosing around, knocking on walls and noticing that there's a hollow space behind some of them?"

That morning she had begun thinking about going back to Five Rocks for Christmas. Her family would surely appreciate a visit, and she wouldn't be taking any vacations once she had boarders. It would also give her a chance to question Mr. Carmichael about Mourning and discuss Jettie's property. Perhaps he would even have some money for her. But as she stared at the river she realized it was a bad idea. If winter came early, the river and Lake Erie could freeze over while she was gone, leaving her stuck in Five Rocks until the spring thaw. She'd heard of people driving sleighs along the frozen banks, but could think of few things less appealing than shivering under buffalo robes, in constant fear of falling through the ice into the lake.

It suddenly occurred to Olivia that she had no idea where Mr. Fletcher lived. "Do your accommodations ... When you get back, will you have a place for Mrs. Fletcher?"

"That ain't no problem. I sleep on the floor."

"No need for that. There are plenty of beds upstairs. The two of you are welcome to stay here, if you can stand the smell of paint. I assume you'll be living here for a while anyway, once we're open. If you like, you can choose one of the rooms on the second floor. Take one of the two that face the back. I don't know who my other boarders are going to be, and I don't want any strangers in a room that has a view of the barn."

He nodded.

"Well, you'd better get to it. You might as well go home and start making whatever arrangements you need to make. The sooner you leave, the sooner you'll be back, and you want to get your traveling done before the snow comes." She offered him her hand. "I wish you and Mrs. Fletcher a safe journey. I'm going right now to speak with Mr. Wentworth, explain everything and get him looking for someone to accompany you. I'm so thankful you can do this. I haven't been able to sleep at night, worrying how I'll be able to take in a house full of boarders without any help." She turned and skipped down the porch steps.

He stood, looking dumbfounded. "When you gonna look over the buggy I be thinkin' to buy?" he called after her.

"No need for that. If it looks good to you and the price is reasonable, go ahead and buy it." She hopped to get her foot in the stirrup. "I trust your judgment. I certainly don't know anything about picking one out. Waiting for me to look at it would be a waste of time." She threw her leg over Sandy's back. "There are no end of buggies for sale and plenty of young white men needing work, so I don't see why you shouldn't be ready to leave in a day or two."

Ten days later, when Olivia went to the livery after breakfast to saddle up her horse, Mr. Thompson came out of his office.

"Last night that Nigra fella you got working for you brung back the team he's been using. Must have left that buggy he bought over to your place."

"Oh. That's good. I'll have to start thinking about buying a team. Or a horse anyway." She tried to hide the excitement in her voice. She would have told Mr. Thompson about Bayliss going down south to bring his wife back, but knew she had to get out of the habit of volunteering information. She might as well start now.

"'Fore he brought the team back, Finney seen him turn up your drive. Had a woman on the seat next to him. Said she was a scrawny little thing. Black as coal. Then he must have walked the team into town."

"Oh. That so?" She kept her voice disinterested.

"Must have left that woman at your place."

"I don't know about that." She shrugged.

She busied herself with Sandy and then rode out of the livery, straight to the boarding house. When she turned up the drive she saw a thin, barefoot woman with a kerchief around her head. She was bending over a pail to wring out a work dress and hang it on the line. The woman heard the clop of Sandy's hooves and looked up, an expression of fear on her face.

Olivia dismounted at a distance and slowly approached her. "Hullo. You must be Mrs. Fletcher. I am Olivia Killion."

"Oh, Miss Killion, my Bayliss done told me 'bout you, 'bout all you done for us." She took Olivia's hand in both of hers and seemed inclined to fall to her knees, though to Olivia's great relief she remained upright. "God bless you, Miss. I ain't got no words what can

236

thank you. One day I been working in the kitchen and hear a buggy comin', and who be driving it but my Bayliss? Ain't three days go by 'fore I be in that buggy with him, on my way to freedom."

Olivia heard pounding from inside the house. "Mr. Fletcher's working already?"

"Oh yes Miss. He got his mind set that ever thing gonna be ready 'fore Christmas."

"Have you gotten settled in all right? I assume you're staying here?"

"Yes Miss." Mrs. Fletcher looked frightened again. "Bayliss say that be all right."

"Of course. Of course it's all right. I hope he told you how much I'm going to need your help." Olivia shivered and looked down at the woman's bare feet and thin cotton dress. "Aren't you freezing?"

"It surely be cold up north in Michigan. But Bayliss, he gonna get me some clothes, soon as them stores in town open up."

"Didn't Master Drew or his wife give you anything to take?"

"I ain't got but my two dresses, but Bayliss had a blanket in the buggy, so I been fine."

Olivia's first impulse was to throw Mrs. Fletcher in the saddle behind her and ride straight to *Chez Mademoiselle Lafleur* for clothes and footwear, but she quickly dismissed that notion. No one should have to go into their new hometown for the first time looking that pitiful, half-dressed and no shoes.

"But surely you aren't going to walk all the way into town barefoot."

"Ain't no thing. I custom to that."

"No, no. That's no way to start a new life. I'm going to bring you some shoes and other things," Olivia said. "You go wrap yourself in your blanket until I get back."

"I ain't no lazy bones, Miss," she said anxiously. "I'm a start workin' right away."

Olivia turned to look into her eyes. "Mrs. Fletcher,

237

don't worry. You're going to have plenty of work to do. But you had a long journey, and all you need to do now is get some rest. Besides, you'll make yourself sick standing out here in the cold. Then what good will you be to me?" She touched the woman's arm and spoke more softly. "You're free now. You don't have to be afraid of anyone. Certainly not of me. I want you to go get your blanket, wrap yourself up in it, and sit there on the porch enjoying the day. Don't you dare move until I get back. Just sit there watching the river and remembering everything about this day. The first day of your new life." After a pause, Olivia asked, "Have you had anything to eat?"

"Yes Miss." Maryam Fletcher stared at the ground, looking bewildered. "Bayliss done get us some victuals on the way."

"Say good morning to Mr. Fletcher for me. I'll be back lickety-click."

Olivia rode off and soon returned with moccasins, warm stockings, a woolen dress, and a sweater bulging out of her saddle pack. A pot and frying pan were tied across her back. Long tin containers filled with soup and porridge dangled from either side of a thin rope that hung over Sandy's back. Mrs. Fletcher was sitting on the porch, obediently huddled under a blanket. Olivia freed herself from the kitchenware and handed the moccasins to Mrs. Fletcher.

"I didn't know your size," she said, "but thought these might do until you can get some proper shoes." Then she handed her the rest of the clothing and went inside to put the food in the kitchen and look for Mr. Fletcher. She found him upstairs doing something to one of the windows.

"Good morning. It's wonderful to see you safely back. Your wife is a lovely woman."

He straightened up and looked as uncomfortable in Olivia's presence as his wife did.

"Did you have any trouble with your wife's master?"

"No, Miss. My Master Stuart, he surely be most unusual. I be ascared Maryam's Master Drew ain't gonna let her go, so I go see Master Stuart first. He say I's right to be ascared. It don't matter none what Master Drew promised – that one white man what don't hold with no niggers going free, not on no 'ccount. So Master Stuart say he gonna tell Master Drew that it be him wantin' to buy Maryam. So I give him the money, and I's surely ascared he maybe gonna put it in his pocket and that be the end of everything. Like what most white men gonna do to a colored." Then he blinked nervously. "Down south, I mean. Them white men down south. But he done just like he said and they ain't no trouble at all. Master Drew right glad to sell Maryam, 'ccount of she ain't so young no more."

"And no patrols bothered you?"

"We seen two a them, but they don't do nothin' 'cept look at our papers and wish us a good day. Young fella Mr. Wentworth sent with me be a big boy, look like he coulda knocked them chasers down to Louisiana with one punch."

Olivia smiled, relieved that he had no horrifying stories to tell.

He stared at the floor. "We both so full a thanks to you, Miss Killion. I can't hardly believe my Maryam be here. Just two weeks ago I been figuring it take me another two years to save up that money, and Lord knows what can happen to a body in two years. Master Drew could sell her off and I never find her. I'm a pay you back that money, ever cent. I ain't got no words to thank you enough –"

"Mr. Fletcher, I know you're both grateful, but please don't feel that you have to keep saying so. You're already paying me back. The kitchen is beautiful. All of your work is. You're not beholden to me. If not for you I would never have such a lovely home. What I can't understand is why on earth you're working this morning –"

"I been gone long enough, when I should a been working."

"Bosh. What I want you to do now is put your tools away. I don't want to see you working any more today. Or for the next two days. Spend them with your wife. Take her into town and get her some warm clothes and whatever else you need. I brought one fry pan and one pot. They're in the kitchen. There's also a tin of beef soup and another one of porridge. And a skin of cider."

"That be most kind of you."

"I've already bought all the things we'll need to equip the kitchen. Ordered them from two stores on Jefferson – Wetmore's Crockery and Payment's Dry Goods. When I get back to town I'll go tell them to deliver it all, so don't be surprised if you find crates on the porch. Just put the boxes in the kitchen and use whatever you need. I'll leave buying food up to you. It's a beautiful day to show Mrs. Fletcher around Detroit. Might even warm up enough to take a ride on one of the ferry boats." She turned to leave.

He cleared his throat and said, "Miss Killion, Lord know you be the most kind-hearted woman ..." He paused, obviously searching for words.

"Is something wrong?" Olivia asked.

"Well, Miss Killion, truth be, you 'bout collapsed my Maryam's poor heart, callin' her 'Mrs.' and tellin' her to sit on the porch of a white lady's house, right out front where anyone can see."

"Oh."

"Folks be gettin' used to freedom fast enough, but ain't *no one* get used to *nothin'* that fast. Week ago she been working in Master Drew's kitchen. Some days she be out in the fields, overseer with his big black whip standin' over her. She don't know her place, he gonna whip her bloody. Then I come and bring her to this crazy white woman – waitin' on her, aksin' if she be hungry, sayin' she gonna go get her some shoes. Done took all the courage she got, talkin' to you like she done.

And she ain't never had no shoes. Not never in her life. Now she think she done somethin' wrong, gonna be in trouble, cause she ain't got none."

"Oh. I'm sorry. So what should I do?"

He sighed. "Call her Maryam. And me Bayliss. Or Fletcher. No more Mr. and Mrs. And maybe ..." He hesitated.

"Maybe what?"

He took a deep breath. "I know it ain't my place to aks and it sound uppity to my own ears, but if I ain't gonna do no work ..."

"Please Mr. ... I mean Bayliss, tell me how I can be helpful."

"Maybe you could stop comin' 'round here for a few days. I's sorry to aks you that ..."

"No, no." She held her raised palm out toward him. "It's perfectly all right. I'm the one who needs to apologize, for being such a blockhead. Acting like she's some tourist, up here to see the sights. I should have thought about what a big change this is. I should have realized how much the two of you need time alone together."

He smiled and shook his head. "Indeed," he said. "You know, Miss Killion, we ain't never in our lives had no time alone together. Not five minutes. Not even the night we been wed. Ain't never been in a room alone together. Master Stuart give me leave to visit her 'bout ever week, but she ain't got her own cabin. She sharin' it with another family."

Olivia paled. "Oh. I never thought about that. I guess there are a lot of things I never thought about. Please tell me if I do or say anything else that makes this more difficult for her."

"She be fine. Freedom be easy to get custom to."

"So I'll see you on Thursday." She briefly placed her hand on his forearm, smiled, and left the room.

When she came onto the porch Maryam leapt to her feet, watching Olivia warily.

241

"Hullo again, Maryam," Olivia said. "I'm afraid I have to be gone for a few days, so you and Bayliss will have to manage here on your own, but I'll see you again on Thursday. I'm glad to welcome you and hope you will feel at home here." Olivia smiled, walked back to her horse, and rode straight to Michelle's shop.

She waited impatiently for a customer to leave and then dragged Michelle to the table in the back room and sat her down to hear about the Fletchers' arrival.

"I can't get my mind settled on it," Olivia said. "Here's this woman – overnight her life has changed. It's like a miracle. You should see the way she looks at me, like she can't decide whether to flee for her life or fall down and worship me, like I must be either the devil or the Messiah."

"Well sure, it would be a big change, especially all of a sudden like that," Michelle said. "But I don't see what you're so upset about. It's a good thing. She's here now. Fletcher's right. She'll get used to it fast enough."

"I'm not upset about her. I'm nothing but happy for her. I know she'll get used to the way things are here. It's just the idea ... I mean, all I did was lend them some money. That's all. What's that to me? Nothing. I know he'll pay me back. And that tiny little thing, that required no effort of me, changed their whole lives."

"And so?"

"So, it makes you wonder – how many other times might there have been a person in your life, someone who needed something that would have made all the difference to them, some tiny little thing, and you didn't help."

Michelle stood and held out her hands, palms up. "Jesus, Mary, and Joseph. I ain't never known no one enjoys feeling guilty as much as you do. You should a been born a man. Then you could become a priest and beat your back with one a them little whips they got. You did help Fletcher's wife, so why don't you try feeling good about that? Like old Hershey says, you just went and saved a whole world."

Chapter Twenty-Six

A thick envelope arrived containing pages of Mabel's recipes, and for the next three days Olivia was in Michelle's kitchen from dawn to dark trying them out. She and Michelle couldn't consume all the food she prepared, so she offered free samples to every customer who came into the shop. She appropriated Michelle's counter for serving from pots and tins and made little tents of card paper on which she wrote what they contained. The first day's menu was Beef-Steak Pie and Chicken and Dumplings. On the second day she offered A-La-Mode Beef, Chicken Pudding, Collared Pork, and Stewed Mushrooms. On the third day she prepared only desserts: Crullers, Indian Batter Cakes, and Charlotte Russe. She gained confidence as she watched people gobble down her food. Word of this strange phenomenon spread, and soon men were shyly slipping through the door and doing a bad job of pretending to shop before gravitating to the counter.

"You're welcome," Olivia said as she handed them a plate. "I would appreciate your honest opinion of each dish."

Their comments were all enthusiastic, but she thought the most sincere compliment she received was the man who went to stand in the corner while he licked his plate.

"Starting in January I'll be serving meals at OK Accommodations, out on the west side of town," she told them. "Very reasonably priced. Be sure to tell your friends and family."

After Michelle closed up on the third day, Olivia put a note in the window – "The food sampling is over, until the opening of **OK Accommodations** in January."

Back in Michelle's kitchen, Olivia leafed through the papers Mabel had sent. "I wish I'd had these in the summer, when there was fresh fruit. She's got recipes here for after dinner drinks – Peach Cordial and Raspberry Cordial and then there's something she calls 'Cherry Bounce.'" She smiled. "What a name, all I can picture is Mabel bouncing down the front stairs after a few cups of it." Olivia tossed the pages down on the table. "This stuff sounds so easy to make. All you do is put the fruit and sugar and some spices in a demi-john, pour gallons of whiskey or wine over it, and let it sit around for six months."

"That's nothing but a rum pot, girly girl. I mean, she says whiskey instead of rum, but it's the same thing. Don't need no recipe for that. Anyone on the street will tell you how to make a rum pot. Everyone's grandma's got one in the cellar. No better excuse for having a drink. Grandma only drinks it for the fruit, of course. The alcohol is a necessary evil, for preserving it. You can go ahead and make one. They still got peaches in the market."

"I know, I saw them, but they're all dried out."

"So they've been resting in someone's cellar for a while. What does that matter? Dryer they are, the more whiskey they'll soak up. Come winter, the evenings are going to be long. Me and Hershey will help you finish that up, dry peaches or not."

On Thursday she returned to the boarding house and found Mr. Abraham's Conestoga wagon standing in the drive. She barely took the time to tether Sandy to the rail as she rushed inside.

"Mr. Abraham! Mr. Abraham!" She felt like a little girl whose favorite uncle had returned.

Feet clomped on the stairs and there stood the pudgy little man, his eyes closed into down-turned half-moons, the way they did when he smiled.

"Hullo, *mamaleh*, how have you been?"

"I'm fine. Better than fine. Grand. I hope you were up there picking out your room."

"As a matter of fact, this is exactly what I was doing. I thought I might ask you for the one on the second floor next to the Fletchers'. It also is facing the back. Is that suitable?"

"Yes, that's perfect. Move in now if you want, if you can stand all the mess. I have clean sheets and blankets over in Michelle's storeroom." She would have given him an enthusiastic hug, but forbidden that, she turned excitedly toward the kitchen. "Come, come. I have a surprise for you."

He followed her and watched as she opened the door of the bake cabinet, which she had painted a grey-blue. She stooped down to indicate the bottom two shelves, which were stacked with dishes and pans, still in their brown paper wrapping.

"Those are for you. Brand new. Michelle told me about all those rules you have – you know, about your food. So these things are just for you. No one else is allowed to use them. You can buy whatever else you need and keep it in there."

For once he seemed speechless and finally uttered a simple, "Thank you, dearest girl."

"There are four white plates and bowls and four brown. Michelle told me how you can't eat meat on the same ones you eat other stuff on. But both pans look alike, so I guess you'll just have to remember which one you cooked meat in. Maybe you can make a scratch on it or something." She straightened up, put her fists on her hips, and frowned. "I have to say, you certainly do have a lot of rules to follow. I can't imagine how you keep it all straight. I'd forever be getting all mixed up. Some day you're going to have to explain to me why on earth ... But anyway, you can keep your food in there too. All I got so far is tea and coffee." She bent to rummage in the cabinet again. "Oh, and here are a few lumps of sugar and some salt. So you can make yourself a cup of something now if you want. The stove isn't lit, but there's dry wood and kindling out back. Matches are up there on that shelf." She nodded. "You'll just have to make yourself at home. Seeing as I'm not officially open, you're not yet my boarder, entitled to be waited on." She smiled. "You're just my friend."

He stood looking at her, wearing a strange expression.

"Is something wrong?" she asked. "Aren't those dishes all right?"

"They are perfect. And the best gift anyone ever gave to me."

Neither of them spoke for a moment, and Olivia began to feel awkward.

"There's a jug of cider if you're thirsty," she offered. "I mean, if you're allowed to drink that."

"That sounds good. Who would make a rule against cider?"

She took one of "his" tin cups from the cupboard and worked the pump handle to rinse it. Then she reached to the top cupboard and took another cup for herself.

"You bring the cider." She nodded at the earthenware jug on the table. "I'd as soon sit on the porch, while we still can, but it is chilly out there. Do you mind?"

"No. That is fine for me."

She glanced up the stairs as she passed them. "It's so quiet. Isn't Mr. Fletcher up there?"

"On the top floor. Painting. His wife is helping him."

"Should we call them down to join us?" She pulled the front door open, set the cups on the round wooden table Mr. Fletcher had built, and sat on one of the four chairs that went with it.

"I think it isn't so good to interrupt a painter." Mr. Abraham seated himself. "He's probably wanting to finish a first coat for the whole room. Don't you want to go up and see how he is doing?"

"Oh, I don't like to bother him. Make him feel like I'm checking up on him."

Mr. Abraham picked up the book lying on the table and read out its title – *The American Frugal Housewife* by Lydia Maria Child." He raised his eyebrows.

Olivia smiled and poured the cider. "That was a present from Michelle, so she could fool with me. Mrs. Child tells you to do silly things, like always pick up bits of twine and paper, you know, save every little thing. Even tells you to take your clothesline down every night, to make it last longer. She must think women don't have enough to do. A friend of mine says that the insane asylums are all filled up with farmers' wives. I think it must be with ones who were trying to follow Mrs. Child's advice."

Mr. Abraham smiled and raised his glass.

"Though I do admit some of the things she says are sensible." Olivia raised her own glass, took a sip, and then took the book from Mr. Abraham to read from a dog-eared page: "In early childhood, you lay the foundation of poverty or riches, in the habits you give your children. Teach them to save everything – not for their own use, for that would make them selfish – but for some use. Teach them to share everything with their playmates; but never allow them to destroy anything."

"That's making sense."

She paused and looked up at him. "She even mentions something about Jews."

"Not how to boil them alive, I hope."

Olivia rifled through the pages. "Here it is: 'Pack your butter in a clean, scalded firkin, cover it with strong brine, and spread a cloth all over the top, and it will keep good until the Jews get into Grand Isle.'" She snapped the volume shut and looked up at him. "That's something mean-spirited, isn't it?"

He smiled. "Yes, it is. I don't know where is this Grand Isle place, but she is thinking it is a wonderful

247

place that the Jews are crying to get into. Of course, since they are Jews, no one is wanting them around and will never let them in. So she is saying that your butter will keep until forever."

"That's what I thought." Olivia set the book back on the table. "She doesn't have any good food in there. If she had her frugal way, we'd bake with dust and ash instead of flour. I got a different cookbook from the library. That one sure isn't for poor people. Cream, cream, and more cream. You're going to be sorry you can't eat my cakes. So how is your family?"

"Thanks to God, they are all well."

"Were you born in America?"

"Yes."

"So ... I hope you don't mind me asking, but how come you speak English the way you do?"

"You don't like my English?" She flushed, and he quickly said, "It's okay. I know what you mean. I have mistakes."

She nodded. "Mostly the same mistakes. Like you say 'he is thinking' instead of 'he thinks' or 'you must to go' or 'you can to go' instead of 'you can go' and 'you must go.' How come?"

He sighed. "On my father's side they are very American. They are a few generations in this country. They changed their name from Abraham to Avery and are speaking good English. But my mother's parents were immigrants. They are speaking Yiddish, wearing clothes like me, and celebrating the Jewish holidays. So we can to say – pardon me, we can say – there was tension between these two families. The Averys were embarrassed when the Rosenblums were coming to their neighborhood, with their beards and black hats. And the Rosenblums said the Averys were ashamed to be Jewish. My parents chose to live near the Rosenblums, so where I grew up everyone was speaking Yiddish and when I was older I never tried to lose my accent. Or fix my mistakes. I changed my name from

Avery back to Abraham. I try to be proud to be as I am."

It's like Mourning talking like coloreds, she thought.

"Can you explain some of your rules to me?" she asked.

"I don't know where to begin."

"Well, I've been thinking about the rule that you can't touch any woman who isn't your wife."

"I thought you are liking that one."

"But what about those Children of Israel in the Bible. They did all kinds of touching. Look at King David and Bathsheba. Didn't they have the same rules back then?"

"Ah, but what he was doing is written as an example of how a man must not to behave. And he got a punishment, no matter that he was the king."

"And Abraham? He had a child with another woman."

"First, that was before God gave to Moses the Torah. Second, lots of the things in the Bible we aren't doing any more. We aren't throwing stones at people to kill them if they work on the Sabbath."

"Do you think people are supposed to enjoy ... amorous congress?" She blurted out the question and turned red.

He quickly recovered from the shock and smiled. "An unusual welcome back you are giving to me. You better to pour me another cup of cider."

She filled their glasses and apologized for making him uncomfortable. "It's just that you're the only person I know who talks about ... real things."

"It's all right, *mamaleh*. I know you have no mamma to ask. I will answer your question. What is between men and women is a serious matter. Because from that children are coming into the world. So you must only to do that with a woman you are married to. A woman that you are taking responsibility for her children. As far as enjoying – it seems to depend on what religion you have." He switched to his teasing

249

tone of voice. "The Arabians – those poor fellows have many wives, as many as they want – but still they are believing that only in heaven they will have a good time with women. As for the Christians – if we are judging by the Yankees around here, they aren't enjoying anything anywhere, not up in heaven and not down on earth. But I must to say that the French are a different story. But Jews are allowed – no not allowed, obligated – to enjoy that part of life. And to be making sure their wife also does. Of course you know what the Jew-haters are saying about that."

She waited for him to answer.

"Of course Jews are enjoying to do that – it's free."

Her face remained blank and he explained. "People are saying about Jews that they are always grabbing for money. But never mind about that. To answer your question seriously, physical love is a great gift God gave to us. To despise that pleasure is a sin, not a virtue. But a man must not to be irresponsible and temptation is all around him. Everywhere he is looking there are pretty women he might very much like to touch. That's all right. What is in his thoughts doesn't matter, so long as he isn't doing that. But a person should try his best to not have the thoughts. Not to put himself where there is temptation. Evil is easily finding its way into a person's mind and staying there. You understand?"

Olivia nodded. She turned away from Mr. Abraham and gazed out over the river, remembering Filmore Stubblefield kneeling over her on that bed in their barn. The way his expression had changed, as if a frightening mask had suddenly covered his face. Iola put that evil in his mind, Olivia thought. Iola, together with the whiskey and my helplessness, brought something out in him – something he probably could have lived his whole life and never known was there.

"Are you all right?" Mr. Abraham asked her.

"Yes." She turned back to him.

"You are looking so sad all of a sudden."

"I'm fine. Just a little tired. And this is my least favorite time of the year. The trees all stark and bare. I just finished reading that ghoulish story everyone was talking about last year – *The Fall of the House of Usher*. The way everything looks all gray now reminds me of that story."

"Olivia." He spoke slowly. "I didn't mean to say that something happening between a man and a woman is evil."

She forced a smile to her face and nodded.

"Everyone is always fighting a battle between what their bodies are wanting to do and what their minds are saying they should to do. Just remember, the body is God's creation. It is giving us life. Giving us pleasure. And sometimes we don't do what we should. All of us are sometimes weak. We are making mistakes. So we are trying harder the next time. You know, the rabbis say, when your time comes and you are standing before The Holy One Blessed Is He, the question He is asking is not 'Olivia, why weren't you Queen Esther?' or ..." He paused, searching for a name that might mean something to Olivia. "Or 'Olivia, why weren't you Dolley Madison?' You know what He will ask you?"

She shook her head.

"Olivia, why weren't you Olivia Killion?"

"I don't understand what you mean."

"He made you as you are. Some gifts. Some flaws. Some weaknesses. Some talents. He is wanting you to be that person. Live your life. Enjoy it. Use the talents and gifts. Know the weaknesses and flaws. Be the best Olivia Killion you can, with what God gave you."

The door opened behind them, and Bayliss and Maryam Fletcher stepped onto the porch. Olivia gave them a wide smile, pleased to see them and even more pleased for the awkward conversation she had begun to be brought to an end.

"Hello, there you are. Just in time for some cider. Maryam, could you bring some cups?"

Maryam nodded and went back into the house. Olivia spoke to Mr. Fletcher in a whisper. "I don't like it, bossing her like that. I would have been glad to get the cups, but –"

"Miss Killion," Bayliss interrupted her, "'Scuse me for saying so, but that be a fool thing to say. How she gonna work for you, you ain't gonna boss her? You be her boss. You s'pose to tell her what to do. You done that right, in a kindly voice. Now she know what you want of her, and she feel safe and happy cause she know how to do it. You just hold your horses. She gonna turn uppity faster than you think."

Olivia laughed. "So how's the work going?"

"Right fine. I'm painting. Started at the top and working my way down. They's still some windows don't open easy, but I'm a get to them."

Maryam returned with the cups and seated herself next to her husband.

"Well, good," Olivia said. "I guess I need to start advertising for boarders. Can I say the end of January?"

"I be done way 'fore that. I still be pushing for Christmas."

She waved a dismissive hand. "I prefer to have my first Detroit Christmas at Michelle's and not start off cooking a big Christmas dinner for strangers. But can I tell people the rooms will be ready sometime in January?"

"Yes, Miss."

"Maryam, at your Master's house, did you sometimes do the laundry?"

She nodded.

"That's good. That will be your main job. We will provide fresh bedding for our boarders every two weeks. That means ten sets of sheets every fourteen days. And we will give each a clean towel once a week."

"Most places are not so generous," Mr. Abraham said. "They are changing the sheets only once a month. Some places aren't even changing them between boarders, if the month isn't up."

"And aren't those places infested with all kinds of bugs? That's not going to happen here." Olivia thought for a moment. "Well, maybe every three weeks would be enough. That is a big pile of laundry. Bayliss, can you make sure that before we open Maryam has everything she'll need for the laundry? She'll need a lot more lines. During the winter she'll have to hang it in the barn. And I haven't even thought about where she'll do it. Lord, I can't have all that mess in the kitchen while I'm trying to cook."

"She do it out in the barn," Mr. Fletcher said, his tone implying that should be obvious.

Olivia nodded and remembered herself carrying all those buckets of water up the hill in Fae's Landing. Maryam looked so frail. "Please, buy a wagon she can use to haul the buckets, and grade the path from the back door to the barn." She turned to Mr. Abraham. "Do we have to put the sheets back on the bed for them, or can the boarders be expected to make up the beds for themselves?"

"Whatever you are deciding is the way it is. I think it is fine if Maryam is leaving the clean sheets in the rooms. For me I can say, if you are giving me clean sheets every three weeks, I'm glad to put the sheets on all the beds for you."

Olivia turned back to Maryam. "All right, so you don't have to bother making the beds. I would like you to sweep the entire house twice a week, and dust the common areas. I'll have two buckets in the kitchen, one for the compost pile and one for trash to burn. I'd like you to see that those are emptied every evening and that the surfaces in the kitchen are wiped clean and the floor swept and mopped. And I think that's enough to start out with. I have no idea how much time all that will take. Just work at your normal pace. I don't expect you to work more than eight or nine hours a day. I want you to be sure to tell me if I've given you too much to do. But if you finish all those chores sooner than that, then you could help me in the kitchen. Does that sound all right to you?"

Both Fletchers nodded.

"How am I going to get fire wood?" Olivia looked back and forth between the two men. "I can gather enough kindling from the woods and there's a big pile of split logs out back, but that pile won't look so big once the snow comes. And I don't look forward to splitting another log in this lifetime."

"You either are hiring someone to chop it for you, or you are ordering cord wood from one of the companies that sell it," Mr. Abraham said. "If you like, I can to see about that for you. See which is cheaper and who is giving you the best deal."

"Oh thank you. And I wanted to ask you another favor. I know we could get snowed in for days, even weeks, if it's a hard winter. Could I take advantage of your big wagon to bring in supplies? You know, sacks of flour, sugar, beans. Tins of oil."

"Of course."

"That's why I put up that storeroom in the barn," Mr. Fletcher said. "Locked up tight to keep out both the people and the raccoons."

"I'm so glad you did. I never would have thought of it. My goodness, I can't imagine doing this all on my own, without all of you. As for wages, Maryam, I don't know how much I should pay you. Mr. Abraham, is that something you could find out? And you ask around too." She looked at the Fletchers. "Talk to people you know, women who do similar work."

"We best get back to work," Bayliss said, and both Fletchers rose. "I nailed together a sign, like you wanted," he said. "It be out in the barn. I painted it white, but left the letters for you to paint, like you said. Paint and brush be next to it."

"I think I must to be going too." Mr. Abraham stood up.

"Oh, but I thought you were going to stay here."

"I am, since you are kind enough to invite me. But I have some business to settle in town."

"Do you think you'll have time enough to stop at Michelle's on the way back and pick up your bedding? You could bring all of it actually. There are four big bundles in the back of her shop."

"Happy to do that."

Olivia watched him drive off and thought what a difference it made, having the right people in one's life. Everything became so easy. Then, smiling, she strode back to the barn and picked up the wooden sign Bayliss had made, a large rectangle nailed to two pointed stakes. She knew she shouldn't paint while still in her dress, but couldn't be bothered to change. And she wanted it done that day, so it could dry in the barn for a while before she put it up. She had made a card paper stencil and used it to copy thick black and red letters:

Olivia Killion ACCOMODATIONS
Clean Quiet Rooms
Full Board
Daily Transport to Downtown

She left space for the additional line that she hoped to be able to add next summer:

Indoor Water Closet and Shower

Chapter Twenty-Seven

Olivia would prepare Christmas dinner for five: herself, Michelle, Mr. Abraham, Slim Johnny, and Michelle's girl Sara May. It would be her first real test, a preview of cooking for nine boarders every day. For Mr. Abraham she planned two fish dishes from the library cookbook: Boiled Whitefish a la Mackinac and Fried Whitefish. The side dishes – creamed baby onions and scalloped potatoes – would be cooked in new pans, so Mr. Abraham would also be able to partake of them. The rest of the guests would have stuffed turkey and gravy. Dessert would be lemon meringue pie and her favorite – Charlotte Russe – made the real way, in a mold lined with lady fingers and filled with Bavarian cream. She would have none of the modern version – sponge cake with a spoonful of whipped cream plopped on it.

Then another, unexpected, guest was added to the list: Jeremy Kincaid. About a week before the holiday, Olivia's old neighbor from Fae's Landing was in Detroit and looked for her. He started at the United States Hotel, from there was directed to Michelle's shop, and Michelle told him how to get to OK Accommodations. He found Olivia in trousers, work shirt, and flat cap, working a scythe over the brown weeds in front of the house.

She squinted into the sun as he approached and recognized his red horse Ernest before she did him. "Jeremy, hullo, how good to see you. Have you had news of Mourning?"

"No, sorry I can't say that. Just thought I'd stop by to see how you're getting on." He shaded his eyes with one hand and looked up at the house. "Grand place you've got here."

She turned and proudly followed his gaze. "Yes. I love it." She lay down the scythe, retrieved her coat from the hitching rail, and put it on as he dismounted. "Come, there's hay and water for Ernest in the barn. I can offer you coffee, tea, water, or cider."

"Cider sounds good."

"Is it too cold for you to sit on the porch?" she asked. Their breath hung in the air, but she hated to go inside.

"Fine with me." He led Ernest around back to the barn.

She went inside and returned with cider and a plate of bread and butter.

"Are you hungry?" she asked when he reappeared and took the chair opposite her. "There's food inside. Venison or eggs."

"This is plenty." He picked a slice of bread from the plate and took a bite. "See you finally got the hang of it."

"No more bake kettle for me. I have a real oven. So have you heard anything new about what might have happened to the Stubblefields?"

"No, but folks are saying that the state is going to auction off their land."

"Oh. No family turned up?"

'Uh-uh. Not a one."

"How soon will the auction be?"

"Couldn't say. Guess they have to wait a while longer. I don't know what the law says. Why, you want to buy it?" he asked with a grin.

She surprised herself by saying, "I might. If it's going cheap."

He stared at her for a moment, wearing an expression she couldn't decipher.

"Are you planning to bid on it?" she asked.

"Me? Noooo. I'm no farmer. In fact, I've been asked to give more lectures over at the university."

"That's wonderful for you."

"It's not a real job. Not yet. But they're offering free lectures for the community and have hired me to give the first series. Soon enough they'll have a faculty of the sciences."

She nodded and smiled. "That's grand. You'll be good at that. All the girls will be sweet on you."

"Actually, I brought a draft of the first talk I'll be giving. Forgot it in the saddle bag. I'll go get it for you to read." He started to rise.

"I don't have time now," she lied. "I need to clean myself up. A couple of potential boarders are supposed to come to look at the rooms. And before they get here, I want to post my new sign. But tell me, where are you having your Christmas dinner?"

He looked uncomfortable with the question, and she didn't wait for him to answer. "I only ask because I'm making dinner for a few friends. You'd be most welcome to join us, and then you could practice giving your lecture to a real audience, after dessert." She felt a twinge of guilt for inflicting this on Michelle and her friends, but rationalized that by then they would be three sheets in the wind and wouldn't mind if someone stood up to read them the train schedule. And with other people around, Olivia would feel less obligated to comment. Anyway, it wasn't impossible that it would be interesting. One could hope that Jeremy lectured about animals the way he talked about them, and not the way he wrote about them.

"Kind of you to ask. I believe I will gratefully accept that invitation. Unless the weather's bad, of course. Don't wait for me then. Why are you bothering to cut those weeds? They'll be buried under a foot of snow soon enough."

"I know, but in case it doesn't snow in the next few days, I want the place to look nice and tidy when people come to see about a room."

"Waste of energy, if you ask me. Bare doesn't look much better. But you do need to get your sign posted. I would have ridden past the place, if you hadn't been out front. Almost needed a sign to know it was you, in those duds."

"Well, it's all painted and ready," she said, ignoring his remark about her attire. "That's next on my list of things to do today. Feel like helping me with it?'

"Surely do."

They brought the sign, shovel, and sledge hammer from the barn, and Jeremy selected a spot. It was closer to the road than Olivia would have chosen, but she realized he was right, as the whole point of having a sign was to draw the attention of people on the road. He dug two holes for the stakes, and she held the sign while he pounded it in. She took a few steps back to admire it and saw Bayliss step onto the porch, come to see who was making all the racket.

"Bayliss, come look. Isn't it grand? This is Jeremy Kincaid, an old neighbor of mine."

"Not that old." Jeremy laughed and shook Mr. Fletcher's hand.

Mr. Fletcher assured her that the sign was indeed a marvel, told her he had finished painting the last room on the second story of the house, and went back in to start on Olivia's room.

"Your boy doing a good job?" Jeremy nodded at Mr. Fletcher's back.

"Oh yes, Mr. Fletcher is a godsend. I don't know what I'd do without him."

"You know you're in a city now. If you don't keep your eye on these people, they'll rob you blind."

Olivia didn't know if by "these people" he meant everyone who lived in a city, workmen, or coloreds. She didn't want to know.

"Time I was going. Let you get ready to meet your boarders," he said. "And I'll see you Christmas Eve."

"We won't be eating here," she said. "Come to Michelle's shop."

She waved as she watched him ride off and suddenly realized what had caused the idea of sharing a life with the once much-admired Jeremy Kincaid to lose its

259

appeal. It was simple. She tried, and found it impossible, to imagine a little black boy crawling up the front steps of one of those fancy houses in Ann Arbor.

At noon on the day of Christmas Eve a great racket commenced – the streets were suddenly filled with men blowing horns and firing guns. Olivia rushed out of the kitchen to join Michelle on the sidewalk.

"What happened? What's wrong?"

"Ain't nothin' to be ascared of," Michelle said. "Just the Germans showing their Christmas spirit. They carry on like this all day. Some of 'em all night. I'm going to close up now, like everyone else. You 'bout done cooking?"

"Almost. With what I can do ahead."

"Pretty soon they're starting a pony race down on Jefferson Avenue. Everyone goes. Slim Johnny's taking bets."

Olivia returned to the kitchen to check on the turkey and finish breading the fish. Then she followed Michelle down toward the river to watch the race. When they turned onto Jefferson Avenue, where the entire population of Detroit did indeed seem to have congregated, Michelle easily made her way through the crowd, stopping often to chat with people. Olivia hung back, careful to stay far enough behind to avoid having to join in Michelle's socializing.

The street was so mobbed that Olivia couldn't have seen much of the race had she wanted to. She slowly backed away, extricating herself from the mass of bodies, most of them unwashed men in rough clothing. A touch on her shoulder startled her, but it was only Slim Johnny asking who she wanted to wager on. She smiled, shook her head, and further removed herself from the crowd. She was not, however, without entertainment. A large group of Indians was coming up the street, wearing long army coats and the funny hats one of the milliners was passing out to them. All were having a grand time and Olivia was fascinated by their bursts of wild dancing. She soon heard thundering horses' hooves and the crowd grew louder. Jubilant shouts told her the race must be over and she hoped they could now go home.

"There you are." Michelle linked her arm through Olivia's. "What are you doing way back here?"

"I was watching the Indians. You know, there aren't so many women here." Olivia glanced around nervously, noting how many of the men were drunk.

"So?"

"I'm just saying." She felt rebuked, knowing Michelle already thought her a terrible spoil-sport.

But Michelle made no teasing remark. She spoke with a few more people she knew and then turned to Olivia and said, "Come on, let's go home."

On their way Olivia asked Michelle which church she wanted to go to.

"Church? Do I look like a big church-goer to you?"

"But it's Christmas."

"So? The Yankees around here don't even celebrate Christmas."

"I thought everybody goes to church on Christmas. We stopped going every Sunday when I was little, after my mother died, but we still went on Christmas Eve."

"So what kind of a church did you go to?"

"When my mother was alive, we went to the Congregational church. And that stayed 'our church.' The one we were always absent from, if you know what I mean."

"Yes, I know what you mean. That's the minister you have to cross the street to avoid. None of the others are going to tell you how much they're looking forward to seeing you on Sunday."

"Exactly." Olivia smiled. "But my Mammo Killion, my father's mother, was always real upset that we didn't go to the Catholic church. She loved to make fun of the Quakers in Five Rocks, with all their simplicity."

Olivia tried to produce an imitation of an old woman's voice. "Phoo. What's so grand about simplicity? You want I should feed you a complicated dinner of chicken and dumplings, or would you prefer a nice simple piece of stale bread? Phoo. Gammy bunch of fools. Everyone gets some kind of religion jammed down their throat – might as well stick with the one what's got all the good art and music. Empty room. Phoo. Any more simple, they'd be out in the barn."

Michelle grinned and said, "They say Ste. Anne's has a beautiful Midnight Mass. I guess, seeing as this is your first Christmas away from home, I could go with you, if you want."

For a moment Olivia was tempted to tell Michelle about spending last Christmas with Mrs. Place and why she had been hiding in her house. But she just smiled and said, "Would you really?"

"I'm French, ain't I? All the frogs are Catholic. And them priests got some good ideas. Letting you do whatever you want and then forgiving you, long as you mumble enough prayers. And they got the worst hell. You get to imagine everyone you hate burning in it."

Olivia flushed. Not a day passed that she didn't imagine Iola tormented in flames, turning crispy and then disappearing.

"I'd wager you've pictured that sister-in-law of yours in it."

"Mabel? No, my word, never. I don't hate Mabel." Olivia pulled her woolen scarf tighter around her head. "Though she certainly can be annoying. You should have seen the way she flounced into our house on the day our father died. The women from the Congregational Church had just come for his Sunday best, so they could get him dressed and laid out on the table in the parlor. Then Mabel comes in rustling her bustle. She pulls me aside and asks, 'What on the good Lord's earth possessed you to give them that suit?'

"I say, 'I don't know, Mabel. I guess I think it looks

the nicest on him. Besides, it's brand new.' And she says, 'Well, that's just the point, now isn't it? Why would you want to put a brand new five-dollar suit under the ground?'"

"Thought you might want to auction off his clothes, did she?"

"Who knows what goes through that woman's mind? Then she pats my arms and says, 'I know you meant well, dear, but next time a question like that comes up, you come and ask me what to do. Just like I was your big sister.'" Olivia made a face like a hissing cat. The same face she had made at Mabel's back that day.

"I guess she'll be waiting a lot of Tuesdays for you to ask her for sisterly advice."

Remembering how kind Mabel had been when she came home, Olivia added, "But she's not always so awful. She can surprise you and be real nice."

Soon after they returned to the shop Jeremy rapped on the front window.

"Mr. Kincaid, how good of you to come." Michelle let him in and planted loud kisses on both his cheeks. Olivia watched from the back doorway as Michelle relieved him of his coat and the coffee beans and wine he had brought.

"It's you who are good to have me."

Michelle was wearing what she called her "best titty dress" and Olivia smiled, watching the effort it took for Jeremy to keep his eyes off her bosom. "Come back to the kitchen," Michelle said. "It's warmer, there's coffee, and Olivia's desperate attempts at food preparation make a good show."

Olivia took Jeremy's hand and greeted him warmly, but did not lean forward to kiss him. The three of them had a companionable cup of coffee, and Olivia was surprised by how comfortable it felt, setting the table together and waiting for the other guests. Half an hour before those guests were to arrive Olivia began frying up the pieces of white fish and several times had to rap Jeremy's knuckles with her wooden spatula.

"Stop that," she scolded. "Mr. Abraham can't have any of the turkey. If you keep gobbling up all the fish, he'll go hungry. Why don't you take the turkey out, since you're the one will be in charge of carving it?"

The dinner was a success, though they made an unlikely group. Mr. Abraham in his neat black suit and trimmed beard, Slim Johnny not much more than a skeleton with long stringy hair and pock-marked face, Sara May who barely spoke a word, and Jeremy the professor – but they seemed glad enough of one another's company and got on well. Olivia's food was pronounced delicious by all, and Olivia found Jeremy's lecture about the mating habits of wolves entertaining, especially when accompanied by the bawdy remarks of Michelle and Slim Johnny. Mr. Abraham sat through it still as a schoolboy and occasionally raised his hand to ask a question. When it was nearing midnight Michelle asked Olivia if she still wanted to go to church.

"Maybe next year," she replied, worn out from the long day.

"I think it is time for us to wish you a happy holiday and a good night." Mr. Abraham pushed his chair back.

"I didn't know Jews celebrate Christmas," Jeremy said.

"We don't. But any excuse to share a meal with friends is a happy occasion for me."

"I didn't even know there were any Jews in these parts," Jeremy said. "Did you just come out from New York?"

"No. My family has been in Michigan for a few generations, so I think longer than you. One of my ancestors was indeed the first Jew that came to Detroit, in 1762. He was a fur trader and Chapman Abraham was his name. He was even captured by the Indians, while they were making a siege of Detroit, but they traded him back for an Indian chief."

264

"You're right, that's longer than me." Jeremy's chair scraped as he rose.

All the guests soon departed after a lengthy exchange of hugs and holiday wishes, the dishes were cleared, and Michelle went out to the shop to lock up. There she found the gifts someone had left by the door.

"These are from Hershey," she said after they opened the packages, which each contained a paisley shawl – blues and greens for Michelle and reds and oranges for Olivia. "He gets them in Cleveland."

Olivia draped the shawl over her shoulders and admired it in the mirror.

"Tell me." Michelle came to stand beside her. "Are you and Jeremy ..?"

Olivia took a moment to answer, remembering how she had once longed for his touch. She searched her heart for any remnant of feeling, found none, and turned to face Michelle.

"No. There was never anything between us. We were just neighbors. If you have an interest in him, feel free to pursue it. I think he would like to find a wife. He seems to believe that a professor requires one."

"What's a hoity-toity professor's wife gotta do?"

"I don't know." Olivia shrugged. "I would suppose look respectable – no great titty dresses – and drink tea with the other professors' wives."

"Sounds a hell of a lot easier than being a French fashion expert."

Chapter Twenty-Eight

A week later Olivia moved into OK Accommodations. She loved her enormous bedroom. The double bed had night tables on either side, and the other side of the room was like a little parlor, with sofa, table and two armchairs. The attached dressing room was almost as big as her old bedroom in Five Rocks. It had hanging space, a bureau, a dressing table, and a framed, full-length mirror.

Mr. Fletcher had made sure her bedroom door closed tightly – so she would not be disturbed by boarders returning late at night or leaving early in the morning – and put a heavy dead bolt on it. He also put locks on each of the sash windows. He'd wanted to put wooden bars on them so Olivia would be safe in hot weather when the windows remained open, but she wouldn't hear of it. She didn't want to live in a room that looked like a jail cell and she couldn't know when she or somebody else might need to climb in or out of a window.

OK Accommodations officially opened on Monday, January 9, 1843. Not all of the rooms were occupied. On the ground floor, in one of the two rooms that used to be the dining room, was tiny, grey-haired Miss Jeanie Streeter, a retired school teacher and activist in the temperance movement. Olivia had inherited her from Mrs. Rafferty and warned her that she had no intention of banning alcohol from the premises. Miss Streeter had shrugged and smiled, saying she knew there were drunkards everywhere. She'd been staying at the Steamboat Hotel while the work on the house was being done and was happy to be home again. Olivia didn't know much about her, other than that she had grown up in North Carolina and might therefore be assumed to be pro-slavery. She was, however, hard of hearing so Olivia didn't think she posed much of a threat. In any case, Mr. Abraham reminded her, the last thing Olivia wanted was a house full of known abolitionists. Miss Streeter spent most of her days in the parlor, peering through thick spectacles to do what she called quilling – curling tiny strips of thick paper around quills and gluing them into astonishingly elaborate designs that she framed and then sold or gave away.

In the room next to Miss Streeter was Mrs. Effie

May Porter, a widow who, together with her husband, used to run one of the hotel dining rooms. She would turn out to be a godsend of recipes and advice. Mrs. Porter was a sturdy-looking woman, her dark hair only beginning to gray. She also spent a lot of time in the parlor, being impatient with Miss Streeter.

On the second floor were Bayliss and Maryam Fletcher, Mr. Abraham, and a young couple – Derek and Meghan Gage. The Gages were newly-weds, just arrived from upstate New York, who hoped to buy one of the ribbon farms on the riverfront. They mostly kept to themselves. Meghan took in work from one of the local dressmakers, but stayed in her room to do it. Derek worked long hours at a sawmill and sash factory not far from the house. The two other rooms on the second floor were still unoccupied.

Olivia had rented the small rooms on the third story to single men. Andy O'Donnell tended bar at the Corktown Tavern and Olivia barely saw him. He slept most of the morning and then tended to disappear, only occasionally sitting in the parlor to play his banjo, the strains of which brought both Miss Streeter and Mrs. Porter in to join him. Olivia would also come in, both to enjoy the music and to watch the two older women flirt with the good-natured, pudgy young man, who reeked of whiskey and the opium he smoked each night to help him sleep. Olivia prayed that he was keeping his promise and obeying the one rule she was strict about – no smoking inside or near the house or barn. The only one of her boarders who owned a horse, Andy was a source of concern to Olivia. She would never know when he might suddenly appear in the barn, at any hour of the night.

Next door to Andy was Dominick Ballou, the handsome son of a Chippewa mother and French Voyageur. Dominick had his own pirogue and worked long hours at the port. Olivia saw little of the swarthy young man, which was just as well, since she found his intense dark eyes extremely unsettling.

Before anyone else moved in, Olivia had shown Mr. Abraham the menu she was planning for the first week.

"No, no, no." He raised his voice. "You must not to give them a choice. What are you thinking? They are eating what you put on the table. And you must not to give so many dishes at each meal. I know you aren't wanting to be a skinflint, but you aren't charging enough rent to feed them like this."

"But I can't have my boarders going hungry."

"No, no one is going hungry. You are making a lot of whatever you are serving them, but not so many different things. You will wear yourself out. One day you are giving them venison and rice and beans for dinner. And leftover venison and rice and beans for supper. The next day pork roast and potatoes for dinner and supper. The next day chicken and dumplings."

Olivia didn't argue, but looked doubtful. "What about breakfast? Should I tell them they all have to come at the same time?"

"This is the way in most places I am staying. But this is your house. Your rules. And you know those two young men upstairs aren't eating breakfast at the time when Miss Streeter and Mrs. Porter are getting up."

"I know. I thought I'd put out bread, jam, and butter for everyone to serve themselves –"

"No, no, no." He interrupted her. "No one is going in the kitchen when you are not there. No one opens your cupboards. You are giving them a plate with some bread and jam and butter on it. You will maybe give them more, but they must to ask you for it. Otherwise you are finding things disappearing faster than you can buy them."

"You think these people would steal from me?"

He shrugged. "Why find out things about people that you are not wanting to know. We must to give our fellow human beings the least chances to disappoint us."

"All right." She sighed and continued, "I'll personally give them bread, jam, and butter. And for those who are here between eight and ten, I'll prepare eggs and bacon between those hours. I'll brew one big pot of coffee in the morning and one in the afternoon and when it's gone, it's gone. And I'll offer to pack a lunch for Mr. Gage and Mr. Ballou, if they don't want to come back here to eat. I don't know about Mr. O'Donnell, with the hours he works. I guess I'll just have to come to some kind of arrangement with him."

"Before you are getting too generous, remember you will have two more boarders, at least, maybe four, if couples are taking the other two rooms."

"But if I do like you say about dinner and supper ... that sounds so easy. With Maryam taking care of the laundry and cleaning, I won't have much to do all day."

"Believe me, you will be plenty of busy. Once you see what it is costing you to feed all these mouths day after day, you are spending most of your time finding ways to save money."

"Like how?"

"Once you told me how you were shooting a deer. A barrel filled with venison in your barn is a lot of free meals. And there are plenty of fishes in the river. Get Fletcher to sink some pilings and build you a little dock down there and then you will buy a trot line or net. And you have so much land. Of course in the summer you are growing your own vegetables. You already have some fruit trees out there."

"I do?"

"I think so. Two apple and two peach. You must to plant many more. And grape and berry vines. Why not ask Bayliss to build a chicken coop? And you already have a barn just waiting for a cow."

She smiled and shook her head. "You're trying to put me back on the farm. At least here I have a well and pump handle."

269

Olivia threw a party the evening she declared OK Accommodations officially open. She served pie, cake, cider, and wine to about twenty people, having told each of her boarders to invite a few friends. Michelle came with Slim Johnny and Sara May. Andy O'Donnell played his banjo, and Dominick Ballou surprised everyone by joining in on his harmonica. Most of the music was of the foot-stomping variety, but when Dominick played a tremulous solo of "Amazing Grace" the room grew silent. Listening to Mourning's favorite tune, Olivia had to wipe away tears with a napkin.

She had made a trip to the bank to extend a hand-written invitation to Mr. Wentworth and his wife. The banker came, unaccompanied by Mrs. Wentworth, but with a surprise guest – Zach Faraday. Olivia and Mr. Faraday greeted one another as if they were being introduced for the first time. She chatted with him for a moment and then made a point of being busy with her other guests. Mr. Wentworth soon slipped out of the parlor with Mr. Faraday and showed him around the house and barn. When Olivia next saw Mr. Faraday, he came over to tell her that her house was lovely and he was sorry that he had to be going. Later Mr. Wentworth touched Olivia's elbow and asked her to come out to the front yard. While they shivered in the cold, he pointed at the roof, as if he were telling her something about the house.

"Mr. Faraday will deliver a parcel soon," the banker said. "I can't tell you what night, but it should be within a week. The parcel will consist of a single item. He will bring it through the woods on horseback, deposit it in the barn, and leave. You won't see Mr. Faraday at all. He will arrive late at night, but you needn't watch for him. Neither will you ever see the parcel. You will only know that it's arrived because one morning you'll find a strange horse in your barn. And you won't know when the parcel has left. Do not look for it. It requires no care. But there are a few things you must do."

She nodded, listening intently.

"Sometime tomorrow go out and hang some warm blankets on the clothes line in the barn, as if you're airing them out. If you don't have extra blankets, you need to buy some, because the ones you leave on the line will stay hidden in the barn, for other parcels to use. We should have thought of this before, but don't you go trying to open that door and put them in. Just leave them on the clothes line and forget about them."

She nodded and he went on. "And every evening check that the trough is full of water and there are three skins of drinking water next to it. If there is any danger at your house – agents or unexpected guests that you feel wary of – you are to light a lantern in your bedroom and place it in the window that looks out at the barn."

"So that's why Bayliss put such a wide sill on that window."

"When the danger passes, put out the lantern. That's all. Otherwise, go about your normal routine. There's only one other thing for you to do – on the morning that you find the horse, take it into town as soon as possible. Just leave it at Finney's barn. No need to explain anything to anyone. Not to your boarders either. If any of them see the horse and ask about it, say a friend left it there and change the subject. In general, you should try to get your tenants used to minding their own business."

"All right."

"Do you have any questions?"

"No, no questions." She shook her head. "But Mr. Faraday should know that Mr. O'Donnell comes home at all hours, and he's on horseback so he goes into the barn."

"All right. I'll advise him of that, but that shouldn't present a problem. They'll hear a horse coming in plenty of time to get out of sight."

"And tell him that Mr. O'Donnell is a poor sleeper

and smokes some opium just about every night, so he'll still be in the yard for a while after he's tended to his horse."

"I'll tell him." Mr. Wentworth smiled. "That's good. You're thinking right, alert to possible risks. The hard part for some folks is keeping their face straight and not going to check on things. But Mr. Faraday and his friends have been doing this for a long time. You can feel safe. Put your trust in them and just go about your business. If they haven't asked you to do anything, then there's nothing you need to do. By the way, Bayliss and Maryam won't ask you any questions, and there's no need to involve them in anything."

"No, of course not."

For the next two nights Olivia barely slept; she couldn't help getting up to watch out the window. The third night she collapsed into bed and slept soundly. When she woke in the morning she hurriedly wrapped a coat around her shoulders and rushed to the barn, but found no strange horse. She straightened the blankets on the line and looked around with a sigh.

After serving breakfast, washing up, and then sitting with Miss Streeter for a few minutes to watch her do her quilling, Olivia began preparing dinner. She jumped when someone rapped loudly on the front door. Wiping her hands on her apron, she went to open it and found Jeremy on her threshold.

"Oh, hullo. How are you?" She pulled the door wide open, and he greeted her with a wide smile.

"Oh my." She looked at the sky behind him. "I didn't notice when I was out before. It looks like it's finally going to snow."

"Looks like." He stepped inside. "I was wondering if you rent rooms by the day. I have to be in Detroit for a few days."

"I do offer hospitality to my old neighbors, but I *don't* charge them rent. Two of the rooms on the second floor are unoccupied. You're most welcome to one of them."

"Truth is, I'd like to take my meals here too and would feel a lot better doing that if you'd let me pay you something."

"For staying a few days and nights? Certainly not. Go get Ernest settled in the barn."

"There's something I have to do in town first. I just wanted to make sure you have room for me tonight."

"Dinner is at two."

When Jeremy returned for dinner, Olivia clearly heard the clopping of Ernest's hooves. Yes, Mr. Wentworth was right, when you're listening for someone coming, you hear them. The parcel would have ample warning to hide, either in the woods or in the barn.

When Jeremy came in from the barn he had her blankets over his arm, neatly folded. "Thought you'd want these inside." He held them out. "It's getting colder. If we get much moisture in the air, they could turn into a sheet of ice out there."

"Thanks. Just set them on that chair by the door."

She set dinner on the table – platters of fried fish and potatoes with cheese – and picked up the old school bell she kept on the cabinet and rang it.

"Where'd you get that thing?" Jeremy asked.

"Detroit is amazing. Anything you can imagine, you can find someone selling it. There's a store that sells nothing but bells. Every kind of bell you could think of."

They sat: Jeremy, Olivia, the Fletchers, Mrs. Porter, Miss Streeter, and Mrs. Gage. Miss Streeter said grace as usual and while they ate Jeremy gave a series of short impromptu lectures. Somehow he managed to empty his plate and have seconds, though he never seemed to stop talking long enough to breathe, let alone ingest nourishment. He expressed no interest in anyone else in the room, but no one seemed to mind. Maryam and Bayliss always looked relieved to have other people carry the conversation, and the white women smiled and nodded. Miss Streeter clutched Jeremy's arm so often, Olivia thought she might leave a bruise. After the meal Jeremy rose and bowed to Olivia.

"My thanks and compliments. That was a delicious meal and even better company. I'm going back into town if you need anything."

Company? Olivia thought. He means audience. I think he's getting worse. That university has him more puffed up than usual.

But she smiled, a gracious hostess. "If you want, you could stop in at Michelle's," she said. "Ask her to come for supper. I'm sure she'd love to see you again, and we could play a little Three Card Brag."

"Sounds like a grand idea."

He and Michelle returned towards dusk. Olivia watched them ride up the drive, Michelle in the saddle behind him, no sunlight between his back and her chest. Olivia remembered herself in that position, praying for Ernest to stop and make her lurch forward.

Jeremy took Ernest to the barn and Michelle stomped up the back stairs to the kitchen where Olivia was peeling potatoes. Michelle removed the pack she had on her back, took out two bottles of wine, and set them on the table.

"Those are from Jeremy. This," she said, pulling out a bottle of peach cordial, "Is from me. I've got my nightdress in there too. You don't mind if I stay the night, do you? He'll take me back to town with him in the morning."

"Of course I don't mind." Olivia turned and dried her hands. "There's another empty room, right next to his."

"Who knows?" Michelle said, raising her eyebrows. "Maybe I won't need it. We'll see how the evening goes."

It took Olivia a moment to grasp her meaning. "But

you hardly know him."

"You sure you wouldn't care?" Michelle moved closer to look into Olivia's face.

"No. No, I wouldn't mind. I promise you. It's not a thing to me. But I'd mind for you. If you're wanting to think about marrying him –"

"Marrying him? Go on, girly girl, I was just fooling about that. Can you see me drinking tea in the parlor with a bunch of swells? Even if he would have me, which he wouldn't."

"How is it you've never gotten married?' Olivia broke her rule about prying, but Michelle didn't seem to mind.

"Never found anyone that fit. Then I went and ruined myself. Came out here to Detroit to make a new start and ruined myself all over again." She was smiling, keeping her voice light. "But don't worry none, being used and cast aside by your Mr. Kincaid would be a step up for me. Up till now most of the men I've chosen were more likely to take my life than improve it. But he's a good sort." She nodded toward the barn. "Won't do me no harm. Only thing is – I'm not so sure he's given up hope on you." She stared into Olivia's eyes again. "Can you really say you don't care?"

"Really." Olivia made a cross over her heart. "When I first met him," she said and flushed, peeking out the window to make sure he wasn't coming, "I thought about him all the time. How my whole life would change, if he would just have the good sense to fall in love with me. But back then he never showed a drib of interest."

"Looking for someone to fix your life," Michelle said, nodding. "Choose a man, choose a life."

"They say that in Michigan, too?"

"Say that everywhere. And I guess it's true, but I didn't want to believe it had to be like that. I thought I could make my life the way I wanted it, and then find someone I could see being in it. That's what men do, isn't it? So why can't we?" She smiled wryly. "But don't be feeling bad for me. I got no envy for all them women that twist themselves up to fit into some man's pocket." She turned away and made her voice light again. "But I do believe it's high time I chose a better class of man to be disappointed by." She winked and they heard Jeremy's boots on the back stairs.

Chapter Twenty-Nine

Later that evening, while Olivia was getting out the playing cards and Michelle was putting bottles of peach cordial and whiskey on the table, the back door opened and Mr. Abraham came in. Back from peddling his wares in Pontiac and Mount Clemens, he called out cheery greetings, stomped his feet on the mat, and headed for the warmth of the stove. Then Mrs. Porter peeked in and asked them to deal her in. Jeremy gallantly pulled up a chair for her.

"Do you know how to play Three Card Brag?" he asked her and then picked up a deck of cards, riffle shuffled it, and showed off making a bridge.

"I certainly do, young man."

Michelle emptied a bag of apricot pits on the table and passed out ten to each one. "We use these to bet."

"How much is each worth?" Mrs. Porter asked.

"Oh, don't worry," Olivia said. "We aren't playing for money."

"Not playing for money? Then what's the point?"

"It's just a friendly game," Michelle said.

"I can't imagine anything more boring." Mrs. Porter frowned and shook her head. "I say four bits apiece." She held up one of the pits.

"That puts $25 on the table," Mr. Abraham said.

"Isn't that nice for you, you learned your numbers. What's the problem? Afraid of an old lady?" She stared down her nose at him like a stern schoolteacher. Then she smiled and patted his arm. "Don't worry. It's only money."

Olivia, Michelle, and Jeremy exchanged amused glances and finally declared each apricot pit to be worth five cents. Mrs. Porter reached for the second deck and performed an impressive riffle shuffle and bridge of her own. Then she slammed the deck down in front of Jeremy, commanding, "Cut."

It took less than two hours for all the pits to find their way to the pile sitting in front of Mrs. Porter, but no one was complaining. The evening's entertainment had been well worth the loss of half a dollar each. They'd hidden their smiles as Mrs. Porter finished off most of the bottle of peach cordial. She began by holding her thumb and forefinger up together, almost touching, and asking for "just a teeny-tiny little sip, just to clear my throat." But she never failed to nod her head when Mr. Abraham politely, and with a straight face, offered to pour her "just one more little pinch" and then filled her cup to the brim. Finally they were all yawning and tossed the cards into a pile that Michelle gathered up. Mr. Abraham rose and asked to have a few words with Olivia.

"So let's us go into the parlor," Jeremy said to the women.

When they were alone in the kitchen, Olivia whispered to Mr. Abraham, "Wait just one second. There's something I have to do. I've been wondering all evening when I'd get the chance." She grabbed the blankets from the chair by the door and slipped outside into the dark, tiptoeing down the stairs. She shivered in the cold as she strode quickly to the barn and returned them to the clothes line, bunching them up far from the door and thinking she did not envy the man or woman who would have to spend a night in this freezing cold. She paused to stroke Sandy and murmur a few words and on her way out left the barn door open wide enough for a horse and rider to walk straight in, silent in the night.

"Good news I have for you," Mr. Abraham said when she returned. "Our friend at the bank had a letter from your lawyer in Pennsylvania. He said to inform you that the house and business sold quickly and you would understand what is he talking about."

His curiosity was obvious, but she volunteered no explanation.

"And because of this you are receiving some money as soon as he can make arrangements to send it. So meanwhile the banker wants to buy a sleigh for you. And a horse to pull it, if you didn't buy one for the buggy yet."

She shook her head. "No, I didn't have enough money left for a horse. But I'd be glad to get one now."

"Good. He saw a sleigh he thinks is good for what you need. You will pay him back when the money is coming, but he wants to buy it now, because soon you can to be deep in the snow. People think a hard winter is coming."

Olivia hadn't often ridden in a sleigh, but the times she had it was lovely, flying through the woods in falling snow. "Well, I think it's a grand idea. He can go ahead and buy it. And a horse too. Maybe I'll go into town tomorrow, stop by to see him."

Mr. Abraham put his head through the doorway and looked up the corridor. "Maybe not tomorrow. From what the banker told me, I think that the day *after* tomorrow you will be going to the town anyway."

"Oh, yes." She froze for a moment. "I forgot about that other thing I have to do." So tomorrow night Mr. Faraday would arrive with his parcel and leave a horse for her to return to Finney. She shivered again, thinking about how cold it was outside.

"And," he said, his voice so low she could barely hear him, "in two more nights after that you can to expect another delivery. Three sets of the dishes you ordered." He held up three fingers.

278

"So there will be three horses to return?"

"No, just one. They will ride together and manage with Mr. Faraday's horse and one more."

She nodded and then turned to stoke the stove and put a kettle on. She resumed speaking in a natural voice. "Do you go driving around in your wagon all winter?" she asked him.

"Not so much. Soon you will have the pleasure of much of my company. By spring Mrs. Porter will clean my pockets. I used to stay the winters in Cleveland with my family, but the last few years ..." He lowered his voice again. "There are some deliveries that are better to make in bad weather."

"How can that be?"

He moved closer to her. "The wind isn't blowing so well from the south when there's two feet of snow on the ground," he said. "So there is less new baggage, and so fewer villains searching for baggage. Those sissy Kentucky boys can't to survive a Michigan winter." He smiled. "But many parcels are in a safe place, still waiting for delivery. After this week you probably won't get any more until the river is freezing hard. Then maybe a lot. Once you have a sleigh, we can to take them right from here, straight over the river to heaven. Swoosh." He made a swishing motion with his hand.

"So that's why the sleigh."

He nodded. "And now I am tired and saying good night."

Olivia joined the others in the parlor. Michelle and Jeremy soon said their good nights and mounted the stairs. Olivia sat with Mrs. Porter for a few minutes and then watched from the window as she drunkenly wobbled to the outhouse. When she returned, Olivia stepped outside to help her up the steps and into her bedroom. Unabashed, the older woman removed her dress and petticoat and handed them to Olivia to hang up. Then Olivia tucked her into bed like a little girl.

The next morning the house was quiet. Olivia went

to the barn and was relieved to find Ernest still there, assuring her that Jeremy was not an early riser. Tomorrow she would likely have the much-anticipated strange horse out of sight before Mr. Kincaid was up and around. She went back in and found Maryam in the parlor sweeping.

"Good morning," Olivia said. "If I'm not here tomorrow morning, do you think you could prepare breakfast for the guests?"

Maryam went on sweeping without looking up. "Yes Miss."

"Thank you. I appreciate the way you're always willing to help."

"Yes Miss."

"Maryam, is everything all right?"

"Yes Miss."

Olivia turned and shook her head as she left the room. For the last few days Maryam seemed to have stopped speaking with her, other than Yes Miss. When Bayliss came back from his job in town tomorrow she would have to ask him what was bothering his wife.

Jeremy soon came down and poured himself a cup of coffee. Michelle appeared not long afterward. Olivia watched them out of the corner of her eye, but the way they spoke and moved past one another did not lead her to believe that Michelle had paid a visit to his room. They were soon waving good-bye, Michelle snuggled up against Jeremy's back, but Olivia didn't think that meant anything. She had been wrapped around him like that when they arrived yesterday.

The hours passed slowly. Olivia prepared a beef-steak pie for dinner and, needing to stay busy, made additional crusts and filled them with apples for two pies. Only Olivia, Miss Streeter, and Mrs. Porter were at the table for dinner. Maryam took her plate up to her room, as did Mrs. Gage. Olivia thought most of the winter was likely to be like this. Mr. Gage would not be inclined to walk through snow drifts for Olivia's cooking. But what about Mr. Ballou? What did he do after the river froze? Maybe he would be here all the time. She tried to imagine what they might be talking about if he were at the table now, training those dark eyes on them.

It snowed all night. In the morning Olivia looked out her bedroom window and saw tracks, only partially hidden by the delicate shower of flakes that still danced in the wind. Two horses had entered the barn from the woods, and only one had left. Deeper, more recent tracks told her it hadn't been long since Mr. Abraham had driven off in his wagon. She could only guess that he had taken the parcel with him. She dressed hurriedly, put on a thick black winter coat and boots, and wrapped a red scarf around her head.

When she pulled the barn door open, an enormous black stallion blinked at her. She stroked his neck and fed him an apple. "Hey boy, aren't you a giant? This right here must be your saddle. Are you going to let me put it on you? I know you're not going to give me any trouble, going to take the bit like a good boy, aren't you? We've got to get out of here quick. Don't worry, Sandy, I've got an apple for you too. Sorry, Ernest, I forgot about you."

While she hurriedly saddled both horses she glanced up at the clothesline. The blankets had disappeared. After feeding Sandy an apple Olivia wound the black stallion's long lead around her saddle horn. She mounted in the barn and rode slowly down the drive to the road. The snow muffled the sound of the hooves and she hoped no one was watching. She resisted the urge to look behind her to see if any of the curtains were moving. If someone was watching her, it was better not to be seen looking nervously over her shoulder. The stallion clopped along obediently and once they were far enough up the road she stopped and turned to speak to him. "You about scared me to death when I came in the barn, the way you look so fierce and all, but in fact you are one good horse."

Heavy snow began falling again, but she was soon at Finney's barn where she wordlessly handed over the stallion. Afterwards she stopped at the bank. Mr. Wentworth wasn't in yet, so she left a message that the purchase he wanted to make was fine with her. Then she entered one of the shops to buy some groceries, the excuse she would have ready for having gone into town. But when she arrived home no one asked where she had been. The house was quiet, other than the soft tones of Miss Streeter and Mrs. Porter conversing in the parlor. Maryam had cleaned up the breakfast mess and Olivia sat at the table alone, feeling somewhat despondent. She had expected this business of helping fugitives to be more ... more what? Idiot, she scolded herself, you want excitement? Excitement means some poor soul's life is in danger. You should be thanking God for every minute of boredom you get. She rose to join the women in the parlor and idly picked up the book on the end table next to Miss Streeter.

"Oh, you're reading 'The Legend of Sleepy Hollow,'" Olivia said. "I've always meant to get that from the library. There is a man in my town that the children call Ichabod Crane and run away. Is Mr. Crane such a frightening character?"

"I wouldn't say he is frightening at all. Frightening is what happens to him. They probably do that because of the way this man looks."

"What does Ichabod Crane look like?"

Miss Streeter picked up the book and thumbed back toward the beginning. "The cognomen of Crane was not inapplicable to his person," she read. "He was tall, but exceedingly lank, with narrow shoulders, long arms, hands that dangled a mile out of his sleeves, feet that might have served for shovels, and his whole frame most loosely hung together. His head was small, and flat at the top, with huge ears ..." She put the book down and looked at Olivia.

"Other than the flat head, that's a pretty good description of him." Olivia smiled, fondly remembering Mr. Carmichael loping down Main Street. She wished she had an attorney that she trusted like him here in Detroit and vaguely wondered how he would get Jettie's money to the bank. "I'd like to read that book when you're finished, if you don't mind."

"Why of course, dear."

That afternoon Bayliss glided up the drive in a black sleigh pulled by a sturdy fleabitten-gray work horse. Olivia stepped out onto the porch and waved enthusiastically. "We should all go for a ride," she called.

"Best get Fleabag here settled in her new home," he called back.

"You didn't really name her Fleabag, did you?" Olivia asked when she joined him in the barn.

"Ain't mine to name." He stroked the horse's neck and the animal nodded agreeably. "But ain't no mind to her what we be callin' her."

"Poor old Fleabag." Olivia gave her the apple she had brought. "Don't worry. We'll take good care of you."

"You got any practice driving a sleigh?" Bayliss asked.

Olivia shook her head.

"You got time, I can give you a lesson bit later."

"That would be fine. Tell me, Bayliss, don't we need a team? I mean, can one horse pull enough weight? What if the sleigh has four or five people in it? Like everyone wants to ride into town with me?"

"Nah, don't need no team. One horse can pull you a quarter ton of manure over bare earth and hardly notice she done it. You be puttin' her on ice and snow, she gonna pull twice that easy. An extra horse – that just add more weight on the ice, help you fall through into that freezin' cold river." It was the closest he had come to acknowledging outright that he knew why she needed a sleigh.

"Oh my. I hadn't thought of that. Tell me, Bayliss, is Maryam angry with me?"

He stared at the ground and sucked his front teeth for a moment. "No Miss. How she gonna be angry with you?"

"The last few days she hasn't been talking to me. Nothing but 'Yes, Miss. Yes, Miss.' Doesn't eat with us either. Takes her plate up to your room. Did I do something wrong?"

"No, Miss Killion, you ain't done nothin' wrong."

"Has anyone else here been unkind to her?"

"No, Miss."

"Don't you start with 'No Miss, Yes Miss.' Can't you tell me what's bothering her?"

It took him a while to speak. "It just ... few times I took her into town some white folks been ... unkind."

"I'm sorry to hear that." She waited for him to go on. When he didn't speak again, she pressed him. "I still don't understand. Why isn't she talking to me?"

He sighed. "Colored folks down south ... they be thinkin' the white folks up here be different. Then she get here and you be the only Michigan white folks she seen and you indeed different. So when she go into town she 'spectin' they ain't no difference between white folks and colored folks. She don't know that some white women gonna 'spect her to step aside on the sidewalk, some white men gonna say things to her what they ain't never gonna say to no white woman."

They were both silent for a moment before he went on. "In her mind she know you ain't been nothin' but kind to her, so no, she ain't angry. Ain't never gonna be angry with the woman what bought her out of slavery. But right now she be hurtin' bad. It what happen to colored folk what come up here. First they be feelin' like they landed smack in God's heaven – no one beatin' 'em outa bed before sunrise, standin' over 'em with a whip. But then they slowly start to understand – no matter how much better it be here, they still ain't just plain folks. They's still niggers. Only now they ain't no heaven they can dream 'bout runnin' off to. They already in what s'pose to be heaven. So now they know – ain't no place on God's earth they can run to where they ain't gonna be a nigger. Make 'em bitter."

"But surely she must know how many white people are trying to help. Trying to change things."

He remained silent for a moment and then looked her in the face for the first time and sounded almost angry himself. "Ain't enough."

That statement hung between them for a moment. She felt a small surge of resentment. How could they be so ungrateful?

When Bayliss spoke again his tone was still hard, but less aggressive. "You white folks got laws what let them slave-catchers come drag us back down there. You be buyin' their cotton and smokin' their tobacco. And you got your own laws what say coloreds got to register, pay a bond. You be payin' a colored man less than a white for doin' the just exact same work. Hotel don't want to give us a room, they don't got to. Tavern or store don't got to serve us." He paused again and then spoke quietly. "Just cause things be better up here, that ain't sayin' they be right. Just cause a men ain't a devil, that don't make him good."

Olivia pursed her lips and studied the ground, feeling lost. First she'd been at fault for being too kind to Maryam. Now she was judged for all the sins ... What did these people expect of her?

"But don't worry you none, Miss Killion. Maryam, she gonna get custom to the way things be and go back to normal. We best start learnin' you to drive this sleigh."

It was a dark evening in the beginning of February

285

when Mr. Abraham said to Olivia, "It's time to see how good a teacher is Bayliss. Tonight you are driving the sleigh over to Windsor."

She paled. "I've never driven on the river in daylight. I've never driven on ice at all. Just on snow."

"Not to worry, *maidaleh.*" He waved a hand. "The snow on the river is deeper than it is on the ground. And you are not running into rocks and stumps. Nothing but nice smooth ice." He cut a path through the air with his flat palm.

"Except for the cracks in the ice that you can't see because they're under all the snow."

"Better you should not to see them. If the ice breaks, we're sunk. In the drink. No one is outrunning the cracks."

She turned to scowl at him.

"Don't worry. It's true that ice is breaking faster than horses are running, but this ice is thicker than Mrs. Rafferty's backside. Many wagons full of coal are driving over it every day. The ice, I mean, not her backside. We won't fall in the water. I promise, like you say, on my heart."

"Cross my heart."

"All right. Cross my heart."

They put on coats and boots. Out in the barn Olivia started filling a lantern with oil.

"No need for that," he said.

"How do you think we're going to see where we're going?"

"You are seeing as much as you need. We have only to go a small way west, to the place where Bayliss made for you a nice slide down to the river. This is the main thing you must to learn tonight – how to find that ramp in the dark."

"Don't you think a lantern would make that a whole lot easier?"

He turned and stared at her. "And what, my dear, usually clever girl, is the reason we are going at night?"

She flushed and said, "So they can't see us."

He nodded. "Even if someone is in the woods watching the house, you can to keep some hope that they aren't seeing you. You are waiting until a few hours before sunrise. Remember, while you are snuggling under your quilt, they are for hours watching in the cold, dreaming about their bed. Then your sleigh is swooshing out of the barn. If they are still awake and seeing it at all, they are wondering if it was real, or just a shadow and the wind in the trees. If they were dreaming. Meanwhile you are flying like an angel. With practice you are going down the road and onto the river in two, not more than three minutes. Then you only must to make it halfway across, to the international line. They can't to stop you after that. Of course if you want to help them, a lantern is a very excellent idea. Or maybe a drummer boy marching ahead of you?"

"All right. All right."

That night and the next two Olivia practiced getting the sleigh onto the river. The ramp Bayliss had made was easy enough to find and solved the mystery of what he and his workers had done with all the dirt they'd dug out of her barn. The slope was steep and frightened her, going both up and down, but Fleabag never balked. It was beautiful out on the white desert, a mist of snow swirling about them, the stars bright overhead. All she had to do was turn Fleabag's head toward the lights of Windsor, say Giddap, and relax. The horse did the rest. Olivia finally stopped imagining a loud crack beneath them, the sickening gurgle of the sleigh flooded with water, and the frozen blackness closing over her head as the weight of the buffalo robes pulled her to the bottom of the river. She doubted she would be able to find the ramp on the banks of Windsor without Mr. Abraham at her side, but what did that matter? Once she was over there she could drive back and forth all night and light a lantern that would lead the good people to them.

287

A few days later Olivia was preparing for bed when she looked out the window and saw Mr. Abraham's wagon fly up the drive and into the barn. She was still pulling on her thick woolen robe, preparing to go see what was wrong, when she heard tapping on her window. She yanked it open and Mr. Abraham, his hat and beard covered with newly fallen snow, whispered, "We must to hurry. I brought three parcels who must to come inside. Where is everyone?"

"The Gages aren't here. They went to Pontiac to visit family," Olivia whispered back. "Miss Streeter and Mrs. Porter went to bed about an hour ago. Mr. O'Donnell is at work, but you never know when he will come home. And Mr. Ballou ... I'm not sure. I think he came in and went up to his room."

"So I'm bringing them in, God bless."

Chapter Thirty

"It's a family," Mr. Abraham whispered, standing on the small wooden bench Bayliss had built and put under her window. "One child. God bless. God bless. You stay there and help them in."

Olivia watched him retreat into the dark. She had never seen him so rattled. A moment later a little girl, her head covered with short pigtails, was crawling into Olivia's arms. At first touch Olivia realized the child was burning up with fever. She gently laid her on the bed and put a hand to her forehead.

"Hullo, sweetie, what's your name?"

"Cordelia."

"That's a pretty name. My name's Olivia. How old are you?"

"Seven and a half."

"Oh my stars, such a big girl. Listen Cordelia, honey, you and your mama and papa are going to stay here for a while, until you feel better. First thing we have to do is get you out of these wet clothes." She covered the child with the quilt. "Is it all right if I help you get them off? You can stay under the covers so no one will see you."

Cordelia cooperated while the white lady bunched up the sodden garments and slipped them over her head. Then Cordelia turned and curled up on her side and Olivia gave her back a brisk rub through the quilt. The mother and father, both young and slim, easily slipped through the window without any assistance. They stood staring wide-eyed at Olivia while Mr. Abraham completed what was for him a struggle. He finally pulled his leg in, straightened up, and tugged the window and curtain shut. Then he turned to Olivia, who gave the girl's back one last pat and stood.

"Miss Killion, these are the Quattros."

"Hullo," Olivia nodded to them. Mr. Quattro was almost skeletal and nervous-looking. His wife kept her face blank, seeming resigned to whatever was to come. They both returned Olivia's nod.

Mr. Abraham was still agitated. "Phillip didn't know three agents were following on his tail while he was driving the Quattros to Finney's. Those agents are searching the hotel now."

"Tell me later. Right now let's get them into some dry clothes and something hot into Cordelia's stomach," Olivia said.

"Yes, sure. But first we must to think about what to do if they are coming here. The agents."

"Why would they come here? If anyone had followed you, they'd be banging the door down by now."

"It's not meaning they won't come later, when they finish searching Finney's. You never know who is saying things. You know what the Gages are telling people about this house? Or Mr. Ballou? Maybe those agents know who I am. I told you they caught me once, with slaves in my wagon. And now I am staying here, so that is putting you on their list. And even if they aren't suspecting, these people are riding around looking for the kind of places they would choose to hide someone. Big isolated houses with barns and close to the river. They know as good as Mr. Wentworth how to spot a good place for a station. And Finney heard them say they have spies watching the river, in the day and night."

"I see. So the Quattros can't go to Windsor as long as those agents are still in Detroit." Olivia was thinking out loud. "And they certainly can't stay out in the barn. Not in this cold, even if Cordelia weren't ill."

Mr. Abraham started to say something, but she held up her hand, wanting a moment to think.

Finally she said, "This room is the only place they can stay." She turned and motioned for the Quattros to follow her into the dressing room. She shoved her dresses aside and showed them how to find and open the door to the hiding place. "There's no room to do anything but stand up," she said. "And it will be dark. But you shouldn't have to stay in there for long." Then she turned and opened a crate in a corner of the dressing room. "There are all different sizes of clothing in there. I'll go into the bedroom while the two of you try to find something to change into, and something for Cordelia."

She closed the door to the dressing room behind her and rejoined Mr. Abraham.

"So?" She looked at him and whispered. "What happened?"

"They came yesterday and were supposed to wait a few hours in Finney's barn and go over last night, soon as it was starting to be dark." He stepped closer so Olivia could hear him. "But then the little girl – she was feeling poorly. Finney was thinking it was dangerous for her to be outside in the cold wind with such a fever and then it started raining, so he was thinking there was no harm in waiting one more day. So he put them in one of the hotel rooms and was trying to find a doctor to come. Then from nowhere, three agents were taking over his hotel, demanding to search. One watching outside, one in the lobby, and one going room to room. "

"So how did the Quattros get away?"

"Out the window and down a rope. Some of Finney's people made a big rumpus out front."

"That sick little girl climbed down a rope in the rain?" Olivia shivered. "And you just happened to be there?"

"No. But Finney knew I was in town doing business and sent a rider to look for me. Have you thought how to explain that box of clothing to the agents if they find it?" he asked.

She nodded. "It's got an address on it, in New York. Those things were left behind by some boarders, and the box is all ready to send to them. I'm just waiting for them to forward the cost of shipping it."

"I always am saying you are a clever girl."

Olivia walked to the bed and put her hand on Cordelia's forehead. "She's on fire. We'll have to wake up Maryam. She said she knows about medicines."

The Quattros stepped back into the bedroom, wearing clothes that were much too big for them, but at least clean and dry. Olivia reached for their wet clothing and stooped to pick Cordelia's soggy garments from the floor.

"Excuse me," Olivia whispered. "I want to put these things with the rest of the laundry. I'll be right back."

When she returned, the Quattros had dressed their daughter and were sitting on the bed whispering to her.

"Did you bring any other things with you?" Olivia asked them. "Leave anything in the wagon?" They shook their heads no. Olivia couldn't help shaking her head along with them. She still couldn't get over the idea of people who, literally, had nothing but the clothes on their backs.

"So this room is going to be your home, until those catchers give up looking for you and we can take you over to Windsor. There are other people living in this house that we don't know if we can trust, so you will have to be very, very quiet and always keep the windows locked and the curtains closed. You must always pay attention, and if you hear anyone come into the house, you have to go in there." She nodded toward the hiding place. "Cordelia, honey, I know you don't feel good, but I'm going to ask you to get up for just a minute. I want you to know where you have to go if the bad men come. I want you to see what it's like and how you can get out, so you won't be scared. Can you do that for us?"

The Quattro family remained in the hiding place for a few minutes before letting themselves out. Cordelia assured them that she hadn't been scared and would keep quiet if the white devils came.

"I have to be sick," Olivia said, staring at the wall while she thought. "There's no other way."

"What are you talking about?" Mr. Abraham asked.

"As long as they are here, I have to stay in my room, pretend to be sick. I mean, there's no way they can keep absolutely silent for days on end. And there's the parlor right there." She pointed at the front wall. "Miss Street and Mrs. Porter are in there all day long. But if I'm sick in my room, they'll think it's me making whatever noise they hear. And someone has to be in here with the Quattros. If not and they have to hide, who's going to push the dresses back to hide the door? And what about food? It's the only explanation for Maryam carrying trays of food into my room." She paused for a moment. "So Maryam will have to know."

"Yes," Mr. Abraham said. "She must to know. She will have to stall the agents if they are coming. She's got her freedom papers?"

"Yes, they're here and I showed them to Mr. Wentworth's attorney, so he can vouch for her, need be.

Those agents do have to knock on the door, don't they?" Olivia asked. "I mean, they can't just come barging in?"

"No, they can't to do that. They must to identify themselves and tell you for what they're looking. You must to let them in, but whoever is answering the door can take some time, ask a lot of questions."

Olivia turned to the Quattros. "So you understand, I'll be staying in this room together with you. Lucky for us we have the dressing room, so we can give each other some privacy. You still have to be very, very quiet." She looked at Cordelia, who nodded. "I'll sleep here on the sofa and the three of you will have to share the bed."

The Quattros looked a bit stunned, and Olivia thought they may have expected to be told to sleep on the floor.

"A woman named Maryam who works for me will bring us food, but I'm the only one who will open the door to take the trays from her. We can trust her, but it's better for her if she can truthfully say she never saw you. The kitchen is right across the hall, so she should be able to find times to bring food without being seen. Otherwise people will be wondering how Miss Killion, sick as the poor thing is, is eating like such a horse."

Mr. Abraham was nodding in admiration. "It's a very good idea, about you being sick. When Maryam is making medicine for Cordelia, they are thinking it's for you. Very excellent."

"Yes, I know. I'm a clever girl," Olivia said and turned back to the Quattros. "All right, let's say you are sitting here eating your dinner and someone pounds on the front door. What do you do?"

"Go in there." Mr. Quattro pointed toward the hiding place.

"That's it?"

He shrugged.

"And leave three plates of food sitting here?"

"No Miss, I see, we take them with us. Hide them in

293

there with us."

"Yes, but not all of them. Leave one plate with food on it."

"Why for, Miss?"

"They're going to smell food when they come in the room, especially with all the windows closed. But one plate, they'll think is mine. They don't have dogs, do they?" she asked Mr. Abraham.

"Praise God, no."

"And try not to panic." Olivia turned back to the Quattros. "You'll have plenty of time to get yourselves in there, nice and slow. Quiet. Remember, the bolt will always be on the door and I can take my good time opening it. I'm sick in bed, after all, and have to dress myself."

Mr. Abraham said he should go upstairs and wake Maryam. Olivia slid the bolt, opened the door a crack to peek at the empty hallway, and then held the door open to let him out. Olivia and the Quattros sat in silence for some time until they heard Maryam's voice whisper, "It me." She came in and set a tray on the table. It held a teapot, four tin cups, and a fifth cup filled with something hot and strong-smelling.

"That be for the fever." Maryam pointed at the cup. "I be back with food in a bit."

Mrs. Quattro sat on the bed with Cordelia, blowing the heat from the cup of steaming medicine. Her husband sat stiffly on one of the chairs. They all drank in silence. There was a tap on the door and Olivia heard Mr. Abraham's whispered "It's me" and let him in.

"From now on this is me or Maryam." He tapped twice quickly, then a pause, then a single tap. "I'm going upstairs now," he said. "I don't think you are needing any help from me. You, my lady, were born to be a spy."

"You're looking pale. Do you feel all right?"

"Yes, yes. It's just … I have to admit, it gave me the shakes, seeing those agents."

"You saw them?"

"I had to drive past Finney's with the Quattros in the bottom of my wagon. All three of those devils were out front in the street, showing their papers to the men who were hollering about kidnappers. All I could think about was before … and now with a little girl in there."

"Don't let yourself think about that other time," she said, a little too loudly, and then lowered her voice. "Just think about little Cordelia over there, safe in my bed, and how you were able to rescue her. Were there a lot of people who came to protest against those agents?"

"Not so many. But enough to get their attention."

"What did they look like? The agents?"

"Like people I am not wanting to meet."

"Did one of them have long, dark wavy hair and a mustache?"

"I should remember their hair? I wasn't looking for a new friend."

"How about a bright red waistcoat? You'd have noticed that, wouldn't you?"

"Yes, if you are mentioning it … not red, but the tall one was wearing a bright colored waistcoat. Purple, I think. Yes, you are right. I saw that."

"With a ruffled shirt?"

"Yes. Very fancy-shmancy that one was."

"Please try to think again. Did that one, the tall one, have long wavy hair? Lots of hair. Like a lion."

He shrugged. "It maybe could be. Why?"

"I'm afraid he might be the man who was following me and Phillip when we brought that family from Backwoods. Lord, if he comes here and recognizes me, they'll tear the house apart."

Chapter Thirty-One

Maryam soon returned with food, and Olivia asked her to bring two pitchers of water, two water skins, and another chamber pot. Then it was late and Olivia said they might as well try to get some rest. She went into the dressing room to change into her winter nightdress, took a quilt from a wicker basket, and settled herself on the sofa. The Quattros arranged themselves, and the room was soon quiet except for Mrs. Quattro murmuring to Cordelia.

Olivia couldn't stop rehearsing the scene in her mind, the way it might happen: shouting and loud pounding on the front door wakes them and she is first out of bed, moving quickly, but not too quickly, silently pushing the dresses aside and opening the door to the hiding place. The father picks up Cordelia while the mother whispers soothing words and rubs the little girl's back. Cordelia remains asleep on her father's shoulder and they are safely shut away by the time someone begins banging on the bedroom door. Olivia remembers to stand near the bed before she calls out, asking who on earth it is, trying to sound as if she just woke up, using a low, hoarse voice that is different from the girlish one she spoke with during her first encounter with the handsome agent. While she talks, she scrutinizes the room, looking for anything out of place. She hasn't forgotten to fold the quilt away and move her tin cup from the table by the sofa to the nightstand.

For what seemed hours she thought it through, over and over, forgetting that she wasn't alone in the room until Mr. Quattro began snoring. That reminder of their presence made it even more difficult to sleep.

Nonsense, she scolded, remember how well you rested on that hard old deck of a steamship full of strangers. But then I had Mourning with me, she wanted to shout and suddenly felt like crying. It had been months since she'd allowed herself self-pity, since she'd felt so lonely. No, I am not going to do this, she thought. Mr. Abraham is such a good friend and so is Michelle. I should be grateful, not feeling sorry for myself. I'm the adventurous traveler. The one who helps other people. Not a weepy dishrag.

But listening to that mother with her daughter, Olivia couldn't help thinking about Little Boy, the way he smiled, laughed, and made that little gurgling sound. He was over a year old, must be crawling all over the place, even standing up. She no longer allowed herself to imagine him in her own arms – only in those of a kind-hearted black woman who was singing to him. Olivia never gave the woman a face, but she had a lovely voice.

There were no intruders that night. Olivia woke before dawn and peeked out the window, thanking God when she saw that the rain had turned to snow; the tracks leading from the barn to her window were hidden under an untouched blanket of white. Before the boarders began shuffling around, Maryam brought breakfast and more medicine and emptied the chamber pots. Then Mr. Abraham's secret knock came on the door – two quick, pause, and one more – and he told her he was going to walk into town to see what folks were saying.

Olivia spent the slowly passing hours trying to read. Mr. Quattro managed to sleep through most of the morning, as did Cordelia. When she was awake, her mother tried to engage her in guessing games, but the child lay listlessly on the bed. Maryam's medicine did not seem to be making her feel any better.

After they'd had a cold dinner of venison and bread and cheese, Olivia took a Bible from the bookshelf and removed a folded sheet of paper from it. On it she'd written: September 18, 1842   Greenstreet – Caleb, Maribelle, and Josiah – of Kentucky. From Backwoods, Michigan to Detroit, Michigan and then to Windsor, Ontario. She sat on the edge of the bed and held it out to the Quattros before she remembered it was highly unlikely that either of them could read.

"Those are the names of another family I helped," she said. "Their names and the date they were here and where they came from and where they went. I assure you, I didn't put any of it on paper until I knew they were safe in Canada. I know you don't like to tell your real names or where you're from, and I understand the danger you see in that. But I believe you need to think about the future. How are all the slaves who escape ever going to find one another? Someone else from your family might come to Canada, be living on the other side of a hill, and you'd never know." She paused a moment while they glanced at one another and then went on. "Come spring I intend to go over to Windsor and convince someone to set up a registry, keep records of all the coloreds who come from the United States, all their relations and where those relations were living the last they knew."

"Once we be in Canada that be fine," Mr. Quattro said. "But we ain't suppose to tell nothin' 'bout ourselves long as we be here."

"Yes, I know. But unfortunately I don't think anyone in Canada is likely to ask you for that information. So I would like to write down the first names of your parents and brothers and sisters and aunts and uncles, because if there are many, I won't be able to remember all of them. And I can't see any danger in a list of first names. Even if someone found it, I'd say it's a list of people I'm planning to invite to a party. They'd never know the difference."

Mr. Quattro looked skeptical and shook his head, but his wife jerked her knee to jostle his. "Course we got to do that. Mary said her and Harold be comin' soon.

How you think we ever gonna know where they at?"

They were reciting names to Olivia when Mr. Abraham rapped on the door again. "It's not good," he said. "One of them is still at Finney's, but the other two are on horseback looking for houses like yours. And I think there are more than three of them – they are paying people to help them."

"Oh." Olivia's face fell and she wondered what was so special about the Quattro family. "I was hoping to take Cordelia to see a doctor. Her fever hasn't gone down at all. She's been drinking water and tea, but doesn't want to eat anything."

He shook his head. "You can't even to think about that."

"Well, you go get a doctor, bring him back here. Say it's for me. I am supposed to be sick, after all."

He shook his head again. "I looked for the doctor we know we can trust, but he's away, delivering a baby on somebody's farm or something. And when I was coming home now I saw tracks on the road. A single rider passed your house and then turned around and came back before he went into the woods. He must to be watching the house. His tracks didn't stop by the ramp to the river, so I think he didn't notice it, thank God for the snow, but I think you are receiving a visitor soon."

Olivia folded the paper and returned the Bible to the shelf. "We're ready for him, far as I can see." She surveyed the room.

"God let it be so." Mr. Abraham turned toward the door. "I am going to bring in some firewood."

When he slid the bolt open and turned the handle, the door was pushed into him, almost knocking him over. Mrs. Porter stood in the doorway. "I thought so," she said, keeping her voice low, and stepped into the room. "All that whispering. And the Jew drummer barging into your room at all hours. You people must think I'm deaf as a biscuit."

They all froze, but Olivia quickly recovered and stepped over to close the door behind the older woman. "Mrs. Porter, please, you can't turn them in." Olivia tried to take her hand. "This poor child is deathly ill, just burning up. I know you have a Christian heart. You can't –"

"Turn them in? Stop babbling hogwash. What makes you think I'd turn them in? I sure am a Christian and not one who holds with the way some of them preacher devils twist the Scriptures. Our Lord Jesus never meant for no man to be another man's slave."

She walked over to put her hand on Cordelia's forehead while Olivia bolted the door. Mr. Abraham drew closer to Mrs. Porter and explained why he couldn't bring a doctor or take the child into town. "It seems they must to wait here a few more days."

"At the risk of this child's life." Mrs. Porter shook her head. "One thing you can do is get her into a tub of water. Not hot, just lukewarm. Even on the chilly side. That usually gets it down, though there ain't nothing to say it won't shoot right back up."

"Oh, yes, I should have thought ... I remember hearing that," Olivia said. "Mrs. Porter, can you please find Maryam and ask her to prepare a bath for me? A cool one, like you said. And then, please, please, go sit with Miss Streeter, just like any other day."

"All right. I'll go keep her company, but you don't have to pay much mind about her. That one *is* deaf as a biscuit. You really think there are catchers on the way here?"

"Yes, it's quite likely."

Mrs. Porter looked around the room and shrugged. "I guess you think you know what you're doing."

After she left the room Mr. Abraham asked Olivia if she'd lost her mind, asking for a bath. "What if she's in the tub when they come?"

"What does that matter? There'll be plenty of time to get her out. You're forgetting that I'm the one

Maryam is making the bath for. So of course I'll have the bolt on the door, and of course it will take me some time to get out of the tub and make myself presentable. We'll put some warm clothes in the hiding place. All the Quattros will have to do is wrap Cordelia in a towel and whisk her in there."

And that was how it happened. Mrs. Quattro was just about to lift her daughter out of the tub when the agent came. They barely heard his knock on the front door. It wasn't wild pounding and shouting as Olivia had imagined, but polite. A visitor come to call.

"Go," Olivia mouthed to Mrs. Quattro. "Leave me one towel."

The family was safely hidden away, as was Olivia's bedding, before the rap came on the bedroom door. Olivia stood near the tub and asked, "What is it, Maryam? I haven't finished my bath yet. But I do believe it has brought my fever down." Olivia kept her voice low, trying to sound hoarse.

"They be a gentleman here to see you, Miss."

"A gentleman? Do you mean Mr. Kincaid? Or Mr. Wentworth?"

"No Miss. A gentleman what I ain't never seen before."

"My stars, I can't imagine who would be calling in this weather. Did you tell him that I'm not well?"

"Yes, Miss. And I try tellin' him he gotta wait in the parlor, but he be standin' here next to me."

A deep male voice broke in. "I apologize for the intrusion, Miss. Are you the owner of this establishment?"

Olivia recognized his voice immediately, remembered his violet-blue eyes and high cheekbones. And that lustrous mane of hair.

"May I ask who is inquiring?" Olivia bent to put her hand in the tub and make splashing sounds, leaving a small puddle on the floor. Then she scrutinized the room again. The Quattros had forgotten nothing.

"My name is Jared Dansbury, and I surely do apologize for the intrusion. I have been commissioned by the State of Kentucky to return fugitive slaves to their rightful owners. As such, I carry papers granting me the power to search all establishments suspected of harboring any such fugitives. Again I apologize, but that includes your bedroom."

"It's a shameful profession you've chosen for yourself," Olivia said.

"That may be so, in your eyes, but your state legislature has seen fit to protect the property rights of my employer and oblige you to assist me in this endeavor."

Olivia splashed some more. "Go ahead. Carry on with your search. We've nothing to hide here. You might as well begin upstairs while I clothe myself."

"If you don't mind, Miss, I prefer to begin with your room. I'll wait right here."

Olivia bent down and stuck her head in the tub to wet her hair. Then she straightened, pulled it back from her face, and wrapped the towel around it. While waiting as long as she thought it would have taken to dry and dress herself she turned down the quilt on the bed, so he would see that it was empty before she got into it. Then she slid the wooden bolt, opened the door with her back to it, and quickly moved toward the bed.

"This is completely unacceptable, barging into a lady's private bedroom," she said to the air behind her. "Even if I were healthy, which I am not."

"You go ahead and make yourself comfortable, Miss. I'll be out of your way in a minute."

Olivia lay down on her side, half of her face pressed into the pillow, and pulled the quilt up to cover most of what remained exposed. The agent looked out both windows and then crouched to look under the bed. Olivia held her breath when he went into the dressing room and opened wicker baskets. When he began rapping on the walls she thought her head would

302

explode. She was as furious as she was afraid. Why was he checking this one room so thoroughly? Danged Mrs. Porter must have said something to him. I'll strangle her with my own hands, Olivia thought. But Mr. Dansbury soon stepped back into the bedroom.

"I beg your pardon again for the intrusion," he said. "And hope you feel better soon. I'll have a look around the rest of the house and barn and be on my way."

"Whoever you're looking for, I hope they're having a nice dinner in Windsor," Olivia said.

"Law's the law. Weren't so many of you Yankees breaking it, we wouldn't have to suspect all of you," he replied and left the room, pulling the door closed behind him.

Olivia threw the quilt off her face and took a few deep breaths. There didn't seem to be anything she could do, other than lie in bed and wait for him to be gone. She sighed. Such a handsome-looking man. So well-mannered. And such a devil.

His footsteps were heavy as he went up the stairs, but much quieter coming down. Olivia felt certain he was outside her door, listening, and paled when she heard rustling noises coming from the hiding place. She groaned loudly and called out for Maryam. No one came to the door, and she called again. She heard people walking around, and then the front door opened and closed.

"He be gone." Maryam opened the door to Olivia's room. She was normally bare-headed, but now had a red scarf wrapped around her head.

"Thank God. Come in and bolt the door behind you." Olivia rose from the bed and asked, "Was it you who let that man in?"

"Yes, Miss."

"Not Mrs. Porter?"

"No Miss, when he come she be in the parlor with Miss Streeter."

"And did she talk to him at all?"

"No Miss."

"You're sure."

"I let him in and he tole me what he be wantin' and I tole him you be sick and ain't receivin' no visitors and he tole me he ain't no visitor and he gonna search the whole house and 'ccordin' to the law he got to tell you that and aks me where you be at and he come with me to your door."

"Did Mrs. Porter come out of the parlor? Could she have given him some kind of signal?"

"Not 'less she got magic powers. She ain't never got off her chair."

Olivia frowned. "Do you have any idea what made him want to search this room first?"

"No Miss. 'Cept that what I gonna do, if I be that agent. Case the person I be chasin' be in here and gonna go out the window. Special with you bein' in here with the bolt on."

"Yes, you're right. It's probably just that." Then Olivia frowned again, staring at Maryam and looking confused. "Isn't that Mrs. Porter's dress you're wearing?" The bright red and blue plaid garment was far too big for Maryam.

"Yes Miss, that surely so. 'Fore that man come she give it to me, tell me you say I gotta put it on."

"And the scarf on your head?"

Maryam nodded. "She put it on me."

Olivia was puzzled, but would have to ask about it later. "Did you watch that man leave?"

"Yes, Miss, he get on his horse and go that way." She pointed toward Detroit.

"That doesn't mean he didn't sneak back into the woods. But what does it matter? He can watch the house all he wants, there's not going to be anything for him to see." Olivia paced back and forth, thinking out loud. "I guess I might as well tell them to come out. Could you go brew up some more medicine?"

"Yes Miss."

When Olivia opened the door and told the Quattros it was safe to come out, both parents looked distressed. Cordelia lay over her father's shoulder like a limp rag doll.

"She spit up all the water she drank," Mrs. Quattro said. "She like to be on fire."

Olivia put her hand on the child's forehead and pulled it back in alarm. "Oh my, I've never felt anyone so hot." She stood feeling useless.

There was a knock on the door. Two, pause, one. Olivia opened it and Mr. Abraham came in. "How's the little girl?"

"Not good. Not good at all. She needs a doctor," Olivia said.

He paused, looking uncertainly at Olivia before he spoke. "Mrs. Porter has an idea. Come with me into the kitchen for a minute. Please."

Olivia did as he asked and heard Maryam go to the parlor and tell Mrs. Porter that Miss Killion wanted to have a word.

"What's going on?" Olivia asked Mr. Abraham's back. He was pouring two cups of tea.

"I am just wanting some company. Sit here with me for a few minutes. Don't worry. The front and back doors, they are both locked and bolted.

He began telling stories about his last trip, and Olivia stared at him as if he had lost his mind. Maryam silently slipped into the kitchen and began arranging some things on a tray.

"Tell me, Maryam," Mr. Abraham said, "that man checked your freedom papers, didn't he?"

Maryam turned to face them and nodded her head. Mr. Abraham's gaze stayed on her for a moment and then he asked Olivia, "That dress is looking terrible on her, don't you think?"

Olivia glanced at Maryam and said, "Yes, yes, it's much too big." Then she turned back to him, exasperated. "But what are we going to do about poor

Cordelia?"

"Why don't you ask Maryam?"

"What do you mean?"

Maryam came over to the table, and Olivia looked up at her. "What does he mean? Do you have some other kind of medicine?"

Mr. Abraham slapped his palm on the table. "She's right," he said, obviously having a hard time keeping his voice down. "She may be an *alte yachne,* but she's a clever *alte yachne.*"

"What is the matter with you?" Olivia asked.

"What is the matter with your eyes, dear girl? Nothing! Nothing at all! You have perfect vision, but you didn't notice. And if you didn't notice, so you think the Kentucky cracker is going to notice?"

"Notice what?" Olivia turned to Maryam for an explanation. Then her chin fell and she stood up. "You're not Maryam!"

Mrs. Quattro removed the red scarf from her head.

"She said so." Mr. Abraham looked like he might get up and do a little dance. "Mrs. Porter said so and she was right. People are never looking at servant's faces, even if they're white. If you put her in the right costume —"

"I still don't know what you are talking about."

"You want to take the little girl to a doctor in Detroit? Mrs. Porter had a better idea. You and Maryam here ..." he extended his arm toward Mrs. Quattro, "and Mrs. Porter are taking her to a doctor in Canada. If your prissy boy in his ruffled shirt is down on the road waiting to stop the sleigh, she is telling him she's taking you to the doctor. You are lying in the back seat, your head on a pillow in Maryam's lap, all covered up with buffalo robes. The little girl is underneath the seat, wrapped in fur, safe from the cold by all the robes over you."

"What if he wants to search the sleigh?"

"Why? He is looking for a family. There's no place to

306

hide even one adult on that sleigh. And he knows you are sick, and he already intruded on you once today. And the last thing he is expecting is you to drive a fugitive out, in broad daylight, when he just was searching your house. Anyway, you think a ruffled shirt is going to argue with the *alte yachne*?"

"But if the ruffled shirt is watching the house, how are we going to get Cordelia from the house into the sleigh?" Olivia asked.

"We didn't think of that yet."

Mrs. Porter had come to stand in the doorway and they all remained silent, thinking.

"The laundry," Olivia said at last. "We have mountains of dirty sheets. If Maryam wasn't busy taking care of me, that's where she'd be right now, out in the barn doing laundry. So she'll pretend that's what she's going to do. She'll carry armloads of sheets out there. Then she'll come back in for the tub, the one I had my bath in. It's not a laundry tub, but what does a man know about that? Poor little Cordelia is thin as a rail, doesn't weigh much of anything. She can curl right up in the bottom of the tub, a pile of laundry on top of her. Mrs. Quattro will open the back door and Mrs. Porter will say, real loud, 'Here, let me help you with that' and they'll carry the tub to the barn, each holding one handle, and then Mrs. Porter will say, 'But you can't start on laundry now. We've got to get poor Miss Killion to a doctor.'" Olivia looked up at Mrs. Porter. "You do know how to drive a sleigh?"

"Do bears like berries?"

"And I assume you know where the doctor's office is? A doctor we dare take her to?" Olivia asked her.

"I told you. You're not going to go to a doctor in Detroit," Mr. Abraham said. "You're going to take her right over the ice, to the promised land."

"And we'll leave Mrs. Quattro there with Cordelia." Olivia nodded, as if saying "Now I understand."

"Not so many folks are bringing fugitives back from

Canada with them."

"But what about Mr. Quattro?"

"He must to stay here until the crackers leave. Not in your bedroom, of course."

"There's no other place he can stay," Olivia said, "He can sleep on a quilt on the floor of the dressing room." She looked up at Mrs. Quattro. "Do you want to do this? Go by yourself?"

She nodded. "My baby be real sick."

Olivia thought for a moment and then wondered out loud. "I don't know if we dare use Bayliss's ramp. We can't turn to the right, if they're supposed to be taking me to a doctor. There is nothing in that direction. We have to turn toward Detroit."

"There's a big ramp right before Hog Island," Mr. Abraham said.

"But the river's so wide there."

"Yes. You're right about that." He thought for a moment. "There is also a ramp between here and town, by the saw mill. Go toward Detroit and if you are feeling safe, use that one. If you are feeling like someone is watching after you, keep going to Hog Island. If that isn't feeling good to you, you can to turn around. Use the saw mill ramp on the way back. Or go to the bottom of your drive and then race for your ramp."

When they rounded the first bend the ruffled shirt was indeed waiting by the side of the road. Driving like a teamster, Mrs. Porter gave him her best scowl, but the agent only tipped his hat as they swooshed by. A few minutes later they neared the saw mill and Mrs. Porter made a sharp turn toward the water, bumped down the ramp, and raced across the river. No hooves pounded after them and they were soon past the magic line.

Olivia sat up, squeezed Mrs. Quattro's shoulder, and said, "Cordelia can get up. You're free now."

Mrs. Quattro helped her daughter off the floor and

into her lap. She put her hand to her forehead and then hugged her, wrapping the buffalo robes tight. "Oh baby, you got the fever. But we gonna get you to a doctor in two licks."

"Where's Pappa?" Cordelia murmured. "Why didn't Pappa come?"

Mrs. Porter easily found the escarpment up the bank, but had to stop and ask several people for help finding the address Mr. Abraham had given her. Soon Mrs. Quattro stepped over the threshold of a large Victorian home and turned to wave good-bye. Olivia limply raised her own hand, overwhelmed by the absurdity of it – for one day their lives had been intimately entwined; now Olivia was unlikely to ever see her again. Man is a bewildering creature, she thought.

Olivia moved into the front seat and they drove back toward the river. Though happy that mother and daughter were now safe, she felt more let down than exhilarated.

"That was a brilliant idea, putting Maryam in that dress so when Mrs. Quattro changed into it he'd think she was Maryam," Olivia said. "And I'm truly grateful for all your help and the way you put your own self at risk, driving us here."

"Ain't no thing."

"But there's one thing I want to ask you."

"So ask."

"Why were you so unkind to Mr. Abraham, calling him 'the Jew drummer'?"

"He's a Jew ain't he?"

Olivia made an exasperated face.

"And he's a drummer, ain't he? Peddles his goods all over hell and back. So I'd say that makes him a Jew drummer. What's unkind about saying so?"

"But when you say 'Jew drummer' like that, it sounds as if you think there's something wrong with being a Jew."

"Don't sound like no such thing." Mrs. Porter was obviously offended. "If you think it's an insult to call someone a Jew, then I'd say you's the one what thinks there's something wrong with being one."

Olivia remained silent for a moment. "So you don't dislike him?"

"No, I think he's fine company. I can say the two most important things about him – he's funny and a terrible card player."

Olivia kept quiet the rest of the way home. Feeling as if she had been trapped in her room for days, she tried to enjoy the fresh air and scenery, but her view consisted mainly of a blizzard of snowflakes and the backside of a buffalo hide. She was exhausted and welcomed the prospect of a good night's sleep, followed by nothing but routine and boredom.

Chapter Thirty-Two

The Kentucky crackers had apparently gone south to wait for the spring thaw, and Olivia's wish for boredom was fulfilled. Parcels were regularly delivered and picked up, but usually on the same day and without her setting eyes on them. She did nothing but leave food and water in the barn. She did ferry a few small groups of fugitives over the frozen river, but those trips were uneventful. When in Windsor she always tried to learn what had become of little Cordelia, but found no one in Canada who could tell her anything about a mother with a sick little girl. She also tried to convince people to begin keeping lists. They listened politely, but Olivia doubted her advice would be taken.

Her house grew empty. First the Gages purchased a farm and left. Then Bayliss announced that he and Maryam were moving into town.

"I still gonna come out here regular ever week, see what repairs you need doin'," Bayliss assured her. "But

I don't want Maryam workin' no more. 'Sides it gonna do her good to be in town. See more of other free black folks."

Olivia later learned that their departure had been at the urging of Mr. Wentworth, who thought the presence of black boarders called too much attention to the house. Olivia hired a white girl named Janie Renfro to replace Maryam, but Janie didn't want to live in and walked or rode her horse to work every day. She was a good worker, but chattered incessantly and Olivia sorely missed Maryam's silent glare.

Late one afternoon Olivia saw Michelle trudging up the drive in the snow and brought a pair of slippers and a blanket to wrap her in. They sat at the kitchen table drinking coffee until Michelle asked for something a little stronger. Olivia poured her a whiskey and then cocked her head and stared at her friend.

"Something's different about you," she said. "Did you cut your hair or something?"

"Stopped painting my face," she said and took a drink of whiskey. "Jeremy didn't like it." She set the glass down hard and stared at Olivia, waiting for her reaction.

"Oh. So you and Jeremy –"

"He's been staying with me the last few days. Stopped in the shop and took me out for supper. Then the snow started coming down hard ... and he just stayed."

Olivia smiled and put her hand on Michelle's. "I told you. I'm happy for you. I mean, as long as you're happy. You are, aren't you?"

"Yes. I been lonely for a man in my bed, and he's the best one what's ever been there."

"All right, so I am happy for you. As long as he doesn't carry you off to Ann Arbor."

"No." Michelle visibly relaxed and took a roll of cloth containing a few cigarettes from her bag. "You have to let me smoke in here today," she said and Olivia raised her hands in surrender. "My butt's way too froze to sit out on that porch. 'Sides I deserve some consideration for once – that was a hard sentence to get out of my mouth." She lit the cigarette, inhaled, and leaned back in her chair to exhale at the ceiling. "No, I think he's pretty much given up on that professor business. Oh, they'll pay him something to give his talks, but he's figured out that they ain't about to give him a full-time job and a house like them professors. I don't think he really wanted one any way. He liked the idea of it, but he loves that cabin of his."

"Have you been there?"

"Uh-huh, we rode out one day when the weather warn't too bad."

"Wait until you see it in the spring. Oh my stars, you'll get to use his shower. I am jealous of that!"

Michelle smiled. "We'll invite you out for a scrub."

"Maybe some evening after supper I'll come into town and the three of us can have a drink together. Or you two come here for supper and play some cards. Just tell me what night."

A wide smile spread across Michelle's face. She looks like a young girl, Olivia thought.

"So how are you doing here, with all these empty rooms?" Michelle asked.

"I didn't know you were keeping track. It's quiet, but I keep myself busy."

"I meant money-wise, little girl," Michelle said.

"Just about breaking even."

"So why ain't you in town, putting up notices, telling all the shopkeepers you're looking for boarders? I'll tell you who you got to talk to, soon as the ships start coming in all them cariole drivers what work the port and get folks right off the boat. You promise 'em two bits for every boarder they bring you, this place will be bursting."

"I will. I will. Just as soon as we get some sunshine."

"What are you, some kind of reverse vampyre?"

Michelle bared her teeth.

"Still reading your penny dreadfuls, are you? You should try an actual book some time."

"And you should try running a business like you actually want to make money. Hershey's going to be leaving for his spring circuit soon. Then you'll have another empty room and probably won't even be covering your expenses. Course, why shouldn't you feed these people out of your own pocket?"

"I'll fill the rooms, don't worry. You know, I've never thought of it before," Olivia mused, "but it's strange, isn't it, that Mr. Abraham stays the winter here, instead of in Cleveland with his family."

"I suppose so. A person could forget he's got a wife, way he never talks about her. They must be one a them couples what get along all right, long as they don't got to actually see each other."

"He must be lonely."

"He has been known to patronize Mr. James Slaughter's bawdy house. On more than one occasion."

Olivia's mouth fell open. "That can't be true. Not Mr. Abraham!"

"You think he ain't human? That ain't even a nice thing to say about a man. If his wife don't want him around, then he ain't doing no one no harm. We all got our flaws and weaknesses. Needs. We got our needs. By the way, speaking of flaws, don't be making the mistake of feeling free to talk about ..." Michelle leaned forward and lowered her voice "... your packages in front of Jeremy. I don't mean he'd go turn us in, but he ain't no abolitionist, and he could get careless and flap his jaws without intending no harm. Just watch what you say around him."

"Of course I will. I watch what I say around everyone. But what makes you think that about him?" Olivia was of the same opinion, but interested in hearing Michelle's reasons.

"Things I heard him say. Like, 'You want to keep

wearing your cheap cotton, don't you?' Or 'You think they were better off in Africa?' Things like that."

Later it started snowing and Olivia insisted on taking Michelle back to town in the buggy. When she returned home she sat on the porch in the dark, her enjoyment of the stars greater than the discomfort of the bitter cold.

Lord, human beings are hard to know, she thought. I'm not allowed to poke Mr. Abraham in the arm, but he can visit that bawdy house? Then she remembered how many secrets she had and sighed. Just mind your own business, she told herself. That's all you can do. And be kind. If everyone would just mind their own business and be kind to one another, this world wouldn't be the mess it is.

One evening in mid-April Mr. Abraham came home and announced that the first boat from Buffalo had docked. Olivia's spirits rose. Winter was officially over, even if there were still large chunks of ice floating on the river. The port would soon be humming again; they were no longer cut off from the world. She hadn't realized how much she missed being able to walk along Atwater Street, immersed in all that awful shouting and commotion. Mr. Abraham had already restocked his wagon and tomorrow would start on a short trip to the cities farther north before leaving on his grand circuit.

The next morning Olivia looked out the window and saw a bright blue sky. She put on trousers, took Sally for her morning ride, and then went into her room to change. But why on earth should a person wear a cumbersome dress and petticoats to fry bacon and scrub the floor? No reason, she decided. Her boarders were accustomed to seeing her in men's clothing when she rode or worked outside, but she had not yet ventured into the parlor dressed that way. Too bad for them, she thought, they'll just have to get used to it. She strode into the parlor and asked the women if they were

314

ready for their breakfast. Their blank faces stared her up and down.

It was Mrs. Porter who finally spoke. "We were starting to wonder if you were ever going to ask." She pushed herself up out of the chair. "Let me give you a hand. Fry up a heap of onions."

Later that day, after Olivia had fed them a dinner of fried chicken and mashed potatoes, she went out to sit on the porch. Still in her trousers, she put her feet up on the rail, tipped her chair to balance on its hind legs, and enjoyed the clear sky. It was still cold, but not intolerably so. She'd wrapped a scarf around her head and face, but even so thought she'd better go in soon, before she got an ear ache.

She heard horse's hooves, but paid them no mind. There were no parcels in the barn and so no reason for passing strangers to be of concern to her. Then a colorfully painted, two-wheeled cariole turned up the drive. A tall, thin passenger stood on the footboard behind the driver. He wore a proper black overcoat, but appeared to have a dead animal wrapped around his head.

Lord, she thought, that driver is bringing me a boarder, but he's some kind of wild man. Michelle should watch who she advertises for. But as Olivia stared, she thought there was something oddly familiar about this stranger. When the cariole came to a stop she watched the passenger descend into the slush of melting ice and snow, picking one foot after the other high in the air. She'd know those knobby knees anywhere.

"Mr. Carmichael!" She rushed down the steps. "I can't believe you came all this way."

Thrilled to see someone bringing news from home, she would have thrown her arms around him, but he was that much taller and did not cooperate by bending down.

"Miss Killion?" He blinked. "Yes, of course it's you. I thought that must be a young hired boy, sitting up there on the porch."

"Sure it's me." She pushed the scarf back. "I knew it was you, even with that bobcat wrapped around your head."

"I beg your pardon. I'll have you know this is genuine coyote." He removed the furry hat and held it out for her to admire. In addition to the long earflaps, the animal's legs and tail hung down the back. "A rugged-looking fellow was selling them on the boat. I thought it must be the latest in Michigan pioneer fashion."

She grinned and then bent down, as if searching under the tiny carriage. "Where are your bags?"

"I left them at the hotel."

"What hotel? Of course you're staying here."

"I would be most happy to. That was my intention, if you have a room available, but I didn't wish to presume. This good fellow will return to the hotel and bring my cases to me." He spoke to the driver who nodded and turned around.

"You must be tired after your trip," she said. "Did you get much sleep on the boat?"

"A bit. I slept well in the hotel last night."

"Oh, you mean you arrived in Detroit yesterday? You must have been on one of the first boats to arrive."

"The first one out of Erie."

She turned and led him up the steps, straight past the parlor where the women were sitting, and back to the kitchen. Let them be curious for a while. "There's plenty of fried chicken if you're hungry."

"No. Thank you. I had my dinner in town."

She worked the pump handle to set a glass of water in front of him and moved the kettle onto the stovetop. "That coffee will be hot in a lick." She bit her lip before asking, "Did Mourning ever come back to talk to you any more?"

He set his ball of fur in the chair next to him and folded his hands on the table. "No," he said. "I'm sorry to say I haven't heard anything of him. I trust you've been well?" He cleared his throat, obviously uncomfortable.

"Me? Yes. As a horse." She turned to face him and paused before continuing in a more subdued tone. "I've made some friends here, and they've helped me to ... to be better than I was. And having this house ... it's been good for me."

"I'm glad to know that." He blinked and looked away. "Oh, I should tell you that I've brought your money." Back on safe ground, his voice regained its assurance. "The proceeds from the sale of Mrs. Place's properties."

She gave him a blank look. "You mean you have it in your pocket?"

He smiled. "No. I assure you that I got a better price than would fit in my pockets. I did have it on my person, in gold, during the trip. Do you know that they make a special vest consisting of rows of pockets, especially for the transport of gold coins? One wears it under one's shirt. I'd been thinking of transferring the money through the bank, but when I saw one of those vests in a store over in South Valley, I decided to bring it myself. Good excuse for seeing Detroit. And you." He looked away.

Olivia's heart dove for the floor. Dear Mr. Carmichael can't be here to court me, can he? Lord, and me running out there, trying to get my arms around him. What must he think? But how could he think that? He's old. Olivia did not know his age. She'd always simply thought of him as old. He'd been an adult, her father's widowed lawyer, for as long as she could remember herself.

She forced herself to smile and said, "Lucky no one pushed you overboard with all that gold on you. They would have turned you into a sunken treasure." She kept her smile, but couldn't help feeling sad, remembering Mourning saying something similar about the bags of gold coins she'd been wearing under her skirts when they traveled together. "So did you see much of Detroit?"

"First thing off the boat I went to the bank to see your Mr. Wentworth. He's a good sort. Most accommodating. Put off another appointment and made time to speak with me, free me of that vest. He and I will sort out getting this house in your name free and clear. What remains of the money will go into an account that you can draw on. I can't tell you what the balance of that account might be at the moment, but if you'd like we can go see him tomorrow. He'll have worked it out – exactly how much is owed to him for expenses and what remains."

Olivia nodded and he continued, "Afterward I walked along the waterfront for a while and up Woodward Avenue to that large park. I can see why you decided to stay here. It's quite a city."

"I can't walk anywhere in Detroit without seeing something new. Even if I've been up and down that street a thousand times. Tomorrow after breakfast we'll go see Mr. Wentworth, and then I'll show you around. I have a buggy out in the barn."

They grew more comfortable as they spoke about practicalities and then her family, town gossip, and Mrs. Place. He told her about the funeral; it had been much as Olivia imagined it.

She grew melancholy for a moment, remembering her father's funeral. It had been January and the gravediggers had set a fire to thaw the ground, dug a few inches, set another fire, and dug some more – until they finally got past the frost line and could go down deep enough. The ceremony was short. While watching the coffin being lowered into that scorched gouge in the earth Olivia shed her first tears. It isn't fair, she'd been thinking. Everyone else gets to go back home and warm

318

their hands at the stove in the kitchen, but he has to stay down there all alone, under all that ice. He must be so cold. But she'd known she was mostly crying for herself. I'm glad I wasn't there to see them bury Jettie, she thought. It would be too hard, crying for both of us. She shook the sadness off, reminding herself, it what we all come to anyway. Might as well enjoy the blue sky while we're still under it.

"Did Jetty have someone taking care of her?"

"Yes. A colored girl from The Bottoms over by South Valley. Good-natured young woman. She went to get Doc Gaylin at the end. He sat with Mrs. Place for a few hours, before she passed over."

"That's good." Olivia's voice caught. "I always worried about her being alone like she was, even when she wasn't sick. What if she fell down the stairs?"

She was glad for the distraction of hooves in the drive. The cariole had returned with the cases. Olivia showed Mr. Carmichael the three empty rooms on the second floor that were his to choose from. He tried all the mattresses and decided on the one Bayliss and Maryam had shared.

"Let me pay you now for the first week." He became awkward again.

"You can't possibly believe I would charge you rent."

"Of course you will. I won't stay otherwise. But we needn't discuss that now," he said.

She looked into his face and then quickly away, unsettled by the longing she thought she saw there.

"I'll go fill the pitcher." She lifted it out of the basin on the bureau. "There are towels in the wardrobe."

When she returned with the hot water, she said, "I'm sure you could use some rest, and I have to start getting supper together. I'll call you when it's ready. Or feel free to come down to the parlor. I'll introduce you to the boarders."

She frowned as she descended to the kitchen. She'd always been grateful to Mr. Carmichael, trusted him with her problems, and known he was on her side. And on Mourning's side. But why on earth had he come out here? And for how long? He said he wanted to pay for the first week. Just how many weeks did he intend to stay? And how did she draw the line between hospitality and leading him to believe she might return whatever feeling he may have?

I'm being ridiculous, worrying about nothing, she argued with herself. I'm a little girl to him. He's never thought of me in any other way. Why wouldn't he leap at a good excuse for getting out of Podunk Five Rocks and seeing such an exciting city? I have to stop imagining problems where none exist. She could imagine what Michelle would have said – "Girl, when Jesus comes back to save our eternal souls, you'll find ten reasons to fret about what good can possibly come of that."

Olivia decided to bake a cake in Mr. Carmichael's honor. She was humming in the kitchen – a tune Mourning used to play on his harmonica – but paused when she heard footsteps descending the stairs. To her relief, Mr. Carmichael did not come looking for her, but went straight to the parlor to join the women. Only a few minutes passed before Olivia heard them giggling. She shook her head and resumed humming. She considered Mr. Carmichael to be many good things that did not include funny But, she reminded herself, it doesn't take much to entertain people who've been cooped up in a house together through a long Michigan winter. When the table was set she opened a bottle of wine and carried a tray into the parlor.

"I see you've met Mr. Carmichael." She handed Miss Streeter a glass of cider, poured wine for everyone else, and raised her own glass. "For me a visit from anyone from back home would be cause for celebration, but Mr. Carmichael's arrival is a very special occasion. And I hope he's planning to stay for a while." She avoided looking at him while she spoke.

For once Olivia did not have to make an effort to keep the supper conversation going. The women were more than pleased to have someone new to talk to. After helping herself to a second glass of wine, Mrs. Porter leaned toward Olivia and spoke loudly. "I was just saying how Detroit is famous for its hotels. Best hotels in the country, outside of New York City. So I'd like to ask the use of the buggy tomorrow, if you don't mind, so I can show them to Luther."

Olivia gave her a blank look. "Who's Luther?"

"Luther." Mrs. Porter's eyebrows joined together. When Olivia's expression didn't change, Mrs. Porter bobbed her head toward Mr. Carmichael. "Luther. Him. Your friend."

Mr. Carmichael raised his eyebrows and shrugged his shoulders.

Olivia was both amused and embarrassed. "My stars, I never realized that I didn't even know your Christian name. You were always Mr. Carmichael to me." Then Olivia turned to Mrs. Porter. "Regarding the buggy, that will be just fine. Mr. Carmichael – *Luther* – and I have something to do in town tomorrow, and you're welcome to ride along. While we tend to our business, you can do your own shopping. Then later we can meet at Michelle's shop, and you can show Mr. Carmichael all the fancy hotels while I visit with her."

After the meal Mr. Carmichael lingered in the kitchen and insisted on helping Olivia with the washing up.

"I brought some of the things you asked for," he said as he hung the dish towel on its hook, "from Mrs. Place's house."

"How kind of you. I certainly never meant for you to have to carry them all this way."

"I had plenty of room for them. Except for the clock and knitting basket. I left those back in my office. I'll go fetch the rest now, if you like."

She nodded eagerly and he soon returned with a

large cloth bag. He removed what looked like a clump of tissue paper and unwrapped her mother's brush and comb.

"Oh thank you. These are the most important. They were my mother's." Olivia ran her fingers over them. "I can't thank you enough."

Next out of the bag came a wooden box containing Jettie's china figurines: a Flamenco dancer in black and red ruffles, a colorful geisha, a Hindu woman wrapped in an orange sari with a purple jewel on her forehead, a Dutch girl in big wooden shoes and white cap, and a dark-skinned woman carrying a stalk of bananas on her head.

"She loved these so much." Olivia stood them in a row on the table. "I'm going to put them in the china cupboard in the parlor."

Then he handed her Jettie's shiny, low-cut red dress. Olivia stood and held it to her body. "Oh my goodness, just look at it. I wonder when she last had a chance to wear it. I always wanted to ask to try it on, but couldn't let on I knew it existed without admitting I'd gone snooping through her closet the first day I was at her house."

"I'm sure you would look fetching in it." Mr. Carmichael took a step closer and draped Jettie's white feather boa around Olivia's shoulders.

She took a nervous step away and let the dress and boa fall over the back of the chair. "I'm sure I can't imagine any occasion I'd have to wear it."

He had also remembered to bring the pictures Jettie had cut out of a journal and tacked to the walls of her kitchen. They were unwrinkled, having been pressed between two thin slats of wood.

"I never cared for these much, but they will remind me of her the most." Slightly teary-eyed, Olivia sat down and held each one up in turn. "Of all the hours I sat in her kitchen staring at them. I guess I'll put them in my room."

Last out of the bag were Jettie's perfume and the volume of Wordsworth.

"Well," Olivia said and stood. "Thank you again for bringing everything. I guess we'd better get some rest. It seems we'll have a long day tomorrow. And thank you for helping in the kitchen."

"My pleasure. I've been at home in a kitchen for a long time. Since my Clarissa passed."

"So you cook for yourself?"

"Yes. At first I had a woman come in, but I like my privacy better than that. Nowadays I take some meals at Sorenson's Saloon. Occasionally have one over at Mrs. Monroe's. But mostly it's simpler to tend to myself."

"At least you'll have a vacation from it while you're here. I'm sorry to say, but I don't remember your wife at all."

"You wouldn't. It's been eleven years since I lost her, barely a year after we married. You were just a little girl."

Olivia stared over his shoulder for a moment, brows furrowed. "Maybe I do remember her, a little. Did she have red hair?"

He nodded.

"Yes, I do recall her coming into the store. Tobey and I used to make fun of the way Avis fell all over himself every time he saw her. She was real pretty."

"Yes, she was."

Olivia looked into his face and could think of nothing else to say. The schoolchildren were right, he did fit Mr. Irving's description of Ichabod Crane, with his long nose and big ears. So homely there was something endearing about him.

"Before you retire ..." Mr. Carmichael reached back into the bag. "I have one more thing in here. For your birthday."

"How did you know today's my birthday?" Olivia's eyes opened wide. "I didn't tell anyone."

"I'm your attorney. We don't want anyone confusing the owner of this property with some other Olivia Killion, so I went to your church for the baptismal record. Happy Birthday." He removed from the bag a rectangular box of wood and demonstrated how it folded out into a game board.

"I don't know what to say. You are too kind to me." She picked up the board smiling. On one side it was checkers, which she knew how to play. "What's this on the other side?" she asked when she turned it over.

"Backgammon. I'll be happy to teach you. Now that I've seen your front porch, I know you have the perfect place for a game on a summer evening."

"You're right about that. I love sitting there watching the river. It's a lovely gift. Thank you," she said, hoping he didn't plan to still be here when summer came, months from now.

"And lastly ..." He handed her another rectangular shape, wrapped in gingham. When she removed the cloth her mouth fell open. She was holding a stack of three framed photographs – one of Tobey, Avis, and Mabel in their parlor; one of Main Street, focusing on Killion's General Store; and one of Mrs. Place's house and bakery shop.

"How did you ... this is wonderful ... the best present ... but how did you?"

He looked pleased but uncomfortable. "I wish I could take credit for a Herculean effort, but a man drove into town one day, in a wagon that was piled high with his equipment. All I did was pay him to produce the photographs."

"Didn't people wonder why you were having a picture made of my family?"

"I told them it was for you. And when someone asked why I wanted a picture of Mrs. Place's house, I said it was to show to prospective buyers. I'm glad you're pleased with them."

She stared at the photographs. If only she had

likenesses of Little Boy and Mourning. "They are the best present anyone ever got."

"I am glad you like them." He folded the empty bag and stepped away from the table. "As you said, we'd best get some sleep."

Chapter Thirty-Three

The next morning Olivia took Sandy for a quick ride, served breakfast to her guests, did the washing up, tended the fires, and made two beef-steak pies for Janie Renfro to bake and serve for dinner. Then she harnessed Fleabag to the buggy and climbed into the back seat, knowing Mrs. Porter would want to sit with Mr. Carmichael up front, where she could point out every building and hole in the road.

When they arrived at the bank Mr. Wentworth greeted Mr. Carmichael warmly, the two men seeming to have taken an immediate liking to one another. The banker ushered Olivia and Mr. Carmichael into his office, but the two men were in such agreement regarding the arrangement of Olivia's affairs that she felt pleasantly extraneous – and bored. She interrupted them, saying she needed something from the store across the street and would come back later.

When she returned they had a stack of papers for her to sign and she walked out of the office feeling light-headed. Two years ago she couldn't have imagined enjoying such financial security. She couldn't stop taking inventory in her head, over and over. Not a cent did she owe to anyone. Her lovely boarding house sat on a beautiful piece of land. The farm in Fae's Landing would one day be worth some money. She owned her own buggy, sleigh, and two horses. And there were still hundreds of dollars in her account. The handshakes and signatures on documents made it all real, and she felt like a millionaire.

All these worldly goods wouldn't buy happiness. She knew that. They couldn't make her old dream of a wagon full of children, with a big yellow dog chasing along beside them, come true. Not in this lifetime. Not with all the secrets she had to keep. But better to be a lonely spinster with her own house and money in the bank than a homeless lonely spinster without a penny to her name. She would make a life, enjoying the company of her friends and doing what she could to help others. And one day Mourning Free would come knocking on her door. She felt certain of that. She at least would know what had happened to him and perhaps, just perhaps, would get to see Little Boy again. She made bargains with God every night – all the good deeds she would do, if only He would make that happen.

Olivia and Mr. Carmichael still had time before they were to meet Mrs. Porter at Michelle's shop, and Olivia asked what he would like to see first.

"Is there anything left of Fort Pontchartrain?"

"No, that's long gone. But I could show you where it used to stand. Or how about starting at Ste. Anne's church? It's not the original one they built inside the fort, but it's real pretty. I'll tell you the stories about Father Gabriel Richard. He's the Jesuit priest who started all the schools in Detroit. In his school everyone learned together – whites and Indians and boys and girls."

"That sounds fine."

So they visited the church and she told him the stories every Detroiter loved to repeat about the pipe organ and printing press the Jesuit priest had brought through hundreds of miles of wilderness. Olivia especially liked the one about the British arresting Father Gabriel and Tecumseh forcing them to let him go.

"So what would you like to see next?" Olivia asked when they came out of the church.

"I believe Mrs. Porter has more than enough sight-seeing in store for me." Mr. Carmichael took his watch out of his pocket and clicked it open. "I wouldn't mind stopping somewhere for a beer."

She directed him west on the Chicago Road, toward the Corktown Tavern.

"There are lots of closer places," Olivia said when they were settled at the table, "but this is my favorite. I like to eavesdrop on the Irish people – the way they talk reminds me of my Mammo and Daddo Killion."

The waiter came and Mr. Carmichael asked what she would like. She hesitated before answering, "I'll also have a beer."

The waiter quickly moved to the bar and returned with two tall glasses.

Olivia took a sip of hers and said, "Michelle – the friend of mine you're going to meet – I wrote about her in my journal."

"Yes, I remember. The woman who was so kind to you when you happened into her shop."

Olivia nodded. "And Jeremy Kincaid is likely to be there with her. I wrote about him too."

"Oh? The neighbor for whom you had such strong feelings?"

"I thought I did ... until after ... you know. Then all that seemed nonsense. And I know I'll never get married. I don't think I was cut out for it anyhow, but after all that's happened I have no interest in any kind of relationship like that with a man."

"That's a harsh sentence to impose upon yourself."

"No. Not if it's the right thing. And it doesn't have to be lonely. I remember what Mourning once said to me, when I was moping because Jeremy didn't want to be more than a friend." In a poor imitation of Mourning's voice she quoted him, "Having the person you care about as a friend ain't nothin'," and then switched back to her own voice. "Now I believe he was talking about him and me as much as he was about Jeremy. But either way he was right. I see that now. A true friend can be as important as a husband. Maybe more."

She watched him, hoping not to see terrible disappointment on his face. She wanted their friendship to be simple. Uncomplicated. Like with Mr. Abraham. It would be wonderful to have another man she could talk to. Maybe the next stop on Mr. Carmichael's tour of Detroit should be Mr. Slaughter's bawdy house.

"What about you? Why didn't you ever marry again?" It was absurd to be asking Mr. Carmichael, her father's attorney, such a personal question. But it felt like the way to steer their relationship in a safe direction.

"I never met anyone I thought I could love like Clarissa. We grew up together, in South Valley. Our families lived across the street from one another."

"What on earth possessed you to move to Five Rocks?"

"That was Clarissa's idea. After I started practicing the law. Said it was better to be a big fish in a small pond. And she was right about that. I made a good living, being the only attorney in town. Everyone was my client."

"Who's taking care of things while you're gone?"

"Your friend, Billy Adams."

"That dim-wit passed the bar?" She flushed, ashamed, but only a little, of speaking so unkindly of her former classmate.

"Mr. Adams is not lacking in intelligence." He paused to drink. "For some reason I have failed to understand, he reads slowly. But that does not make him stupid. He has a good memory and good judgment. And he perseveres when faced with difficulty. Like you." He smiled. "And my clients find him agreeable."

"Unlike me," Olivia said and raised her glass again.

"Why would you say that?"

"You live in Five Rocks. You know I never had any

328

friends. And the way the old biddies gossiped about me."

"No, I don't know about friends. How would I know what efforts you invested in seeking friendship or what results they yielded? And I do not frequently socialize with your old biddies. I do recall hearing some unkind remarks about you teaching Mourning to read and write. About you spending too much time with him in general. But what do you care? I can only guess that the last thing in the world you would wish yourself to be is the type of girl who wins their approval. As for girls your age, if they were unkind to you I must assume that stemmed from jealously. You were pretty, smart, Miss Evans' pet, and the daughter of Old Man Killion, one of the wealthier men in town."

"I can't have been all that wonderful. No young men ever came to call on me."

"I don't suppose it occurred to you that they might have been afraid to?"

Olivia feared that he was about to add "like me" and quickly steered the conversation back to a more comfortable topic – gossip about her old town. After a while she allowed herself to smile and say, "People in Five Rocks were lucky you moved there. You're so kind, so honest. I always knew I could trust you. And I feel lucky you came out here. Not because of the money and things you brought. It's good to see you. I don't have many people I can talk to like this. I'd be real sorry if that ever changed."

Mrs. Porter was waiting for them at *Chez Mademoiselle Lafleur*. Olivia introduced Mr. Carmichael to Michelle, and the two of them conversed for a short time while Olivia poked around the shop and went to the kitchen to pump herself a drink of water. Finally Mrs. Porter grew impatient and asked Mr. Carmichael if he didn't think it was time they got started on his grand tour of Detroit's magnificent hotels. Olivia was glad to see them drive off, eager to be alone with Michelle. She repeated most of the conversation she'd had with Mr. Carmichael at the tavern.

"This will sound terribly conceited," Olivia said, "but I'm afraid he may have come all this way because of feelings he has for me."

"Lord, girl, you are hopeless. Of course the man is in love with you. A cat can see that. I saw it just from watching him open the door for you. From the way his eyes follow you when he thinks you ain't looking. How many lawyers you think are gonna travel across the Great Lakes to hand deliver a bunch of old junk to one of their clients?"

"So what am I supposed to do?"

"You already did it. That little speech you gave him is all you can do."

"But you know how good he's been to me. I want to treat him nicely, make him feel at home in my house."

"Of course you're going to make him feel at home. Be as sweet as you want. Just don't go giggling and batting your eyes. Since you got no clue how to do that no how, that shouldn't be a problem."

"I don't want to mislead him."

"Act like you feel like acting. That's all you can do. He already understands you're not interested. You just told him outright, before he had a chance to make a fool of himself asking. Right there you already spared his feelings."

"Will you and Jeremy come out tonight? Play some cards with us? I could come get you in the buggy."

"Sure, we'll come, but no need for the buggy. Ernest will do just fine. I love hanging on to Jeremy while I got my legs wrapped around that big old horse."

After supper that evening Olivia was alone, standing at the kitchen window, when Ernest clopped up the drive. Michelle had some kind of wooden contraption fastened to her back. Jeremy swung his right leg over Ernest's head and dismounted first, so he could hold the box while Michelle loosened the straps holding it to her. Must be another of his inventions, Olivia thought.

"What have you got in there? Your grandmother's bone china?" Olivia teased as she opened the back door for them.

"Something you're gonna like way more than some old plates." Michelle laughed. Olivia had never seen her look so happy.

Jeremy set the box on the table, and Olivia couldn't help noticing that he looked good too. They both seemed younger. At ease. While Michelle took two bottles of wine from the pouch she was carrying, Olivia lifted the top of the box and peeked in.

"You baked a cake?" She looked at Michelle, more than surprised.

"Me make that? Not likely. I'd have to close the shop for a week. No, no, girly girl, this is no mere cake." She removed the lid of the box, lifted up an elaborate concoction of pastry and whipped cream, and began speaking in her fake French accent.

"Behold a *Gâteau St. Honoré*, the queen of fine French pastries, prepared by special rush order in honor of the birthday of everyone's favorite landlady, the beloved Miss Olivia Killion." She set it on the table and began a short lecture. "Here at the bottom we see the layer of delicate puff pastry, covered with the smoothest, richest *crème pâtissière*."

Mimicking the role of the vulgar American, Olivia asked, "And what're them balls a dough 'round the edge?"

"Dough? No, no, *Mademoiselle*, no. Those are profiteroles of *pâte à choux*, the lightest of light puff pastries, filled with the finest whipped cream, and covered with a delicate icing of caramelized sugar."

"And all them squiggly doo-bobs in the middle?"

"A carefully piped crown of the most divine *crème*

chantilly, topped with delicately crafted curls of rich dark *chocolat*."

"Is it only for looking at?" Mr. Carmichael had appeared in the doorway, wearing a smoking jacket of dark green velvet.

"Ah, here is the gentleman who knows when a celebration is called for," Michelle said and glided over to kiss his cheek. "I will admit that a party was his idea. However, unimaginative Scotsman that he is, all he said was, 'Could you please bring a cake?' It was I who envisioned this work of art."

Jeremy was grinning. "You going to quit with your fooling so we can pour the wine and play some cards?"

"Play cards? How much longer do you expect me to keep my fingers out of that whipped cream?" Olivia asked.

"Alas, the plebian wants to destroy it already." Michelle turned to get plates from the cupboard.

Olivia moved toward the door, lightly touching Mr. Carmichael's arm to indicate that she wished to pass. "Mrs. Porter isn't going to want to miss this. I'll see if she and Miss Streeter are still awake." She stepped up the hall to rap on their doors and assured them they were perfectly welcome to join the party as they were. "We'll pretend not to notice your dressing gowns, and tomorrow you can go on pretending not to notice my trousers. And this is not my boring old ginger cake. This is something special."

The two women came in time to admire the *Gâteau St. Honoré* and then Michelle cut it, taking care that each serving contained two of the glazed profiteroles. Jeremy poured wine – Miss Streeter refused and Mrs. Porter asked for her usual "tiny nip" – and they touched glasses.

"To your health. Long life."

Michelle removed a small box from her pocket and pushed it over the table to Olivia. It contained a delicate gold chain with a pendant of turquoise stone. Olivia rose and went to the window, looking at her reflection as she held the necklace up to her throat.

"It's lovely." She squeezed Michelle's shoulder. "Thank you." Then she sat and looked around the table, letting her eyes rest on each of them. "Having all you good friends in my life – it makes such a difference."

They all nodded and smiled, but the room fell into a brief awkward silence. Then Mr. Carmichael cleared his throat and said, "There is a gift I would like to give you, but for that you will have to accompany me to Detroit tomorrow."

"Well, doesn't that suit the present I want to give her just fine," Mrs. Porter said and turned toward Olivia. "You take the day off tomorrow. Day after, too. Tell me what you got laid in and me and Janie will do the cooking and washing up."

"I can't ask you to do that."

"Why not? Be good to get back in a kitchen, and that way you can go gallivanting 'round town tomorrow without having to worry about getting back here. Two days I said, mind you." She held up two fingers. "Kitchen won't feel good much longer than that."

"That's a wonderful present." Olivia leaned across Michelle to pat Mrs. Porter's arm. "So now can we finally eat?" Olivia asked and they all picked up their forks.

"Who is Saint Honoré?" Mrs. Porter asked between enthusiastic mouthfuls.

"Saint Honoré or Honoratus is the patron saint of bakers and pastry chefs," Michelle said.

Mrs. Porter emitted a little snort. "Trust the frogs to have one of those. But I admit it wouldn't be no punishment to eat this every day."

"You scrape your plate any more, you're going to wear a hole in it," Miss Streeter said.

Mrs. Porter and Miss Streeter soon retired, and Jeremy shuffled the cards. Already light-headed, Olivia drained her wine glass and thought, maybe this is what happy feels like. She didn't want the feeling to end and nudged her glass toward the wine bottle sitting in front of Mr. Carmichael. He raised his eyebrows, but smiled and filled it again.

"Uh-oh, watch out for girly girl tonight," Michelle said.

"Yes, you better," Olivia said. "I plan to discover what it feels like to drink too much."

Michelle shook her head. "Leave it to you to turn getting canned into some kind of school work."

"You shush and hold on to your cards. Canned or not, tonight I am invincible."

For a few hours they all drank too much and laughed and didn't mind if most of what they said was nonsense. The usually formal Mr. Carmichael was surprisingly relaxed.

While he was filling Olivia's glass for the fourth time, she said to Michelle and Jeremy, "I bet you two can't guess what this man's Christian name is." She nodded her head toward Mr. Carmichael. "Even if I give you a little hint." Her words were slurred. "It starts with an L."

They tried Lawrence, Lionel, Lazar, Lewis, Lloyd, Linus, Leonard, Leonardo, Leopold, Leroy, Lester, Lemuel, Leighton, Laban, and even Loxley and Lancelot before giving up.

"Knew you couldn't guess. Who would guess an awful name like Luther? *Luther*. What kind of parents name a defenseless little baby *Luther*?" She looked at Mr. Carmichael as if he were to blame for allowing his mother and father to do such a thing.

His face was blank, but his eyes looked amused rather than insulted.

"What's wrong with Luther?" Jeremy asked.

"I would never, not in a million billion years, give my child a dreary old name like Luther. Not unless I was counting on him growing up to be an undertaker." Olivia took a sip of wine and turned her gaze back on

Mr. Carmichael. "You sure don't look like a Luther. Course, whenever someone dies, there you are."

Mr. Carmichael repressed a smile. "Is there another name you would prefer?"

"How about your middle name? Is it any better? You signed your letters L. A. Carmichael. What's the A stand for?"

Mr. Carmichael had obvious difficulty keeping his face straight. "I doubt you will be more fond of it."

"So what is it?"

He barely managed to get out the two syllables – Angus – before he and the others exploded into laughter. For long minutes they held their sides and wiped their eyes. When the hilarity subsided Olivia said, "That's grand. They named you for the devil and a cow," and they were reduced to tears again.

"You're confusing Luther with Lucifer," Jeremy managed to get out.

"Same thing." Olivia waved a dismissive hand. But the physical effort of laughing so hard seemed to have had a sobering effect and she looked over at Mr. Carmichael. "Sorry. I didn't mean to hurt your feelings."

"You haven't. You, I allow to call me anything you please." He seemed to regret the words as he spoke and glanced away, eyes averted. Olivia was dismayed to see him recoil that way, like a dog staying out of kicking range.

Michelle stepped in to fill the silence by chattering about the boats coming into the port. She soon declared that it was getting late, and she and Jeremy rose to leave. Olivia and Mr. Carmichael stood at the back door, watching their drunken attempts to climb onto Ernest and then waving good-bye as they started down the drive. Olivia was clearing away the last of the dishes when large raindrops began splattering against the windows.

"Oh my. Even if those two manage to stay on the

horse, they're going to get good and soaked," Olivia said.

"I'll be retiring as well," Mr. Carmichael said.

"Do you feel like going out on the porch to watch the sky?" she asked him. "I know it's cold out there, but just for a few minutes?"

He extended his arm in an "after you" gesture.

He held her coat for her, and by the time they stepped outside it was pouring, sheets of rain slanting in under the roof of the porch, wetting their feet. Thunder rumbled in the distance, and black clouds were blowing in from Lake Erie.

"Sideways rain," Olivia said. "That's what Tobey used to call it, when the wind was blowing like this. I love a good storm." She hugged herself, getting cold and wet. "They come up so quickly here."

Great bolts of lightning struck the black surface of the river, one after the other. The display of power – the stunning clash of air, water, and fire – was humbling.

"Makes you feel small, doesn't it?" she said. "Like all the problems you think are so big don't count for anything. Makes you wonder how God could care what we do or not."

"I thought you were undecided as to His existence."

"There has to be something, doesn't there?" She looked up at the sky and shivered.

"We'd better go in before you catch your death." He held the door for her, and they removed their shoes in the front hallway. When he straightened up he said, "I also feel lucky that I came here. I think it will be a fine vacation."

"Good. You deserve one." She stood on her toes and kissed his cheek before saying good night.

Chapter Thirty-Four

The next morning after breakfast Olivia told Mrs. Porter what meals she had planned and showed her where to find things. "Janie knows, if you have any trouble." She bent at the window to check on the weather. "Will you look at that sky. Not a cloud in it. You've got the craziest weather out here. Janie should try to get some of the laundry done. Oh, and please don't use any of the dishes in this bottom cupboard here. They belong to Mr. Abraham. And don't forget to make enough to leave a meal out at night for Mr. Ballou and Mr. O'Donnell."

"Shoo. You get." Mrs. Porter waved the back of her hand at Olivia. "You forgot I used to feed dozens of people every day. Hundreds."

"All right, then. I will."

Mr. Carmichael had brushed and harnessed Fleabag, and the buggy awaited Olivia in the front drive. She was headed for the door when Miss Streeter timidly stepped out of the parlor.

"Excuse me, Miss Killion. I wanted to give you this before you go." She handed Olivia one of her quilling pictures – intricate coils and hair-thin curls of colored paper crafted into a bright spring bouquet.

"Oh thank you. How lovely." Olivia marveled at the delicacy of the work. "I don't know how you do this. And the colors in this one are so bright." She set it on the mantle in the parlor, stood back to admire it, and gave Miss Streeter a hug before going to join Mr. Carmichael in the buggy.

The sun glinted brightly off every surface, reflecting the remnants of last night's storm. "Could we ask for a more glorious day?" she asked.

He smiled and said, "Giddap."

Neither of them felt the need to speak until Mr.

Carmichael turned onto Jefferson Avenue and said, "Yesterday, while we were at Michelle's, she showed me some of your sketches. One of that church we'd just been to and another one of City Hall."

"She kept those?"

"Of course. She thinks they're quite good, as do I. Then, while Mrs. Porter was giving me my tour, I noticed the shop of a portrait painter and paid it a visit. That's it, up there on the corner of Griswold. See the sign, F. E. Cohen? He paints landscapes and historical scenes, as well as portraits. Creates beautiful panels for the passenger ships. Flamboyant young fellow and very talented. Quite good-looking too, in a Bohemian sort of way."

"Since when are you a matchmaker?" she asked. "Anyway, I told you, I have no interest."

"That was not at all my intention." He turned to look at her. "I fear that what I'd like to suggest may cause you to feel uncomfortable, but please don't. It would give me great pleasure to purchase whatever drawing materials you require. Perhaps you would like to paint as well. Mr. Cohen isn't in the business of selling artists' supplies, but he's a most congenial fellow and willing to accommodate. He even agreed to give you a few lessons in the use of those supplies, if that is necessary and of interest to you."

She thought for a moment before replying. "I am uncomfortable with that. Especially since you've already helped me so much and given me so many presents – and why should you give me anything at all?"

Mr. Carmichael opened his mouth to speak, but Olivia rushed on. "But right before Mr. Abraham left on his trip, we had a long talk about giving and receiving. He said it's easier to be gracious about giving than taking, because we don't like to feel beholden or needy. We want to be the generous one, the one who gives to other people, to whom everyone else is beholden. But he said that is prideful. We all need each other and mustn't deny someone else the satisfaction of being a giver."

Mr. Carmichael nodded. "He's right about that. It would be selfish of you to deny me an almost forgotten pleasure. It's been a long time since I've felt like giving anyone a gift."

Olivia smiled and then shrugged. "Of course, Mr. Abraham wasn't talking about birthday presents. He meant giving to people in need. He said most folks are only generous to the people they like and admire, and those are usually the ones least in need of assistance. Real generosity is when you see someone who is destitute or sick, but that person is nasty, mean-spirited, and dirty. Maybe he smells so bad that you don't feel at all inclined to stop and see if you can assist. All you want to do is run away, and you don't think that's a bad thing to do because what that needy person deserves is probably a kick in the pants, not a helping hand. But to a man with a good heart the only thing that matters is how much they need that helping hand."

"I look forward to meeting your Mr. Abraham. Perhaps out of respect for him, you could extend his thoughts to include birthday gifts."

"That's exactly what I was thinking." Olivia grinned. "Since I'm finding it hard to turn down such a wonderful gift."

"All right. Let's go introduce you to Mr. Cohen."

"Did you really like my sketches? Honest?"

"Yes, I did. Honest. I would be most glad to have one of them – some scene of the city – to take home and hang in my office. I can think of no better souvenir of this trip. And you shouldn't waste a moment wondering what an art critic might say. All that matters is that you enjoy creating them, and your friends enjoy having them." He grew silent for a moment and then continued, his voice wistful. "I remember your mother, down by the river with her easel. She always looked so

339

happy on those days."

His words struck Olivia silent. Motionless. She grew cold, as if something were draining out of her. At first she felt nothing; then resentment welled up. Don't worry about what an art critic might say? So he thinks my drawings are terrible, and he and Michelle are humoring me? All that matters is that I enjoy making them? How pathetic does he think I am? She blinked and clenched her fists. Lonely old Ichabod Crane thinks he has to pity me? I have made more of a life than he has, in his dusty office with the tin roof. And he has no right to speak of my mother that way. Happy on those days, indeed. As if most of her life passed in misery. How dare he make her someone he pitied? And me? He thinks I need his presents? He can take them, along with his big flapping elephant ears, and go home, sit in his empty house and feel sorry for no one but himself.

Poor Mr. Carmichael, one small voice in her mind scolded. What's wrong with you? He didn't mean anything. He's only being kind, like always.

But when she turned to look at him, her face was stone. "I suppose you think I'm the same way – not right in the head. You and the biddies. There goes crazy Nola June's daughter. Just like that mother of hers." Olivia's voice grew shrill. "Best humor her, buy her some paints and brushes, keep her busy. You wouldn't want to find her swinging in the pantry, kicking the wind, like that lunatic mother of hers."

She was horrified, but couldn't stop the words. He turned toward her, pale and frightened, and she began pounding her fists against his chest.

He tried to grasp her wrists. "What did I ... I don't ... Your mother was a lovely woman ... I know she was often indisposed –"

"Shut up, shut up."

A man passing on the street hesitantly approached the buggy. "You folks need help?"

"No, we're fine." Mr. Carmichael motioned with his

head for the man to continue on his way. "Just some bad news from home."

"Shut up, shut up, shut up." Olivia continued shouting, but her voice grew weaker. "There wasn't anything wrong with her." She began to sob. "There wasn't anything wrong with her. She was a good mother. There was no reason for her to want to die. My father loved her. Jettie said so." Her last words were barely audible, and her head fell forward, resting on Mr. Carmichael's chest. He hesitated before allowing his arms to lightly encase her. "And there's nothing wrong with me. Nothing. It wasn't my fault. It wasn't my fault. There wasn't any reason for them to do that to me."

"No, there wasn't." He gently rocked back and forth and patted her back. "There was no reason at all. Shh. It's all right."

Her anger dissipated and she sat up and rubbed her eyes, mortified, unable to look at him, wishing she could wipe her nose on something, even her petticoat. "Oh Lord, I'm sorry –"

"Shh, don't be." He removed the hand that was still on her shoulder it. "It's all right."

"I don't know what came over me, making such a scene," she mumbled.

He tried to make his voice light. "At least you chose good weather for it. Everyone's still got their windows closed. And you owe no explanation to anyone. When my Clarissa died, I felt like beating someone to a pulp."

"But you didn't."

"I think I can survive that level of assault on my person. Do you feel better now?"

She nodded. "I've never behaved like that before." She stuck her head out and looked down the street, relieved to find no one near them. She finally managed to look at him, a brief glance. "I suppose it's funny – a woman trying to convince you she's not a lunatic by having a conniption fit."

"You are no lunatic. I assure I have witnessed far more extreme behavior from people who have not experienced anything close to as terrible as you have. Losing your mother when you were so young and then your father, and then the horror out there. And with no one to talk to most of the time. Anger and fear stay with us longer than we imagine. It's good that you let some of it out," he said. "I'm only sorry that I said something to upset you."

"Oh Lord, there's no reason for you to apologize." Olivia shook her head and took a deep breath. "I am crazy. I hope I didn't hurt you."

"I'm perfectly fine. Should I take you home?"

She shook her head. Still feeling ashamed, her voice strained, she did her best to sound like a normal young woman teasing her companion. "Are you trying to get out of buying me those brushes and paints?"

"Certainly not." He picked up the reins.

She stayed his hand with hers. "Can we sit here for a while longer?" He released the reins and they sat in silence until she asked, almost in a whisper, "Did you know that my mother hanged herself?"

"No." He grew pale again. "No one ever told me that."

She sat up straighter, arranged her clothing, and ran her hand over her hair. "I just wondered if everyone else knew. I only found out when Mourning told me one night, while we were sitting outside by the fire. He knew because he was with my father when he came home and found her." She shook herself lightly, just a quiver. "But let's not talk about it any more now. Let's go see your flamboyant portrait painter."

After they had spent over an hour with the good-natured but eccentric Mr. Cohen, Mr. Carmichael gathered up her purchases and declared himself ready for a beer. "Would you like to go to your Irish tavern?" he asked.

"Why don't we just go to King's? It's right over on

342

the corner of Woodward."

After they had been served beer and sandwiches, it was Mr. Carmichael's turn to take a deep breath. "There's something I need to tell you."

"All right," she said, trying to mask her unease.

"But first, I've been wanting to ask – would you mind if I called you Olivia?"

"No, of course not." She hoped the rest of the conversation would be that easy.

"Except –" He smiled sheepishly. "I can't very well ask you to call me Luther."

She flushed red. "Oh my stars, I'm so sorry about that too. I was just being a drunken fool. Luther is a perfectly good name."

"No, it isn't. It does sound like an undertaker. You could choose a new one."

"Me, make up a new name for you?"

"Why not?"

"How on earth would I do that?"

He shrugged. "There's always Ichabod."

She grinned. "So you know that's what the schoolchildren call you?"

"I'm not deaf."

"I'll have to think on it. One thing for sure – it won't be Ichabod. But if you ever get a horse, I definitely think you should name him Gunpowder. So what did you want to talk about?"

He cleared his throat. "Through my correspondence with Mr. Wentworth regarding your inheritance from Mrs. Place, it became clear that he knew, courtesy of your friend Michelle, that I had manufactured a Free Man of Color paper for Mourning –"

"Oh heavens, I've gotten you into trouble. I'm so sorry. I never would have told her – I mean I didn't tell her, not your name, not ever. I promise. I never said your name, just that my lawyer from back home made a paper like that, and I never, ever would have said anything at all, except I never dreamed Michelle would

343

meet you, not in a million years, I mean who could have guessed you'd come all the way out here –"

"Calm down. It's all right. I'm not in any trouble. That's not what this conversation is about. It's about Mr. Wentworth wanting me to stay here for a while and make more of those papers – for people in Michigan."

"But they'd have a Pennsylvania stamp on them."

"That doesn't matter. It even makes sense. There are more free coloreds in Pennsylvania than in just about any state. Why wouldn't some of them want to come out to Michigan, just like all the whites who are pouring onto those steamboats? So that's one of the reasons I came here. After I first contacted him, he and Michelle figured out that I must be *that* lawyer. The one with the precious official stamp."

"How'd you come by that stamp, anyway?"

"Stole it from an office in Philadelphia a long time ago."

"You're one surprise after another." She was partly relieved and partly disappointed to discover that he had not plowed the waters of Lake Erie solely for the purpose of seeing her. Perhaps those longing looks had been entirely in her imagination. Not even Ichabod Crane was interested in her.

"Are you saying he wrote that in a letter? Asked you make those papers?" She raised her eyebrows.

"Not outright. He mentioned only that I had provided an important document to a friend of yours and that he knew of many people who would find such a document useful. But I understood his intention."

"So you brought the stamp with you?"

"I would have done so in any case. I always keep it on my person. Anyway, what I need to tell you is that I may be staying in Detroit for a few weeks. Even months. And I want to ask if it would be convenient for you to have me staying at your house for that long."

"Of course it wouldn't be *convenient*. It would be grand."

344

"Are you certain?"

"Of course. Why not? Unless you'd rather stay somewhere else," she said, unsure how she really felt about this prospect.

Now I know what it's like to be on the other side, she thought. How poor Jeremy must have felt, trying to be a good neighbor without giving me false hopes about his feelings.

"Who's going to take care of your lawyer business, if you stay here?" she asked.

"Billy Adams manages most things well enough on his own. If there's an emergency, I'll be only two or three days away."

"Plus the two weeks it will take his letter to get here, telling you that there's an emergency."

He shrugged. "Mr. Adams will just have to manage."

Olivia paled. "What about your safe? Now that you're gone, can he open it?"

"Yes, but you needn't worry. I forgot to mention that your papers are no longer in it. They are safe in a depository box at Mr. Wentworth's bank, to which only I hold a key. When I leave, you'll decide whether you prefer them to stay here or for me to take them back to Five Rocks."

They finished their sandwiches in comfortable silence, and then Olivia asked if he felt like going home.

"Actually, I've been thinking of visiting one of the public baths I've noticed. What would you think about that?"

"You mean go have a bath? Now?"

"Obviously not together." He smiled.

She pulled her bottom lip up over the top, perplexed. "You know, I've seen their advertisements, but it's not something I've ever thought of doing. You want a bath, you fill a tub at home, you know?" She thought another moment. "But I think it's a grand idea. A nice hot bath without all the bother. Tucker's Toilet Saloon is right over there."

"I was thinking about Whitsey's Baths, up near the Michigan Garden. Their sign says everything is brand new and they have salt baths, as well as fresh water."

"Why would anyone want salt in their bath?"

"Folks say it's relaxing. Helps soak out your aches and pains. I don't believe you remain with the salt on your skin, but wash it off after the bath."

"All right, let's go get clean and relaxed."

Lying in steaming hot water – of which she had not carried a single drop – in a tub so deep and long that she could stretch out in it, Olivia thought Mr. Carmichael was a genius. She would have to make a habit of this. The last lingering effects of her outburst soaked away and this was well worth having to ride home in the cold with her hair all wet.

"What next?" Mr. Carmichael asked when they were back in the buggy.

"A lie down sounds good to me." Olivia yawned. "And then good old Mrs. Porter serving us our supper."

"I can second that."

"Too bad you didn't bring your coyote hat," she said. "That would feel pretty good on my wet head about now."

"I'll gladly leave it for you when I return to Five Rocks. I can't quite see myself walking up Main Street in it."

When he turned up the drive she suddenly sat up straighter and said, "Lucas."

"Pardon?"

"Lucas is a nice name. It even sounds like a nickname for Luther. Matches the initials on your letter paper too. What do you think about that?"

He tipped his head in approval.

"But I won't be able to say it. My mouth is never going to agree to call you anything but Mr. Carmichael. I just can't. It would feel disrespectful, what with you being older and an attorney and all."

Chapter Thirty-Five

Olivia's life settled into a familiar routine. She rode and cared for Sandy, cooked and cleaned, gathered kindling, and tended her vegetable garden. Every few weeks she hunted until she took a deer. She kept chickens in the coop Bayliss built and planted apple, pear, and peach trees, a row of grape vines, and raspberries. The work kept her busy, but not exhausted. Parcels arrived and continued on their way without incident. Michelle and Jeremy often came to spend the evening. One day Olivia found a stranger holding his hat on her porch and struggled through a lengthy and puzzling conversation before realizing that he had come to court her. A gentleman caller at last. She drove him away by mumbling something about her fiancée from back home who would soon be arriving, but derived immense gratification from the fact that a nice-looking young man had made the effort. So she was not repulsive after all. Though she did suspect that the large home she owned may have contributed to his motivations for paying her a visit.

In all it was not an unpleasant life, but at the end of each busy day came the evening, when she sat on the porch watching the boats go by, her heart longing for one of them to deliver Mourning and their child to her.

Weeks passed and Mr. Carmichael made no mention of how long he intended to remain in Detroit, but Olivia was in no hurry for him to leave. He had stopped bringing her gifts and paying her compliments. He seemed to have taken some sort of job at the bank. He left the house early each morning, returned home for dinner, and then drove back to the city. Then he began taking his evening meal with Mr. Wentworth and his wife, returning home after Olivia was asleep. Olivia gave him the use of the buggy in a mutually beneficial arrangement. The other boarders enjoyed the transportation into town and back that he provided, and he was always willing to stop at a dry goods or the Washington market for whatever Olivia needed. Once a week Olivia left Janie in charge and rode into town with Mr. Carmichael. She spent the morning shopping or drawing, had dinner at King's with Michelle, and sometimes stopped in at Mr. Cohen's shop to show him her sketches and watch him paint.

Mr. Carmichael seemed much busier than the forgery of a stack of Free Man of Color papers would have kept him. Olivia wondered how deeply involved with the Underground Railroad and Anti-Slavery Movement he had become, but he never spoke with her about it. She assumed Mr. Wentworth must have told him that her house was a station on the railroad, but she wanted to be certain. So one morning she went into the bank.

"I guess you must have told Mr. Carmichael about my house," she said to Mr. Wentworth, once they were alone in his office. "But I want to be sure. I mean, the weather's getting so beautiful, I'm surprised I haven't been receiving more packages."

"Oh you will. This week. I'm expecting Zach Faraday this morning, to tell me about the deliveries he has coming."

"Have you heard any talk of slave catchers in the area?"

"No, none at all. Why?"

"Twice in the last month I've seen someone on the road in front of my house. A single rider, just sitting on his horse watching. Both times I stepped out onto the porch to shake a rug and have a look at him. He just sat there staring at me for a few minutes before he turned around and disappeared."

"I'll have Finney ask around, but I don't know of any strangers in town with southern accents."

"I wanted you to know, just in case, but I don't really think it's one of them. I couldn't tell for sure, the way he had his hat pulled down and with the sun in my eyes, but I think he was colored."

"That doesn't mean anything. They have plenty of villainous colored men in their employ. But you're right. It could simply be someone stopping to admire your house. Or thinking how easy it would be to rob. Do you lock up at night?"

"I don't always remember, but I'll be sure to from now on."

"As for your Mr. Carmichael, of course I have spoken with him regarding your part in our organization. Now that he comes into town every day, he'll be the one to inform you when a package is on its way. Save Zach Faraday or someone else the trip out to your place. And you certainly can count on him for any assistance that might become necessary. We all have to thank you for bringing him to us." He stood. "He's taking on more and more of our legal work."

Olivia nodded. "I thought he probably had. And there's something maybe you could ask him to do. I've tried to convince folks over in Windsor to start a register with the names of all the coloreds who pass through here, to help relatives find each other. They pretty much ignore me, but if a lawyer like Mr. Carmichael were to speak to them about it and say it was you asking them to do it, they'd be sure to listen."

"Fine idea. I'll discuss it with Mr. Carmichael. I can't tell you how pleased I am that he's decided to make his home in Detroit. I know it gives him great satisfaction, being able to help. Of course our Miss Anderson must have played no small part in that decision," he said and winked.

"Miss Anderson?" Olivia's face was blank. Mr. Carmichael was moving to Detroit? He had a lady friend? Olivia was no less stunned by having the usually staid and solemn Mr. Wentworth wink at her.

"Oh dear. I hope I haven't let a cat out of its bag," he said. "I assumed you knew they've been keeping company. Gloria Anderson is from one of our best families."

Out on the sidewalk Olivia smiled to herself, wondering if Miss Anderson called him Lucas.

"You're in good spirits," a male voice said.

"Mr. Faraday. How are you? Mr. Wentworth just told me he'd be seeing you today."

"Yes, I'm a little late. Stopped by Whipple's Hotel. Did you know they have an elephant penned up out back? A real elephant."

"Yes, I heard about that. And that he's charging two bits for entrance to see it. I might just go have a look."

They chatted for a few minutes and then Mr. Faraday said he'd better keep his appointment. But then he snapped his fingers and turned back.

"Wait. I almost forgot," he said. "Remember when you first came into my store, you were trying to find that fellow called Mourning Free?" Olivia tensed and nodded. "Well, his last name isn't Free, but there is a black man name of Mourning in Backwoods. I was at Springer's Livery a few weeks back and noticed he had a new hand brushing down the horses. Then Jake Springer called the fellow Mourning, so I asked if he might be Mourning Free. The fellow said no. Said his last name was Jackson. Then he suddenly remembered a reason why he had to go home."

"Jackson was his parents' slave name," Olivia said, almost in a whisper.

Zach Faraday nodded. "That makes some sense. After he was gone, I realized I should have mentioned your name. Maybe he's got a reason for making himself hard to find, but maybe he's also got a reason to trust you. So I found out from Jake Springer where he lives. He's renting a little house on the road north out of town. On the way to the Abbot place."

Olivia was holding her breath.

"A few days later I rode past there and saw him outside, chopping wood. So I stopped. Said I may have been mistaken about the last name, but I had a message for someone named Mourning from a pretty young white woman. A Miss Olivia Killion. He didn't say anything, but he listened hard while I repeated the message – that Mr. Carmichael has some important papers for him. Then I hope you don't mind, but I also told him that both Miss Killion and Mr. Carmichael are in Detroit. That Miss Killion has a boarding house called OK Accommodations and that Mr. Carmichael is currently boarding there."

"What did he say?"

"Nothing at all. But he took in every word I said. I could see that."

"It's strange to think of him renting a house," she said, more to herself than to Mr. Faraday. "It would be more like him to be sleeping up in the loft of the livery."

"With his family?"

Olivia blinked. "He has a family? A child? There with him?"

"There was a little baby on a blanket. I assumed it was his. And a young woman was hanging up laundry."

Olivia's mind raced. She didn't want to be mistaken. Little boy would be almost 14 months old. Shouldn't he be walking?

"A little tiny baby? Like a newborn? Or older?"

He shrugged. "Sorry. I wasn't paying much mind to the child." He turned away again. "I shouldn't keep Mr. Wentworth waiting. Listen, if you want to send another message, it's no thing for me to ride up there again."

"Thank you. Maybe I will. And thank you for going there in the first place. That was kind of you."

She didn't want to send another message. She had to see for herself. She decided to wait a week, give herself time to think it through, but there was no real question of whether or not she would go; she had to. No matter that Mourning was unlikely to welcome a visit from her. If he wanted to see her, he knew where she was. Had known for at least a month. Thirty days of

351

getting up each morning and deciding this would not be the day that he went to talk to Olivia.

What would she say to him? Did his wife, if that woman was his wife, know who Olivia was? Should Olivia go to Mourning's home? Wouldn't it be better to look for him at the livery, where there might be a chance of talking to him alone? No, that would be a mistake. Little Boy wouldn't be at the livery, and if Mourning refused to take her to see him, she couldn't very well show up at his home after that.

It would also be a mistake, or at least unfair, to go to his home while he was at work. She had complicated Mourning's life more than enough. If that woman was his wife, the last thing he needed was Olivia confronting her alone. Who knew what he had told her about Little Boy?

It took a while for Olivia to begin internalizing the concept "Mourning's wife." She had often imagined him marrying and Little Boy with a new mother, but that was only supposed to happen in some distant future. First Saint Olivia would ride up to rescue father and son from poverty and hopelessness. Eventually she would grant him permission to take a wife. Not blatantly – her consent would be given through subtle signs and hints – but in this fantasy Olivia wielded a great deal of control. Now she stared at the bleak fact that she had none. On the question of whether and how often Olivia might see the child, Mourning would certainly acquiesce to his wife.

The day before she rode to Backwoods Olivia went to the bank and withdrew $300 from her account. That night she was almost asleep when she suddenly sat up in bed. That rider in the road, the man watching her house – that had been Mourning. She was certain of it. He had come all the way here, but never knocked on her door. Why? Had he just wanted to see that she was well? He already knew that from Mr. Faraday.

And then she knew. He had stayed out there,

waiting, until she looked out and saw him – and, more importantly, saw him ride away. It was his way of saying, "Look, here I am, alive and well. You can stop searching. But I choose not to come up there. It would be too hard. Too complicated. It's easier this way for all of us. Whatever important papers Mr. Carmichael has can wait."

And there was another reason he came. She was also certain of that. He simply needed to put his eyes on her. The same way she needed to put hers on him.

She left late in the day, so she would arrive in Backwoods toward evening, when Mourning and his wife were both likely to be home and Little Boy would still be awake. She stopped at Zach Faraday's store to say hullo.

"I'd like to ask a favor of you," Olivia said before she left, pressing the $300 into Mr. Faraday's hand. "To ride up to Mourning Jackson's place again – not now, in a few days – and give him this money. It's all right to say it's from me. It's what's owing to him."

There were no trees to hide behind on the road to the Abbot place. She rode slowly and stopped a short distance from the house, which sat a good thirty paces back from the road. There was no one in the yard, but she sensed motion inside and waited. The woman came out first. She wore a plain dress of bleached muslin and something white wrapped around her head. Olivia squinted at her. Why did this woman look so familiar?

Then she remembered. At The Bottoms in South Valley, when she'd gone back looking for Little Boy, there had been a young woman in a dress and headdress like that. She had been kind, had brought a dipper of water to Olivia and a bucket for her horse. While Olivia begged them to let her see her baby the woman's eyes were sad, not hostile like the others. Was this the same woman? Olivia remembered her being very pretty. Like an Egyptian queen. What was her name? Laisha. Her name was Laisha.

Laisha froze mid-step and stared at the rider on the horse. Olivia removed her hat. She was wearing trousers and worried that she might be mistaken for a boy, but no, that day at The Bottoms she had also been in men's clothing. Laisha watched Olivia for a moment and then slightly raised one hand before turning back toward the house. She wasn't running for help. She walked slowly, deliberately. She disappeared into the house and then came back out with the child in her arms. She walked part of the way toward Olivia and stopped, standing sideways to the road. She raised the boy up, not as if putting him on display, but to rub her nose against his belly and make him laugh.

The pressure in Olivia's chest was suffocating, and then she grew numb. How can that be my child? Olivia wondered. He looks as if he belongs with that woman over there. I wonder what she calls him. What need does he have of me? This is his home. Where his parents live.

Mourning had emerged from the house wearing his floppy hat, but removed it and tossed it aside. Olivia's gaze locked on him.

How will I ever take my eyes from him? I can't do this. I can't ride away.

She forced herself to remember the words she had repeated all the way here – Life is long. I don't know when, but one day he will knock on my door. Alone or with his family, but he will come. He will bring my child to me, to touch, to hold. Not now. He can't do it now. He knows I can't do it now. But some day. As long as we draw breath, nothing in this life is final.

Mourning took Little Boy from Laisha and tickled him. More of that gurgling laughter. Then Laisha reclaimed the baby and walked back to the house. Mourning remained standing in the yard alone, and Olivia devoured him with her eyes. Neither moved for a long while. Then Mourning lifted his finger to his hatless forehead before he turned away. He vanished into the house and closed the door. When Laisha looked out again the road was empty.

The End

Olivia's story begins in *Olivia, Mourning*, Book 1 of the Olivia series, which is available as both eBook and paperback at .amazon.com.

In today's book market word-of-mouth and customer recommendations are crucial to success. If you enjoyed *The Way the World Is,* please consider taking the time to post even a brief review on Amazon and/or Goodreads.

If you would like to receive an email when Book 3 of the Olivia Series - *Whatever Happened to Mourning Free?* - is released, sign up to follow the author's blog at http://yaelpolitis.wordpress.com
Or sign up to **Stay Up to Date** regarding new releases by Yael Politis on her Amazon Author page:
http://www.amazon.com/Yael-Politis/e/B002BOA5NU/ref=ntt_athr_dp_pel_1

Other books by Yael Politis
Olivia, Mourning (Book 1 of the Olivia Series)
The Lonely Tree

If you would like to know more about this author and read reviews and excerpts of her work, visit:
http://yaelpolitis.wordpress.com

You can contact her by email at: poliyael@gmail.com.

Olivia, Mourning
Book 1 of the Olivia Series

Olivia wants the 80 acres in far off Michigan that her father's will left to whichever of his offspring claims the land. As Olivia says, "I'm sprung off him just as much as Avis or Tobey." The problem: she's seventeen, female, and it's 1841.

Mourning Free, Olivia's trusted childhood friend, knows how to run a farm and is also sorely in need of a new start in life. The problem: though born in a free state, he's the orphaned son of runaway slaves.

Not without qualms, they set off together. All goes well, despite the drudgery of survival in an isolated log cabin. Incapable of acknowledging her feelings for Mourning, Olivia thinks her biggest problem is her unrequited romantic interest in their young neighbor.
Until her world falls apart.

Strong-willed, vulnerable, and compassionate, Olivia is a compelling protagonist on a journey to find a way to do the right thing in a world in which so much is wrong.

What Midwest Book Review Says
Olivia, Mourning, Book 1 of the 'Olivia' series, is historical fiction at its best ... a compelling, gripping saga that deliciously wraps what could be predictable elements in a cloak of many choices. It's all about options and consequences – and is a heartfelt story especially recommended for readers who enjoy headstrong protagonists tasked with making their own way in the world."
D. Donovan, Senior eBook Reviewer, MBR

The Lonely Tree

British Mandate Palestine and Israel – 1934-1967

Tonia's parents take her to live on Kfar Etzion, an isolated and struggling religious kibbutz south of Jerusalem. Fifteen-year-old Tonia does not believe that their dream of establishing a Jewish state will ever come to be. Life on the kibbutz is harsh and Tonia dreams of security and a little comfort, though material wealth for its own sake is not what she longs for. She wants something simple – to be able to bring up her own children under a roof of her own, in a place where they won't feel constantly threatened. She is determined to seek this different life in America – as soon as she is old enough – even though that means turning her back on her love for Amos Amrani, a handsome young Yemenite who belongs to the Jewish underground.

Much of this novel takes place in Kfar Etzion, during its establishment, siege, and fall to the Arab Legion during hostilities immediately prior to Israel's War of Independence – resulting in the massacre of its surviving defenders. A later part of the story is set in Grand Rapids, Michigan, where Tonia tries to find her new life.

This is one of very few English novels that take place in British Mandate Palestine and the only one that tells the story of Kfar Etzion. While the characters are fictional, historical events are accurately portrayed. The Lonely Tree, however, does not read like a history book. It is a character-driven love story with no political agenda.

See reviews and an excerpt at:
yaelpolitis.wordpress.com/the-lonely-tree

What the Reviewers are Saying

For me this book is one of the reading highlights of the year, a powerful story that stayed with me long after I finished reading." *Christoph Fischer, Author, Amazon Top 500 Reviewer*

"The most moving book I have read this year." *Catherine Cavendish, Author, Blogger/Reviewer*

"You will find not a single dull paragraph in this entire work ... a vivid account of the forces that drive both human idealism and human destructiveness." *Gold Dust Magazine, UK*

10076414R00209

Made in the USA
San Bernardino, CA
04 April 2014